REWIND

Also by Catherine Ryan Howard

Distress Signals

The Liar's Girl

Catherine Ryan Howard was born in Cork, Ireland, in 1982. Her debut novel *Distress Signals* was published by Corvus in 2016 while Catherine was studying English literature at Trinity College Dublin. It went on to be shortlisted for both the IBA Books Are My Bag Crime Novel of the Year and the CWA John Creasey/New Blood Dagger. Her second novel, *The Liar's Girl*, was published to critical acclaim in 2018 and is shortlisted for a Mystery Writers of America 2019 Edgar Award for Best Novel. She is currently based in Dublin.

REWIND

CATHERINE
RYAN HOWARD

CORVUS

First published in Great Britain in 2019 by Corvus, an imprint of
Atlantic Books Ltd.

10 9 8 7 6 5 4 3 2 1

A CIP catalogue record for this book is available from the
British Library.

Hardback ISBN: 978 1 83895 055 2
Trade paperback ISBN: 978 1 78649 656 0
E-book ISBN: 978 1 78649 657 7

Printed and bound in Great Britain by Clays Ltd, Elcograf S.p.A.

Corvus
An imprint of Atlantic Books Ltd
Ormond House
26–27 Boswell Street
London
WC1N 3JZ

www.corvus-books.co.uk

To Mum, for introducing me to books

In a room of shadows, a woman sleeps.

She is the bulge on the right side of the double bed. Strands of dark hair splayed across a pillow. One bare arm outside the sheets, a wedding band visible on her ring finger.

Unaware that she isn't alone.

This room is an unfamiliar one for her, even more so in the dark. Were she to wake up right now she might lift her head, prop herself up on her elbows and turn her head to look around it. Gradually her eyes would adjust and shapes would emerge from the dark.

After a moment, she would remember where she was and why she had gone there.

How long would it take her to see the shape that doesn't belong?

It stands stock still in the corner, arms down by its sides. The clothes are dark and bulky – layers, perhaps against the winter cold. Gloves on the hands, a balaclava on the head. The balaclava is twisted slightly to one side so the eyes are barely visible and the slit for the mouth shows only some cheek.

Watching.

Watching and waiting.

Waiting to use the knife with the long, serrated blade pressed against its side.

Time passes.

The sleeping woman stirs – her legs move; she turns over; the arm slips beneath the covers – but she does not wake. The dark figure moves closer to the bed until it is standing beside it, looming over her. She does not wake. The gloved hand that isn't holding the knife reaches out and gently strokes the woman's face and still, she does not wake.

catherine ryan howard

The intruder makes a circle with a thumb and middle finger and flicks the woman's cheek, hard, because – it's clear now – it *wants* her to be awake.

A moment's delay.

Then a frenzy of motion.

The woman's eyes open. Her body rises, head and shoulders lifting from the pillows, legs rising beneath the sheets. She opens her mouth as if to scream but the figure clamps a hand over it, pushing her back down. The hand that's holding the knife lifts to pull back the sheets with a finger. The woman is wearing a pair of shorts and a camisole top, her pale limbs are bare, exposed now. She sees the blade and her efforts to get away instantly intensify. Now her arms are flailing wildly, her legs kicking, her whole body jerking and contorting and squirming in the bed, fingers clawing at the balaclava—

The knife rises slowly in the air and then comes back down quickly, with force, plunging through the thin material of the woman's top and disappearing into the concave flesh of her stomach.

Lifts again. Down again.

Into the chest.

Lifts again. Down again.

A slash across the woman's forearm.

Lifts again. Down again.

Deep into the right side of her neck, just under the jawline.

The intruder steps back.

The woman's hands go to her neck and almost immediately her fingers are stained by the blood that flows from the wound there. Her mouth is open as if in a silent scream.

Dark, spreading stains.

She turns, rolling on to her right side. Her uninjured arm reaches out, past the edge of the bed, towards the intruder, as if asking for help.

The figure in black bends to lay the knife on the bedside table before going to the chest of drawers pushed against the wall opposite the foot of the bed and destroying the camera hidden there.

REWIND

0:00:17

It took Natalie most of the day to get away from Dublin City. From *all* cities. Cork was the last one she'd seen. She'd taken the train there first thing this morning, then transferred to this bus. It had snaked through Midleton – goodbye towns, too – and onwards, ambling along narrow, winding roads, the kind where the single white line painted down the middle was already more gone than still there. By the time she caught her first glimpse of the sea, she was 300 kilometres from her own front door. The traffic had thinned to the occasional passing car but the road twisted so much that the driver felt the need to blast the horn before each and every bend.

Natalie watched the bars signalling reception in the corner of her phone's screen disappear one by one. She'd already lost her mobile data; it had dropped out somewhere between Castlemartyr and Ladysbridge. The device in her hand was now rendered almost useless. She pushed through the urge to connect to the bus company's wifi for the last few minutes of the journey and let the phone slip into the depths of her handbag instead.

For all of a minute it felt like peace, a welcome release.

Then her fingers started to twitch and her palms grew clammy.

Natalie turned to concentrate intently on the view out the window. There was a stretch of smooth, grey sea wedged between the horizon and the darkening sky, marred only by two blots, one large, one small. Islands. She could just about make out the lighthouse sitting atop the larger one, looking like the nib of a fine pen from this distance. Then the bus took a hard right and there were only fields and trees and neat, old-fashioned bungalows, all surrounded by low pebble-dashed walls and set close to the road.

Then a sign for THE KILN DESIGN STORE & CAFÉ 500m.

Another one right behind it: WELCOME TO SHANAMORE.

She was here.

For the entire journey, a burning heat had been rushing against the back of Natalie's legs from a grille beneath her seat. She was desperate for some cold, fresh air but also to stay on the bus, to let it take her back out of here again, to go home and talk to Mike and to forget about this while there was still time to.

But when the bus lurched to a stop, she got up and got off it.

She wasn't prepared for the icy blast of late November air that pricked at her skin and instantly infiltrated her clothes. Gasping at the shock of it after the thick heat of the bus, Natalie hurried to pull on the coat she'd carried outside draped over an arm.

The train journey from Dublin to Cork had been just under three hours and she'd spent it obsessing over images of Shanamore she'd found online. This was having a disconcerting effect now that she was here. It was as if she was touring the set of a movie she'd watched a hundred times: everything was strangely familiar and yet totally foreign at the same time.

The bus had stopped outside the entrance to the car park of The Kiln, a trendy design store shaped like a barn that presumably flogged its locally produced crafts to well-heeled foreigners and its flat whites to local farmers. Its car park was the only smooth stretch of tarmacadam surface in Natalie's line of sight. There was the church, rising up behind her, the tallest thing for miles. There was the small public park alongside it, although in real life the rubbish bins had beer bottles in them and the picnic tables were liberally spotted with dried bird shit. The dull, sparse grass sloped away from her, falling to the level of the next bend in the road. Beyond it, the logo of a service station glowed bright against the dark sky. Directly opposite was a row of squat terraced houses bookended by two pubs. One of them was perfect Instagram fodder, the other was in dire need of knocking down.

Next to the picturesque pub was the mouth of a small road. Natalie could see a giant pothole at its start, concrete crumbling at its edges, the crater filled with murky water. When she lifted her eyes, she saw a cardboard sign had been tacked to the nearest telephone pole: SHANAMORE COTTAGES, 1KM. It pointed down the potholed road.

Everything else in her eyeline was hedge or tree or sky.

The light was fading. Natalie didn't wear a watch but she figured she'd turned off her phone ten minutes ago, at the most, and it had been just after five o'clock then. She needed to get to the cottages before it got *actually* dark.

She set off, pulling her case behind her.

Plastic wheels against crumbling tarmacadam produced a hollow, rumbling noise. In the dead quiet, the noise she was making seemed to grow louder and louder. At least, she thought, the road was relatively straight, so any oncoming cars would see her before they hit her – she hoped.

When Natalie finally spotted the sign marking the entrance to Shanamore Cottages, she guessed it was fifteen minutes since she'd got off the bus. Pretty much the length of the walk that Google Maps had promised, then. The cottages, however, were not entirely as advertised.

Individually, the six of them were identifiable from the images she'd seen online. Which is to say, they didn't look much like cottages at all. Each one was an identical assembly of cubes. Some smooth, unpainted cement and some thick, green-ish glass. The smallest cube was the entranceway, a space about the size of two telephone boxes, where the only non-glass piece was the wooden slab of a front door. A larger cube behind it formed the home's ground level, with mini cubes making a couple of postmodern bay windows, one at the front and one at the side. Another cube half its size formed the second storey, pushed a few feet to the rear. The entire front section of that cube – the master bedroom, from what Natalie remembered of the website – was made of glass.

But it was obvious now that the photos online had been taken at carefully considered angles. Their frames had conveniently omitted the breeze-block shell of an unfinished McMansion sitting in the overgrown field next door, and they didn't convey at all just how close together the cottages were. They were sitting in two rows of three, facing each other, with only the narrowest of laneways separating each one from its immediate neighbour. Natalie suspected that if you stood in one of those lanes and stretched your arms out, you'd touch a cottage on each side. She'd found an old newspaper article online, property section, which suggested these were the work of an ambitious young architect who'd qualified at the height of the Boom and had been gifted a swathe of Daddy's land. Crowding it with cottages must have been him trying to get as much bang for his buck as he could. If that was his plan, it hadn't worked. The cottages had stood empty for years, no buyer willing to be the first, until some foreign investment firm had bought the lot for a song and turned the entire estate into a holiday 'village' of short-term lets instead.

Movement.

A man had emerged from the nearest cottage and was striding towards her. The house had a sign in the front window that Natalie couldn't read in the dim but she thought it might say RECEPTION.

He waved, called out, 'Marie?'

He must be Andrew, the manager.

Natalie waved back. 'That's me.'

Marie was her middle name. She'd made the booking over the phone just a few hours ago, giving her first name as Marie and her last as Kerr – Mike's last name, her married one, which she never used. If she had to produce a credit card now or show some photo ID the jig would be up, but maybe the check-in procedure at Shanamore Cottages was more of a casual operation. She'd only needed to give a name and a telephone number to secure her reservation, after all.

There was a red hatchback sitting in Andrew's driveway and he met her at its rear. The car's licence plate was almost completely obscured by a thick layer of dried mud.

'Welcome to Shanamore,' he said.

It had a streak of apology in it.

They shook hands, limply, Natalie conscious of the fact that hers was warm and damp from dragging her case.

Andrew was wearing dark corduroy trousers and a thick, Aran-style sweater that seemed much too big for his wiry frame;

he gripped the too-long cuffs of it in his palms with the tips of his fingers. His dark hair was long and flopped in front of his eyes, the kind of style the boys at school used to have back when Natalie was in it. (Curtains? Isn't that what they called it?) It all conspired to create a first impression of youth and boyishness but here, up close, Natalie could see that this man was easily her age, late twenties, early thirties.

'You found us all right?' he asked.

'No problem at all.'

He looked around, behind her. 'You didn't *walk* here?'

'Only up the road,' she said. 'The bus dropped me off by The Kiln.'

'You've been here before? To Shanamore?'

'No, never.'

'And you're *not* here to make pottery – right?'

He'd already asked her this on the phone. There was a local potter who offered week-long classes and had some arrangement whereby attendees got a discount if they stayed here.

'No.' Natalie smiled. 'I'm just after a few days' peace and quiet, that's all.'

'Well, let me show you to your cottage.'

They started walking, him leading the way.

'You live on site?' she asked.

'Yep.'

'All year round?'

'All year round.'

'And you said on the phone you only keep one or two of these open at this time of the year?'

'It's easier that way,' Andrew said. 'Makes more sense.'

'So can I ask which one …?'

Andrew pulled a key from his pocket and held it up to the light. It had a large '6' printed on its plastic tag.

Natalie tried to keep her expression neutral while her entire body flooded with relief.

———

She didn't know what she would've done if he'd shown her to a different cottage. She'd had vague notions of finding a way to get inside No. 6 by other means, later, or making up some complaint that would necessitate a move there first thing in the morning. But mostly she'd tried to not worry about this detail. Now, finally, she could stop.

No. 6 was the cottage directly opposite Andrew's, No. 1. He unlocked the front door and hurried inside ahead of her. There was no hall or foyer; you were immediately in the living room, facing the foot of the stairs. The entire ground floor of the cottage was one big, open space.

'Meant to do this earlier,' he muttered as he scurried about the room, turning on lights. Two floor lamps, the pendant hanging over the dining table, spots recessed in the ceiling positioned strategically over faded prints of Shanamore Strand in cheap IKEA frames. He pushed a button and transformed the pane of black glass stuck low on the (fake) chimney breast into a scene of (fake) glowing fire. He fiddled with the thermostat until the nearest radiator started to splutter and click. Plumped a sofa cushion. Straightened the coffee table.

Natalie stepped inside, closing the door behind her, and watched him move around the room. He reminded her of an air steward in the galley before trolley service: practised to the point of automation.

'Oh,' he said suddenly, 'I forgot your welcome basket.'

Before Natalie could respond, he was gone and the front door was closing with a *thunk* for the second time in as many minutes.

She parked her suitcase and advanced into the room.

Two three-seater black leather couches and a matching armchair were arranged in a U-shape around the fire and the flat-screen TV that hung above it. Behind the furthest couch, at the rear of the ground floor, was a solid wood dining table with space for eight and beyond that, the clinically white cabinets of an ultra-modern kitchen. Their glossy finish made them gleam in the lights.

9

The only walls were the exterior ones. The one at the rear was made entirely of glass, a huge window with one door inset. The staircase clung to the side wall and had only air between its steps and no railing; Natalie felt nervous just looking at it. Floor-to-ceiling windows interrupted the remaining two walls. It was dark enough outside now for all the glass to be showing only interior reflections.

Natalie touched a hand to one of the cushions on the armchair and felt cold with a hint of damp.

And a lump forming in her throat.

A squeeze of heartbreak in her chest.

This can't be the place ... Can it?

The door swung open. Andrew was back, carrying a small wicker basket. The air swirled and changed, suddenly charged with the presence of another person, chilled with the draught the open door was letting in.

He looked at her, eyebrows raised, awaiting a verdict.

'It's nice,' she said. 'Lovely.'

'Good. Glad you like it. Sorry about the cold. I should've put on the heating earlier. It should warm up pretty quick.' He set the basket on the coffee table. 'So – any questions?'

'No, no. I think I'm all set.'

She smiled. His eyes met hers and she realised it was for the first time. Eye contact, evidently, wasn't his thing. Andrew proved this by looking away again almost immediately.

Then he gave a little wave, turned on his heel and left.

The *thunk* of the front door locking shut echoed around the house again and then everything was quiet and still.

Too quiet and still.

Natalie cast about for a remote control but couldn't find one, so she went to the TV and randomly pressed the slim buttons hidden on its side until loud voices boomed into the space, banishing the silence.

She took a quick inventory of the contents of the wicker basket. A box of Irish soda bread mix; six mismatched eggs; a bag of Cork Coffee Roaster's 'Rebel' blend; a bar of chocolate with a pencil sketch of Shanamore Strand on the label; a single bottle of beer from the Franciscan Well; a small carton of milk.

She was patting her coat pockets for the hard shape of her phone before she even realised she was doing it. It was like a muscle memory, a tic. But she didn't need a photo of the basket. She didn't need any photos at all, because she wouldn't be posting online about this trip.

For a change.

A search of the kitchen turned up a drawer filled with things swiped but not consumed by previous guests: hardened sachets of salt and pepper, a few pouches of ketchup and mayonnaise, individually wrapped teabags.

Natalie supposed she could bake the bread and have it toasted with scrambled eggs, but she was missing a crucial ingredient: being arsed enough to. She wasn't even hungry, not really. So she made herself a cup of hot, sweet tea and took it to one of the couches, and idly ate her way through the chocolate bar square by square without even taking off her coat.

What she was really doing, she knew, was stalling. Putting off going upstairs. Because being here in the cottage was one thing, but to see the bed, to have to – at some point – get *into* it …

On the TV, the talk show had been replaced by a *Friends* rerun. The one with the wedding dresses.

By the time Phoebe and Monica had persuaded Rachel to get into one too, it was pitch black outside.

Natalie got up to draw the curtains.

According to the front window there was nothing out there in the night except for a buttery gold square directly opposite: a view into Andrew's living room via the window at the front of his cottage. Same layout, same furniture, just all turned the other way around like a mirror image. There was no sign of him and no lights on upstairs, although his car was still parked in the drive.

She pulled the curtains closed until their edges overlapped. The material was thin, the orbs of the streetlights easily filtering through.

There was nothing to cover the wall of black glass, yawning like the mouth of a great abyss at the rear of the cottage. Either the owners were trying to save money or they thought there was no need for window dressings when all that was behind the house was a patio, a few feet of communal garden and a hedgerow. But it made Natalie uneasy. What was on the other side of that hedge? She couldn't tell in the dark.

There could be another house looking directly into hers.

There could be someone looking at her right now.

As Natalie stood at the glass, contemplating this, it morphed from a mere lack of privacy into a structural vulnerability. How strong was that glass? Could someone hurl a rock through it? What would she do if someone did?

Here it comes, she thought. The Anxiety Train. Express service to Crazytown unless she applied the brakes. Natalie tried to, now, telling herself that the glass was fine and that there was no one out there. That hundreds if not thousands of people had stayed in Shanamore Cottages before her and nothing had happened to any of them. That if it were daytime, she wouldn't even have noticed this. This wouldn't even be a thing.

She silently repeated this several times until she felt herself relax.

But she also wished she'd found a bottle of wine in that bloody wicker basket.

It was when she turned to go back to the couch that the shelf beneath the coffee table revealed itself and the several small piles of books on it. Natalie knelt on the floor and started pulling them out, appraising each one. Battered paperbacks. Airport bestsellers, for the most part. A newish copy of *Jurassic Park*. Two or three in a foreign language.

A library of left-behind holiday reads.

Natalie stopped and stared at the narrow, hard, cornflower-blue spine.

And she knew. She knew even before she reached out and picked it up and turned it over in her hands: it wasn't just a copy of *Percy Bysshe Shelley selected by Fiona Sampson*. It was *her* copy.

Their copy, hers and Mike's.

Then she opened it and got confirmation.

Stuck on the first page was the bookplate she'd bought in the Keats–Shelley House by the Spanish Steps, along with the book itself, a few years before. It was stuck on slightly askew because Natalie had done it quickly, surreptitiously, in the doorway of the gift shop, before Mike could catch her in the act. The *For my M* she'd scrawled beneath the sticker was in a messy version of her handwriting for the same reason. When she'd presented it to him that night over a candlelit dinner off the Via Veneto, the first thing he'd said was, 'When did you buy this?' The next question he'd asked her was if she'd marry him, the proposal his plan for their supposedly last-minute weekend away in Rome all along.

Last week she'd been arranging the bookshelves in the room she was supposed to be using as a home office when it had occurred to her that she hadn't seen that book in a while. When she'd asked him about it, Mike had reminded her that there were a few things they hadn't seen since the move. He'd said it was probably down the bottom of a box they hadn't unpacked yet. He'd seemed confident that it would show up soon.

Natalie clutched the book to her chest as if it were something precious. And it was, but not for the reasons it had been in the past.

Now, it was evidence.

Now, she had proof.

———

The clock on the TV screen said it was almost eight. Natalie decided to have a bath. It would warm her up and give the cottage time to warm up too. Afterwards, she'd crawl into bed and let herself sink into a night of blissful sleep. She could face facts tomorrow.

She'd have to face the bed now, though.

Reluctant to put the poetry book back with the others or to leave it out, Natalie pulled open drawers in the kitchen until she found a relatively empty one and then slipped it in there. After double-checking the doors and windows were locked, she turned out the living-room lights and lugged her case up the stairs. She kept her free hand on the wall to steady herself and tried not to focus on the empty space between the steps or the yawning open space to the right of them.

There were two closed doors at the top, one off either side of the small, carpeted landing. The bathroom was through the one on the right. Simple, white and very clean. There were no windows save for a tiny frosted square above the sink. Natalie dropped the plug in the bath and ran the tap until it got hot, adding a few drops from the miniature bottle of shower gel that had been left on the edge.

She sat on the closed lid of the toilet and watched the bubbles grow.

Until an alien noise pierced the air.

BEEP-BEEP-BEEP-BEEP-BEEP.

Her phone, Natalie realised on a delay.

Had it always been that loud? And that annoying? She got up to retrieve it from her bag, which she'd dropped in the doorway. A single bar of service had appeared on screen, letting a flood of text messages and notifications come through. The newest one said she had a voicemail.

Natalie put the phone to her ear and played it.

It was him.

'Nat, where are you? What's going on? I'm—'

She threw the phone across the room and watched as it smacked off the tiled wall, dropped into the bath water and sank beneath the bubbles.

Natalie blinked.

Had she really just done that?

She'd done it unthinkingly, or rather *before* she could think about it, and now, in the moment immediately after, she felt like she might throw up.

No phone? The idea made her feel clammy, anxious, unmoored. *No phone. No phone. No phone.* She couldn't contact anyone and no one could contact her. No one even knew where she was—

But that had been her plan, hadn't it? She had intended to turn off the phone while she was here. This would make things easier now.

Simpler. She wouldn't be *able* to turn it back on, so she wouldn't need to waste any energy trying to stop herself from doing it.

This was a good thing, even if it didn't feel that way.

Natalie found the phone beneath the water – the screen, somehow, had remained intact – and put it in the plastic bin under the sink.

The bath wasn't full yet. She pictured herself lying in there with the breach of the bedroom still ahead of her and decided that wasn't the right recipe for relaxation. She should go in there now. Just get it over with.

It was only a bed, for God's sake. An inanimate piece of furniture. She crossed the landing.

The bedroom was cold with a hint of damp, just like downstairs, and just like downstairs, this space had a gaping wall of glass. The difference was that this one was to the front of the cottage.

There was an amber streetlight right outside and it lit the room well enough to see the outlines of everything in it, but Natalie flicked on the ceiling light to get a better look. The bed was king-sized, the sheets plain white and pulled smooth across the mattress. She got down on her hands and knees to look underneath it, imagining that she'd see the glint of a cufflink or a lost earring, like people do in the movies.

There was nothing.

It didn't matter. She had the poetry book.

The bed faced built-in wardrobes with mirrored doors. There was a dressing table, a small TV screen mounted on the wall and a table and two tub-style armchairs set right in front of the wall of glass, just in case you wanted to play a game of Exhibit in a Zoo.

This wall of glass, at least, had curtains. Natalie was pulling them closed when she caught a flicker of movement in her peripheral vision: someone moving in the downstairs window of Andrew's cottage. But when she looked, there was no one there.

She wondered what Andrew's deal was. Was he from Shanamore? Did he live alone over there? She hadn't seen a wedding ring or any evidence of children. And there was something about him, something she couldn't quite articulate, that made it hard for her to believe he wasn't alone and easy to assume that he was.

The wall of black glass that fronted the second storey of Andrew's cottage – his bedroom window – suddenly lit up with a flash of eerie blue light, revealing—

A woman.

Standing at the window, looking out.

Natalie yanked the curtains closed, then immediately regretted being so obvious about it.

There'd barely been time to collect an impression but it was definitely a woman she'd seen, not Andrew. She was wearing a skirt. Knee-length, maybe. And her hair was pulled back from her face, perhaps in a ponytail …

'No,' Natalie said aloud, catching herself. *Don't start down that road.* She'd only seen this woman for a fraction of second; she couldn't describe her in any detail with any certainty. And she didn't think she'd been wearing glasses. The light that revealed her was so odd, it was as if she was lit from the chest up—

Natalie realised what the weird blue light had been, where it had been coming from.

The woman's phone.

That had been *all* the light, which meant that until some call or message had lit up that phone's screen, that woman had just been standing there in total darkness, at the window, in Andrew's bedroom.

Watching.

Watching Natalie.

FASTFORWARD

0:00:41

Three loud knocks, knuckles on a door.

'Audrey?' a voice said. 'You up?'

She wasn't. Audrey was half-awake, aware of real-world intrusions but desperate to hang on to the warm, wispy tendrils of sleep, to delay another morning for just a few moments more.

She clamped her eyelids shut, turned over and burrowed deeper into the warm cocoon of her bed.

'Aud?' Louder now, more demanding: 'Aud*rey*?'

The voice was coming from the other side of the bedroom door, the handle of which wasn't a full foot from Audrey's head. It belonged to Dee, her younger sister.

And, technically speaking, her current landlord.

'I'm coming in,' Dee warned. But this was followed by a *clink* and a dull *thump*; she'd tried the door and discovered that it was locked. 'Audrey, for God's sake. Open this bloody door before I have to—'

Audrey reached out an arm and turned the key in the lock.

The door swung open immediately, the white light from the landing banishing the grey dim of the box room in one fell swoop.

The next thing Audrey saw was a cup of steaming coffee seemingly hovering in mid-air.

'Is that for me?'

'It wasn't,' Dee said. 'But you can have it.'

Audrey pulled herself into a half-sitting position and gratefully took the cup of coffee, slurping up a mouthful.

She stole a sideways glance at her sister as she did. Dee was standing in the doorway, arms folded, surveying the roomscape with a frown. She was already dressed for work in her trademark black suit, barely there make-up and neat, gleaming hair; Audrey so rarely saw her in casual clothes these days that whenever she did, it was disorientating, like meeting one of your primary-school teachers outside of school.

'It looks a lot worse than it is,' Audrey said.

The box room was a small square narrowed by a set of built-in wardrobes along one wall and the single bed pushed against the opposite one. The strip of floor that remained was mostly hidden by a thick layer, several strata deep, of books, clothes, papers. The bad news for Audrey was that this mess matched up perfectly with the shaft of bright light coming from the open door, an unwelcome Newgrange.

'What amazes me,' Dee said, 'is how quickly it descends into this.'

'An almost thirty-year-old shouldn't be able to fit into a space this size. It'd be weird if it *didn't* look like this, if you ask me.'

'Speaking of—'

'Jesus, Dee,' Audrey said, 'I am *not* having a party. How many more times—'

'We've accepted an offer, Aud. As of ten minutes ago. Five grand above the asking price, which is more than we thought we'd get. Especially after all this time.'

Audrey's stomach sank.

She said, 'That's great. Wow. Congratulations.'

'Thank you.' Dee smiled briefly. 'It is great, yeah. But it comes with a condition. The buyers' own house is already sold and *their* buyer is anxious to move in, so they want to move in here, like, yesterday. We've, ah ... We've agreed to be out in three weeks.'

'Three *weeks*?'

'I know, it's a bit crazy.'

'But you haven't found a house yet – have you?'

'No, not yet.' Dee touched a hand to the doorframe and then turned to look at where her fingers had landed, as if fascinated by some imperfection in the wood she'd just detected there. 'Alan and I ... We can stay with his parents. They've offered us their spare room.'

'Oh.'

'Maybe there's a friend you can stay with, just until—'

'Don't worry about it,' Audrey said. 'I'll sort something out.'

'I'll ask around at work. Maybe you could get a room-share. And if you need help with a deposit—'

Audrey reflexively raised a hand in a *stop* gesture, silencing Dee. She didn't want to talk about borrowing money from her little sister two weeks before her own thirtieth birthday. Their living situation was shameful enough.

'I'll be fine. *Any*way …' Audrey threw back the blankets and swung her legs out of bed. 'I better get going. What time is it?'

'You know,' Dee said, 'I think this is actually going to be a good thing.'

Audrey felt the aftertaste of the coffee turn bitter on her tongue.

'I wanted to help you,' Dee continued, 'but I don't think I *was* helping you. That's the thing. You're just not— I mean, you never were—'

'*Hungry enough*,' Audrey finished. She'd heard the same line from Dee umpteen times before. 'Because I'm just too comfortable, aren't I? I need to struggle. Well' – she stood up, thrusting the coffee cup back at Dee who only narrowly avoided getting her white shirt flecked with coffee drops – 'in three weeks I'll be homeless and destitute, so that should probably do it, don't you think?'

Dee rolled her eyes. 'Oh, come *on*.'

'No, no. You're right. You're totally right.' Audrey began angrily smoothing the pillows and pulling the corners of the duvet to the edges of the bed. 'I'm just *way* too comfortable here, living in the ten square feet my little sister rented to me, doing a job that's, like, a million miles away from the one I want to have, working forty hours a week just to pay off a loan I took out to get a Masters that, so far, has been of absolutely *no* use to me at all. While also slowly dying of shame. Yep, you're absolutely right.' She stopped and turned to face her sister. 'I've got it *cushy*.'

'You just don't want to hear the truth. You never have. Because, God forbid, it interferes with your dreams and mantras and your vision boards.'

'What's your point, Dee? That I'm a great big failure? Is that it?'

'I don't think you *can* fail if you've never even *tried*.'

'You should put that on a poster. One of those motivational ones. With a sunset. You could sell them on Etsy. You'd make a fortune.'

'Aud, you—'

'I *am* trying, Dee. I *have* been trying. All this time. As hard as I possibly can.'

'Have you?'

'*Yes.*'

Dee held out her left arm and rotated it until Audrey could see the face of her slim, silver watch.

Audrey blinked at it. 'Oh, for …'

She'd overslept.

She was an hour late for work and counting.

————

By skipping a shower and taking a cab she could ill afford, Audrey made it to the office just in time for what they called the 'Now' meeting, held every morning at nine thirty. ThePaper.ie was run out of Hive, a trendy open-plan co-working space off Leeson Street that was populated with beanbags in primary colours, complimentary fruit water stations and men who dressed for their cycle to work as they would for the Tour de France.

The rest of the Ents team were already gathered around AltaVista, a giant slab of a conference table named after an early internet search engine. Audrey was confident that she was the only member of the team who knew what AltaVista actually was. The rest of them would probably keel over if they knew she was old enough to have *used* it.

Everyone was heads down, their eyes fixed on their phones. Audrey slipped into one of two vacant seats – the other one, at the head of the table, awaited the imminent arrival of their boss, Joel – and took out her phone too.

She had a new email. It was from Joel, a master of devastating brevity. The message consisted of only one word. All caps, no punctuation.

LATE

It had been sent three minutes ago. Audrey wanted to twist in her seat and see where Joel was watching them from, but if he'd seen her come in, he'd see her do that too. Besides, it was no mystery. His vantage point was most likely his office, a tiny box made entirely of glass partitions, parked in the middle of Level 1. His very own Panopticon.

Audrey deleted the email and swiped at her phone's screen until Daft, the property-search app, had started downloading itself to the device.

Three weeks. She had three weeks to find a place she could afford that didn't also look like it had been a drug den in a previous life or had the potential to be a crime scene at some point in the future. Audrey knew what was ahead of her; she'd seen the TV documentaries, read the reports. Professionals sleeping in bunk-beds. Bedsits that offered the convenience of being able to work the microwave without having to get off the toilet. A queue of fifty-odd twenty-somethings waiting obediently outside every half-decent listing, eyeing up their competition, trying to assess where they were likely to come in this latest round of Dublin's Private Tenancy Pageant, founded in 1999 and back now, bigger than ever, after a little devastating-economic-downturn break that was already fading from everyone's memories. Audrey did some mental arithmetic and then entered what she thought she could stretch to, rent-wise, in the Search box. The only result was a single bedroom in a house in Stillorgan. There were no photos at all, which probably meant the place looked like an episode of *Hoarders* featuring Fred and Rosemary West. Yet in the five days since the listing had gone up, it had been viewed almost fifteen thousand times.

'Morning all.'

Joel had appeared as if from nowhere, like he did every morning. The man didn't arrive so much as materialise.

Audrey slipped the phone into her pocket and waited to catch his eye so she could mouth a *sorry* at him but, before she could, he said her name, sending a ripple of interest running around the table like an electrical current. Then:

'My office. Straight after this.'

Audrey just about managed a weak nod of acknowledgement. She'd never been called into his office before. She must really be in trouble.

'Right,' Joel said then, loudly, signalling the meeting's start. 'Everybody ready?' He sat down and flipped open his laptop, tapped a key and started reading from the screen. 'Here's what we've got so far. Rumour has it there's a snap of a certain rugby star and a certain girlfriend of *another* certain rugby star getting up to no good in The Grayson on Saturday night. Snap as in Snapchat. Find it for me. That's our top priority. Across the pond: Lena got a tattoo with no bra on and some magazine has a video of it. Embed is our friend. Across the other, smaller pond: Piers thinks KK shouldn't have used a Snapchat filter on O'Hare, so we have the snap *and* we have a screen-grab from the show there. That's two paras already and you haven't even had to make anything up yet. Fresh in from the paps: some actress going somewhere with no make-up on. One of the models going somewhere with not enough make-up on. An *X-Factor* reject going somewhere with *lots* of make-up on. Danni, I'm going to give those last three to you.'

Danielle, sitting directly across from Audrey, lifted a flattened hand to her forehead in a mock military salute. She was the team's MVP when it came to coming up with different angles on *Woman Somewhere On Celebrity Spectrum Goes About Her Daily Life*. For Christmas last year, they'd got her a T-shirt with STEPS OUT AMID, her favourite phrase, printed on the front.

'And we're trying something new this week,' Joel continued. 'Find someone interesting, scour the 'Gram for shots taken at home with lots of background and use them to flesh out "Inside the home of ..." pieces. Our angle should be "this person clearly gets paid way too much of the licence fee because look how swanky their home is despite them being utterly shit" or "secret shame of the washed-up former star forced to live in a three-bed semi". Okay?'

Audrey nodded along absently with the other bobbing heads. Her mind had started to wander. What was she going to say to Joel? He always seemed to expect more of her than he did of the others, presumably because she was older, more mature, more *sensible*, and on every other day she appreciated that distinction. But now she feared it might mean she was in actual trouble for a silly infraction.

It was excruciating to care about something that mattered so little. Audrey didn't know which was worse: having to do this job or the prospect of losing it.

The Paper was an online news site that had started life as a content aggregating upstart during the Celtic Tiger, when Ireland suddenly got money and discovered feta cheese and flat whites and investment properties in Bulgaria and everyone collectively lost their minds. But the arrival of the Bust coincided with the arrival of the smartphone and, after pivoting away from its original website into an app and mobile offering, The Paper had survived – and thrived. It now employed a team of reporters who wrote original pieces and broke actual news in 250-word Lean Cuisine-style stories, just the right portion size for the eternally distracted Millennial scrolling through his phone while in line for a burrito bowl.

The problem was that Audrey wasn't one of those reporters. Her job was in The Paper's entertainment section, infamous for doing the opposite of their Serious News colleagues upstairs: squeezing 250 words out of nothing of import at all. Usually a single, pixelated paparazzi shot and an allusion to some unsubstantiated rumours that just about stayed within the legal lines. Their model was the universally despised but yet also phenomenally successful Sidebar of Shame. They worked to traffic targets – clicks – set by the Powers That Be each morning. Every minute counted and every story had to pull its weight. It was the only position a newly graduated and totally inexperienced Audrey was offered that was even remotely related to what she wanted to do. What she'd decided to finally *try* to do, aged twenty-eight, after nearly a decade in recruitment.

What she really wanted was only one floor away: the rest of The Paper's staff, the ones who wrote about the actual news, had the whole of Level 2, upstairs.

Audrey would get there.

That was the plan.

And so, for now, she would suck it up. She would spend her days coming up with different ways to say 'Famous woman goes outside, does mundane things' and she would do it well. She would bide her time until an opportunity arose.

That's what Dee didn't understand, that waiting *was* trying.

Snap.

Joel had closed his laptop.

Audrey had zoned out on half the meeting.

'Let's get those clicks,' he said to the group. Then to her: 'Let's go.'

She got up and followed him away from the table.

Joel's office was so small that the only seat was the one behind his desk, so Audrey stood in the doorway, facing him.

He had barely sat down when she blurted out, 'I'm so sorry I was late today. I don't know what happened, but it won't happen again. I promise.'

'Good, but this isn't about that.' Joel rested his elbows on the desktop. 'Audrey, I may have a story for you. It's a bit TMN for us, this …' TMN was Too Much News, Joel's shorthand for stories that had some viable content for Ents but mostly involved details their core readership would skim. Like when celebrities made speeches at the United Nations. What they wore: yes, in excruciating detail. What they said: no one cares. 'But upstairs aren't interested and I don't want to let it go to waste. You'd get the by-line. You'd be off the click-factory for the day. And if you strike the right tone – if you can get the balance right – I can probably get it listed on the main page as well as in Ents, so, you know …' He turned his palms to the ceiling. 'Actual news.'

'I'll do it,' Audrey said.

Joel snorted. 'I haven't told you what it is yet.'

'Whatever it is, I'll do it.'

'I'm sure you will. The question is *can* you?' Joel paused. 'Do you know who Natalie O'Connor is?'

Of all the things Audrey thought he was going to say next, that had been the very last one.

'Yes,' she said. '*Of* her, anyway.'

Audrey wasn't about to admit it to Joel – or anyone else – but she had spent hours of her life scrolling through Natalie O'Connor's life on Instagram. Dubliner Natalie was beautiful. Glossy. Perfect. *Nice*. Living in an *Ideal Homes* spread and married to a Prince Charming in a non-problematic way. She had thousands of followers and had parlayed her popularity into a lifestyle brand called And Breathe. Its website flogged scented candles made by hard-to-pronounce brands and un-ironically shared articles with titles like 'Digital Detox: What Happened When I Put Down My Phone and Picked Up My Life'. Since both Natalie O'Connor and Audrey were the same age – since they'd both had the same amount of time to get their lives in order – it was, inevitably, a depressing spectator sport.

What had Natalie done?

Audrey was thinking *scandal*. A few exposés had hit the blogging world recently. Girls with caterpillar eyebrows getting paid thousands to say beauty products worked when what actually worked was Photoshop. Someone caught pretending a hotel room was the inside of her own home. Becoming the face of a national stop-smoking campaign and then getting pictured on Grafton Street at 3 a.m. lighting a fresh Marlboro off your last one.

'Natalie is missing,' Joel said. 'She's *been* missing for a week. And her husband didn't bother to tell anyone that – including the Gardaí – until today.'

———

Audrey walked back to AltaVista with her eyes fixed firmly on the floor. She grabbed her coat and laptop bag from her vacated chair, studiously ignoring the searching looks of everyone else still sitting there. Their collective curiosity pulsed in the air like a bass-line, but Audrey wasn't going to enlighten them. This was *her* story.

There was a Starbucks five minutes' walk away and a Starbucks ten minutes' walk away. In Audrey's experience, no one from Hive could be bothered to trek to the further one, so it was the perfect place to work undisturbed. She ordered a large filter coffee, the one item at the intersection of *lowest price* and *longest lasting*. She was starving but couldn't stretch to any overpriced, barely defrosted pastries after forking out for that cab this morning, but she thought there might be a half-melted cereal bar thingy in the bottom of her bag if she got desperate. She settled into a low armchair in the far corner of the café's upper level, her laptop balanced on her knees.

The first thing Audrey did was open a new Word document and copy the text from the Garda press release into its blank white space. It was the standard fare.

> Gardaí are appealing for the public's help in finding a Dublin woman missing since 5 November. Natalie O'Connor, 30, was last seen at her home on Sydney Parade Avenue in Sandymount on Monday 5 November at approximately 8 a.m. O'Connor is described as being 5'5" in height with long brown hair and brown eyes. Anyone with information is asked to contact Donnybrook Garda Station on …

The Paper got sent at least one of these notices from the Garda Press Office every week and only the personal details ever changed. Joel had explained to her that it was largely up to the family of the missing person whether or not to release an appeal like that, so this didn't mean that the Gardaí were out in their crinkly white overalls combing the Wicklow Mountains for decomposing Natalie parts. Whatever this incident was, it probably fell somewhere on a spectrum between personal crisis and a domestic dispute. This appeal was destined to become one of the thousands of missing person reports Gardaí released each year that were followed a few days later by the good news that the public could stand down. Which was why, for The Paper, this wasn't really news. But Joel had recognised the name and seen an opportunity.

One hundred thousand of them, to be exact.

That's how many followers Natalie O'Connor had on Instagram. With no updates from the woman herself, those followers would be desperate for information and they'd look for it in the same place they found everything else: online. If Audrey could come up with a few plausible explanations for Natalie's week-long disappearance and put them in virtual print without incurring the wrath of the legal department, those 100,000 clicks – and perhaps many more besides – would be theirs.

And Joel would love her for it.

She chugged some coffee and then did a bog-standard Google search for Natalie's name.

There was less than a page's worth of relevant results. Two bare-bones news stories from that morning, which were basically the Garda appeal, an old interview about her diet with an Irish glossy magazine and a somewhat snarky article by a broadsheet listing Ireland's top-ten influencers arranged in descending order by their follower numbers that had been published six months ago.

Behold the strange, self-regulating confinement of Internet fame.

There seemed to be no Twitter account for Natalie and no Facebook profile, at least none that were publicly accessible. Instagram, then, was going to be the start and end of Audrey's research.

She picked up her phone and tapped on the app's icon.

Since April 2012, Natalie O'Connor had posted well over 3,000 photographs to Instagram. It took Audrey nine minutes and a very real risk of Repetitive Strain Injury to scroll down to the start of the stream. The posts there were badly lit and often blurry pictures of an entirely different girl altogether.

Natalie the missing person was unfailingly elegant, wearing glowing make-up on perfect skin, sporting shiny raven hair in sleek waves and a wardrobe that was Dry Clean Only. But Natalie from six years ago had over-plucked eyebrows, streaky yellow highlights and a wardrobe of fast fashion that didn't look like it would survive more than one spin in the wash.

Audrey took a screenshot of the very first post: a selfie of Natalie wearing an ill-fitting mini-dress, taken in a mirror that inadvertently captured a messy bedroom with clothes scattered on the floor and mismatched sheets on an unmade bed.

Scrolling back up, it was easy to track the woman's transformation. The quality of the photos got better – and Natalie herself started to *look* better, glossier, more put-together – but what was in the photos changed too. A careful curation set in, gradually narrowing the range of images to just three subjects: places Natalie went, outfits she wore and shots of the inside of her immaculate home.

Mike, her husband, rarely featured in the photos but was often credited with taking them, the perfectly compliant Instagram Husband. He made most of his appearances in a series of shots from their wedding day. Him and Natalie on the shores of some impossibly picturesque lake, every last pixel perfect.

Audrey banked another screenshot: a close-up of the newlyweds gazing adoringly into each other's eyes, not a pore nor a smudge of make-up or a stray hair in sight.

Then she scrolled back up to the very top. The most recent post was a picture of a grooved, hard-shell suitcase in pastel pink, parked on a hardwood floor in a hallway filled with natural light. A smaller, matching bag was leaning against it and a crimson passport was resting on top of that. The caption read:

> Taking a few days to myself. I hate to be one of those insufferable people who tell you they're taking a break from their phone and social media by posting to social media using their phone, but I don't want you thinking I've mysteriously disappeared. Sometimes I just need to live up to my own brand. Back soon! #outoftheoffice #timeout #andbreathe

Audrey took a screenshot of that too, then moved on to the comments Natalie's followers had left underneath.

> Nice! Enjoy!
> You deserve it x
> Where did you get your case?
> Omg where are you going?
> LOVE the suitcase! Where's it from?
> Where can we buy that case?

> O fuck off who cares
> Another all expenses paid trip I suppose. Fugly bitch.
> Jesus get over yourself!! Like anyone would even
> notice.
> But you've barely been posting as it is!!
> She's probably not even going anywhere.
> #attentionseekermuch
> FRESH OUT OF FUCKS OVER HERE!
> This is probably her cover story for going off to get her
> lips done like the rest of them …

By Thursday, three days after the post had been published, the insults and the demands to know where the suitcase was from had fallen away and followers were using the comments to talk to each other about Natalie's absence.

> This is so weird. She always updates, even when she's
> travelling. I know she said she was taking a break but
> still …
> --- SO weird. Wonder what's going on.
> --- Friend of a friend knows her BFF and she said no
> one can get a hold of her.
> --- WTF???

Audrey kept scrolling. She stopped when she saw that, sometime on Friday, Mike had left a comment.

> This is Mike, Natalie's husband. If anyone has been in
> contact with Natalie since last Monday can they please
> email me at m.kerr@seacapital.ie. I'd really appreciate
> it. Thank you.

Audrey thought that was a truly terrible idea. If the other comments were indicative of the kind of responses Mike was likely to get, she could only imagine the sea of molten shite that was clogging up his inbox right now. And that was if anyone had actually seen his comment, hidden as it was hundreds of comments deep under a week-old post.

She checked Mike's Instagram account, but there were no posts on it yet. He'd evidently set it up just so he could leave that comment. This also suggested he didn't have access to Natalie's account, which explained why there'd been no appeal for information on Instagram, where a hundred thousand people who were borderline obsessed with Natalie would have seen it straightaway and started spreading the news.

You couldn't walk down the street in this country without someone who knew someone who knew you catching you in the act; as a teenager, Audrey had learned that lesson the hard way. Ireland was the opposite of the Witness Protection Programme. So why hadn't Natalie been spotted when so many people knew who she was?

Audrey ran a search, first for Natalie's name and then for #AndBreathe, across all of Instagram. She carefully picked her way through the results, hoping she might stumble upon a blurry picture of Natalie taken from across a street, or maybe even a smiling selfie she'd acquiesced to taking with a fan. There was nothing.

She went back to Mike's comment on the suitcase photo. There were a number of responses to it, all about as helpful as you'd expect.

> OMG is she okay???!?!!
> Whoa, shit just got real here …
> Oh PLEASE. This is just some stunt. Pathetic!
> How do we know that's really her husband?
> Maybe she was trying to get away from HIM – if you've
> seen her, DON'T email him!

Audrey searched for Natalie's name on Twitter and Facebook too, just to see if she'd stumble across a discussion of any interesting rumours or the like, but found nothing useful.

She sat back, drank her cooling coffee and thought about what she knew.

She had more than enough material to make a story for The Paper, and at least three angles to choose from. Acid-tongued internet trolls force popular Irish Instagrammer into hiding. Followers of Irish Instagrammer speculate about reasons behind her sudden disappearance. Desperate husband of missing Irish Instagrammer pleads for her followers to help him find his wife. She could pick any one of them, tone down the showbiz sensationalism, and it would do the job.

And that's what she *should* do, starting right now: the job she'd been assigned. *Just* that. She knew Joel was waiting impatiently to see the fruits of her labour.

But ...

This was the opportunity she'd been waiting for. Wasn't it? Why she'd stuck it out on the Ents team all this time? Did just doing what had been asked of her qualify as seizing this opportunity with both hands?

Audrey kept thinking about Mike's email address: *m.kerr@ seacapital.ie.*

The Ents team never interacted with anyone. No emails, no interviews, no statements. They scraped together stories out of pre-existing material, already posted in the public domain: pictures, rumours, tweets. Aside from college projects, Audrey had never actually conducted an interview.

But no matter which way she assembled the shape of her Natalie O'Connor story in her head, there was a gaping hole in the middle, an unanswered question that would distract the reader.

It was distracting *her*, right now.

Why had Mike Kerr waited a week to report his wife missing?

She opened a browser window on her laptop and navigated to the Sea Capital website. Mike Kerr smiled warmly at her from the top of a page entitled MEET OUR TEAM. He looked like he belonged in the pages of a clothing catalogue – a pricey, aspirationally trendy, middle-class one. Underneath a long bio extolling all of his academic and professional accomplishments was a telephone number, complete with extension.

Before Audrey could think too much about it, she plugged the number into her phone and pressed CALL.

It rang once, clicked, then rang two more times. She thought that might suggest the call was getting forwarded to another number. She hoped it wasn't a reception desk or a voicemail.

A male voice answered.

'Yeah? Hello?'

'Ah, hi. Is this, ah … Is this Mike? Mike Kerr?'

'Yeah, who's this?'

'My name's Audrey. Audrey Coughlan. I'm, ah, writing a piece about Natalie – about the appeal – and I'm wondering if you would—'

'What do you mean, writing a piece?' He sounded suspicious now. He'd sounded merely impatient before. 'Are you a reporter?'

'Yes,' she said, while wondering if that was even true. Could she actually call herself a reporter? On this story she could, yeah. That's why it was important to do it right. She added, 'With ThePaper.ie,' then braced herself for abuse or a dial-tone. When neither came, she pushed on. 'I thought, maybe, if you don't mind, I could ask you a couple of quick questions? It won't take l—'

'That's fine.'

'Great.' She punched the air. 'Thank you.'

'I'm at home now. Does that suit?'

'Now would be great, yeah.' Audrey was pulling her laptop closer to her, trying to open up a new blank document with just the fingers of her left hand. It was harder than it seemed. 'I'll just—'

'I'll text you the address.'

Audrey pressed the phone into her ear, thinking she'd misheard. 'Sorry?'

'Are you in the city centre? We're in Sandymount.'

She'd been anticipating that if Mike was willing to answer questions at all, he'd do it over the phone. It hadn't occurred to her to do it in person.

She didn't *need* to do it in person, but …

Natalie O'Connor's husband was inviting her to their house. The one Audrey had drooled over on Instagram. The one where Natalie had, apparently, been seen last.

'That'd be perfect,' she said, slapping down the laptop's lid. 'Text me the address and I'll head there now.'

REWIND

0:00:30

The room was dark. Andrew was cold. His neck was stiff and hurting, his mouth fuzzy and dry. He could hear a quiet but insistent hissing noise, like a radio stuck between stations.

It was the middle of the night, gone 2 a.m. according to his watch. He'd fallen asleep in an awkward half-sitting position on the couch, long enough ago for the timed heating system to have switched itself off.

The hissing was coming from his laptop, sitting facing him on the coffee table. Its screen was filled with static, the noise the accompanying soundtrack.

Was that what had woken him up?

Andrew gulped down what was left in the can of Coke he'd opened earlier, washing away the fuzzy feeling in his mouth and replacing it with an uncomfortable fizz that stretched all the way down his oesophagus and into his otherwise empty stomach.

Then he pulled the laptop on to his knees.

What had happened to the feed? He clicked the ESC button to exit full-screen mode, shrinking the static to a rectangle in the middle of his desktop, floating amid folders with labels like 'Accounts 2017' and 'Website Images', and a shortcut to OPERA, the booking system he used for the cottages. A status warning was now flashing red underneath it:

NO SIGNAL DETECTED.

Andrew frowned. He'd never seen it do that before.

He clicked the REWIND button, rubbing at his eyes as the feed skipped backwards.

A minute back there was still only static.

Five minutes back: still, only static.

Andrew used the trackpad to move the starting point to a half-hour ago and clicked PLAY to start the footage from there.

A view of a bedroom.

Not a total malfunction then. Andrew let his shoulders drop in relief.

He re-entered Full Screen Mode and sat back to watch the footage play out.

There she was: a bulge on the right side of the double bed. Strands of dark hair splayed across a pillow. One bare arm outside the sheets, her wedding band visible on her ring finger.

Exactly as she'd been when he'd last looked, when he'd *been* looking, watching, after she'd fallen asleep but before he had.

What had happened since?

The image on screen was in greyscale, glowing eerily: night-vision. The camera automatically switched to it whenever the room into which it was pointed went dark. The lens was concealed behind the face of a digital alarm clock that Andrew always set on top of the chest of drawers at the foot of the bed and then crossed his fingers that his guests wouldn't move it. It captured a view of the bed, one of the bedside tables and a slice of empty wall—

Andrew bolted upright, just catching the laptop before it slid off his knees and on to the floor.

There's someone there.

On the screen. In the room.

Someone *else*.

Standing very still on the left-hand side of the bed, looking down at the woman sleeping in it.

A figure, clad all in black.

Something black was even covering their face – a balaclava, Andrew realised. And they were wearing gloves. And holding a—

They have a knife.

Andrew couldn't fathom what was happening. The longer he looked, the less the scene made sense to him. Was this even real?

Then the attack started and he knew that it must be.

The real thing was so different to the movies. There was no sound, for starters. The hidden camera did have the ability to record audio but because of where it was positioned inside the alarm clock, it was almost completely prevented from doing so. If Andrew turned the volume all the way up and plugged in some headphones, he'd hear *something*, faintly, but watching it like this on the laptop, the footage was effectively silent.

He didn't *want* to hear the audio that went with this.

What was really disconcerting was how the frame didn't change. There were no cut-aways, no artful camera angles or considered lighting schemes. Nothing left to the imagination. No edits for relief.

And yet Andrew didn't look away.

He couldn't. It was as if some kind of paralysis had come over him, pinning his body to the couch, gluing his eyes to the screen.

It went on forever.

The violence left her lying face-down, one bare arm and one bare leg hanging over the edge of the bed. Blood everywhere. Her flesh was a mess of slashes and punctures, a flap of it hanging off her neck like the lapel of an unzipped coat. Skin torn and broken and pushed inwards by the blade. Crimson blooms, spreading, growing, joining up. Splatters on the fabric headboard, a spray of blood across the wall above it.

Bile rushed up into Andrew's throat and he gagged, spewing a clear, bitter fluid tinged with brown – the Coca-Cola – all over his laptop's screen, down his clothes, on to his chin.

But there was worse to come because, then, the killer turned to face the camera.

The figure began moving slowly, purposefully, towards the lens, the form growing bigger, an ominous black shadow spreading across the screen like a solar eclipse.

Andrew blinked in confusion. He caught the blur of a black glove, fingers outstretched, reaching—

Then static. And the warning.

NO SIGNAL DETECTED.

This intruder, this *killer*, had destroyed the camera.

And while Andrew had many questions now – Who was that? How had they got in? Why her? Was she still alive? Were they still *here*? What should he do? – the most troubling one was this: How had they known the camera was there?

PAUSE

0:00:38

Jennifer spins her phone around on her desk with an index finger and thinks back to the night she first met him.

A Tuesday night in April, it was. Half a year ago now. Sycamore House was unusually busy because the big-name hotel across the road had some kind of medical conference on, and whoever had organised it hadn't done it very well, and there were overbookings.

Some woman (the *front desk manager*, excuse you) had called to see if Jennifer had any vacancies and when she said she did, asked if she'd take four or five of their reservations. Jennifer didn't like the way the woman was talking down to her, as if a purpose-built property filled with identical rooms was somehow more work than a guesthouse converted from an actual house. This woman was able to take any free room and check any guest into it, knowing they'd get what they'd expect. Jennifer had to get a look at their luggage, chat them up a bit to find out where they were from and pore over their reservation for clues to their status before she could decide whether they'd get the big room with no view but a new shower or the small room with traffic noise but a good bed.

In the end, she went with what was good business. She said yes, quoting the *front desk manager* a rate of one hundred and fifty euro a night, double what they were actually charging.

They'd arrived together, three men and one woman, less than five minutes later, annoyed and frustrated. Jennifer had sympathised with them, agreeing that it was terrible that the hotel had let this happen. She served them tea and coffee and shortbread biscuits that she said were homemade but which she'd actually bought from Aldi, smacking the pack off the countertop in the kitchen to rough them up a bit. While they munched on them, Jennifer had Niall, her bellboy of sorts, take the luggage up to the rooms, turn on the lights and turn up the heating.

Meanwhile, she showed them the endless breakfast menu and gave them maps, and even printed out some tickets the woman needed for her bus back to the airport in three days' time. As she did, she felt their attitude towards her change. *Warm*. Like most professionals, they'd greeted her initially with chilly indifference, seeing her not as an equal but as a lowly member of the service industry, only there to meet their every need.

For years, she'd forgiven this behaviour, but nowadays, she tended to hold people's first impressions against them.

Tomorrow morning, she'd spit in their eggs.

Things had quietened down after that. She'd sent Niall home. She'd fixed herself a cup of coffee and spent some time on the staff rota. She'd swapped her tailored blazer for a cardigan that wrapped around her waist. They had a couple of rooms left but she'd doubted they'd sell them. She was thinking of locking the outer door and going up to bed when *he'd* walked in.

He wanted a single room, one night. No car. One small piece of luggage: a gym bag. He gave her a mobile number and an address that was practically around the corner. She traced a finger across the raised lettering on his credit card.

MR MICHAEL KERR.

Jennifer had always believed that the idea of love at first sight was absolute horseshit. At thirty-nine, she knew for sure it was. Love was not about knowing in an instant but about knowing someone well, an intimacy that could only grow over time, and to mistake physical attraction for that feeling was silly and immature. But the first time Jennifer had looked into *his* eyes, she'd realised there was a third option: the promise of love at first sight.

She just knew — she absolutely *knew* — that this was merely the opening scene of their story.

What she didn't know was all the twists and turns their story would take. How many times in the weeks and months ahead she'd consider walking away. Leaving it be. Leaving him.

How she'd find herself forced to become the kind of woman she'd never thought she'd be: the *other* one.

The kind who, inevitably, gives her married man an ultimatum: her or me.

Now, Jennifer picks up her phone and looks for the umpteenth time at the text message Mike sent her less than an hour ago.

> Sorry to bother you but I'm having trouble contacting
> Natalie. If you've heard from her, can you let me know?
> Thanks, M.

It's a group text. Jennifer, obviously, will not respond. That wouldn't look good for either of them. But she does wonder: why did he send it to *her*? Did he mean to?

She realises it then: this is his way of letting her know his decision.

It's not what's *in* the message that matters, but the message itself. He's telling her that his marriage is over without actually typing the words. Mike is a good man, a respectful man. He's not going to come and tell her that their life together can now begin when his wife's side of the bed is still warm. He will wait. But in the meantime, he wants her to know that things have changed.

That they *will* change.

Jennifer smiles, knowing she is about to get everything she wants. Finally.

REWIND
0:00:20

When Natalie awoke the next morning she found the bedroom bright with wintry sun; the thin curtains hadn't even put up a fight. She was reaching for the bedside table before she could even form a conscious thought, the habit of her morning ritual so engrained, but then she had two: she remembered that she'd destroyed her phone the night before and she realised the heating must have gone off overnight. The air in the room was a cold, sharp shock against her bare skin. Natalie retracted her arm and snuggled deep into the cocoon of the duvet, but sleep had left her. She was wide awake, having slept solidly for the first time in weeks.

She wondered how Mike had slept.

Last night.

Some other night, here in this very same bed.

The thought was enough to propel her out of it.

As she descended the stairs, Natalie was taken aback by the absolute silence. The white noise she was so used to back in Dublin – engines, horns, sirens – was entirely absent here. The ground floor of the house was transformed in the daylight, the curtains no longer offering comfort and privacy but looking more like a messy stain that needed removing. When she pulled them back, the space filled with golden light. The neutral palette and bare white walls inside heightened the colours outside – blue sky, grey-brown tree branches, green grass – as if the floor-to-ceiling windows were screens and some amazing filter had artificially enhanced the view.

But it was even colder down here than it'd been upstairs. Natalie hurried to turn on the heating, turning it all the way up. She thought she should go for a walk on the beach and wondered if she'd brought enough warm things to wear to do that without freezing.

There was a grimy espresso pot in the back of a kitchen cupboard.

She gave it a good scrub and set about making coffee on the stove.

While she waited for it to boil, she opened the drawer she'd put the poetry book in the night before. It was almost a surprise to find it still sitting there. She touched a hand to its cover and felt reassured by its solidness.

It was real. It wasn't a figment of her imagination. Because that's what he'd say: that she was imagining things. That she was losing it. That she was paranoid.

That's what he'd *been* saying for weeks.

Mike. Her partner, her love, her everything. The man who'd told her every day for nearly ten years that she was his everything too. They'd been best friends, then a couple, then a team. An incredible team. They'd been on their way to building something special (an empire, Mike liked to half-joke), a business that would give them the kind of wonderful, easy life Natalie secretly feared no one deserved. But something had gone wrong somewhere along the line and no matter how forensically she studied her memories, she couldn't trace its origins. She'd missed it entirely and now it was too late.

And she missed *him*. Was missing him, now. It was a physical ache, a heaviness in her chest. She longed to feel his arms around her, to bury her face in his chest, to tell him what was wrong so he could try to make it better. But this time, *he* was what was wrong. So whenever she pictured the man that she loved, another, identical man stepped in front of him, blocking her view. She couldn't ignore this other man, couldn't move him, couldn't see around him. But she could hear the man at the back telling her she was seeing things, repeatedly insisting that there was no other man there.

The espresso pot began to hiss.

Natalie closed the drawer.

The coffee was thick and black and much stronger than she liked – at home, there was a machine that swallowed a capsule and then spluttered out a mug made just right – but it was hot and it had caffeine in it and two out of three wasn't bad. She held the cup with two hands and turned to go and sit at the table—

A man.

47

At the window.

The cup slid from Natalie's fingers.

There was a man standing outside the wall of glass. Not five feet from her. Nose pressed against the glass. Looking in. *Searching.*

Natalie jumped as scalding hot coffee splattered her stockinged feet but she didn't – couldn't – take her eyes off him.

He was older. Greasy dark hair, longish and wild. A heavy coat, the kind with lots of pockets and zips. Old, loose jeans, muddied and ripped. A ruddy, lined face aged by the elements.

What the—

He was trying the handle.

Natalie could feel her heart thundering in her chest, hear the rush of blood in her ears. But she couldn't move. Her whole body had locked up in fright. She could only watch as the handle wriggled, but – thank God – didn't depress.

The door was locked. She'd double-checked that before going upstairs the night before.

My phone my phone my phone.

But her phone was dead. Drowned. Useless. And anyway, who would she ring? Everyone she knew was hundreds of miles away. The Gardaí, then. But she was in the middle of nowhere. She probably wouldn't even have reception.

The man's eyes found hers. He jerked away from the door and then, after a beat, started waving his hands about and mouthing something, shouting something through the glass.

At first, Natalie couldn't make out the words. It was as if she was underwater and had to fight her way back to the surface, back to the present tense. But then:

'Sorry!'

That's what the man was shouting, holding his hands up like cops do on TV. *See? I'm not armed.*

'Thought it was empty,' he said, tapping the window with a fingernail.

She stared at him.

'Handyman.' He pointed at his chest. Then he pointed at her.

Behind her. 'Microwave.'

Natalie turned to look. There was a microwave on the countertop, its power cable ending in a bouquet of frayed electrical wires.

Her shoulders sagged. *For feck's sake.*

She gave a little wave to show the man that she understood, then put a hand to her chest and laughed to signal that he had absolutely frightened the living shite out of her, but hey, no harm done. *Except maybe knock next time, asshole? Or go to the* front *door?*

'Sorry. Again.' His breath left a blur of condensation on the glass. Then he said, 'I'll come back,' turned, and was gone.

––––––––

The cup had hit the edge of the rug under the dining table, which was good because it hadn't broken but which was bad because it had left a large, spreading stain soaking into the fibres. By the time Natalie had taken care of that and showered and dressed, the clock on the TV screen was telling her it was almost eight and she was wondering what she should do next.

What was Mike doing now?

What did he think *she* was doing?

She didn't quite know herself. This was, admittedly, a hare-brained scheme. Natalie hadn't given it a lot of thought and that approach, yesterday, had felt right, because there'd been way too much thinking going on lately. *Over*thinking. About everything, all the time. It had been a relief to do something different, to *be* different. Yesterday morning she'd watched Mike walk out of their front door and, not long afterwards, some unseen force had propelled her out the front door too. And down the road. On to a bus. To the train station. All the way here, to Shanamore. But what now?

She'd found the book. Was that enough? Or would he find a way to explain *that* away too?

Outside, a car door slammed.

When she went to the window, Natalie saw Andrew loading

boxes into the boot of his car. On impulse, she grabbed her coat and hurried outside.

Andrew was bent over, leaning into the boot, when Natalie called out, 'Morning!' The word hadn't even got all the way out of her mouth when she realised her mistake. The sound startled him and he jerked upwards, whacking his forehead off the underside of the boot's lid.

'Sorry!' She half-ran to close the distance between them. 'God, I'm so sorry—Are you okay?'

Andrew regarded her coldly.

Then he pulled his hand from his head and they both looked at that.

Clean. No blood.

Natalie exhaled.

'I'm so sorry,' she said again. 'Are you all right?'

He grumbled something that sounded like, 'Fine,' and rubbed at the spot where his scalp had made contact with the car. 'What did you …? What do you want?'

'I'm, ah …' What she wanted was to ask him the question, to ask him straight out about Mike, but now that she was standing here, the words wouldn't come. She scrambled for an alternative. 'I'm looking for directions to the beach?'

Andrew pointed over her shoulder. 'Back down the road, turn left. Keep walking and you'll reach the Far Strand. That's the smaller beach. The Front Strand is the main one, where the hotel is. You can walk from one to the other. The tide will be out. You'll have a grand stretch of sand.'

Natalie didn't know what she'd do with a grand stretch of sand – or what she was supposed to do with it – but she thanked him for the information.

'And that Kiln place, it opens at …?'

'Nine,' he said.

'Is it only ever you on reception?'

Andrew looked taken aback. She'd just blurted it out; now, replaying the question in her head, Natalie realised it had the air of a complaint.

'What I meant,' she said quickly, 'is do you meet every guest? Just because' — she stuck a hand into her bag and started feeling around for her wallet – 'a friend of mine stayed here. At least, I think it was here. Maybe you'd recognise him?' She had the wallet out now. She flipped it open and slid the picture of her and Mike, taken at a wedding they'd been to last year, out of one of the card slots. She'd folded it in half so she was hidden on its back side. 'This is him. Michael. Mike.'

She didn't want Andrew to take the photo in case he opened it out fully, but she was also worried her hands might start to shake. Because this was it. The truth. Coming straight for her.

Andrew was frowning at the photo.

'Ring any bells?' she asked. 'I'm sure it was here he said he stayed ...'

'You could just ask him,' he said flatly.

'Yes.' Natalie smiled. 'Yes, of course. I could. I just thought—'

'It wasn't here.'

She raised her eyebrows. 'No?'

'No.'

'He couldn't have checked in without meeting you? Maybe someone else was on reception or—'

'I check everyone in.'

'Oh. Okay.'

Andrew glanced up at his own bedroom window then, prompting Natalie to do the same. There was no one there that she could see. She wondered if the woman from last night was still in Andrew's cottage and who she was to Andrew.

And who she was.

'Well,' she said, 'thanks anyway.'

As she turned to go back to her cottage, it occurred to her how odd it was that Andrew could be as sure as he'd seemed when he'd just glanced at a photograph. Would Mike have *asked* Andrew to lie? The idea of him doing such a thing made no sense. It would turn the man she'd known for nearly a decade into a total stranger. And even if she could find a way to reconcile *that* absurdity, why would

51

Mike have been preparing for a day when she came here and asked Andrew the question?

But then the poetry book, and everything else ...

Mike *had* been here. He must have been. So what other explanation could there be?

It was only after she'd gone back inside that she realised she'd never told Andrew about the handyman.

There wasn't much to do in Shanamore. Go to the beach. Go to The Kiln. Go to the pub. Two of those three things had people in them Natalie could potentially talk to, but those same two things weren't open yet.

It took her half an hour to reach the Far Strand. The journey wasn't the pleasant morning walk she'd been anticipating. Shanamore's idea of a footpath was a few inches of space between the edge of the road's crumbling surface and the muddy ditch that ran alongside. Keeping both feet within its parameters meant constantly ducking thorny branches while cars and trucks whipped past at such high speed that Natalie felt like she'd been unwittingly cast in a dangerous-driving commercial and absolute carnage awaited her up ahead. Each blind bend was a little death.

The beach wasn't worth the risk. The tide was out, as Andrew had promised, but the 'grand stretch' of sand was rippled with pools of brown water and tangles of drying, dirty seaweed that seemed to have pinned an ocean's worth of discarded plastic to the sand. Between her and that was a band of bleached pebbles, flecked, if you stopped to examine them, with cigarette buts and ring-pulls. The waves were too far away for her to hear them crashing and there was no one around except one or two distant dog-walkers. The icy wind whipped her hair and sandblasted her skin, and her eyes watered.

Again, she thought: Here? Really, Mike? This?

But the sky was blue and Natalie liked the smell of the sea, so she continued to walk, shoulders hunched against the wind, until she reached the Front Strand. She stopped at the first bench she came to on the path above the beach and sat down to take in the view, her coat pulled tightly around her.

At this range, the tiny blot of an island she'd seen yesterday was now a jagged tower of rock rising out of the sea. The winding road that connected the dock to the lighthouse was a crisscross of angular scars on its skin. The second, smaller island huddled behind it.

A shadow fell across her: a tall, looming shape.

It – he – said, 'Well, hello again.'

Natalie looked up.

She didn't recognise the man grinning down at her. But when he said, 'Gave you a bit of a fright this morning, didn't I?' the penny dropped: he was the Peeping Tom turned maintenance man who'd almost caused her a coronary.

'Oh.' Natalie smiled tightly. 'Yes. Hi.'

'Mind if I …?' Without waiting for a response, he sat down next to her on the bench. Inches apart, even though there was plenty of room to leave a couple of feet between them. He stuck out a hand. 'Richard.'

After mentally playing out the potential consequences of alternative responses, Natalie opted for the path of least resistance: she shook it.

'N—Marie.'

He squeezed her hand in his for a moment longer than was necessary. His skin felt ice-cold against hers.

'Gorgeous morning, isn't it?' Richard said then, turning to look out over the water. 'Weather like this, it blows all the cobwebs away.'

Natalie studied him. Up close, he didn't look quite as old and dishevelled as he had during their earlier encounter. Late forties, she'd guess. He was in different clothes now. Wool trousers and a thick, padded jacket with a logo on its sleeve. But his face was deeply lined and rough with grey stubble, and the skin on the side of his nose was red raw and looked sore. His hair seemed even more wild here, whipping about in the sea breeze, but although it was long and there seemed to be lots of it, it looked matted with grease and patches of pink scalp showed through. His lips were badly chapped.

'I prefer it here this time of the year,' he was saying now. 'We have the place to ourselves. No bloody tourists, eh?' He smiled at her, revealing a row of honey-coloured teeth jostling with each other for space. 'No offence.'

Natalie shifted her weight on the bench, trying to open up more space between them without being obvious about it.

'You down here on your own, then?'

'Yes,' she said. 'Just fancied a walk.'

'I meant here in Shanamore.'

She knew he had. 'My husband's coming later today.' The lie came easily. He was a stranger who knew exactly where she was staying and where she was staying, *alone*, was in the middle of nowhere.

And he had access to it.

'What does he do then, this husband?'

'Finance.'

Richard snorted. 'Lovely, we *all* do a bit of finance.'

Sweetheart, love, darling. Natalie was well used to these so-called terms of endearment from delivery men, waiters, the barista at her local coffee shop. They barely registered with her; she didn't think it was worth fighting the feminist fight for what was, for most offenders, a verbal tic, a habit, an innocent if intensely annoying way of speaking to women that had slipped into their vocabulary and put down roots, especially when there was so much more important stuff to fight for. But there was something about that *lovely*, something intimate and yet also … Was it infantile? It made her skin crawl.

She realised that Richard hadn't said anything else and was looking at her expectantly.

'He works for a venture fund,' she said.

'I know what *that* is.' His tone implied he thought she didn't think he would. 'Bet he makes a lot of dough doing that, eh?'

She felt his eyes travel down the side of her face and on to her neck and she was grateful for the winter coat that obscured the lines of her body and covered up the rest of her skin.

A scan of the beach clocked only two other people, a couple, and they were some distance away and walking in the opposite direction. It wasn't worth the risk to be rude.

A few moments more so her departure wouldn't look too abrupt, and then she was out of here.

'He works very hard,' she said. 'So you work up at the cottages?'

'I do a lot of things.'

Again, there was an indignant air about his answer, as if she'd *accused* him of working there.

His accent was British, the ex-Etonian RADA-actor kind. Geography-wise, she wouldn't have a clue, but he sounded posh. And not Irish at all.

'How long have you lived in Shanamore?'

'Oh.' Richard shrugged. 'A while.'

'It's nice.'

'It's lonely.'

Natalie didn't take the bait.

And enough was enough. She moved as if to get up. 'Well—'

He turned, surprised. 'You're not off already?'

'I was just stopping for a second, I wasn't …' *You don't owe him an explanation.* 'Yes, I am. Well, it was nice—'

'You've got your car?' Richard made a show of looking around.

Natalie stood up, brushing something imaginary from her coat. 'I'm walking.'

'I'll give you a lift.' A statement, not an offer.

'Thanks, but I want to walk.'

'I'll walk with you.' Richard smiled as if he was doing her a favour, generously changing his plans to accommodate hers. 'It's no trouble.'

Natalie scanned the beach. The couple were even further away now, just a dark dot in the distance.

She said, 'But you have your car.'

'I do.' Richard stood up now, too. 'It's down at the Far Strand.'

And there, finally, was her out. He was assuming that she was walking back the way she'd come, in the direction of his parked car.

'Oh, I'm not heading back yet.' Natalie pointed over her shoulder, down the beach. She didn't even know what was down there, but anywhere in the opposite direction to where he was going would do. 'I'm going to keep going.'

'That's all right,' Richard said, 'I'll walk with you.'

'There's really no—'

'I'll keep you company. Then I can drop you back to the cottages whenever you're ready to go.'

Natalie bit her lip. She wanted to scream.

'Otherwise it's a fair old walk,' he went on, 'and that road isn't very safe for pedestrians. The speed of some of those cars—'

'No offence,' she said, cutting him off and hating herself for the polite smile she couldn't help but temper this with, 'but I'd rather be alone. Thanks anyway. Have a good day.'

Richard's face hardened.

She took a couple of steps back.

He didn't move to follow, but he held up a hand in a frozen wave and said, slowly and deliberately, 'I'll be sure and get that microwave fixed for you.'

He locked eyes with her as he said this, turning whatever unease she'd been feeling up to eleven.

Natalie moved abruptly and started walking, not knowing exactly where she was going, only that it was away from him. Where was this fabled hotel supposed to be? She felt for the key of the cottage in her pocket, manoeuvring her hand until the plastic tag was in her palm and the sharp end of the key was poking up between her fingers.

Just in case.

She could feel Richard's gaze boring holes into her back.

But … Could she *really*? Or was she just overreacting? *Imagining things*, again? She pictured herself recounting what had just happened to someone who wasn't there. *Well, he came up to me and said it was a gorgeous morning and then offered me a lift back to the cottages because the road is a bit dangerous for walkers and, oh, he said he'd make sure to get the broken thing in my cottage fixed because that's his job.*

She could see Mike in her mind's eye, hands on his hips, looking at the ceiling, lips pressed together. Trying to think of a way to say that she was losing her grip on reality without actually saying that. A *new* way.

'Fucking bitch,' Richard spat from behind her.

Nope, right the first time.

Natalie picked up her pace.

The Front Strand was just one long beach disappearing around a bend into the Far Strand at the west end and, from what she could see, ending in a bank of sand dunes up ahead of her, to the east. The footpath she was on ran parallel to the water. There was a large car park with two or three cars, all empty; a neglected children's playground and some low-slung buildings off in the distance that might be a shop and a pub or café or something, but were all shuttered up. That was it. Everything else was fields and road or things that looked to be very far away. Shanamore itself was forty-five minutes' walk – at *least* – back the way she'd come, and she was getting further and further away from it with every step.

But she wasn't going back to where *he* was. Not a chance.

She saw it then. A bus stop.

It was on the other side of the playground, by the main road: a lonely red pole with a dinner-plate-sized Bus Éireann logo tacked on top. The bus that had brought her here yesterday had driven past here on the way to Shanamore. Logic dictated that it would do the same today. But how often?

Natalie was steps from the stop when she heard an approaching car slow behind her. For a second she worried it was Richard but when she turned she saw, sitting somewhat incongruously in the driver's seat of a monstrous Jeep, a woman who looked like she might have her photo under 'Kindly Grandmother' in the dictionary. The passenger-side window was sliding down with an electronic *buzz* and the woman was leaning over.

'You need a lift, love?' she called. 'That bus won't be here for hours. I'm going as far as the village if that's any good to you?'

It was better than good. Natalie skipped the obligatory round of polite refusals, eagerly pulled open the door and got in the car, awash with relief.

Kindly Grandmother was Nettie, who lived in nearby Ballycotton. She and her husband were retired but ran a B&B from their house during the summer months. They talked about the weather and the lack of public transport in rural areas and how good the cake was in the café in The Kiln.

It was after nine now; The Kiln would be open. Natalie asked if Nettie wouldn't mind dropping her off there.

'Not at all, love. Sure it's on the way.'

The Kiln's car park was nearly full and a couple were walking up the steps into the shop. It felt like Grafton Street compared to the beach. But when Natalie entered The Kiln – its interior seemed to have both the ceiling height and the respectful hush of a church or a cathedral – she found that the place was practically deserted. There was just the couple she'd followed up the steps, a bored cashier rearranging leaflets at the register and, down the far end, a waitress in an empty café area.

She wondered who owned all the cars outside.

Then Natalie saw the very last thing she was expecting to see here, in The Kiln, in Shanamore.

A picture of her own face smiling up at her.

FASTFORWARD

0:00:44

Audrey arrived at Mike and Natalie's home just as someone else was leaving it: a blonde woman, wearing a long, beige trench coat cinched tightly at the waist and a pair of those thick-framed designer glasses that manage to look both ridiculous and incredibly chic all at once. She turned and walked off in the opposite direction, towards the beach. Audrey wondered if maybe the woman was one of Natalie's friends. She made a mental note to check Natalie's Instagram connections for women who looked like that later.

Sydney Parade Avenue seemed relatively quiet for a residential street so close to the city centre and abutted by two busy roads. There was a steady flow of traffic but no horns or sirens, and no pedestrians once the blonde woman had disappeared around a bend in the road. The Kerr–O'Connor home was an elegant red-brick Edwardian semi-D with a stained-glass window in its front door and what looked like new sash windows in a tasteful sage green. A loose gravel drive pushed the house back from the road and immaculately manicured hedging served as a buffer from it. It was picture-perfect except for the fact that all the blinds were drawn and one of the two vehicles parked outside was a Garda car.

The listing for the house was still online. Audrey had checked. It didn't reveal how much the house had actually sold for, but the asking price had been just a few euro shy of seven figures. Crazy money for the square footage, but par for the course in this, Ireland's most expensive postcode.

As Audrey walked up the drive, each step made a conspicuously loud crunching sound on the loose gravel underfoot. The rattan welcome mat said *Our neighbours have better stuff*.

She rang the doorbell and stepped back to wait.

An electronic *ding* from her coat pocket signalled the arrival of a new email. A message from Joel. This time he was no words and all punctuation.

???

Audrey was hurriedly typing *Got something, more soon* when the front door opened and she and Mike Kerr were face-to-face.

He looked a bit dishevelled, like he'd just woken up from a nap, but otherwise he was the man in Natalie O'Connor's wedding photos. Tall and broad-shouldered and attractive, but in a generic, forgettable kind of way. If she'd seen him committing a crime, she mused now, she'd find him hard to describe to police. He was in need of a shave and either didn't know or didn't care that he'd dripped coffee or some other brown liquid down the front of his shirt.

He blinked at her in confusion.

'Audrey,' she said, sticking out a hand. 'Coughlan. From The Paper? We spoke on the phone.'

'Right, right,' Mike said. 'Yes. Sorry. Come in, come in.'

Inside the house was quiet and cold. What little light was coming through the blinds was weak and thin. Shadows fell everywhere. The difference between what Audrey had seen of this house online and what she was looking at now was the difference between the dress on the model on the dodgy website and the dress that arrived, creased and wrinkly and shapeless, in the post a month later postmarked China. Natalie O'Connor had clearly applied a few filters in her time.

Mike led her down the hall, towards the rear of the house. As they passed the open door of what looked like the living room, Audrey caught a glimpse of the occupants: one man and one woman, both in Garda uniforms. She was standing in front of the fireplace, he was sitting on the couch. Both of them looked up as they passed. It was somewhat disconcerting to encounter uniformed Gardaí in someone's home and Audrey was reminded that she was totally winging it here and potentially way out of her depth.

Her palms began to sweat.

Mike took her into the kitchen, an enormous, clinically white space, clearly a new extension to the original house. The blinds were up on these windows and there was an enormous skylight above the dining table, so it wasn't quite as gloomy as the front of the house. But Audrey could detect a faint rotting-food smell; somewhere there was a rubbish bin that needed emptying or a fridge in need of a clear-out. There were soiled dishes in the sink and a pizza box on the counter, stained with splotches of grease.

Mike indicated that she should take a seat at the dining table.

Audrey obeyed and then set about getting what she needed out of her bag. Her notebook. A pen. Her phone so she could record the conversation. She did this slowly, to give herself a chance to gather her thoughts. She'd start by asking the questions she'd come up with on the way here, the ones she'd hastily scribbled down in the bus shelter around the corner. But she should also remember to study him, to try to gauge his emotional state, to see what she could glean from his demeanour. And not to upset him. Unless ... Would it be better if he *did* get upset? Would that make a better story?

Audrey began to wish that she'd talked to Joel before she'd left the office, got his advice.

Mike sat down across from her.

Too late now.

'So,' she said, 'thanks so much for agreeing to talk to me.' She smiled, then realised this wasn't a smiling situation. And she should probably say ... 'I'm so sorry about Natalie.' But that made it sound like she was offering her condolences. *Shit.* 'I mean, I was sorry to hear that she'd ...' What? What was the end of that sentence? Natalie could be luxuriating in a five-star spa resort on the lakes of Killarney for all anyone knew. 'I know this must be a very stressful time for you.' *Okay, good.* 'And a very frustrating one.' *Better.* 'But because we're an online news site, I think we're best placed to reach Natalie's followers. Much more so than the traditional media outlets. So we can get the details out there, amplify the Garda appeal. We can help. We will help. With *your* help.' Oh, that was good. Where had she pulled that from? She should write that one down.

'Yeah,' Mike said. He had folded his arms. 'Let's just get this over with.'

For a second Audrey was wounded that she'd failed to endear herself to her subject, but this wasn't a social call. She set her phone recording and pushed it across the table, closer to him. She flipped to the page in her notebook with her questions. Most of them were barely legible.

She closed the notebook again. Took a deep breath.

'So,' she said. 'Mike. Right. Let's start at the beginning. When did you first realise that Natalie was missing?'

'I don't know that she *is* missing.' When he saw the confusion on Audrey's face, Mike added, 'Just because *I* don't know where she is doesn't mean she's missing. Does it?'

Audrey thought that since he was her husband and he hadn't seen or heard from his wife in a week and there was a Garda appeal out for information on her whereabouts, that's exactly what it meant.

'Okay … Well, then, when did you last see her? Let's start there.'

'Monday morning.'

'Here in the house?'

'Here in this kitchen.'

'How did she seem?'

Mike's eyes narrowed. 'I thought this was about asking the public for help.'

'It is, but—'

'Then why do you need to know how she *seemed*?' He rolled his eyes. Combined with the folded arms, messed-up hair and stained T-shirt, the gesture gave him the distinctive air of Sullen Teenager. 'You don't.'

Audrey hadn't expected Mike to be this prickly but then maybe he was right to be. ThePaper.ie could help disseminate the appeal for information on Natalie's whereabouts, yes, but only if it came wrapped up in something that appealed to their core readership. A story that was, on some level, an attempt to tear Natalie down.

Maybe Mike knew this.

Maybe this was just him trying to protect his wife.

'Had you any contact with her after that?' Audrey asked. Yes/no questions were probably a safer bet at this juncture. 'After you saw her on Monday morning, I mean.'

Mike shook his head. 'No.'

'She didn't leave a note?'

'No.'

'Did you try to contact her?'

'Of *course* I did.'

'By phone?'

'Repeatedly. There was no answer. Then it started going straight to voicemail. I sent her messages too, but there was no response.'

'Did any of those messages have read receipts?'

'She never read them,' Mike said. 'By the morning after, they weren't even getting delivered. She must have turned her phone off.'

'Do you've any idea where she might have gone?'

'No.'

'Has she done anything like this before?'

'No.'

'Why did you wait a week to report it to the Gardaí?'

'Because this isn't—' Mike stopped, exhaled. She sensed he was either nearing the end of his patience or regretting inviting her here, or both. 'This isn't *that*, okay?'

'Not what?'

'You know ...' He waved a hand, as if the thing they were talking about was tangible and sitting on the table between them. 'Something bad.'

Audrey waited.

'Look,' Mike continued, 'she cancelled things, okay? She had an event on Thursday – last Thursday – and first thing Monday, that morning, she cancelled it. She called the organisers on the phone and sent an email apologising. And then there was that post, with the suitcase ...' He shrugged. 'She just needed some time off, that's all.'

'But why not tell you that?' Audrey said. 'Do you think?'

Mike looked away. 'I don't know.'

Because maybe she needed time off from you, too, Audrey thought.

She said, 'So, you last see her on Monday morning and you called the Gardaí on …?'

'Natalie's parents called them on Friday,' Mike said. 'I was going to give it until today, but they didn't want to wait.'

'Why did you want to?'

'Because I didn't want this,' Mike said, pointing at Audrey. 'Or them.' Pointing towards the living room. The two uniformed Gardaí in there.

'But surely you want to know where she is, that she's safe.'

'Of *course* I do,' Mike said, loud enough for it to qualify as shouting. 'That's why I'm doing this, why I'm talking to you.' He shook his head. 'For all the bloody good it's doing.'

Audrey let a beat pass.

'When you saw her,' she said then, 'do you know if it was before or after she put that post with the suitcase up on Instagram? The one with the note about her taking a break? Because I read some of the comments on it and, God, they were awful.'

'Never read the comments.'

'Is that what Natalie says?'

'It's what *I* say to *her*. All the time.'

'Does she listen to you? Maybe she read the ones on that post and got upset, and that had something to do with why she left.'

Mike shook his head. 'It wasn't that.' Before Audrey could ask the obvious question, he'd pushed on. 'Look, Nat values her privacy, okay? I know that seems like a weird thing for someone in her position to claim, but she does. Everything that goes up online is carefully chosen. That pink suitcase? That's not even hers. Not the one she uses, anyway. She points out the things to people that she wants them to see and she keeps everything else for herself. For *us*. We live a private life, ironically. And I want her to come home, to come back, but I don't believe that I have to go against her wishes in order to do that, okay? We're appealing for information here, not sharing it. We should be able to do this without, you know, you printing her diaries or whatever.'

'When you say "her wishes", you mean …?'

'She wanted *more* privacy, not to be more exposed than she ever had.'

'But surely she would've known that if she left, and told no one where she was going, that it would—'

'I *know*,' Mike said. 'I know.' He threw up his hands. 'I'm just trying to do my best here, okay? I don't know why she left without telling me. Maybe she didn't. I mean, maybe she did tell me. I was thinking, she could've called and left a voicemail, but, like, accidentally rang the wrong number or something?'

It took Audrey a moment to realise he was actually asking her this.

'I suppose,' she said. 'Yeah. That's possible. But, ah, wouldn't she have heard the voicemail greeting and realised it wasn't you?'

It was written all over Mike's face: he hadn't thought of that.

'The Gardaí are here,' Audrey said to change the subject.

'Yeah … Our next-door neighbour called them.'

Audrey was confused. 'About Natalie?'

'No. She, ah, she saw some woman creeping around the back garden earlier. While I was out. She called 999 to report a break-in.' He sighed. 'It was probably just one of Natalie's crazy followers. She has a few.'

'But surely they don't know where she lives?'

'You'd hope not. But there, um …' Mike hesitated. 'There was an incident a couple of weeks back. This woman knocked on the door. Natalie thought it was a neighbour and invited her in.'

'What happened?' Audrey said. 'Who was she?'

Two loud electronic notes rang out: the doorbell. Mike got up so fast that his chair's legs screeched on the floor.

As he hurried out of the kitchen, Audrey sank back into her chair, deflated. Just when things were getting interesting … She pressed PAUSE on her phone.

She could hear the front door opening, then voices in the hall. The shuffle of footsteps. The voices moved away and then were muffled suddenly by the closing of an interior door. It sounded like someone had arrived and Mike had gone with them into the living room where the two Gardaí already were.

Audrey looked around the kitchen.

She drummed her fingers on the table, deciding.

Decided.

As quietly as she could, she grabbed her phone and started a circuit of the room, snapping pictures as she went. She took a few shots of the noticeboard on the wall, close enough so she'd be able to read all the little notes, receipts, postcards and trinkets stuck on there. She flipped through the little piles of paper that sat on the countertop – the post, probably picked up from the hall and dropped here. Bills mostly, addressed to Michael Kerr, and a couple of Jiffy Bags with Natalie's name handwritten on them in Sharpie. One had been stamped with the name of a well-known magazine and another with the logo of a high-end department store. She took photos of both, just in case. She checked cupboards and peeked quickly into junk drawers. For what, she didn't quite know, but she knew she would if and when she found it.

This just felt like something she should be doing.

And also something that she *shouldn't* be doing.

Which, when you worked on the Ents desk at the ThePaper.ie, was about exactly right.

Audrey noted there were no fewer than three different places to leave a note in this kitchen: a floral memo pad on top of the microwave, a chalkboard magnetically attached to the fridge and a reporter's notebook wedged between two travel mugs on the dresser, complete with pen threaded through its coil. And those were just the old-fashioned ways of doing it.

She saw a thin, cornflower-blue hardback book sitting on one of the other kitchen chairs, facedown. It looked like it'd been flung there, mid-read. At first she thought it was one of those Ladybird-style children's books, but when she turned it over she saw that it was in fact a book of poetry. *Percy Bysshe Shelley selected by Fiona Sampson*. She flipped through it. The pages were clean and smooth. No one in this house was obsessively reading their Romantic poets, that was for sure. There was a slightly off-kilter sticker on the inside cover that said, *Keats-Shelley House Rome*. Someone – Natalie, she assumed – had written *For my M* on the title page.

She put the book down on the table and positioned her phone over it so she could snap a pic.

'What are you doing?'

A male voice, but not Mike's.

Audrey looked up. There was a man standing in the doorway. Tall – taller than Mike – with tightly cut black hair. Mid-thirties. Nice eyes, blue ones. Wearing a dark navy suit and standing with his hands in its pockets, impatiently awaiting Audrey's answer.

'I was just …' She could feel her cheeks colouring. 'I'm interviewing Mike. I work for ThePaper.ie.'

'Delighted for you,' the man said flatly. He took what looked like a little wallet from his pocket and flipped it open. All Audrey could see from where she stood was the emblem of An Garda Síochána. 'Interview's over.'

'But I wasn't finished. *We* weren't fin—'

'You can direct any outstanding questions to the Garda Press Office.' He gestured to the hall behind him, towards the front door. 'Off you go.'

Audrey considered digging her heels in and demanding that she speak to Mike himself, but everything about this man – his stance, his tone, his cool authority – told her that would be a pointless exercise. Instead, she sighed grumpily, theatrically, and collected her things.

When she walked past him into the hall, he turned to follow her out.

The door to the living room was nearly fully closed. With her escort following behind her, Audrey didn't have a chance to stop and look in. She could hear the low murmur of voices, including Mike's, but couldn't make out any of the words.

Outside, it was spitting now and there was a third car parked in the drive – unmarked, D-reg – squeezed in lengthways so it blocked the exit of the other two.

She turned back to face the Garda. He had his hand on the front door and was already pulling it closed.

'Can I just—'

But Audrey had to swallow the rest of her complaint.

The door had closed in her face.

'More than eight thousand views,' Joel said, reading from a printout, 'in under an hour.' He looked up. 'That's great, Audrey. Really great. Well done you.'

'Thanks.' She was standing in the doorway of Joel's office again, but this time it was because ThePaper.ie's analytics said she'd just written the site's best performing content that day by far. She was feeling so proud of herself that she feared she might be literally beaming. Wait until she told Dee about *this*. But smug wasn't a good look so she waved a hand and said, 'Well, there *was* a readymade audience for this. I can't take all the credit.'

'I agree,' Joel said, deflating her smugness like a pin in a balloon. 'But it's still a good story.'

She smiled. She'd take that.

The piece that had gone live on the site just before four o'clock that afternoon was actually Audrey's second draft. Joel had handed her back her first with half the lines crossed out and a scribbled note that said, *What do YOU think happened? Decide then arrange facts to imply without getting sued. Don't spell out.*

Audrey thought what had happened was obvious: Mike and Natalie had had a blazing row about something and she'd stormed out of the house in a huff. It explained everything: why she'd cancelled an event and posted the suitcase message but hadn't told her husband where she was going or answered his calls. Why he'd waited to report her disappearance to the Gardaí and why he now seemed so reluctant to speak to the press. In fact, it was the particular strain of his reluctance – embarrassment – that had convinced Audrey of this scenario over, say, him having killed her and buried her body under the patio. He just seemed mortified about the whole thing.

But she couldn't *write* any of that, of course.

Her second piece had briefly recapped Natalie's career as an Irish Instagram star, showcased a few of her most popular posts and then stated the facts about her disappearance. Audrey included a few quotes from Mike about not reporting it because he didn't want to embarrass her and his belief that she had left and was fine. She finished by embedding the suitcase post from Instagram and noting that Natalie had left no note or message for her husband. The average ThePaper.ie reader – suspicious, cynical, convinced of their own cleverness – would surely think there was something to put together out of that juxtaposition.

And then they'd put it together.

Clickity-click.

'So what should I do now?' she asked. 'I thought I could track down her best friend, Carla. She's tagged in a few of Natalie's posts; I should be able to find her online. And maybe I could find out more about that woman who visited the house. That could be a whole separate thing, actually: the crazies who stalk Irish Instagram stars. And I know that guard was being sarcastic but maybe I actually *could* get something out of the Garda Press Office? I mean, I could try?'

Joel shifted in his seat. 'Ah, Audrey, look. You've done great work here. Really. You went above and beyond. I mean, none of us expected you to talk to the husband. Upstairs know you exist now and I know the bossman was personally impressed. That's great for you in the long run. But tomorrow morning, you're back on the Ents desk, okay?'

'What? But there's *loads* more I could dig out on this.'

That had come out far more whiney than Audrey had intended, but she couldn't help herself. She wasn't ready to go back to the click-factory yet. She'd got a taste of what it felt like to write an actual story and now the mere idea of typing *flaunts her curves* or *steps out amid* made her feel a bit sick.

'The story here,' Joel said, 'is that an Irish Instagrammer is missing. And thanks to you, we've covered that. If she doesn't come back, there's nothing to write about. If she does, boring. If anything else happens, that's a crime story that our crime reporters will cover, not you.' His expression softened, probably because he'd realised that the look on Audrey's face was one of abject despair. 'This was the deal from the beginning, Audrey. I'm not breaking news here.' Joel turned to the screen of his laptop, squinted at it, then started typing.

Their conversation was over.

Dejected, Audrey trudged back to her desk.

The chairs on either side of hers were empty but Audrey could see a couple of the Ents team approaching with steaming coffee cups. She put on her headphones to signal that she was Do Not Disturb, booted up her laptop and put her head down. It was nearly five o'clock. Half an hour and she'd be able to leave here, go home and wallow in her own misery.

Then she remembered that it was T-minus three weeks to her having nowhere to live. She'd have to spend the evening figuring out what the hell she was going to do. Searching Daft.ie. Doing her sums.

God, things were so bad she couldn't even *wallow*.

Idly, Audrey opened up her email account.

And immediately saw that something was wrong. She had almost 500 unread messages, all of which had come in since her Natalie O'Connor piece had gone live.

What the ...?

Audrey went to ThePaper.ie homepage. The headline of her story was at the top of it. Directly underneath was her name and thumbnail-sized headshot. Directly beneath *that* was her email address.

Anyone who read the article could contact her and, apparently, many of them had.

She went back to her email account and started scanning the messages.

Most of them fell into the category of feedback, if you were being generous with the term. Someone had actually taken the time to go to their phone or computer and type out the words *Was there supposed to be a story here? Must have missed it.* Or *I hope your school wasn't fee-paying because you are entitled to your money back. So many grammatical errors I couldn't get through the first paragraph.*

PROOFREAD YOUR WORK, idiot. Or *Nice pic bet yr cunt tastes nice.* Ignore. Delete. Block. Repeat as required. Audrey kept going, scanning each one, just in case there was something there.

And there was.

An Orla Sheridan had sent a message at 5:02 p.m., about an hour after the story had gone live. She was a waitress in a café in Shanamore, she said (wherever *that* was), and she claimed she'd talked to Natalie on Tuesday, the day after she'd disappeared from her home.

> It was definitely her. I have her business card. We talked about Instagram and Mike and stuff. When I saw the thing online this morning I rang the Garda number and told them about this and they took my number but no one has called me back. The reason I'm telling you is because I think it's a bit weird. She said Mike had been here recently and asked me if I'd seen him. (I hadn't.) And she said she didn't want anyone to know where she was and asked me not to post anything online about her. She said she was here for 'peace and quiet' but TBH I didn't buy that. And there's a guy here, bit of a creep, who she said tried to come on to her down by the beach. I don't know if that means anything. And the cottages she stayed in are a bit of a weird place to stay by yourself. I don't know, it's all just a bit off.

As she read, Audrey felt a tingle travel down her spine.

She Googled Shanamore. It appeared to be a glorified crossroads near a seaweed-and-stones-strewn East Cork beach that was half an hour's drive from everywhere else. Audrey vaguely recalled a primary school friend from Cork who'd spent her summers there and the rest of the year complaining about having to.

The village appeared to have a church, two pubs, a petrol station and some sort of arty-farty 'design centre' but not much else. Audrey could imagine that, on nice summer days, Shanamore was the quintessential Irish seaside day out. Sand and splashing and maybe a carton of chips for the drive home or a rapidly melting 99. But this was the dead of winter. The place must be cold and desolate and cloaked in darkness by five o'clock. Why would anyone go there now? Natalie's Instagram chronicled mini-breaks to Paris and Rome, monthly trips to London and 'me time' in every spa resort on the island of Ireland. Why would *she*? And go there without telling her husband, and then start asking the locals about him once she'd arrived?

Before Audrey could let her imagination off the leash entirely, she needed proof that Orla wasn't a whacko. She hit REPLY and asked for a scan of Natalie's business card and Orla's phone number.

Five minutes later, she had them.

Orla had also sent a link to a place called Shanamore Cottages. Clicking on it, Audrey discovered a complex of weird-looking holiday homes that definitely *didn't* conjure up images of the Irish seaside. They stank of Celtic Tiger optimism and looked like they'd suffered neglect since. They were closer to the village than the beach and, according to the pictures on the website, there were only six of them, arranged in a U-shape. Their interiors, however, were modern and striking – or at least they appeared to be in the well-lit images on the website. Popular Instagrammers were always being offered free stays and comp'd trips, weren't they? Was it possible that Natalie had been offered a free stay there? Could there be a legitimate reason why she'd kept that a secret?

A thought struck her: what if Natalie O'Connor was there *right now*?

Audrey pulled off her headphones and picked her phone up, then put it back down again. What was she doing, exactly? Joel had told her in no uncertain terms that she was done with Natalie O'Connor. Case closed. Or passed to proper reporters if and when something happened. Tomorrow, for Audrey, it was back to reality.

But …

What harm was there in making a phone call?

She picked up her phone again and tapped out the number from the Shanamore Cottages website.

It rang three times before a male voice answered with a dull 'Hello?'

'Hi,' Audrey said. 'Is that, ah, Shanamore Cottages?'

'Yeah?'

'Great. I hope you can help me ... I'm trying to get in contact with my sister who I believe might be staying with you? We've had a family emergency and she isn't answering her phone. Her name's Natalie O'Connor.'

A beat passed. Then: 'She's not here.'

'Oh.' Audrey made a *tut-tutting* noise. 'Damn. Maybe she left sooner than she planned to. *Was* she there?'

Another beat passed. But this one was followed by a *click*, then the irritating bleep of an engaged tone.

Whoever was answering the phone at Shanamore Cottages had just hung up on her.

PAUSE

0:00:47

Jennifer is in the back office when the email comes in. A bubble of hope rises in her heart when she sees Mike's name, but then pops when she realises the message is just a Google Alert linking to an article that went live on ThePaper.ie an hour ago.

Gardaí appeal for information on missing Instagram star, the headline reads.

Jennifer mumbles some excuse to David, her assistant duty manager on second shift, and walks out of the back office. They've been allocating rooms – or trying to – for a group of ten pensioners arriving on Monday, all of whom want ground-floor rooms in a property that has only four and no lift. It should've been sorted out last week but Jennifer's discovering that while she was off, everyone apparently decided to down tools and take a break.

Only after she's locked herself into an empty cubicle does she click on the link.

Underneath the headline is a picture of Mike and Natalie on their wedding day. Jennifer scrolls past it and starts scanning the text.

There are quotes from Mike. He has *participated* in this article.

Jennifer doesn't know how to feel about that.

She keeps reading.

After some crap about Natalie's 'success' and a rehashing of the Garda appeal, they've pasted in the Instagram post. The suitcase one, Natalie's last. Jennifer knows the caption off by heart, she's read it so many times, convinced on each occasion that *this* time she'll see something different, some word or phrase that suggests Natalie *knew*, that she'd found out about Mike and Jennifer and that's why she'd walked out of the door that morning.

She reads the caption again now, her brain saying the next word before her eyes can see it.

Taking a few days to myself. I hate to be one of those
insufferable people who tell you they're taking a break
from their phone and social media by posting to social
media using their phone, but I don't want you thinking
I've mysteriously disappeared. Sometimes I just need
to live up to my own brand. Back soon! #outoftheoffice
#timeout #andbreathe

Jennifer shakes her head and thinks, What a truckload of absolute
shite. 'Sometimes I just need to live up to my own brand'? What does
that even *mean*?

The Paper understands that Ms O'Connor did not inform
her husband, family or friends of her plans. Mr Kerr says he
learned of them as Ms O'Connor's online followers did: from
her final social media post (above).

Then there's a quote from Mike:

'Natalie values her privacy. I know that seems like a weird
thing for someone in her position to claim, but everything
that goes up online is carefully chosen.'

Carefully chosen. That's a dig at Natalie, it has to be. This makes
Jennifer smile.

In response to questions about why he waited a week to
report his wife missing, Mr Kerr said he believed his wife
had planned to leave their home and was not in danger.
He maintains that he didn't want to 'embarrass' her with
unnecessary media attention. The Paper has confirmed
that Ms O'Connor cancelled an upcoming appointment via
telephone and email before she left her home on the morning
of 5 November.

Jennifer scrolls back up to the wedding picture and puts her thumb over Natalie's face. Mike looks so handsome in a tux. He'll look even better in one on *their* wedding day.

They haven't spoken about it yet, but they don't need to. There's an understanding: this is it, for both of them. They've made enough mistakes on the way here. They won't make another one by letting each other go now.

But their wedding will be small and special. Intimate. *Private*. Not the fucking tasteless sponsor spectacle The Influencer Bitch forced him to suffer through.

Jennifer is suddenly gripped by a desperate need to speak to Mike, so bad that she feels a sharp pain in her chest.

She can't contact him. Not yet. How would it look, for the husband of a missing woman to have a mistress? Everyone would assume the worst. They'd say this was his fault. Natalie would be the wronged woman, the heartbroken wife.

Maybe that's exactly what Natalie had been counting on happening when she left. Maybe her plan had been to draw Jennifer out, into the spotlight. To expose her. To expose the affair.

Well, she isn't going to fall for it.

And anyway, she *has* to stay away now, after that debacle at the house earlier. What was that neighbour even doing, face up against her bedroom window, staring into someone else's back garden? Nosy cow. And after all of it, Mike hadn't even been in.

Jennifer scrolls back up to the top of the page, to the reporter's by-line. *Audrey Coughlan*. A woman, then. She feels a tinge of jealously that's only made worse by the thumbnail picture. The reporter looks younger than Jennifer, and attractive. And she's met Mike.

Actually—

She taps the screen with two fingers, zooming in.

Is that the woman she saw going into Mike's house?

Jennifer had fled when she'd seen the nosy neighbour, but returned later, checking to see if Mike had come home since. His car was in the driveway, so she went for it. If anyone asked, she was just going to say that she was a friend of Natalie's. But when she got to the gate, she'd seen there was another car there too. A fucking Garda car. Either something had happened with Natalie or Mrs Bitch Next Door had gone and called the bloody police. Jennifer had just about managed to execute an abort, stopping and making a face as if she'd zoned out and approached the wrong house, in case anyone was watching, before turning swiftly on her heel and continuing down the road. When she was far enough away, she'd turned back to see if anyone had come out of the house. No one had, but someone was going into it: a woman.

This reporter, Jennifer realises now.

Audrey.

The jealously flares up into a hot, burning streak. This woman, who doesn't know Mike *at all*, was able to waltz inside his house and speak to him. Sit close with him. Be with him.

It's just not fair.

Jennifer's free hand clenches into a fist until she can feel the sharp tips of her manicured nails digging into her palm.

It's irrational, this feeling. She knows that, she isn't stupid. But that doesn't mean she can turn it off like a switch.

And this *Audrey*, she doesn't seem particularly nice, does she? There's a snide tone to the article, when you think about it. *Mr Kerr* says *he learned of them … Mr Kerr* said *he believed … He didn't want to 'embarrass' her*. What the hell are those quotation marks about?

Jennifer scrolls down to the LEAVE A COMMENT button.

Mike would be absolutely horrified if he ever found out about this, but he needn't ever know. He won't — Jennifer already has a user account on ThePaper.ie; her username is a string of random numbers and her profile picture is of a middle-aged man with a ruddy red face and a shaved head. She types:

> So let me get this straight. This self-obsessed self-styled 'influencer' (WTAF?) told her posse of idiotic sycophants that she was leaving, but not her own husband? Why are we even bothering to look for this bitch? And who wrote this 'article'? A child? Go back

> to school. You clearly need more of it. It's not like your
> looks are going to pay the bills, love, that's for sure.

She reads over it once, then clicks SUBMIT.

The action works like the opening of a vent. The anger loses its pressure, then begins to disperse.

She feels better. Calmer.

She can think clearly again.

The Paper claims comments are moderated, but in Jennifer's experience there are, at best, random checks. She's seen all sorts of vitriol on there, from run-of-the-mill whataboutery to hate speech. She's confident no one will intercept her comment before it goes live on the site. She hopes the reporter sees it. That girl could do with being taken down a notch.

Especially when she can't even get the basic facts right.

> The Paper understands that Ms O'Connor did not inform her
> husband, family or friends of her plans.

But Natalie *did* inform her husband.

She left him a note.

PLAY

0:00:57

Three months in and Seanie still wasn't used to the silence.

He was used to waking up in a one-bed apartment overlooking St John's Road, one of the main arteries into Dublin City's centre, to a cacophony of car horns, rumbling HGVs and whining motorbikes executing impatient overtaking. Noise that started before the sun was up. On the other side of the traffic, train tracks from the south and west terminated in Heuston Station, depositing thousands of commuters on to its platforms five days a week. The trains themselves were a constant low hum, their brakes an occasional screech, the commuters attracting the bells of the tram and the rumble of double-decker buses on which they'd continue their journeys. The apartment building was adjacent to a large chain hotel whose delivery trucks started arriving before dawn and continued coming in waves throughout the morning, each one making a *beep-beep-beep* noise as it reversed into the loading bay. The people in the unit next door liked to wake up to talk-radio turned up loud, the shared wall happy to let the voices through but not the words, which, somehow, was worse.

This was not that. This was nothing at all.

It woke Seanie up, this lack of noise. Eyes wide open no later than seven every morning and sometimes as early as five thirty or six. His theory was that he slept better during the night without the interruption of sirens and the like – with no interruptions at all – so he needed less of it. Quality over quantity.

That's what he was telling himself, anyway.

Imelda's sleep was unaffected, so whenever Seanie woke early he didn't move, he just lay there in the dark. In Shanamore it really *was* dark, the nearest street-light being at least thirty metres away and around a bend in the road. He would lie there and listen to her breathing, thinking about the day ahead and what he might do to keep her from realising that *he'd* finally realised that moving here was mistake.

Too. Because she'd realised it already.

She hadn't actually said it to him, but she didn't need to. Since they moved here, Imelda had developed two different settings: the woman who woke up beside him on a Monday morning and the woman who woke up beside him at weekends. On a Monday she had somewhere to go and she had to be there by a certain time, but that wasn't it. It wasn't *just* that. Her eyes were bright. She moved differently. She smiled more. She was excited.

Excited to leave him.

'Not *you*,' she'd corrected him once, when he was so wounded by her enthusiasm to drive hundreds of miles away from him and stay there for the next five days that he'd let it get the better of him, and said something. 'This *place*.'

He'd said, 'This place *is* me.'

A deep sigh. 'You knew this was how it was going to be.'

'You said you'd transfer.'

'I will. I can't yet.'

'Can't or won't?'

'Oh Seanie, for God's sake.' Imelda only ever used his name when she was exasperated by him. 'This was *your* idea.'

He'd been stationed in Store Street when he got wind of it: Shanamore, Co. Cork, population 941, needed a guard. Cutbacks had closed its one-man station three years ago, forcing the lads across the bay in Ballycotton to hold the fort. But the local TDs must have got an earful about it on the doorsteps in the run-up to the last general election, because miraculously the money was there again. The higher-ups liked the idea of appointing someone young and fresh-faced to the post, someone who'd get involved in the local community, someone happy to leave the city's bright lights behind. What attracted Seanie was the fact that the posting came with a house whose weekly rent was what they were currently spending on a takeaway and a bottle of wine of a Friday night.

At home that night that was the detail he'd led with. They'd been saving for a deposit but they both knew it'd be four or five years before they could afford to buy, and even then it might not be anywhere near the city, let alone in the areas they liked. Living in Shanamore, he told Imelda, would get them where they wanted to go, and quicker. They might even manage to save something on top of the deposit.

What he didn't say too much about, to Imelda or to his superiors, was that he knew Shanamore well. A friend of his grandmother's had had a house down there and when he and his siblings were young, they'd got to use it in the summer months. For three or four weeks each year, one week at a time, his mother would pile him and his brother and sister into the car, pick up his grandmother at her gate and drive an hour and a half west from Waterford to a tiny, three-room cottage on an acre by the beach. It had only one bedroom. The children slept in sleeping bags on the living-room floor while the adults shared the double bed. There was never any hot water and only static on the crappy portable TV, but they spent so little time inside the cottage, it didn't matter.

What they did do was run. Around the garden, down the beach, into the sea. One summer a four-man tent materialised and the kids slept in that, in the garden. The hedges that marked the cottage's boundary line were full of blackberries, which they picked and ate despite being warned not to without washing them first. They made friends with the family next door who had children of similar ages. They made more friends in the caravan park, from one-weekend wonders to children who stayed there all summer long. A World Cup meant endless games of football; an Olympic year meant races and throwing sticks; tennis rackets always seemed to appear around the same time each summer. Sometimes their father came with them instead of Nan, and one time Nan and Mam drove them down and then Mam went back home by herself 'for a break' while they tried – and failed – to picture their mother existing back in their house without them running around her feet.

As they grew into teens, they started hanging out in the pub next to the hotel, drinking cans of Coke and playing pool. They gathered on the beach to drink beer. The boys found private places, little spots tucked between beach boulders or shielded by dunes, and girls who could be convinced to go there with them. Eventually Nan couldn't cope with being cooped up in a tiny house with three teenagers and the three teenagers started moaning about having to leave their friends at home, and Seanie's parents realised that they could afford holidays abroad if only the two of them went. So they did, leaving the kids at home and appointing Seanie Chief Babysitter to Cathal, younger by one year and impervious to authority, and Aoife, younger by three, who mostly stayed locked upstairs in her bedroom.

Now there he was, ten years later, selling Shanamore to Imelda like it was the greatest place in the world. Living by the sea, he said. Fresh air. The quiet idyll of the countryside. They'd spend less but live more.

He was particularly proud of that last line. He was almost certain he'd swiped it from a supermarket ad.

But Imelda wasn't sold. She'd miss the buzz of the Big Smoke, she said. She worked in the IFSC and joked about feeling panicked at the thought of no Starbucks or Deliveroo, but they both knew it wasn't entirely a joke. They moved in a large group of friends and every weekend came with a hectic itinerary. Music festivals. Food festivals. Beer gardens and outdoor cinemas and supper clubs. Some new cocktail club or market or food truck. If not that, then a wedding or stag do.

The truth was, Seanie was exhausted by it all. He'd happily have skipped most of these things and he thought maybe they *should*, considering the cost. When a shift clashed with some outing or festival, he'd moan to Imelda but be secretly glad. Besides, for him, the buzz of the big city meant drugs and disorder and assault. He'd spent too much time taking statements from college students outside fast food restaurants in the early hours of Sunday morning, their faces still smeared with grease and slack with too much booze. He'd seen a friend from Templemore get cut in the face with a broken bottle feet from the Spire in the middle of a Wednesday afternoon. He was ready for a quieter life.

He reminded Imelda that Dublin was only a three-hour drive from Shanamore and that there were plenty of spare bedrooms they could bag for an evening if they wanted to stay up there for a night.

He wore her down.

They'd moved here at the end of July when the skies were blue and the air was warm. Imelda was from Clare and had never been to Shanamore; her childhood beaches were the pristine white sands of the Atlantic Coast. Seanie had recalled the Front Strand's seaweed and stones and worried. But when she first caught sight of it – a panorama of shimmering sea revealed as they rounded a bend in the road in from Midleton – she'd whispered, 'Wow' and he'd started to breathe again, silently thanking the weather for cooperating.

That day, Front Strand was filled with cars and people, and the happy cries of children carried on the wind. They stopped to get celebratory ice creams and Seanie pointed out the cottage where he'd stayed as a kid. Buttery yellow fields of rapeseed made every mile between there and Shanamore Village postcard perfect.

When Imelda saw the café sign outside The Kiln, she'd said, 'Oh, thank *God*,' but by then she was grinning. They both were. Stuck on red at Shanamore's only set of traffic lights she'd leaned over and kissed him and said, 'This is a good idea,' and he'd thought that yes, it *was* a good idea, a bloody brilliant one, and everything was going to work out okay. It felt as if they'd moved their lives into a permanent summer, like every day now was going to feel like a holiday.

Their mood that afternoon wasn't even dampened by the absolute state of the house, a seventies bungalow with a mossy slate roof and about as much charm as a chemical toilet. The Office of Public Works had supposedly given the place a once-over prior to their arrival but it was hard to see where the improvements had been made. There was a shit-brown front door at one end, inset with frosted glass. Next to it were two large windows, hung with vertical blinds, the kind you'd see in a doctor's office. The frames looked like they were rotting. A long, brown-green stain dripped down the pebble-dashed wall between the two windows, evidence that the gutter joint above it had come unsealed.

On the other end was another front door, painted navy blue. A Garda shield was mounted beside it and the newest part of the house was sitting in front: a small cement ramp and metal railing. An eyesore of an antenna rose up behind the house, two or maybe even three times its height, held in place by thick tension cables.

Still in the car, they'd turned and looked at each other.

'I can turn around,' Seanie had said.

Imelda had scoffed. 'As if.'

'I would.'

'It's free, Seanie. Practically, anyway. We'll just keep telling ourselves that. And hey, at least you can't complain about your commute.'

Now, in the darkness of their bedroom, she said, 'Is it seven yet?' Her voice was clear and alert. She'd been awake for a while.

Seanie patted his bedside table for his phone. He pressed a button on it, lighting the room with a weak blue glow.

'Almost,' he said. 'Ten to.'

This was her first time waking up here on a Tuesday morning; there'd been a training day yesterday in Cork, so she'd been able to come home afterwards. But all that did was delay the wrenching Monday-morning routine for one more day.

'I think the phone is ringing,' she said.

'Huh?'

'The *other* phone. Listen.' When Seanie did, he heard the faint but unmistakable shrill on the other side of the wall. 'You should go and check it out.'

Imelda pulled back the covers and he reached for her, touching her arm just as she swung her legs on to the floor, about to say, *I'd rather stay here with you*, but the faraway ringing ceased and his mobile began to vibrate angrily.

A Dublin number.

He sat up in the bed to answer it.

'Sergeant Flynn?'

'Yes,' Seanie said. Then louder, clearer, 'Yes?'

'DS Steven O'Reilly, Blackrock. Sorry — I was going to leave a message.' He could've done that on the station phone, Seanie thought. 'You're in Shanamore?'

'I'm the only one who is.'

'Good man, good man.'

'What can I do for you, Sergeant?'

'You've got a place down there. Shanamore Holiday Village or something? Can't read my own bloody handwriting here. Does that ring a bell?'

'Yeah,' Seanie said. 'Shanamore Cottages.'

But it did more than ring a bell. It sounded an alarm.

Because Andrew Gallagher managed those cottages.

Three months in and Seanie had finally got the call he'd been waiting for.

REWIND TO START

0:00:01

The beginning of it all, it was her.

The summer that stretched between the last day of primary school and the first day of secondary felt like the last of its kind in many ways. Andrew turned thirteen at the start of August but didn't want a party, partly because he worried that he couldn't round up enough kids to go to it and partly because he didn't feel well, hadn't felt well all summer in fact, but endlessly jittery and on edge, sometimes with a sharp pain that bisected his stomach and made breathing hurt.

He knew what was causing it. He sometimes felt like he might be many bad things but stupid wasn't one of them. It was *fear*. He was afraid of making the transition from his one-room country school where a handful of children who couldn't remember not knowing each other all sat within the teacher's eyeline, all the time, to a gleaming labyrinth of corridors and classrooms and playing fields, filled with masses of strangers, some of whom lived in houses attached to other houses and some even in little apartments (the idea of a house that didn't have doors out on to the ground ... Andrew couldn't *imagine* what living in such a thing must be like), and some of whom – the Sixth Years – were old enough to marry and vote and even drive.

The thought of moving among them was terrifying. Especially because he knew so little about how to do it and there was no one, really, that he could ask. He'd taken what little he'd gleaned from overheard conversations, TV shows, the time that girl had got the highest marks in all of Ireland in her Leaving Cert exam and the school was on the news, and spent interminable hours dwelling on it, extrapolating what he could, until he'd convinced himself that there were instructions about how to be and what to say and who to say it to, and that everybody else at the school would already have them.

That had to be the reason why no one else seemed as worried

about this as he was. The challenge then would be pretending that he knew these instructions too until he found them out, before he got found out himself.

For the first time in his life he wished he had an older brother.

There was a gang of teenagers always hanging around the village, looking bored. He watched them as they came off their special school bus that deposited them in the church car park at half-past four each day, hours after Andrew had trudged up the lane to his house with his schoolbag hitting the small of his back in a rhythmic *smack-smack-smack*. He couldn't believe they were only a few years older than him, that he'd look like them soon. They seemed like another species, sauntering around in little packs with untucked shirts and hair on their upper lips and sometimes even things drawn in blue biro on their forearms like DIY tattoos. Their faces always seemed to be communicating some silent threat or challenge.

Andrew feared that secondary school would be filled with people like them and no one like him.

He was right to.

When the time came, no one shoved him up against a wall or pulled down his trousers in the yard or stuffed his head in a toilet. That, at least, would have been something. Some acknowledgement. But there was, it turned out, a worse fate: everyone ignored him. He was able to move around the school like a ghost. Sometimes he would go up to a girl (unlikely to retaliate) or a teacher (unlikely to get mad) and touch their arm or face, just to see if they reacted. Could they see him? It seemed they could, but they didn't want to be around them. Even the teachers, after chastising him, would turn and walk away.

But it was the worst in the classroom where he was forced to stay put.

First Years remained in place while their various teachers came to them. On the first day of term, their year-head told them their seats had been pre-assigned. Forced new-friend-making. Chair-legs screeched on linoleum floors as the teacher read names from a printed list.

Andrew got a seat in the front row, by the window. But the seat to his right remained empty.

He watched helplessly as, all around him, newly matched pairs traded old schools, home addresses and favourite video games. He could only sit there, working to keep an expression on his face that hid his upset, and wait for the teacher to notice she had an odd number. The buzz of chatter grew louder and louder until it started to feel like it might be a weapon, one that was gearing up to attack, to try to break him.

He slid out of his chair and approached the teacher.

Some boy called Barry O'Connell was supposed to be there, she said, but he was missing.

That day and all the days that followed.

Andrew did, in a moment of desperation, try to fix it. On that first Friday, after the last bell, he stalled at his desk, packing away his things particularly slowly, and then especially fast, almost panicked, when he saw that at the top of the room the teacher, Mrs O'Mahony, had started to walk out.

'Miss,' he called out, hurrying towards her. 'The chair next to me is still empty.'

'Yes, yes, Andrew,' she'd said, 'I am aware. I think we may have a phantom boy who's gone off to another school. But moving someone else would just leave someone else on their own, and I can't have threes. There'd be too much messing.' She'd smiled and put a hand lightly on his back, steering him out of the classroom. 'Aren't you lucky to have all that space to yourself?'

When it was clear that he couldn't fix it, Andrew tried to make up for it. He found reasons to talk to the other students in the breaks between classes, pretending he needed a pencil or a protractor or a reminder of what they were supposed to have read in preparation. But these never turned into actual conversations. It was stunted, stilted small talk, and its failure rate drained him.

Lunchtime was too much of a minefield even to try. He ate his sandwiches in the toilets and then walked the corridors in a loop, trying to look like he was heading somewhere with a purpose so that anyone who saw him would assume that he was.

The relief of that first Christmas break made him so joyous he felt like he might burst. Almost three weeks of *no school*! His presents were small and Dad wasn't very well so it was, his mother kept saying on the phone, *a quiet one this year*, but Andrew basked in every minute and every hour of not having to sit in that classroom, alone; of every morning he didn't have to get out of bed while it was still dark; of every day he didn't have to board the school bus feeling like it was transporting him to a punishment.

Then, the first day back to school in January, everything changed. Because of *her*.

Caroline.

───────

The first time he saw her she was standing next to Mrs O'Mahony at the top of the class, looking uncertain. She was tall and skinny with spindly legs and knees that seemed like they were the largest part of her. She had her white knee socks pulled all the way up, which even in Andrew's limited experience was a serious, maybe even fatal social infraction. Her eyes were bright blue and her skin was bronzed by some foreign, mixed-up sun that apparently shone in the wintertime, and her hair was the colour of haystacks, poker-straight and so long that it could fall over her shoulders and on to her chest and then down her sides, as if it was flowing out from under her arms. A thick red hairband was holding it back off her face. The most striking thing of all was that she didn't carry a schoolbag like everyone else, but a large, flat cloth-thing made of multi-coloured stripes that hung from her shoulder.

Andrew had never seen anything like her. What *was* she?

But that first moment wasn't the one that changed everything. It was the one after that, when she looked up to Mrs O'Mahony for instruction and said, 'Where should I …?' and Andrew's stomach burned with the knowledge that there was only one empty seat in the room.

'My name is Andrew,' he said as soon as she'd sat down beside him, immediately regretting his haste, his overt display of enthusiasm. But he couldn't waste a chance like this. He figured he had the length of two lessons plus the five-minute break in between before she'd get swept away from him on a tide of louder voices, before the others would get to her and maybe even whisper that he was a loner, a loser, and say she should stay away from him, and nothing was more dangerous to him than the truth.

'Mine's Caroline,' she said.

She reached out her hand and Andrew realised, after a beat, that she intended to shake his with it. He'd never shaken the hand of anyone his own age before. He gripped hers lightly, just for a moment, feeling the warm dryness of her fingers. His were cold.

When she let go she smiled at him and asked him where he lived.

'Shanamore,' he said.

'Where's that?'

'Near Ballycotton.'

Her face lit up. 'That's where *we* live now.'

Her family had just moved from Dubai to her granddad's house, although she also said her granddad had died so Andrew wasn't sure why. Her life sounded like science-fiction to him: she'd lived in Denmark before that, and for a short time, some place near Amsterdam. He couldn't picture those places; they had names he'd heard but he couldn't imagine a reality to go with them. She might as well have told him she'd lived on Saturn's rings. Caroline didn't have to take Irish classes and she was really happy about that. She liked watching *Friends* and had one brother, who was younger, and she was counting down the days until the next Harry Potter book came out.

That weekend, she came bounding up the drive on her bike. *His* drive. She said she'd figured out which house was his by asking in the shop. She'd cycled all the way to Shanamore from Ballycotton, which Andrew knew to be a long, long road. He got his bike and together they cycled to Front Strand and messed around there for the day, throwing stones in the sea, talking about everything and anything.

Afterwards they came back to Shanamore and Caroline strode right into Murphy's, beckoning him to follow, and when he did he saw she'd marched up to the bar and asked Peggy for two Cokes. He barely tasted it, truth be told, so uncomfortable was he being in that adult place without his own adults, and also because he hadn't thought to check if the few coins he had in his pocket added up to the price of a drink. But when they were done Caroline produced a brand-new five-pound note from a shiny wallet and hopped up from her seat before he could even react.

It was dizzying, being with her.

When he got home no one asked Andrew where he'd been and he was glad because how could he even begin to explain it? He went up to his room and closed the door and then the blinds too and he sat there in the dark and just breathed in and out for a while, letting the quiet wash over him again, welcoming it.

All day Sunday, he had a headache.

By Monday morning, the whole thing had started to feel like a strange, impossible dream, the sharp edges of it already blurring and dissipating, like mist, like something he wouldn't be able to hold on to, but when Andrew turned into Class 2H there she was, sitting in the chair beside his, waving at him and then talking at him about some film she'd watched on TV.

That was the beginning.

———

In the twelve months after he first met Caroline, Andrew came to realise that he'd never actually had a friend. Not a real one. Not a *true* one. Not someone he would always choose to be with over not, no matter the circumstances. His classmates back in primary school, the summer kids, Johnny Quirk who'd lived in the house that had been in the field where the American guy was building a new, huge house that supposedly had a pool … He'd always felt, around them, like he was clock-watching, waiting for a polite amount of time to pass before he could make his excuses and go back home, into his room, where he could breathe and unclench and relax. The room was always the better option. When Caroline came along, it was the last place he wanted to be because it was the only place she couldn't be.

At school, their shared desk became a kind of cocoon of sorts, where their friendship could grow without outside interference, without Andrew worrying about whether he'd said or done the wrong thing, or without the ringleaders coming and tempting her away. He knew it would happen eventually and saw the end of the school term rushing towards them like a freight train on tracks they were both tied to. She was pretty and nice and something new and exotic; it was only a matter of time.

The surprise was that when, inevitably, a couple of ringleaders did come to entice her away – an invite to a cinema trip over Easter, that was the first test – she accepted on the condition, on the *assumption*, that Andrew could come along too.

When summer came around again, the first post-Caroline, it didn't feel like the sudden drive off a cliff-edge, wheels spinning helplessly, that Andrew had been dreading. Instead, it was a smooth, gentle path down to the sea.

In the summer sun, something fundamental, tectonic, began to shift beneath his feet.

It started the night a bunch of city kids built a bonfire on the beach. Someone had brought beer, little watery cans of it, a supermarket's own brand. Andrew accepted one. Although he couldn't fathom the attraction, he made sure to agree that it tasted good and then, halfway down the can, realised he was making the same satisfied gasping sounds he'd seen people do on TV.

And then he started to feel the warm, wispy feeling of mild drunkenness, of being protected from all sharp angles, and thinking there could be no consequences, not when the world felt like this. He took Caroline's hand and pulled her towards him, and she put that arm around her shoulders and shifted until she was pressed up against him and then ... Well, he couldn't quite remember the *exact* sequence of events, but then their lips were pressed together and he thought that maybe they were kissing. If that was this? The actual act was wet and weird and made sour by the beer, and kind of mechanical, but the idea was transformative.

That night, when Andrew looked at Caroline in the glow of the setting sun, her hair soft and wavy from the sea, her smiling mouth just inches from his own, close enough to feel the warmth of her breath, he felt a heat growing in his chest until it had nowhere to go, until it started to strain against the skin and bone, pushing, until it hurt. And the world that had been black and white broke open in explosions of colour and Andrew felt really, truly alive.

He saw the *point* of it all now, even while, back at home, a darkness was closing in on his dad.

To everyone else, it must have seemed like he'd been recast, a series regular now played by a different actor without any explanation for the change. Physically he was taller and broader, yes, the stretchmarks on his thighs and arms proving what the awkward length of his school trousers and blazer could have done all by themselves. But the real difference was emanating from somewhere deep inside of him, a confidence he'd never have had if it wasn't for the fact that wrapped around his right hand was Caroline's left.

Better yet, there was a gang of them now, forged in the liquid laziness of the summer months, and the question was never *if* they'd go somewhere together but what they'd do when they did. Movie nights in each other's houses, never Andrew's, most frequently Caroline's. The beach at the weekends. Cinema trips into Midleton with pizza afterwards. The odd school disco, steeped in anticipation for weeks and weeks and then deflating like a loosely tied balloon on the night of.

Andrew had no reason to believe that any of it would ever change.

———

Almost a year to the day after they'd first kissed, Caroline casually told him that her father was getting transferred again and that she'd be starting her third year of secondary school in Frankfurt.

Blood rushed in his ears at the news.

Outwardly, Andrew took his cues from her. She seemed disappointed but not sad, she didn't seem to think this was *that* big a deal, she hadn't heard the ripping sound as Andrew's emotional life came apart at the seams.

'But it'll be a really nice summer,' she said, as if that was a sufficient consolation prize.

He said nothing. He barely reacted. He *did* nothing as, with each day that past, his connection with Caroline crumbled and fell away, both of them in a steady but determined retreat. What was the point in maintaining it now? By the time she left the country they were barely speaking and Andrew had begun to grieve the girl he loved because she had, for all intents and purposes, died, ceased to exist.

And he realised then that it had all been a mere sheen, a temporary finish covering up the truth beneath, which was that he hadn't changed *at all*, not really. He was still that same scared, awkward, uncomfortable boy who'd walked into Class 2H with his shoulders slumped and his eyes down.

And then everything really did fall apart.

His father's health deteriorated. No one had ever actually told him his father was going to die, but now he knew it to be true. It was obvious there could be no coming back from the skeletal figure barely disturbing the hospice bed, the alien thing with sunken eyes and sore, spotted skin that looked nothing at all like the man he knew. The waiting hung over the house like a spectre until it finally happened, two weeks before the Junior Cert exams. Every single person in the village attended the funeral and then, for weeks afterwards, made a point of stopping Andrew and his mother everywhere they went to say to them, 'I suppose it was a relief, in the end, wasn't it?'

School became something Andrew wanted to be done with as soon as possible. His reports started to come home covered in red messages. *Needs to apply himself. It's time for focus now. We all agree Andrew needs more support.* By then, his mother wasn't fit to support anyone. His father's death had tipped her into a drowning depth of grief that had, over time, hardened into a depression. Most days she didn't even leave her room.

Andrew didn't know what to do.

He didn't know how to be. Comprehending the act of living, which seemed to come so naturally to almost everyone around him, felt beyond his reach. Time stretched out ahead of him like an endless, dead field, flat and featureless to the horizon.

He was broken and only Caroline could fix him.

But she wasn't there and she wouldn't come.

FASTFORWARD

0:00:24

The picture was a shot swiped from Natalie's Instagram account, hanging on the wall inside the door of The Kiln in a plain white frame.

She'd taken it – or got Mike to take it – in their old apartment a couple of years ago. Natalie was leaning against a kitchen countertop, wearing a delicate silk robe that had a spray of cherry blossoms embroidered on to one shoulder, drinking coffee from a large mug with a matching design. Behind her, next to a top-of-the-line coffee machine, a clutch of cherry blossoms sat in a tall glass vase. She looked fresh-faced and her hair was gently tousled. It appeared to be like a candid, off-the-cuff shot, but of course it was anything but. The few feet of kitchen visible had had to be cleared and cleaned in preparation. It had taken Natalie a half-hour to put on enough make-up to make it look as though she wasn't wearing any and her I-woke-up-like-this hairstyle had been carefully created with straighteners and sea-salt spray. She didn't even use that coffee machine. She'd been sent the cup she was holding.

There was a neat, handwritten note at the bottom of the frame. *Natalie O'Connor (editor of lifestyle blog And Breathe) loves Cara Homewares!* It was hanging in the middle of a display of similar pictures, all from the online accounts of various Irish models, minor celebrities and *influencers,* showcasing artfully arranged shots of table settings, wall art and jewellery.

Featuring brands they must sell here, Natalie guessed. Good for selling stuff. Bad for someone who didn't want anyone to know she was here.

Although, to be fair, Natalie very much doubted she'd be recognised. That was the beauty of being internet-famous. If she went to a PR event with the usual gang, nervous strangers would constantly approach her. ('Sorry, you'll think I'm a *total* psycho, but I'm actually *obsessed* with your Instagram account ...') Everywhere else, no one gave a damn. No one even knew there was a damn to give. And who was even here to recognise her? The place was deserted.

The Kiln had a vaulted ceiling that rose high above her, a hopscotch pattern of skylights in it filling the space with natural light. Shelving units were stocked with ceramics and display cases with jewellery, and the walls were hung with an array of colourful, delicate things. It seemed a weird thing to find in otherwise sleepy Shanamore. *A destination shopping experience*, the website had said, which was a nice way of warning that aside from this, there was sod all here.

Natalie headed for the café, desperate for a coffee after almost all of the last one had ended up splattered on the cottage's kitchen floor. She chose a table at the very back, by a window that offered a view of the sea in the distance and only fields besides that.

A woman in her early twenties, wearing a white t-shirt and a black apron, followed her to her seat. Natalie ordered a cappuccino and a croissant from her. When the waitress brought them a few minutes later, Natalie had a hand in her bag, ready to pull out the photo of Mike and ask if this woman had seen him here.

But before she could, the waitress said, 'I'm sorry, you'll think I'm a right stalker – but I recognise you. You're Natalie, right? "And Breathe"?'

Natalie cursed silently. But then she thought that, actually, this might be a good thing.

'Busted.' She smiled. 'Hi.'

'I thought it was you. Did you see your picture out there? By the door? That was me. I made that display. The guy who owns this place is, like, sixty-odd so he didn't even know what I was talking about' – the waitress rolled her eyes – 'but I told him to trust me.'

'It looks great. Great idea.'

'Thanks.' The girl blushed. 'I'm Orla, by the way.'

'Nice to meet you, Orla.'

'Is Mike with you?'

Natalie's first reaction was a stirring of unease at the idea that a total stranger could use her husband's name in the same casual way a friend or relative might.

Her second was a surge of adrenalin.

'He's not, no. But funnily enough he *was* here, recently. Did you see him?'

'No.' Orla looked disappointed. 'I don't think I did.'

'Maybe you just didn't recognise him?'

'But I definitely *would*.'

'Perhaps he didn't come in here … You live in the village?'

Orla rolled her eyes again. 'Unfortunately.'

'And you're here full time?'

'And then some. I usually end up working six days a week this time of year because there's no staff. Wait – are you staying up at the cottages?'

Natalie hesitated. 'Well, yes, but … Actually, I'm sort of hiding away for a few days. So I won't be posting about it or anything …'

'No, no, I know.' Orla held up her hands. 'I saw your post. Don't worry, I won't, like, tweet about this or anything.' She laughed when she said this but it was that very thing Natalie was concerned she might do. 'So you've met Andrew, then. He's a bit weird, isn't he?'

'Is he? Do you know him well?'

'Not really,' Orla said. 'But I know that that was his family's land, where the cottages are. He and his mum used to live there. Then she got sick and they decided to sell up. He was renting some bungalow up at the Front Strand for a while, but when the cottages didn't sell and they changed them into holiday homes, he came back. Got the manager job. It suited him, you see. Nice house and back home, so to speak. His mother's got Alzheimer's. She's in a home in Cloyne. So he has to stay near her. His dad died years ago, and he's an only child. Doesn't really have any friends. Doesn't seem to, anyway. He barely leaves those cottages, if you ask me.'

Natalie raised an eyebrow. 'But you *don't* know him well?'

Orla laughed. 'That's Shanamore for you. Everyone knows everyone else's business.'

'And what about the caretaker? Richard?'

'*Caretaker*?' She scoffed at the notion, as if Richard was going around calling himself a CEO. 'Icky Dickie, we call him. Another one of our eligible bachelors. Did he tell you he paints? That's, like, the first thing he says to everyone he meets. Every woman, anyway. Paddy Picasso, he thinks he is.'

'He didn't mention it, actually. What does he paint?'

'I don't have a notion. They all look like spill accidents to me.'

'Do they sell them here?'

'God, no. You couldn't give them away at a car boot sale.'

Natalie told Orla what had happened down by the beach.

'That sounds like him,' she said. 'Thinks he's God's gift and doesn't understand personal space. But he's harmless.'

Natalie didn't think those two statements could agree, but she didn't say it. Instead, she asked, 'Is it always this quiet?'

'In here?' Orla nodded. 'At this time of the year, yeah.'

'But there's all those cars outside ...'

'That's the locals. They park here and hop on the bus up to Cork. Unofficial Park 'n' Ride. The place would be empty otherwise so we leave them to it.' She paused. 'So, how long are you here for?'

'Um, listen, Orla,' Natalie started. She'd lowered her voice and the girl leaned down a little as if to hear better. 'I'd rather you didn't tell anyone that I'm here, you know? I'm by myself, it wouldn't be very—'

'Don't worry,' Orla said firmly, straightening up. 'I understand.' She winked. 'Your secret's safe with me.'

Natalie thanked her.

And didn't believe her.

———

A stranger walks into a saloon. The barman sees him first, stops and stares. Then all his patrons slowly turn around to look too. In the same, single moment, any music and all conversation cease entirely, inexplicably. *Who is this and who do they think they are, coming in here?*

Natalie had always thought those scenes were the reserve of Hollywood movies until she walked into the convenience store attached to the petrol station in Shanamore. There were two men in there already, one behind the counter and one in front of it, and they both fell silent the moment she came through the door. Both then turned to openly stare.

The one she presumed to be a customer was a gruff figure with a bulging belly who took his time looking her up and down. The employee was older, balding and ruddy-faced, and his expression was one of surprise. Natalie realised it then: this wasn't necessarily a stranger-comes-to-town thing. Approaching customers would normally be signalled in advance by the sound of their car engines. She didn't have one. She'd walked here. They were probably just wondering where the hell she'd come from. Still, their conversation didn't resume and she felt them watching as she walked down the aisle, so she didn't dawdle. She moved quickly, picking things up on impulse.

Back at the cottage, having emptied the contents of her single plastic bag on to the dining table, Natalie wished she'd been more methodical. She'd come back with a bottle of wine, a box of homemade lemon tarts, a frozen pizza and a packet of toffees. And the thing she'd spotted as the guy behind the counter rang up her purchases, tapping the buttons on the register until it whirred and clicked, an aural memory from childhood, long since replaced by the red eyes of barcode scanners and little electronic beeps: a pay-as-you-go mobile phone.

It was a chunk of bright blue entombed in one of those thick plastic cases whose opening seems to demand a power tool. It had limited features, actual telephony only. Calls and texts. The keypad was comically oversized while the screen was a fraction of the area she was used to. It was clearly a device aimed at either children or the elderly, or both, but the packaging promised it came fully charged and pre-loaded with twenty-five euro' worth of credit.

With the help of a chopping knife, Natalie freed the phone but didn't turn it on. She left it on the dining table.

She pulled open the drawer where she'd left the poetry book. It was still there, sitting just where she'd left it.

She looked at it, thinking.

Andrew had denied that Mike had stayed here. Orla said she hadn't seen him. Natalie could still ask around in the pub, but what if she got the same response? And she could spend some time checking around the cottage now, looking under the furniture, in between cushions, that sort of thing, yeah, but she'd hardly turn up anything better than the book.

So why was she still here?

Because he might find a way to explain the book away.

But wasn't that, in itself, a kind of answer?

The kind I don't want to have to watch him give me. I need more.

But what if there wasn't more? How long was she going to stay away? How long was she going to stay *here*?

Natalie checked the clock on the TV; it was just after two. There was probably a bus to Cork passing through the village at some point in the afternoon. She could leave now and go and wait for it in the pub. She might just go as far as Cork City, back to civilisation, and then she'd decide what to do next.

She climbed the stairs and went into the bedroom to pack the few meagre items she'd brought with her. She threw her cabin-approved trolley case on the bed, flipped it open, and crossed the landing to go into the bathroom to get—

A noise downstairs.

Natalie froze equidistant between the bedroom and bathroom doors.

Held her breath.

Listened.

When the noise came again, she instantly identified it as a screech of furniture legs on a hardwood floor.

It was one of the chairs around the dining table.

Someone is down there.

A bubble of anger rose in Natalie's throat. If it was that bloody creep Richard, she'd call the goddamn Gardaí on him. But since her only phone was in the kitchen, she'd have to get rid of him first.

She went to the top stair and called out a demanding, 'Hello?'

Silence.

Louder, more forceful: 'I said, *hello*?'

Nothing.

Well, not nothing. No sound, but the air was distinctly charged with the presence of another person.

There was someone down there, she could feel it.

They just weren't answering her.

And then all of Natalie's bravado dissipated in an instant, because she felt ... She didn't even know what the word for it was, but she just had the sense, a feeling, that someone was there and that they—

They didn't want *her* to be.

She retreated back into the bedroom, closing the door behind her. There was no key in the lock. She turned to put her back to the door, pressing her body weight up against it.

Who would break into a house in the middle of the day?

A noise outside.

After a moment's hesitation, Natalie left the door and went to the window. Across the road, Andrew was coming out of his cottage. She knocked on the glass as hard as she could. His head turned towards the sound.

There were two small windows inset in the bedroom's wall of glass. Natalie grabbed the handle of one and yanked it towards her. It didn't open all the way, but enough to let in a blast of cold air. She put her mouth in the opening and shouted, 'Andrew!'

Frowning, he started moving down his drive, coming closer.

'Andrew!' she called again, hoping that whoever was downstairs would hear it, realise they were about to be caught red-handed and get the hell out of Dodge.

He stopped in the middle of the road, in front of her cottage.

'Are you okay?' he called up to her. 'Your front door ...'

'What?' Natalie pushed her face into the opening, trying to look down. The angle made it impossible.

'It's open.'

'Andrew, someone's inside.'

Then Natalie heard a new voice. From downstairs. Or maybe from outside. She couldn't tell if she was hearing it through the door or the window, and there were no discernible words, only a low mumble. But she definitely heard *something* and it hadn't come from Andrew. She was looking at his face.

'Stay there,' he said. 'I'm coming in.'

He disappeared from view.

Natalie went back to the bedroom door and pressed her ear to the gap between the door and the frame to track his movements by sound. She heard footsteps downstairs, moving around the room, then the front door closing firmly. The creak of the stairs as he climbed them. A light, gentle knock on the door.

'Natalie? There's no one there.'

She opened the bedroom door and for a moment they both just stood there, facing each other, saying nothing.

Then he said, 'Come see for yourself.'

Andrew started down the stairs and, after a beat, Natalie followed him.

Although the front door was closed now, the temperature in the cottage had dropped a few degrees.

Andrew stood at the foot of the stairs, arms folded, while Natalie did a circuit of the ground floor.

'You didn't see anyone?' she asked when she was done. 'Not even outside?' He shook his head, *no*. 'Then who opened my front door?'

'Is it possible you didn't close it properly? The wind, maybe ...'

'I closed it.'

But had she? It might have looked closed, it might've just been on the latch. Could she actually remember locking it? No, not the distinct act. But why *wouldn't* she have?

'It could've been Richard,' she said.

Andrew's eyes widened. 'Richard? Richard who?'

'Your caretaker.'

She explained what had happened that morning at the window, and then her later encounter with him down by the beach.

'I see,' Andrew said when she was done. 'I do apologise.'

'Look, I think I might leave. This afternoon. I know I said on the phone yesterday that I'd probably stay two nights but ... Well, my plans have changed.'

Andrew's expression was unreadable.

'There was no one here,' he said.

'I know.'

'I'll have to charge you a cancellation fee.'

Natalie waved a hand. 'That's fine.'

'There was no one here,' he said again, his tone flat. Then he turned and left, closing the front door firmly behind him.

Natalie went to it, checking it had actually closed.

Then she pressed her forehead to the wood and closed her eyes. Her veins felt fizzy with adrenalin.

Voices outside.

Two of them.

Sounded like ... *arguing*?

She went to the window and looked out. She just caught a glimpse of Andrew as the front door of Cottage No.1 swung closed behind him. There was no one else out there. She cracked open the window but she could hear nothing now except the faint, distant rumble of a car engine.

This place was making her *nuts*.

Natalie went into the kitchen and took the bottle of wine from the fridge. One for the road. She needed it after that. She unscrewed the cap and poured herself a generous glass, soothed instantly by the *glug-glug-glug* sound. She took a sip. The weather had done a reasonable job of chilling it on the walk home, so it was cold even though it hadn't been in the fridge long.

It was when she went to put the bottle back that she saw it.

There was a little magnetic memo pad stuck to the fridge door, adorned with the logo of the Irish tourist board. Natalie had noticed it last night, but last night the top page had been blank.

Now there was something written on it in large, messy, urgent block capitals.

LEAVE.

————

Natalie stared at it uncomprehendingly.

She considered the possible explanations. The last guest had left it, she just hadn't seen it before now. (Impossible.) It actually said something else, something that would neutralise it from threatening to merely weird. (Unlikely – the letters were blocky and clear. And why would anyone else be leaving a note on *her* fridge?) It didn't mean what she thought it meant. (What *else* could it mean?)

LEAVE.

Well, Natalie thought, that's exactly what I'm going to do.

What she *had* been doing, anyway.

She moved around the kitchen flinging open cabinets, pulling on drawers, rummaging through the contents of various shelves. She found what she needed wedged in the plate rack above the sink: a slim, navy ring-binder marked GUEST INFORMATION and covered in faintly sticky fingerprints. She threw it on the dining table and started flipping through.

Page after page of text in Comic Sans, decorated with MS Word clip-art circa 1998 and preserved in plastic pockets. How to work the oven; The Kiln's opening times; details of local attractions which, since they included the Jameson Distillery in Midleton and Fota Wildlife Park, didn't seem very local at all. And—

Bingo.

A bus timetable. Ballycotton to Cork, via Shanamore.

But as Natalie traced the list of departure times with a finger, her stomach sank. This couldn't be the actual timetable. It said there were only two buses out of Shanamore on a weekday, one just before eight o'clock in the morning and another at noon. That was it. Departing from Ballycotton offered an extra option in the evening, but that bus apparently bypassed Shanamore.

The clock on the TV said it was just gone three. There was no bus out of Shanamore until tomorrow morning.

She pulled the timetable out of the pocket and turned it over. On the back was the route in the opposite direction. It, too, only stopped in Shanamore twice on a weekday. The evening arrival time matched her own arrival time yesterday, so it seemed to be up to date. She could get a bus to Ballycotton in a few hours' time, but what good would that do? The only thing there was a hotel that, according to her newly discovered Guest Information folder, shut up shop in the off-season.

She whipped through the rest of the binder's contents until she found a small business card taped to the back cover.

BALLYCOTTON TAXI 24.

Okay, new plan. She'd get a taxi to Midleton. Get back inside the sphere of civilisation. The drive should take about half an hour, maybe less. Midleton was an actual town with a train station and a Tesco and a large hotel. She could check into the hotel there tonight, head back to Dublin tomorrow morning. Or maybe she'd get the taxi all the way into Cork, it wasn't *that* much further, and weren't there buses that left from the quays for Dublin Airport all through the night?

She just needed to call the taxi.

The pay-as-you-go phone was sitting on the dining table. Its packaging had promised that it came fully-charged but repeated pressing of the power button did nothing. It had probably been hanging in that shop for years; no wonder.

Natalie plugged the charger into a wall socket and connected it to the phone. The power button began to blink on and off, but the screen stayed off. It probably needed a few minutes.

There was another option, of course. Once the phone was charged, Natalie could just end all this now and call Mike. Tell him where she was, ask him to come and get her. He would. He'd be here in three hours. They'd be back home in another three.

But she'd have to tell him where she was and there could only be one reason why she'd come here.

There'd be no avoiding it then. They'd *have* to talk about it. She wouldn't be able to put it off any longer; she'd have to explain what the hell was going on here. And she'd be on the back foot for that conversation, what with her running off like Nancy Drew and him having to drop everything to come and get her because someone had left a threatening note on her fridge ...

It sounded bonkers.

She'd sound bonkers, telling him it.

But this time, she had proof. *Evidence.* Things she could show him. She had the note and she had the poetry book—

Natalie's insides turned cold with dread.

She'd looked everywhere for that Guest Information folder, and she didn't remember seeing the book. Slowly she moved towards the drawer, knowing what she was going to see before she opened it and looked.

The book was gone.

FASTFORWARD

0:00:52

Audrey didn't know how to connect her mobile phone to the car's Bluetooth system so when Dee called it at 8:45 a.m., she had to pull over to the side of the road so she could answer.

'Morning, sis.'

'*So* sorry to bother you,' Dee said, her overly friendly tone dripping with sarcasm, 'but I was just wondering: where the fuck is my car?'

'Why, do you need it for the first time on a weekday morning ever?'

'Audrey.'

'But you don't, do you?'

'Not. The. *Point*. Where is it? And where the hell are *you*?'

'Well, spoiler alert, sis, but I'm with the car.'

'Audrey.'

'Look, I'm sorry, okay? But I needed it.'

'Oh,' Dee scoffed. 'Well, if you *needed* it ...'

'I left before five. I didn't want to wake you up to ask—'

'Because you knew *exactly* what I'd say.'

'—and you never use it during the week, anyway. It just sits there. And I'm still insured since you guys went to France in the summer, so it'll be fine. Everything's fine. Except for your blood pressure, probably.'

'Where the hell were you going at five in the— Where *are* you?'

Audrey sighed. There was no point lying; Dee would see the mileage when she got back.

'East Cork,' she said quietly.

'What?'

'It's for the story, Dee. Natalie O'Connor.'

'You told us last night that you were off that.'

'What Joel said was that if she came home, it wouldn't be news, and that if something bad happened to her, it'd go to the crime reporter. But he didn't say anything about me finding her.'

Silence bloomed on the line. A van whooshed past Natalie's window at high speed, sending a tremor through the car.

'I'm sure he didn't,' Dee said then. 'Because that's *completely insane.*'

'You won't say that if I find her.'

'No, I think I will. Does Joel know about this?'

'Yep,' Audrey said lightly. 'All about it.'

He didn't. She'd sent him an email saying she'd been sick during the night and was going to visit a GP on the way to work. That would buy her a couple of hours. Enough time, she hoped, to confirm whether or not Natalie had been in Shanamore, maybe even *find* her there, at which point she'd call Joel and say, Surprise!

'You could've asked me for the car,' Dee said.

'You would've said no. And like I said, I only decided to do this at, like, five o'clock this morning. I couldn't sleep over this, Dee. The email from that girl in the café and the guy hanging up on me at the cottages … She *has* to be there. Or to have been last week. I can't just sit back and let someone else find that out, can I? I mean, *you're* the one who said I needed to start trying. *This* is trying.'

'This,' Dee said, 'is grand theft auto.'

But Audrey could hear the smile that had crept into her sister's voice.

'I'll bring it back in one piece, Dee. I promise.'

'You better.' A long, tired sigh. 'Ring me if you need anything. I can transfer some money to your card if you—'

'No, no,' Audrey said quickly. 'I mean, thanks but I'm good.'

Another lie. Her fund for this excursion was the five hundred euro she'd managed to scrape together over the last year, her security deposit for when she eventually moved out. Which, now that D-Day was three weeks away at the most, she really shouldn't be spending and definitely wouldn't have time to replace.

But she'd worry about that later.

Another van screamed past, blaring its horn.

'Dee, I better go before someone runs into the back of me. I'm pulled into the ditch of a boreen here.'

'You're *what*?'

'I'll call you later, okay?'

'Why the hell are you—'

Audrey ended the call, cutting her sister off mid-sentence.

Checking the road behind her was clear, she swung the car back out on to it. It was narrow, potholed and bordered by thick hedgerow on either side. As promised by the sign back in the village, after about a kilometre's worth of it, Shanamore Cottages appeared. The hedgerow had been cut away from the plot on which they stood so they were revealed suddenly, unveiled unexpectedly, a mirage of modernity in the middle of fields and farmlands.

There were three parking spaces just outside the entrance, all empty. In fact, Audrey could only see one other car in the entire complex: a red hatchback parked in the driveway of the closest cottage to the road. A small sign by that cottage's door advised that it was RECEPTION. Audrey pulled into one of the spaces and killed the engine.

The cottages were strange things to look at, a second-cousin-once-removed of actual cottages, at best. Audrey had watched enough episodes of *Grand Designs* while horizontal and hungover to know that these things weren't *blending into the landscape* but screaming blue murder at it.

As soon as she got out of the car, she immediately felt the brunt of the bracing wind. It was so cold it pricked her skin, as if the air was filled with tiny pushpins all vying for a spot on her face.

Granted, it was an icy morning in mid-November, but looking around, Audrey wasn't convinced summer sun would be enough to transform this place into a holiday destination. The cottages had a cold, industrial finish to them and, set only feet apart in this field in the middle of nowhere, they looked like they were huddled together for warmth.

The plot next door, one plot further away from the village, was an abandoned building site, a half-finished house surrounded by a chain-link fence. Soft plastic signs had been tied to the fence at intervals; once upon a time they may have advertised the name of the construction company but now they were ripped to shreds and flapping in the breeze.

The whole place just felt ... *dead*.

Why on earth would Natalie come here?

Why would anyone?

Audrey made it all the way to the front stoop of the RECEPTION cottage before she got her first sign of life: voices coming from inside. It sounded like it was coming from a television.

She pressed the doorbell. Waited.

Nothing.

She knocked on the door as well for good measure. Waited some more.

Still nothing.

She knocked again, harder, rapping her knuckles against the wood three times. The voices stopped abruptly; it must have been the TV. Footsteps approaching the door from its other side. A bolt turning.

The door opened but only three or four inches, revealing a sliver of a man's face.

A youngish man. Tall and skinny. Pale, with purple shadows under his eyes and dark, floppy hair that had fallen into them. He was wearing what looked like a faded pair of flannel pyjamas pants and an off-white T-shirt turning yellow around the collar. And the way he was pushing his body into the gap between the door and its frame, how small that gap was ... She wondered if maybe there was a dog in there that wasn't allowed out or something.

A very *quiet* dog.

'Yes?' he said, squinting at her.

'Hiya.' Audrey smiled as brightly as she could this early in the morning after a night during which she'd barely slept. 'Is this where I check in?'

The man's eyes narrowed. 'We're closed.'

'*Closed?*' That's not what it said on their website.

'I mean, uh, no vacancies. Sorry.' He started to close the door but Audrey reached out and pushed a hand against it.

'But I have a reservation,' she said, pleasant but firm.

She reached into her back pocket and pulled out the piece of paper Dee's printer had spat out just hours earlier. It was confirmation of a reservation for one night's stay at Shanamore Cottages, arriving today, made on Booking.com. Paid in full in advance, non-refundable.

Audrey held it up and watched as the man's eyes started to scan it.

During her MA, she'd spent a summer working in a call centre owned by one of Booking.com's competitors. She knew how the system worked for smaller properties. When you made a reservation online, it got sent to the hotel or wherever as an email. The property then had to see it, read it and manually enter it into their reservation system. It was unlikely this guy had checked his emails yet this morning.

Audrey was counting on it.

'Um ...' He looked back into the cottage. The room behind him was dark; Audrey couldn't see a thing. He turned back to her. 'I'm – I'm not feeling very well, you see, so we're closed.'

'I understand,' Audrey said. 'But I have a reservation. Can't you just give me the key?'

He started shaking his head. 'No, sorry.'

'But I've pre-paid.' She paused. 'Is there a manager I could talk to?'

The door closed, disappearing him back inside. When, not ten seconds later, Audrey heard it opening again, she expected to see someone else – the *actual* manager – but it was the same man.

Only now he was smiling.

'Sorry for the confusion,' he said. 'I have a cottage for you. Check-in isn't until two, though, so the cottage isn't ready right now. Yet, I mean. It wouldn't have been ready anyway, even if I knew you were coming, so ...' He pushed the hair out of his eyes. His fingernails were bitten ragged and looked dirty. 'Can you come back?'

He brought his left hand up to look at his watch, a movement that forced the door open a little wider. Audrey caught a glimpse of a large, gloomy space beyond. She saw a rectangle drawn in light straight ahead and realised then why it was so dark: all the curtains on the ground floor of this cottage were drawn. She must have woken him up. Maybe he really was sick and she'd forced him out of his sick bed. She felt bad about that.

A little bit.

'Sure,' she said. 'When?'

'The earliest I can do is noon.'

'That'd be great.' That was three hours from now. What the hell was she going to do until then? 'Sorry, I didn't get your name ...?'

'Andrew.'

'Andrew,' she repeated. 'Hi. I'm Audrey.'

'I know,' he said. 'It's on your reservation.'

'Ah. Right.'

He looked at her blankly.

'So,' she said, 'the place in the village – The Kiln, is it? Do you know what time it opens?'

'Now,' he said. 'Nine.'

'I'll head there so.' She started to turn.

'Why are you here?'

She turned back. 'Sorry?'

'You here for the pottery?'

'Ah ...'

'Are you taking a class? Over at the pottery.' Andrew was looking her right in the eye now, which she realised he hadn't done before. 'That's why people come here. Normally.'

Audrey had no idea what he was talking about.

'No,' she said breezily. 'Just taking a little road trip. Someone recommended this place to me, so ...' She looked around, realising how unlikely that sounded. 'It seems very quiet.'

'You're my only guest,' Andrew said. Then, abruptly, he stepped back into the gloom and a front door swung shut in Audrey's face for the second time in less than twenty-four hours.

'Visit Ireland,' she muttered to herself as she walked back down the drive. 'The land of a thousand welcomes. Or sometimes, not even one.'

She wasn't quite at the car when her phone began to buzz in her hand. The screen warned there was NO CALLER ID and only one bar of service.

When she answered, a vaguely familiar male voice said, 'Is that Audrey? Audrey Coughlan?'

'Yeah?'

'This is Mike Kerr. Natalie's husband?'

'Oh.' Audrey froze on the spot, lest she lose her remaining bar of mobile phone reception. 'Hi. How are you?'

'I'm calling to apologise. For yesterday. I wasn't very helpful. And then I got called away … You were just doing your job. And your article really did help. I'm told the guards over in Blackrock are getting loads of calls, so … Thank you.'

'Well, that's great. But there's no need to apologise. Really.' Audrey desperately wanted to know what all those calls were about but now that she had Mike on the line, there was something more pressing she wanted to ask him. 'Actually, I'm glad you called. There's something you might be able to help me with. Shanamore. It's a village in East Cork, by the sea. Does that name mean anything to you?'

Silence.

'Mike?'

'Shanamore,' he said, pronouncing each syllable distinctly.

'Yeah. Do you know it?'

'That's what she asked me.'

'Who?'

More silence.

So much that this time Audrey pulled the phone from her ear to check that her service hadn't gone completely.

'Mike?' she prompted. 'Are you still there?'

'Natalie,' he said. 'Natalie asked me. On the morning she left. She asked me if I'd ever heard of Shanamore.'

The inside of The Kiln looked and felt like some kind of modernist church. The only colour in the building itself came from the wooden beams holding up its vaulted ceiling; everything else was a white wall or pale floor tile or a window of grey sky. And it was, like a church, eerily quiet, but in a deliberate, hushed way, as if the items on the shelves and in the display cases – ceramics, blown glass, horrendously oversized jewellery that would surely weigh the wearer down – were ancient religious relics that demanded respect.

There were no customers, just a cashier standing behind a service counter in the centre. She looked up and smiled briefly, then went back to the magazine or catalogue she'd been leafing through.

Through a gap in the shelves at the rear, Audrey could see dining tables and chairs and she thought she could smell coffee. The café. It must be.

It had no customers either. There were only – Audrey counted quickly – eight tables. A glass counter to the left showcased various cakes and pastries, their icing glistening, and above them a large blackboard displayed the menu in chalk. Most of the back wall was an enormous picture window, offering a stunning view of flat fields in the foreground, sea in the middle distance and wintry sky beyond that.

A voice said, 'Take a seat.'

Audrey turned. A girl – woman – had materialised, wearing a black apron with a dusting of flour on it. She looked to be twenty at the most. She wore little to no make-up and her shiny hair seemed to be its natural, mousy-brown colour.

She wasn't wearing a name-tag, but this had to be Orla.

'Thank you,' Audrey said. She pointed to a table whose far end was pushed up against the window. 'Is there all right?'

'Anywhere you like. Menu's on the board. Can I get you something to drink?'

'Ah, I'll have a cappuccino. Please. And actually' – she quickly scanned the blackboard – 'I'll go with the poached eggs on toast.' The prices were half that of Dublin, she might as well take advantage of it.

'Great.' Potentially Orla smiled. 'I'll be right back.'

Audrey took a seat and pulled out her phone. No bars at all now; she had no reception. There was a wifi network called Kiln-Guest, but Audrey didn't want to connect to it. If Joel had detected her deceit and was trying to call or email, it was good to have an excuse. And it was easier to give it if it wasn't also a lie.

She did use her phone to take a few pictures of the café, ensuring beforehand that the device was on silent, so its *click-click-click* wouldn't give her away.

She stopped when she heard footsteps coming out of the kitchen.

'Here you go.' Potentially Orla had returned with the coffee. 'Your eggs will just be a few minutes.'

'Thanks,' Audrey said. 'Sorry – are you Orla, by any chance?'

The girl frowned. 'Yeah?'

'I'm Audrey Coughlan. From ThePaper.ie.'

Confusion bloomed on the girl's face for a second, then shock as the penny dropped.

'Jesus.' Orla started shifting her weight from foot to foot. 'I didn't think you'd actually come here …'

She glanced behind her, towards the store.

'I live nearby,' Audrey lied. 'I was passing through.' She hoped Orla wouldn't question this because she had no clue what was nearby or where you'd be going that would necessitate passing through. 'I'm writing a follow-up to yesterday's story and I could really do with your input. I know you emailed but it's always better for me to hear it from the source, to have a conversation. I won't use your name if you don't want me to. But this would be really helpful, Orla. Not just to me, but to Natalie. And Mike.'

Orla brightened. 'Mike?'

'Yeah,' Audrey said. The girl's whole demeanour had changed; she must be a Mike fan. Or maybe it was just the opportunity to be of service to Irish Instagram's Golden Couple. 'I just spoke to him and I told him there was someone here who had spoken to Natalie and I think …' She lowered her voice to a conspiratorial whisper. 'I think it really reassured him. You know, that someone spoke to her after he last saw her at their house. It'd be a great comfort to him, I'm sure, if I could give him more detail. He'd really appreciate it. He'd appreciate you doing that.'

Orla was chewing on her lip, presumably weighing up her options.

'Okay,' she said eventually. 'Let me get your eggs first.'

But the eggs ended up sitting off to one side, untouched and congealing, while Orla told Audrey what she knew.

She repeated what she'd shared in the email. Natalie had come in here – 'She sat at the same table, come to think of it' – and she and Orla had chatted for a few minutes. Natalie had said she was in Shanamore for peace and quiet. She'd asked why there were so many cars outside but no one in here. 'The locals park here and get the bus into the city,' Orla explained when she saw from Audrey's expression that she had the same question – and she said that Mike had visited the village recently, but she didn't say for what or when. Orla hadn't seen him and she'd told Natalie that.

Natalie had also asked Orla not to tell anyone or post online that she'd seen her in Shanamore, which Audrey scratched two lines under for emphasis in her handwritten notes.

There were new, extra details too. Natalie had seen what Audrey had failed to: there was a framed picture of her, one of her Instagram posts, hanging just inside the door. In it, she was holding a mug from a collection produced locally at the pottery and for sale in store.

'That was my idea,' Orla said, clearly proud. 'And I told her so.'

They'd spoken about Andrew, the delightful young man who'd just shut a door in Audrey's face.

'My host for this evening,' Audrey said wryly. 'He seems a little ... off?'

'Oh, he's a *lot* off, that one.'

But when Audrey asked her to elaborate, Orla just waved a hand and said something enigmatic about the village rumour mill. She seemed only to want to talk about Natalie.

The local creep who'd talked to Natalie down at the beach was named Richard Flynn but he had the much more memorable moniker of Icky Dickie. Again, though, there was no specific, concrete reason for why 'everyone around here' thought this guy was icky – at least, none that Orla was willing to share. It just seemed to be an accepted fact, evidence pending.

But according to Orla, Natalie had thought he was creepy too.

'Where would I find him?' Audrey asked.

'Icky Dickie? Oh, just walk around here for a while. He'll find *you*.' Orla sighed. 'Or – I wouldn't recommend this – he's usually in Murphy's every night. That's the pub across the road. Not the shit one, the completely shit one. How long are you planning on staying?'

'Just tonight, I think.'

'And you're up at the cottages.' Orla looked at her pointedly. 'Like Natalie was.'

'What does that mean?'

'Well …'

'You think something happened to her there?'

'You *don't* think that?'

Audrey didn't. She *had* been assuming that Natalie was still here, holed up in one of the cottages, but if Andrew was to be believed, he had no other guests. So now she was presuming that Natalie had moved on to the next stop on her road trip, The Don't Tell My Husband You Saw Me Tour 2018. Audrey was hoping that she'd find something here, some breadcrumb left behind, that would point her in the direction of it.

But Orla made an interesting point.

Audrey thought of her strange encounter with Andrew, replayed it in her mind, reanalysing his behaviour. But even with him hanging up on her yesterday … If Natalie had said the same thing to him as she'd said to Orla, to not tell anyone that she'd been here, then he was just obeying the wishes of a former guest by denying that she'd stayed there.

The guy was a bit weird, yeah, and not exactly born for the hospitality business, but he was no Norman Bates.

'Is there a Garda station here?' Audrey asked.

'Just down the road.' Orla pointed. 'Past the petrol station.'

'Did you tell them you saw Natalie here?'

'*Him.* We have the sum total of one guard. And no, because the article said to ring the guards in Dublin. At the number on the appeal thingy. Which I did. My dad agreed that was the right thing. We own the shop. Up at the petrol station?'

'What's his name?'

'My *dad*?'

'The guard.'

'Seanie. Seanie Flynn. Sergeant Seanie, we all call him. He's new. Only been here a few months. All the ould fellas give out about him because they think he's fierce young. Too young to be telling them not to drive home from the pub, you know yourself.'

Audrey wrote the name in her notebook.

'And no one's called you back yet? From the Gardaí, I mean.'

Orla shook her head. 'No.'

'And you don't think Natalie could still be here?'

'Nothing happens in this village without everyone else knowing everything about it. Unless Natalie has been locked inside one of those cottages, without food and without leaving for the last week, she's gone. I didn't see her again after last Tuesday. Neither did my dad.'

'Wait,' Audrey said. 'Did your dad see her a *first* time?'

'She was in the shop.'

'When?'

'I think right after she was in here. She bought a phone, he said. One of those pay-as-you-go ones. That's how I know she was in there. Dad was saying to Mum, "You won't believe what I sold today …" Those things have been hanging there for years, you see. Mum was always trying to get him to dump them, they were so old and dusty. I asked him who bought it – because I was thinking, What an eejit, those phones are *relics* – and he said some woman, and I asked him to describe her, and it was her. That's weird, right? Isn't it? Natalie has an iPhone X. She posted about it. So what did she want some crappy old plastic phone for?'

'I don't know,' Audrey said. Her mind was racing.

None of this was adding up. Mike had told her that on the morning she'd left, Natalie had, out of the blue, asked him if he'd heard of Shanamore. He'd said no, never. Then he'd asked her why she'd asked him that, and she'd – in his words – 'clammed up'. Then she posts the suitcase message online and leaves the house. She's already cancelled an appointment she knows she has in three days' time. She comes here, to Shanamore, 160 miles away. She spends at least one night at the cottages. She goes for a walk on the beach. She comes to The Kiln for coffee, meets Orla and asks her not to tell anyone that she's here. She goes to the local shop and buys a crappy phone, even though she makes her living off a phone app and has a top-of-the-range device already. At some point, she leaves the cottages and, possibly, asks the weirdo manager not to tell anyone she's been *there* either. A week later, she's a missing person.

What the hell was going on?

There had to be something that joined all the dots, but Audrey couldn't see it.

Not yet.

'He's in the shop right now,' Orla was saying. 'My dad. You could go talk to him. But, ah, don't tell him I contacted you, okay? He thinks we should all just mind our own business. Just say that you've heard she was here and you're asking around. Show him her picture. You don't get too many new faces this time of the year. He'll remember.' Orla reached across to pick up the plate of untouched eggs and the cup of now cold coffee. 'Let me get you fresh ones.'

'Yeah,' Audrey said absently. 'Thanks.'

Mentally, she was making a to-do list. Visit the shop to talk to Orla's father. Drive to the beach. Ask Andrew about Natalie and check in. Read the other emails you got to see if anyone else spotted Natalie in Shanamore. Talk to the local Garda, Seanie Whatshisname. Go to that pub and look for Sticky Richard. Call Joel before you lose your job.

Movement, in her peripheral vision.

Audrey turned to see a man had entered The Kiln and was walking in through the store, towards the café. He was tall, older, his body shape obscured by the many layers of clothing he wore. She could see a shirt collar peeking above his scarf, and the hem of a woollen jumper through his open jacket. It was one of those adventurer ones, all padding and pockets.

When he reached the café, he pulled a navy wool cap from his head, revealing a head of wild, greying hair. A folded newspaper was tucked under his shoulder. He went straight to a small table in the furthest corner, behind Audrey, leaving a whiff of body odour in his wake.

Just then, Orla re-emerged from the kitchen, carrying Audrey's fresh coffee. Her eyes widened when she saw the newcomer. She looked at Audrey, widening them more.

She seemed to be trying to communicate something, but Audrey had no clue what the message was.

'Morning, Richard,' Orla said then. Her voice was louder than necessary, her pronunciation exaggerated. 'I'll be right with you.'

She put down the coffee in front of Audrey, who'd got the message: *this* was Icky Dickie.

'Hey,' Orla continued, moving towards his table. 'We had a woman in here last week. Natalie O'Connor. The Instagrammer? I saw online last night – she's missing. No one has seen her in a week. Isn't that weird?'

Audrey closed her eyes and silently recited her favourite curse words. Orla was being about as subtle as sriracha sauce.

'That so,' Richard said.

'Did you see her?'

'Did *you*?'

'I did. In here.'

'Well' – there was the smack of paper; it sounded like Richard had opened out the broadsheet to full width and shaken it taut – 'you better tell Sergeant Seanie that then.'

'So you didn't see her?' Orla pressed. 'Because I thought maybe—'

'I didn't see her,' Richard spat, suddenly and loudly, making Audrey flinch. Then, in a more measured tone: 'Now, love: tea. A pot of. Or maybe I'd be quicker making it myself?'

———

There was only one person working in the shop at the petrol station, a sullen teenage boy with a spray of acne on his neck and a Cork GAA jersey whose bright red hue was only exacerbating the issue. Unless Orla's father's name was Benjamin Button, this wasn't him.

Audrey picked up a pre-packed sandwich, a bag of Haribo and three cans of Red Bull. The diet of champions. While paying for them at the counter, she looked up and saw two pay-as-you-go phones in plastic cases hanging from hooks in the wall. Orla hadn't been exaggerating. These were relics, six or seven years old, with screens small enough to suggest they weren't at all smart. Their plastic cases were thick with dust.

'How much for the phones?' Audrey asked Sullen Boy.

He turned around and gaped at them like he'd never seen such things ever before in his whole life. When he lifted one down and turned it over to look at the back, his fingers left streaks in the dust.

'Twenty-five including twenty-five credit.' He held it up. 'You want one?'

'Ah, no. Thanks.'

Audrey *did* want one, because she hoped that maybe if she bought one and brought it back to the cottage and stared at it for long enough, the reason why Natalie had done the same thing might magically reveal itself.

But she had to watch her spending.

And that was a stupid plan.

Afterwards, Audrey drove down to the beach. She parked at the Far Strand where the only access was a narrow road. There was a barrier at the entrance to the car park preventing vehicles taller than an SUV getting through, alongside a rubbish bin overflowing with plastic bags and empty beer cans. There was space for ten or twelve cars and Audrey's was the only one there.

As she parked, she had a thought: had Natalie come here by car?

She'd been assuming she had, seeing as there wasn't exactly a high-speed Metro link from Dublin to Shanamore. But the Garda appeal hadn't mentioned that Natalie's car was missing, so either she didn't have one or it was still at home. If she didn't drive, how did she get here? You'd first have to get from Dublin to Cork, by train or by bus. Had she booked a ticket? Had anyone checked that? Had Mike? Did they share a bank account?

Audrey put a note in her phone to remind herself she had these questions. Then she locked up the car, tied up her coat and headed for the beach.

The tide was in and the wind was high. Grey waves were racing each other up the shore, breaking into white foam explosions. This action had created a narrow strip of smooth, wet sand just beyond the water's reach. After that was an uneven layer of pebbles, larger stones, heaps of dried seaweed and rotting driftwood, flecked with cigarette butts, empty plastic bottles and the odd beer can. There was no one else around and it was absolutely freezing. Gulls squawked loudly overhead, which made Audrey nervous. Her aunt had once been shat on the head by a seagull and it was a sight she'd never forget. There'd been enough gloopy white poop to fill a milk carton.

She stood on the pebbles with her hands dug deep in her pockets, surveying the scene through watery eyes. Behind her, what had looked like a gentle hill on the other side ended suddenly with a jagged cliff face, a drop of thirty or forty feet straight down. Just visible at its peak were the roofs of a few grubby mobile homes. A campsite, presumably closed for the winter.

Although Audrey's childhood summers were spent on beaches on the west coast – Galway, Clare, Kerry – the Irish seaside experience was the same everywhere. She remembered blue skies, splashing in salty water and Tayto sandwiches seasoned with the grit of actual sand. Everything was always warm: the air, the sea, the skin on her nose and the tops of her shoulders. And everything looked like the photos in her mother's old albums, blurry and overexposed, bleached. She knew no Irish summer was invariably warm and sunny and that there must have been times when she and Dee were homicidal and cooped up inside because of rain, but she didn't remember them. Time was a kind editor. Audrey felt sorry for the kids who'd never get a chance to forget their crappy summer days, because their parents uploaded every moment to Instagram, immortalising them for ever.

Shanamore Strand, however, was decidedly *not* Instagram friendly.

Why Natalie O'Connor had chosen to come here was just as big a mystery as where she might be now.

———

Audrey was back at Shanamore Cottages fifteen minutes before noon. She'd walked the beach until she felt sure she was turning blue, killed half an hour in her car typing notes on her laptop and then driven back at thirty miles an hour. Andrew came bounding out of his cottage as soon as she turned into the complex, waving and smiling.

She pulled up at the end of his drive and rolled her window down.

'You can park outside your one,' he said. His voice was friendly now, his face bright; *someone* must have had a shower and a Solpadeine since she'd seen him last. He pointed to the cottage opposite and said, 'Number six.'

Andrew skipped after her car so he was already stationed at the cottage's front door when she got out of it.

'Where'd you go?' he asked. 'The Kiln?'

'Yep. And then the beach.'

'Cold down there today, was it?'

Audrey nodded. 'Absolutely freezing.'

'Good thing I've the heating on for you.' Andrew unlocked the front door of the cottage and pushed it open with a flourish. He motioned for her to enter, smiled. 'Ladies first.'

Audrey mumbled her thanks. The change in his demeanour was a bit off-putting. She silently willed him to take it down a notch, for both their sakes.

Then she stepped inside the cottage and instantly forgave all.

The ground floor of Cottage No. 6 was just that – all one floor, no rooms, open space squared. The air was warm but not stuffy, and dotted around the room were orbs of golden lamp light. A bright, modern kitchen gleamed to the rear. The backs of a set of leather couches separated the kitchen from the living space, which was dominated by a snazzy-looking fire encased behind a sheet of black glass. Above that hung an enormous flat-screen TV.

She was only here for one night and here to *work*, but still, it made a nice change from Dee's box room where the only seat was a lumpy single bed and the TV an 11-inch laptop screen perched on her knees.

'I hope you like it,' Andrew was saying. 'And I must apologise about earlier. I had a migraine. I wasn't myself.' He explained that there was a bedroom and bathroom upstairs, that he'd set the heating to constant but there was a panel in the kitchen Audrey could fiddle with if it got too hot, and that there was a welcome basket 'with a few bits and bobs' in the kitchen.

When she asked if there was wifi, Andrew's face fell.

'There is,' he said, 'but it's not very strong. We get a lot of complaints about it and I have to explain it's this area. It shouldn't be too bad for you, though, you'll be the only one using it. It's when you get, you know, five cottages with families and all the kids are online, and …' He smiled. 'Well, you know yourself.'

'So I'm your only guest,' Audrey said. 'Is that normal for this time of year?'

She was, of course, hoping he'd say, *Yes! Why just last week I had the same thing. Only one guest. Her name was Natalie O'Connor. She checked out on Wednesday morning and told me exactly where she was going. Would you like to know where it was?* But Andrew just said that it was, and she left it at that. She didn't want him to connect her with the phone call he'd got the evening before, asking for Natalie. Not before she had a chance to look around.

She thanked him again and he left her to it, closing the front door of the cottage behind him.

Audrey went exploring.

The large window at the rear of the ground floor looked out on a non descript patch of grass that backed into a thick hedgerow. When she opened the door that led there and looked out, she saw there was a small patio area, complete with wooden picnic-style table and chairs, tinged green by moss.

Back inside, she opened a few kitchen cupboards and found thick, mismatched plates and cups dyed in primary colours, with intricate flourishes that seemed to have been painted on by hand. Swag from The Kiln, it looked like. How very on-brand.

The basket Andrew had left had a bar of chocolate in it; she broke off half and took it with her up the stairs, eating as she went.

The staircase had no handrail, which made each step a little bit scarier than the one before. Andrew had mentioned families staying here. How could they possibly? A young child on *these* stairs? Daring to look down on the hardwood floor from the landing, Audrey wondered how no one had yet fallen to their death.

Maybe someone *had*, she thought idly. And Andrew had got rid of the evidence to avoid the insurance claim and protect his business. That's where Natalie was: under his patio after falling off this death trap of stairs. Audrey hoped not, and not just because that would mean the poor girl was dead. She didn't think that would spin into much of a story. Take out the concealment of a body and you just have a slip and fall, after all.

At the top, she turned into the bedroom.

It was seriously impressive. The bed was enormous and didn't even take up that much of the room. One whole wall of it, the one at the front, was glass. It offered a view of most of the complex and a wedge of the building site next door. In the distance off to the right a sliver of sea was visible, but you'd have to know what you were looking at or you might mistake it for sky.

The bed was calling to her, the sight of it pushing waves of exhaustion over her, leaving a riptide pulling on her arms and legs, whispering, *Have a nap. You could do with it; you barely slept a wink last night.*

She was, she realised now, utterly out of steam. There was plenty on her to-do list but nothing left in the tank with which to *do*. She needed a power-nap. She could have one. A short one.

There was time.

Audrey kicked off her shoes and got into bed.

Sleep came quickly.

———

She dreamed that she was back at the beach, but barefoot. She'd had to walk there like that; the soles of her feet were scratched and bleeding. The pebbles dug into her feet and then the water was rushing up over them, the salt making her wounds sting, and then it was swirling up around her legs, splashing on her chest, reaching for her face—

Knock-knock-knock.

Audrey awoke with a jolt, groggy and disorientated. It took her a moment to remember where she was and why she'd been asleep in an enormous bed, fully-clothed, in the middle of the day. It took her another one to remember that something had woken her. A noise. Three sharp raps ... on the front door?

Was there someone at the door?

She listened but the noise didn't come again.

Audrey climbed out of bed and went to the window, but there was no one out there that she could see and no cars other than Dee's. Andrew's little red one was gone.

The noise must have been in her dream.

She checked her phone: she'd been asleep for nearly two hours. Shit. She should really call Joel. But she needed to pee first.

She crossed the landing into the bathroom. It was clean and bright, with a large bath and a line of miniature bottles of smelly things lined up on its edge.

When Audrey leaned over to inspect them, a flashbulb went off to her right.

She straightened up.

What the hell was that?

Scanning the room, she couldn't see any potential culprit.

She repeated the move, leaning over the bath, and the flash came again.

This time, though, she knew where it was coming from.

There was a plastic bin on the floor under the sink with an unused bin liner folded neatly over the rim — and something else inside it. Something reflective that, when it aligned with the ceiling light and Audrey was in just the right position to see it, looked like a flash of light.

She reached into the bin and closed her hand around the cool, hard thing she found in there, pulled it out.

A phone. An iPhone.

Large and slim, with no HOME button.

Audrey thought it might be the newest model.

Andrew must have missed it when he was cleaning out after the last guest. But why would someone leave their brand-new, very expensive phone in a bin?

She turned it over in her hands, examining it. The device had no scuffs or scratches, but it was as dead as a doornail; pressing the POWER button did nothing.

Hadn't Orla said that Natalie had an iPhone X? Was this hers? Had she stayed in this cottage too?

Knock-knock-knock.

This time, Audrey knew for sure there definitely *was* someone at the front door. She took the bin liner and hastily wrapped the phone in it.

Then she hurried downstairs to see who was there.

It was a stranger.

Wait, no—

Not a stranger. Not entirely. Audrey didn't know him but she'd seen him before. He was tall, with closely shorn dark hair. Mid-thirties. Nice eyes. Blue ones. Wearing a suit.

It was the guard. The one who'd kicked her out of Natalie's house yesterday.

What the hell was *he* doing here?

Going by the expression on his face, he was wondering the exact same thing about her.

PAUSE

0:00:54

Jennifer has a headache, a pulsating throb at the base of her skull. Her eyes hurt and her muscles feel tender and sore, her stomach upset. She wonders if she's getting the flu, even though she's had a shot. All she wants to do is curl up in bed in a pitch-black room and sleep for days, but instead she has to get Sycamore House through the morning rush.

She hates the mornings. Evenings: fine. Jennifer likes the drip-drip-drip of guests into reception and that, if there is such a thing as a rush hour, it's two people at the same time. In the evenings, everyone wants the same thing she does: to end their interaction as quickly as possible. The guests want to go to their rooms so they can get on with their plans and she wants them to go there so she doesn't have to talk to them any longer.

But in the morning, every single warm body in the house seems to open their door and descend the stairs at the exact same time, like a herd of zombies beckoned by a signal only they can hear. Sycamore House serves breakfast from seven until eleven, but everyone wants to have it between eight and nine. What's worse is that as soon as they've stuffed their faces with enough greasy pig bits, slimy eggs and barely browned toast, they all want the same thing: to check out. They line up at reception, clutching their keys in their hands, huffing and puffing, glaring at her with faces that say they are *really* in such an *awful* rush and could she *please* hurry up because, oh, they are *so very* important they just have to get going right *now*.

Dickheads.

Jennifer checks her phone for the umpteenth time: still nothing from Mike. She knows he can hardly call her right now, in the midst of all this, and she knows she's supposed to wait, but …

It's so *hard*.

She wonders if maybe she should send *him* a message. Not anything incriminating, just something everyday, mundane. *Thinking of you*. Something like that. Just so he'd know that she was thinking about him, waiting. That she *would* wait, no matter how long this thing took.

Tap. Tap. Tap.

Jennifer looks up. There's a man standing on the other side of the reception desk, dressed in a suit, tapping his credit card on the counter and scowling. She's no idea how long he's been there, but each tap is sending an echo of dull pain spreading out from her right temple to her left, like sonar.

She forces a smile.

'Good morning, sir. Checking out?'

'If it's not too much trouble.'

'Of course, sir,' she says, ignoring his tone. 'What's the room number?'

He throws the key down with a clatter.

'Thirty-one,' she says, seeing the tag. 'One moment, please.'

Tap. Tap. Tap.

She finds his reservation on the system, but the figures blur and swim before her eyes. She bites down on her lip until the sharp pain there distracts from the dull thumping rhythm in her head.

She asks him, 'Did you enjoy your stay?' even though she doesn't give a shit whether he did or not.

'It was fine.' He exhales loudly. 'Can we hurry this up? I have a meeting.'

Tap. Tap. Tap.

'The room is pre-paid,' she says, eyes squinting at the screen. 'So it's just the cost of breakfast …'

'I *know*. That's why I'm here. Put it on—'

But then he stops, mid-sentence, to stare at Jennifer open-mouthed.

Probably because she just whipped the credit card right out of his hand.

'Thank you,' she says sweetly.

Thirty-one seems uncertain about what she's just done. Is it a rude infraction or just an attempt to speed things up, like he requested? Whatever his conclusion, he doesn't say any more.

Jennifer pulls the credit card machine towards her and slides his card into it.

Her head feels like it's encased in wet cement. Then that the cement has dried and hardened. Then that someone or something is crushing it into dust.

The machine beeps in protest. She's done something wrong.

The double doors to Jennifer's right swing open and Linda, one of the waitresses, comes through, saying, 'You can have a seat in here...' to the large, dark-haired woman – room Fifteen; Jennifer checked her in last night – following behind her. The two women cross behind Thirty-one's back and go into the lounge where there are a few armchairs, a TV and a collection of the morning papers.

Jennifer pushes the CANCEL button on the card machine and starts the process again.

Linda's voice is now offering tea or coffee. The low murmur that follows is presumably the guest's reply. Then: new voices, much louder. They've turned on the TV in there.

Linda reappears, alone. She catches Jennifer's eye and mouths, *Full*. When all the seats in the breakfast room are taken, standard practice is to ply guests with coffee in the lounge until one becomes available.

Thirty-one is huffing and puffing again.

'Is there some reason why this is taking so bloody long?'

'Yes,' Jennifer says. *You're an abominable prick.*

'... *Natalie O'Connor's husband, Michael Kerr* ...'

She freezes.

'I've got a *meeting*,' Thirty-one moans. 'For fuck's sake. Look' – he starts rooting in his pockets – 'give me that back and I'll just give you the cash ...'

His voice fades away. Jennifer leans over the desk to look through the open door of the lounge. She can only see a narrow slice of the TV screen from this angle, but she can see enough. The news is on.

Mike is news.

Jennifer comes out from behind the desk and goes into the lounge.

Mike's face fills the screen. Underneath him, the ticker flashes BREAKING NEWS: HUSBAND OF MISSING INSTAGRAM STAR MAKES DESPERATE SOCIAL MEDIA PLEA.

She reaches out and touches her hand to the screen.

Mike's eyes are red. He's been crying.

No, he *is* crying.

About *Natalie*?

He says the name then, straight into the camera: 'Natalie.' This footage of him is slightly pixelated and confined to a narrow band in the middle of the screen; it must have been recorded on a phone. 'It's okay if you don't want to come home yet. It's fine if you don't want to talk to me. But for your family's sake, for your friends – please, just let *someone* know that you're okay.'

'What the hell is going on here?' Thirty-one's voice demands from behind her. He's followed her into the lounge. 'Give me back my bloody card!'

She looks down and sees that she's carried the credit card machine in here with her. The prick's card is still stuck inside it.

'Natalie,' Mike says in a voice choked with emotion. 'Please. I miss you. I love you.'

Jennifer swings her arm and hurls the machine square at the TV screen with as much force as she can muster.

PLAY

0:00:57

When Seanie ended the call, he heard the shower running. He sat on the edge of the bed for a few moments, listening to it and thinking about what DS O'Reilly had asked him to do.

On the surface, it was a straightforward request: question the proprietor of Shanamore Cottages about a charge on a credit card that may be linked to a missing person. But it sent a cold stone of dread settling into the pit of his stomach, because the proprietor of Shanamore Cottages was Andrew bloody Gallagher.

The two of them face-to-face again, after all these years.

Would Andrew remember him?

Seanie doubted it.

Would Andrew remember Aoife?

He'd better fucking not.

Seanie pulled on a pair of sweats and went into the kitchen to make coffee. He had Imelda's travel mug filled and ready for her when she appeared ten minutes later, hair wet, suit on, eyes bright.

'I meant to say to you,' she said, taking it from him. 'I think from next week, I'm going to go up on Sunday night.'

Seanie said nothing.

'Monday is a wasted day,' she went on. She'd opened a cabinet and was rifling in a box of cereal bars. 'Then I spend the rest of the week racing to catch up. Trish said she doesn't mind me staying the extra day.'

'But you'd only be home two nights a week then.'

She turned to face him and Seanie thought he could actually hear the cogs turning in her brain.

Start an argument now or cut and run?

'It's just an idea,' she said. 'We can talk about it at the weekend.' Imelda crossed the kitchen to kiss him on the cheek. 'I better hit the road. Have a good week.'

144

She didn't ask him who'd been on the phone.

He waited until he heard her car pull out of the drive before he moved. Like Imelda, he had two settings now, too: the Seanie who despaired at the gulf that was opening up between him and his fiancée, and Sergeant Séan Flynn who kept his mind on his work.

Seanie quickly showered, shaved and dressed in his Garda blues. He poured another coffee and went outside, covering the top of the cup with his hand in a futile attempt to keep the icy air from cooling it on him. This time of the year the night liked to linger; the lights of the petrol station still glowed bright white in the gloom.

He let himself into the station, flicked on the lights and cranked the heater up to full blast.

While on the phone with O'Reilly, Seanie had scribbled notes on the only thing in the bedroom that resembled paper: the back page of a thriller he'd been half-heartedly reading for the past couple of weeks. He took the torn-out page from his pocket now, smoothed it out on the desk and copied what he'd written into a clean page in his notebook.

When he logged on to the station's computer, Seanie found an email from DS O'Reilly already in his inbox. He'd sent on the PULSE incident number for Natalie Kerr (O'Connor), age 31, 5'6", slim build, missing from her home address in Sandymount, Dublin 4, since the morning of 5 November. High risk due to possible mental health issues, length of absence and no precedent; the missing person had never done anything like this before, so this behaviour was completely out of character for her. There was also a note that the woman was a public figure with a large online following, which might result in increased media interest. The photo supplied had seemingly been taken on her wedding day, a disembodied arm suggesting that the groom had been in the original but was cropped out here.

He found the same picture had been included in the press release. Seanie printed out a copy of that, too, so he could take it with him. Ideally, though, he'd be going up to the cottages with a picture of the husband ... He did a Google search for Natalie's name and found an article about the disappearance that linked to the woman's Instagram account. It didn't take long to find the full version of the wedding photo there. Seanie took a screenshot and then printed that out too.

He tucked the two loose pages, folded, into his notebook.

By the time he was done, the clock on the wall said it was just after nine.

———

Shanamore Cottages hadn't been here in his childhood summers, but Seanie had taken a walk around the place shortly after his appointment as Shanamore's sole member of An Garda Síochána. A few weeks later, he'd discovered Padraig Slattery's missing ride-along mower parked askew in one of the spots outside the cottages. The culprits were a stag do of Big City Boys who Seanie found still asleep in their beds down at the Strand Hotel when he went there to return the best man's wallet, which had been dropped at the scene of the crime. He'd taken their details and had a few words, but left it at that. There'd been no permanent damage and, by the looks of things, the hangovers would be punishment enough.

Andrew hadn't been there on either occasion. Seanie hadn't seen him there, anyway.

In fact, the first time he'd seen him was at Mass, the uncomfortable jolt of recognition distracting him to the point that Willy Murphy had had to climb over him in the pew to join the queue for Communion, muttering words under his breath that the Lord wouldn't have been too pleased to hear.

Seanie had told himself it couldn't be the same guy. Not after all this time. He'd discreetly tracked him outside afterwards and watched the guy chatting with Father McCarthy, who was only too happy to supply a brief biography when Seanie asked.

Andrew Gallagher was indeed still living in Shanamore after all this time. And working here too, managing the holiday homes they'd built on his family's land.

'Strange boy,' the priest had said of the man who was only a couple of years older than Seanie. 'But he's a lot on his plate, God love him. The mother's in a home near Cloyne now, doesn't know if she's coming or going.'

As Seanie headed up to the road to the complex now, he saw a small silver car pulling out of it. He was getting ready to hail the driver, thinking it was Andrew himself, when he saw the D-reg on the licence plate and then, as the car drew closer, the long head of hair behind the wheel.

A woman.

Seanie didn't recognise her. He assumed she was a guest.

The complex itself was deserted. Seanie parked the car outside Andrew's own cottage and went to ring its bell, but pushing the button didn't make any sound that he could hear.

He knocked, waited.

Knocked again.

The door opened then and there he was: Andrew Gallagher. Dressed in old flannel pyjamas pants and a creased white T-shirt gone pale yellow at the neck, hair hanging in front of his eyes. He barely looked a day older than he had at eighteen. Just paler. More tired.

He was squinting at Seanie. 'Y – yes?'

Seanie flashed his ID, as if the uniform and car weren't enough of a clue.

'Good morning,' he said. 'Andrew, isn't it?'

Andrew's eyes flicked to the Garda car. Seanie had intentionally parked it across the end of his drive, blocking his car in.

'Yes ...' he said hesitantly. 'Is, ah, everything all right?'

'It will be soon. Mind if I come in?'

Panic crossed Andrew's face. 'Well, actually, you s—'

'Won't take long,' Seanie said, moving to step inside, forcing Andrew to open the door fully and step back to let him in.

The ground floor of the house was one big open space. It was dark; Andrew had nearly all the curtains closed. The only daylight was weak and coming from a window at the very rear of the house. And the place was a state. Things were discarded on every available surface – clothes, magazines, shopping bags – and the air smelled of stale food and, faintly, body odour.

'Please excuse the mess,' Andrew said. 'I haven't been well.'

'I'm living in a house full of cardboard boxes at the moment, mate. You're grand.'

That was a lie. He and Imelda had used half of their summer holiday time to make the move, working steadily for a week to unpack every last thing and find a home for it. The exterior of their new home may say, *Body of elderly woman lay undiscovered for weeks*, but inside, it was neat and tidy.

'You're, ah, our new one, right?' Andrew said. He was leaning his back now against the closed front door. 'I keep meaning to call into the station and introduce myself but, ah, you know how it is. Time just gets away from you.'

Seanie thought of the silent desolation outside and wondered what could possibly be taking up Andrew's time.

'Actually,' Seanie said, 'we've met before.'

Andrew frowned. '*Have* we?'

'I used to come here. In the summers. Years ago.'

'I can't say …' He was studying Seanie's face. 'I don't think I remember you. Did we know each other?'

Seanie let a beat pass.

'No, not really,' he said then. 'I just saw you around.'

'Oh.'

Andrew suddenly seemed to realise how dark it was and flicked the switch for the ceiling light. It only served to illuminate more mess and add a few years to his own face; now, Seanie could see that creases and shadows had indeed aged Andrew Gallagher since he'd seen him last.

'You have any guests?' Seanie asked. 'I saw someone drive out just now.'

'Just her.'

'She's on her own?'

'She is,' Andrew said, nodding. 'So … What's this about?'

Seanie lowered himself on to the nearest arm of the sofa and took his notebook from his pocket.

'Do you, by any chance, remember a guest of yours named Michael Kerr? Dublin address. He'd have stayed here a couple of weeks ago.'

Andrew scrunched up his face, as if searching his brain for the answer.

'I got a call,' Seanie continued, 'about a credit card charge. For' – he read from his notes – '€632.41 on the twenty-fourth of October. Would've been a Wednesday, but that's just the day of the charge, of course. He could've arrived before that. Do you remember that guest?'

Andrew blinked rapidly.

'I didn't have anyone here that week,' he said. 'And I don't recognise the name. And that's a lot of money for here, you'd have to stay ages to rack up that. Maybe as long as nine or ten days, this time of the year. It's not like I'd forget that. People rarely stay more than a week, even in the summer. So I'd remember.'

'So, no?' Seanie said.

'Yes. I mean, no. No, I don't remember.'

'How about a Natalie Kerr?'

Again, Andrew made a show of thinking about it.

'No. No, I don't think so.'

'She might have used the name Natalie O'Connor?'

'Like I said, I didn't have anyone here the week before last, so ...' Andrew held up his hands. 'No. Sorry.'

'Can you think of any reason why there'd be a charge on someone's card if they didn't stay here? Could it be a pre-authorisation? Something like that? Do you enter the numbers manually? Could you have made an error?'

'We don't pre-authorise,' Andrew said. 'And I'm very careful.'

'"We"? Does someone else work here with you?'

'Oh.' Andrew smiled. 'No, no. It's just a figure of speech.'

'We all make mistakes from time to time. You could've done it without realising.'

'I'd have noticed it by now. And, like I *said*' – Andrew was getting louder, his tone becoming defensive – 'I didn't put through any charge for that amount.'

Seanie looked around. 'Where's the terminal?'

Andrew pointed to a small console table tucked against the wall behind the door. Seanie could see a handheld credit card machine sitting there amid a mess of paper.

'Does anyone have access to that other than you?' Seanie asked. 'Family? Friends? Other guests, maybe?'

'No.'

'But it's right there. Out in the open.'

'I'm the only one here.'

'You're saying you never have visitors?'

A shadow crossed Andrew's face. 'There's been no one here in the last two weeks,' he said tightly. 'Not inside the house.'

'No one at all?'

'No one at all. Not without me being here too.'

'Well, wait a second now.' Seanie stood up, took a step closer to Andrew. They were the same height but Seanie knew from experience that for some people, the Garda uniform added a couple of inches at least. He hoped Andrew was one of those. 'There was no one here except you, or there was no one here without you? Which is it?'

Andrew looked Seanie right in the eye. It was for the first time: he'd been having a conversation with Seanie's chest, shoulder and boots up until now.

Then he said, 'What's the merchant ID number on this transaction? Have you confirmed it's mine?'

'It says Shanamore Cottages on the statement.' Seanie wasn't sure it did; he was just assuming that, based on what DS O'Reilly had told him.

'So?' Andrew's tone was turning petulant. 'That could be another Shanamore Cottages. Anywhere in the world.'

'The charge was in euro.'

'All charges are in the currency of the bank account they go out of,' Andrew snapped back. 'Have you seen the statement yourself? Did you check to see if this transaction was accompanied by a foreign currency exchange? Have you actually *confirmed* that it originated in euro?'

Seanie suddenly had the feeling he'd been pushed on to the back foot in this conversation and what was weird was that he couldn't quite identify when it had happened.

He pointed at the machine. 'You can print reports, can't you?'

'Not for you.'

'Excuse me?'

Andrew seemed to realise then that being excessively antagonistic with a Garda sergeant might not be the best course of action and his face softened into an apologetic smile.

'I mean,' he said, 'not without a warrant. Data protection and all that. You understand.'

'Of course.' Seanie smiled too. 'Just one more thing.' He pulled one of the printouts from between the pages of his notebook – the wedding photo – and unfolded it. 'Maybe you'd recognise him if you saw him.' He handed the sheet to Andrew. 'That's him there. Michael Kerr.'

Andrew took it and started studying the picture. 'Is that his wife?'

'Yes. Natalie.' Seanie unfolded the press release and handed him that too. 'She's missing.'

A long beat of silence followed while Andrew studied the pages, holding both of them up, close to his face, his eyes darting from one to the other.

Then he said, 'No,' and handed both of them back.

'No, you don't recognise him?'

'No.'

'Or her?'

Andrew shook his head.

'Well,' Seanie said, 'thanks for your help. I suppose we'll have to check the merchant ID. I'll be back if it's yours.'

Andrew didn't respond.

Seanie let himself out and walked to his car without looking back.

He was dialling DS O'Reilly's number before he even had the key in the ignition, even though he knew he'd be halfway back to the village before he got reception on his phone.

Because Seanie had seen Andrew's hands shaking. When he'd taken hold of the printouts, they'd fluttered as if in a breeze.

Andrew was lying.

Again.

Last time, Seanie let him get away with it. Back then, he'd had no choice. But now Seanie was Shanamore's Garda sergeant, and he sure as shit wasn't going to let it happen twice.

———————

He didn't get reception until he was all the way back in the village, and then he got O'Reilly's voicemail. Seanie left a message asking the DS to call him back, anticipating that he would within minutes. But an hour passed. Seanie tried the number again, from the station, and again got a voicemail. He called the Control Room and got transferred to Blackrock, but a member there said O'Reilly was out and suggested he try his mobile. Seanie did, again, but there was no answer. He left a second, more detailed voicemail this time, explaining his suspicion that Andrew Gallagher knew something, potentially about Natalie O'Connor's disappearance, but, at the very least, about that credit card charge, and requesting that O'Reilly touch base with him as soon as possible so they could discuss next steps. By lunchtime, Seanie's phone still hadn't rung and his stomach was growling, the hunger pangs the only thing distracting him more than the lack of a call back.

His options were to go next door and make himself something, cross the road to the petrol station and buy a soggy sandwich or go into the pub and get something hot. It was cold and it was grey, so Seanie opted for Door Number Three. He locked up the station and walked down into the village, his phone clutched in his hand with the volume turned all the way up.

Walking into Murphy's was like moving through a portal to another world, another Ireland, an *older* Ireland. Or channel-surfing on to an episode of *Reeling in the Years* where a few weather-beaten ould fellas were clutching pints of the black stuff and rolling their eyes about the changeover to the decimal system or the introduction of drink-driving laws. It was tiny inside, claustrophobic when it was busy, with only four or five tables outside of the snug and the stools at the bar. There was a TV but it was a small, crappy one with a built-in VHS machine, only turned on for GAA fixtures and, should any blow-in or tourist make the mistake of saying *Sky Sports* or *soccer* to Peggy Murphy, the pub's third-generation proprietor, they'd be lucky not to get a pint glass of left-behind beer and saliva-swill in the face. If you asked for coffee, you got a still-dissolving cup of Nescafé Gold Blend. If you asked for a cocktail, you'd be pointed in the direction of the nearest farm. There were only ever three things on the food menu – stew, soup and sandwiches – and Peggy only served them between noon and three o'clock with absolutely no exceptions. She made one allowance for the modern world, and only because she had no choice but to: the smoking ban had been reluctantly and somewhat loosely implemented. On more than one occasion, Seanie had come through the doors only to be met with the stale, sour stench of cigarette smoke, and caught Peggy furiously spraying air freshener around behind the counter, muttering that the flue must be clogged up again or something.

'Or something,' Seanie would say with a smirk. 'Yeah ...'

A glass of Club Orange would then materialise on the counter and Peggy would tell him, 'On me today, Seanie,' and neither of them would say another word.

He knew to pick his battles.

Murphy's was unusually quiet this lunchtime. There was only Jimmy Sutton, who had the farm just beyond the petrol station, sitting in the far corner with a newspaper and two-thirds of a pint. He looked up as Seanie came in and they exchanged a silent nod. And there was Father McCarthy, sitting in the snug, tucking into a bowl of steaming stew. When he saw Seanie he put down his spoon and moved to get up, but Seanie raised a hand and told him to stay where he was, to enjoy his lunch, and wasn't it fierce cold out there today, because no conversation could conclude until someone made a comment on the weather.

There were a couple of hefty logs in amongst the flames of the fire and just the sound of them cracking and spitting made Seanie feel better. He'd light a fire at home tonight, he decided. Fires felt like company.

He took a stool at the bar and put his phone down face-up on the counter, checking the screen for any missed call notifications. There were none. When Peggy emerged from the back, he ordered a bowl of stew while she poured him his Club Orange without asking if he wanted it. It was safe to assume he did. He never ordered anything else in here, not even when he was off-duty.

'Heard you were up at the cottages this morning,' Peggy said. 'Everything all right?'

'Jesus.' Seanie shook his head. 'That's some going, even for you.'

Peggy cackled. 'You were seen, Seanie boy. That car of yours isn't exactly camouflage.'

'By who?'

'Oh, I couldn't be saying.'

'Well, I can't be saying either.'

She looked at him, waiting.

'I'm starving here, Peggy.'

'Are you now?'

She didn't move.

'Fine,' Seanie said, relenting. 'Everything's fine.'

'Did you see young Andrew?'

'You do know he's older than me, right?'

'Sure you're only a young fella yourself.'

'I wish I was.'

But Peggy wouldn't be deterred. She folded her arms across her ample chest and looked at him expectantly.

'It was just a routine visit, okay, Peg? Nothing to worry about.'

'But I *do* worry about him. You know about his mother, don't you? Mrs Gallagher. God love her, she's in a home over in Cloyne. Doesn't even know her own son from Adam.'

Seanie let a respectful moment of silence pass before he said, 'I'd really love some stew.'

'You're telling me to mind my own business, is it?'

'I'm telling you everything's fine up at the cottages and that the hunger is making me faint.'

Peggy tut-tutted. 'God almighty. I can't let you starve, I suppose. Not when you're already such a skinny little thing. And when there's no one to look after you but me.' She gave his arm a friendly pinch before she disappeared into the back.

Seanie checked his email, just in case O'Reilly had responded to him that way. Nothing. He opened the internet browser and searched for *Natalie O'Connor Kerr*. Three news stories popped up. There was the one he'd already seen, the one from last night, and two new ones that had been published in the last hour. Both of their headlines shouted that Mike Kerr, the husband, had posted a video online begging his wife to come home. There was a link to the video but Seanie didn't want to click on it while sitting at the bar in Murphy's. He may as well project his phone's screen on to the side wall of the church, set up a few rows of chairs and sell tickets.

He put the phone back on the counter, then picked it up again to check the volume was on. It was.

What was O'Reilly doing?

A gust of cold air on the back of Seanie's legs told him someone else had entered the pub. When he half-turned on his stool, he saw Orla Sheridan, the girl who worked in the café across the way and daughter of Peter who owned the petrol station, coming towards him.

'You got a minute, Sean – Sergeant?' The girl was holding her hands in front of her, fingers twitching, shifting her weight from foot to foot.

Nervous.

'Yeah,' Seanie said, indicating the stool next to his. 'Have a seat.'

'Oh, I'm not staying. I'm just on a break. I wanted to tell you something. It's about the woman—'

'Here you go, love.' Peggy had finally reappeared, carrying a bowl of stew. She frowned at Orla before setting the bowl down in front of Seanie, along with cutlery wrapped in a scratchy paper napkin. 'Everything all right?'

'Fine,' Seanie told her. 'It's fine.'

Orla said hi to Peggy, asked her how she was.

'Fine. You?'

'Fine.'

'Well' – Peggy snapped the towel she'd held Seanie's bowl with over her shoulder – 'isn't it great we're all so *fine*.' To Seanie: 'Enjoy your stew, love.'

She turned on her heel and disappeared into the back again.

'She doesn't like me,' Orla whispered. 'She treats me like I personally opened that café. I mean, I just work there. And I actually asked her if she'd anything going in here before I went over there.'

Seanie could feel the juices in his stomach gearing up for a growl. He was trying not to look at the stew but his nostrils were filled with the smell of it.

'So,' he said. 'What is it you wanted to tell me?'

Orla looked around. Out of the corner of his eye, Seanie could see that Jimmy Sutton had put down his newspaper and was openly watching them like they were his own TV screen.

'The woman,' Orla said, keeping her voice low. 'I rang the number like the thing said but no one's called me back, but that reporter came to speak to me this morning and – actually, she's the one who started me thinking about it – maybe I should tell *you*, because it was here?'

Seanie wondered if the smell of the stew was muddling his brain, because he didn't have a clue what Orla was telling him.

'*Natalie O'Connor*,' she clarified. 'I saw her. Here. We talked. She was staying up at the cottages. *After* they say she disappeared.'

Now the pieces of the jigsaw puzzle turned and slotted themselves into place.

'And,' Orla took another scan of the room, then leaned in close enough for Seanie to see the streaks of brownish make-up on her chin, 'Richard Flynn said he never saw her, but she told *me* he talked to her down at the beach. And that he was totally creepy.'

Stew forgotten, Seanie reached into his jacket for his notebook and withdrew the folded pages he'd tucked inside. He opened the photo of Natalie by herself and showed it to Orla.

'I don't need to see a picture,' she said. 'It was her. I *know* her. I follow her. On Instagram. She gave me her card.'

'And this was when, exactly?'

'Last week.'

A piece fell out of the jigsaw puzzle.

'*Last* week? Are you sure?'

The charge on the credit card – which Andrew was denying had come from him, but it must have – had happened before that. Had the missing wife somehow arranged that, in advance of her coming to stay here? Was that a deposit or pre-authorisation for a booking she'd made? Andrew said no but Seanie didn't trust him as far as he could throw him.

'Positive,' Orla said. 'Tuesday of last week. She'd arrived the night before, I think.'

A violent buzzing started then, followed swiftly by a shrill electronic ringing: Seanie's phone.

The screen flashed with DS O'Reilly's number.

At long last.

'Give me a second,' Seanie said. 'I have to take this.' He grabbed the phone and hurried outside.

'Detective?'

'Sorry, Sergeant. I meant to call you back earlier. But we're—'

'She was here,' Seanie blurted out.

A car whizzed past and he spun back towards the pub door, ducking his head against the wall, trying to shield his phone from the noise.

He only caught the end of what O'Reilly said next.

'...why I didn't call back.'

Seanie stuck a finger in his other ear. 'Sorry, what was that?'

'I said I know. We have an Irish Rail ticket and the mobile phone data. Heuston to Kent last Monday afternoon, then the phone was switched off in Shanamore a few hours later. How do *you* know, though? Do you have a sighting?'

'At least one,' Seanie said. 'And I think she might have stayed at those cottages, where the credit card charge came from.'

'Hold that thought, I'm almost there.'

Seanie frowned. 'Where?'

'Shanamore,' O'Reilly said. 'We're just passing Midleton now. We'll meet you at the station.'

REWIND

0:00:04

And then, one day, Caroline came back.

It was in the weeks after the Leaving Cert, four years after she left. Andrew was down on the Front Strand, walking by himself in the last hour of daylight, when he'd spotted her flowing yellow-blonde hair and favourite red headband a little bit further down the beach.

He'd stopped short, blinked, stared. Surely it *couldn't* be.

But when he called out her name, she turned and looked at him.

They'd met at the water's edge, almost at the exact same spot where Andrew had last kissed her. His heart was fit to bursting; his lungs painfully tight in his chest. He'd waited so long for this moment, and he had so many questions – but now that she was here, that he could reach out and touch her, he found himself practically paralysed.

Their conversation was stilted and awkward at first, as if they were meeting as strangers. He supposed that, after all this time, allowances would have to be made. So they talked about Shanamore and plans for their summers and Andrew swallowed back all the questions he had for fear the answers would spoil things, if not the mere act of asking them.

She didn't even mention Germany and neither of them referenced the past. Minute by minute, the world shrunk until they were the only two people left in it. Andrew would've been happy to never see anyone else ever again.

He had two beers left and he let her have them. She'd hated it before but seemed to like it now.

Andrew was already drunk, warm and cocooned, fortified and confident.

No bad consequences. Not now, not tonight.

The evening light was faltering when he took her hand and led her to their special place, the spot they'd so often retreated to when everyone else's voices got too loud, where they'd spent so many hours lying on their backs, looking at the stars, hands reaching under clothes for warm summer skin.

But this time she let him explore places he couldn't see, secret places he hadn't felt before. Afterwards he held her tightly against him while she dozed, and he wondered what he might say to her to get her to stay and never leave him again.

Then:

'Aoife!'

It was completely dark now, the waterline marked only by the broken shards of moonlight shimmering on its surface. The half-moon had turned everything else to indiscriminate shadows and the temperature had dropped dramatically; Andrew suddenly became aware of the fact that he was freezing.

'Aoife!'

The warm body in the crook of his arm started to stir and move.

His nose was in her hair. It smelled of the sea and cigarette smoke, her breath of beer.

He thought, But Caroline doesn't smoke. She hates smoking. When did she start?

'Aoife!'

The voice close now, almost upon them.

'Caroline,' Andrew whispered. 'Someone's coming.'

'Huh?' she said into his chest. 'What?'

'I don't know, but—'

'Aoife!'

She lifted her head and spat, '*Shit.*'

Caroline never used to swear either.

Just then, a levitating circle of white light appeared on the crest of the dune above them: a torch. It swung around and then down, on to them, burning Andrew's eyes with its brightness. Instinctively he put a hand to his face to protect them against it while also trying to see around it.

Who was there?

'What the *fuck*?' a new voice said.

And then another one: 'Jesus Christ …'

Caroline was scrambling to her feet, pressing one hand painfully into Andrew's ribs in a hurry to do it, turning this way and that, looking for – 'My shoes. Where are my shoes? Where are my *shoes*?'

The voice that had swore said, 'Get up.'

'Seanie, for God's sake,' Caroline spat then, towards the light. 'Why don't you mind your own business?'

'You, go with Dave. Right now. *You*, get the fuck *up*.'

Andrew's head was clouded with confusion. Who were these people? Who were they talking to? Why were they so mad? Why were they here at all? He turned to look to Caroline for the answers and saw her face, illuminated in the torch's beam.

And realised that it wasn't Caroline at all.

The boy shouting things at Andrew looked to be younger than him, but he was taller and broader, squaring up as if for a fight.

Andrew just sat there in the sand, stunned, as the clarity of the bitter cold sparred with the warmth of the alcohol in his system, neither of them winning, leaving him dulled and confused and lost as to what was happening, here in the dunes of Front Strand.

Someone else was shouting now, too: the girl who wasn't Caroline. She was stalking off, arms folded across her stomach, spitting expletives at the boy who was shouting at Andrew.

The fists came from above, pummelling the sides of his head, and then came the kicks to his stomach, and the world got smaller and smaller until there were only two things in it: the inside of his head and the pain.

The whole time his attacker kept shouting:

'She's only thirteen, you sick fuck. She's only *thirteen*!'

———

The next time he knew better than to try it with a local girl. The next time, he met her online.

She told him she liked watching *Friends* and she had one brother, younger, and she was wearing a Harry Potter T-shirt in her profile pic.

Her hair was darker and cut to the tips of her shoulders, but Andrew actually liked it better that way. She asked him lots of questions about what his life was like now but he was too embarrassed to admit the truth: that there was nothing to report except wasted time and family tragedies, that he'd never left Shanamore for anything other than brief trips to somewhere else and back again. So instead he told little white lies and gave her the answers he knew she was hoping to hear.

Andrew let months pass before he suggested that they meet in person. She didn't know his real name but, still, he had to be certain before he could even ask.

She didn't react as enthusiastically as he would've hoped, at least not initially. There were a few days of radio silence. She was afraid and he understood that, because he was afraid too. Maybe the end of this was him as raw with pain as he had been when Caroline had left the first time. Maybe the end of this was the end of all things.

But she was worth the risk.

He assured her that they could go at her pace, that he wouldn't pressure her into anything, and he provided a route around every obstacle she raised. Some personal, yes, but mostly logistical.

He reminded her how much he loved her, over and over and over again. He was gently persistent.

One night she said they could move from messages online to a telephone call and when he – finally – got to hear her sweet voice, it was telling him that she wanted to meet.

Her voice was different, both in sound and accent. But if Andrew closed his eyes, he could still hear Caroline.

It would have to do.

He waited for her at the bus station on Parnell Place. They smiled nervously at each other for a moment before Andrew asked if it was all right to give her a hug. She said yes, although the ensuing embrace was stiff and awkward, but that was okay. Baby steps.

Physically she felt just like Caroline had that first time, that first summer. He was pleased. He had made a good choice.

She pointed at her red hairband and said, 'Can I take this off now? I recognised you straightaway.'

He asked her to leave it on.

She had a little bag; Andrew offered to carry it. She called him by someone else's name. She wanted something to drink so they stopped at the nearest café. Andrew was anxious about this unexpected detour, but he wanted to please her. He led the way to a table near the back, as far away as they could get from the window, half-hidden by a display of cakes and pastries.

The man pulling levers on the coffee machine followed them with his eyes.

'Where's your car?' she asked.

'Oh.' He frowned. 'I didn't bring it.'

'But I thought we'd go to Shanamore.'

This surprised him. 'I didn't think … Do you *want* us to go there?'

'I thought we were going to your place.'

He had to admit it then, that he'd booked a hotel room. Here, in the city centre.

She seemed stunned at first, maybe even frightened. Was it too much, too soon? But he assured her, repeatedly, that she was in charge of today. She could stay at the hotel alone tonight, if she wanted.

No, she said. That was okay.

But as they approached the hotel, he began to worry. It was a shabby outfit across the river, near the train station. The décor was outdated and the rooms small and, despite the slight chill in the air outside, the whole building felt like it was slowly suffocating in a stifling heat. But the hotel had two entrances, one at the front and one at the side. They could enter separately and not be seen together, so long as they were careful.

If she was disappointed, she didn't say.

He'd brought two bottles of wine with him. It was lukewarm now and he'd forgotten to bring glasses, so they sipped it from the soft plastic cups they found by the sink in the bathroom. He could tell by the way she wrinkled her nose that she didn't like it, but she drank it anyway.

She set the empty cup down on the nightstand and turned to smile at him, clearly nervous.

rewind

He smiled back.

And then he reached for her hand.

Her underwear was pastel pink with large, cartoon cats on them, trimmed in blue.

A bit childish for a thirteen-year-old, he thought.

————

'Did I tell you someone's coming to look at the house next Tuesday, Andy?' It was late on a Friday evening and Andrew and his mother were at home, sitting in their respective chairs. Hers was the scuffed leather armchair closest to the fire; his was the overstuffed one covered in splotchy red upholstery that looked deep red in his childhood photos. The *Late Late* was on. She needed to be close to the television because her hearing wasn't great and Andrew didn't like being in the heat of the fire, so the chairs were staggered across the floor like same colour squares on a chequerboard. He couldn't see her face around the edge of her chair and she couldn't see his because he was behind her. Conversation was a disembodied but nearby voice that came with no face to read. 'Did I?'

'You did,' Andrew said.

On screen, some young fella was playing guitar. Country music.

'Did I?'

'You did.'

'You'd want to get that upstairs sorted, Andy love.'

'Mmm.'

'I said you'd want to get that upstairs sorted.'

'I heard you the first time.'

The song ended and the studio audience erupted in applause.

'You heard me, yeah,' his mother said. 'So what did you do about it? I told Michael over the road we might take a skip off him tomorrow.'

Andrew rolled his eyes. 'Mam, we don't need it.'

'Sure we can't let them see the place like this, now, can we?'

'They don't care,' he muttered.

'What's that?'

'I said they don't *care*.'

'Who doesn't?'

'They want the *land*, Mam. That's all they're interested in. They're not coming to see the house.'

Now the singer was crossing the set, waving to the audience. The host met him on the main stage and directed him to sit on the couch.

'Who's that now there?' his mother asked. 'Is that the fella who was in the pub in Castlemartyr that time?'

'No, Mam. That's the guy who sang the song before this.'

'Is it?'

'Yeah.'

'Oh, 'tis. Yeah. You're right.'

The singer started talking about making his new album and then told a long, convoluted story about recording some of it in Marrakesh. The punchline was him running into another Irish musician in a hotel out there, one much more famous than him, which just came off as name-dropping. There was an awkward moment when he paused for applause but only a smattering came. The host hurriedly steered him on to another topic and the singer launched into that.

At least a full minute after she'd last spoken, his mother said, 'We might take the skip off him. Michael over the road.'

Andrew was used to this, her picking up conversations and dropping them again like threads. He could never be sure if this meant her memory had begun deteriorating along with the rest of her, staining these gaps with blankness, or if this actually meant that her synapses were firing as well as ever, ready to pick up wherever she'd left off.

'I told you,' he said. 'They won't be coming in.'

'Ah, we'll have to ask them in.'

'They don't *care*. How many more—' He stopped, took a deep breath. 'They're coming to see the site. That's what the agent said. A site visit. They don't care about the house; it's getting knocked down the second we clear out of here.' He snorted. 'They might not even wait until then.'

'I'll still have to offer, Andy love.'

'*Mam*,' he snapped. 'Seriously. Don't.'

On the TV screen, the talk show had gone to a break and now someone was falling asleep on the train across from someone else who'd fallen asleep on the train.

Andrew closed his eyes and toured the ground floor of the house, trying to see it through the eyes of a stranger, trying to see what he and his mother had long stopped seeing for themselves. Her sunken bed that he'd dragged downstairs and wedged in between the three-piece in the living room next door, the living room that had had to become a makeshift bedroom, first for his father and now for her. The soiled dishes and plates piled precariously in the kitchen, pots left on the range with thick, black grease congealing on the handles. The mountain ranges of old newspapers and folded clothes, the piles of boxes of VHS tapes, Christmas decorations and car boot sale china that were reaching for the cigarette-smoke-stained ceiling on every square foot of floor space. He breathed in deep but he couldn't detect the smell he knew was here, knew *must* be here, but which he was apparently impervious to. Now he imagined that those strangers were the estate agent and the developers who wanted to buy their land – a father and son team, he'd heard – and his cheeks burned at the mere thought. No one could come in here.

The best thing for this place was to raze it to the ground, which is exactly what would happen if they managed to get the sale through. They needed it to happen; they needed the money. Andrew picked up odd jobs here and there and he had work down at the hotel during the season, but that was it and it wasn't enough.

And he didn't know how much longer his mother could even live with him. Nursing homes cost money, much more money than he had or could get.

'They need to go upstairs,' she said now. 'Did I tell you that? It's for the view.'

Andrew frowned. 'The view?'

The ad break had ended and now some greasy young politician was waving at the audience from the top of the set's stairs.

'Yeah,' his mother said. 'The view. I told you that.'

She hadn't. But this had a ring of truth to it, of logic. These developers, they were planning to build holiday homes here. You couldn't see the sea from ground level and, two storeys up, you could only see it from certain angles. It made sense that they would want to go to the highest point of the house and see what they could see from there.

'Did you hear me, love?'

'Yeah,' Andrew said absently. His pulse had quickened.

'They need to go upstairs.'

'I heard you.'

'I'm just saying.'

'Mmm.' He had closed his eyes again and was touring the upstairs of the house in his mind's eye, which was even worse than down here, covered as it was in a thick layer of dirt and dust, filled with even more things, choked with even heavier air and—

'You'd want to get rid of that stuff.'

He opened his eyes. 'What?'

'You'd want to get rid of that stuff, I said.'

Andrew almost said, *What stuff?* But he quickly swallowed those words because he didn't want to hear her say the answer, didn't want confirmation that even though it had been months since she'd been upstairs, he'd kept his stuff up there long before that, and although she'd never mentioned it before now, she'd known all along that he had.

What had she seen?

What did she know?

'I pray for you, Andy love. I do.' His mother sighed, long and loud. 'I pray that the good Lord will save your soul.' She paused. 'Did you hear me?'

'Let's get that skip,' he said.

'What was that now?'

'I said, let's get that skip.'

They needed to make the sale. *He* needed to make the sale, he saw now. Because his mother was just hell-bent on interfering with things, wasn't she? She wasn't as stupid as she looked after all.

And it was time, Andrew decided, for her to go into a home.

FASTFORWARD

0:00:10

September had always been Natalie's favourite month. New copybooks, blue skies, fresh starts. On Stephen's Green, the leaves were turning. In the ten minutes it took her to cut through the park, she counted three Instagram Husbands, each one peering intently into a phone that was trained on a girl or a woman who wasn't looking at it or him at all, but away, into the middle distance, smiling with her mouth open, shoulders hunched, head angled to the side, acting as if she didn't even know this perfectly composed shot of her looking glossy and ethereal was even being taken. Natalie had spent the last half-hour with a woman who'd advised her to start posting more photos to Instagram that looked just like that, and she didn't know how she felt about it.

Ellie Fox called herself a *brand manager*. That's what it said on her business cards. She'd given Natalie one at some function long ago, but it was only today that they'd finally sat down for a proper meeting. Now Natalie's head was swarming with the possibilities Ellie's services would offer. Higher ad revenue. Partnerships. Sponsored travel. She'd even mentioned a company who would professionally edit your videos before they went online; if Natalie signed with her, she'd have access to it. Although she'd long suspected some of the big accounts must have that kind of thing at their disposal, it was weird to know for sure, as if someone had just yanked back the curtain. But Natalie knew she needed to wise up, to get smart about things. To treat this endeavour like a business, to scale it up. They had a mortgage now, a whopper of one, and Natalie wanted to get to a place where thinking of the future – five years down the line, ten – didn't automatically make her throat tighten.

Bestseller was relatively empty so Natalie could see immediately that Carla wasn't there. They'd known each other since they were kids and in all that time Carla had never once been *on* time, so it wasn't surprising.

The café was a small space with few tables, but it was cosy and did great coffee and had walls lined with books. Natalie nabbed their usual table, right at the back. She ordered an Americano, which she'd all but drained when Carla came bustling in fifteen minutes later, flushed and apologetic and out of breath.

'Sorry,' she said, leaning down to give Natalie a one-armed hug. 'Work is a fucking nightmare. We're trying to get this funding proposal in …' She flopped down. 'You know what? I'm not even going to get into it. The short version is the place is an absolute shit-show and I really need a coffee the size of my head.' She looked around for a waiter, then back at Natalie. 'Anyway. You. How goes it?'

'Good,' Natalie said. 'I've just come from a meeting. A bit of an exciting one, actually.'

'Oh? What about?'

'Well, this is going to sound weird, but—'

'What can I get for you, ladies?'

A waiter had materialised alongside them.

'A coffee, please,' Carla said to him. 'An Americano. A big one. The biggest one you have.'

Natalie ordered a fresh cup.

'Honestly,' Carla said once he'd left them alone again, 'if I don't get some caffeine into me soon … How can it only be Tuesday? This week feels like a fortnight long already.' She shook her head. 'Anyway. Sorry. I interrupted you. You were saying something's weird?'

'Yeah. I, ah, I met with a manager this morning.'

'A manager of what?'

'Of brands, technically speaking. But really people. She's kind of like an agent.'

Carla raised her eyebrows. 'An *agent*?'

'I know, I know. It sounds like premium arseholery, but I—'

'Why do you need one of those?'

Natalie told herself she was imagining the stress she'd heard on the *you*.

'It's not so much that I *need* one, exactly. More that I could benefit from one. She seems to think I could, anyway. Of course, she would say that, she's trying to get me to hire her. But she was talking about brand partnerships and sponsored holidays and all sorts of stuff. And how it's all about micro-influencers these days. Apparently.'

'Your favourite word,' Carla said wryly.

'Now with added notions.'

'Micro-influencers – what does it even mean?'

'Small-timers,' Natalie explained. 'I think. Basically. The big names with a zillion followers are charging loads, so brands have copped on to the fact that if they get a group of relative nobodies to post about their products instead, they'll get the same audience numbers but for half the price.'

'How many followers do you have now?'

Natalie shifted in her seat. She didn't like saying the figure. Even though it was online for all to see, saying it aloud felt wrong. Obnoxious. Like sharing your annual salary, when your annual salary was a lot.

'I don't know,' she said. 'A hundred thousand or so?' The number was actually 103,149. Natalie had checked before meeting Ellie. Carla's expression was unreadable; a change of subject felt like the safest option. 'Anyway, the manager, she was lovely. You'd like her. You actually might *know* her, she was at Trinity when you were. Ellie Fox?'

Carla shook her head. 'Doesn't ring a bell.'

A beat passed.

'So what's going on at work, then?' Natalie asked. 'Same shit or new shit?'

'Same shit, but more of it than ever.' Carla's boss was a tyrant on the verge of retirement who delighted in making life hell for all his subordinates. He'd made her hate what had once been her dream job. But as a civil servant, her best option was to grin and bear it until the bastard's pension kicked in a few months from now. 'Maybe I should get in on this Instagram thing. What do you think? Is there a gap in the market for a thirty-one-year-old who lives with her parents, works in a museum and spends all day dreaming of violent ways to kill her boss?'

Natalie felt herself bristle at *this Instagram thing* and then immediately admonished herself for being overly sensitive.

'I'm sure there is,' she said. '*I'd* follow you.'

The coffee arrived. Carla downed a gulp of hers like it was cold water in the desert.

'He's worse than ever,' she said then, wiping foam from her mouth. 'I'm not sure how much longer I can hang on for. Really. You don't know how bloody lucky you are, Nat.'

Natalie thought that she did, actually. But she didn't correct Carla. Now wasn't the time.

'Hey,' she said instead, 'I've an idea. I've been invited to this drinks thing on Friday night at the Westbury. They said I can bring a plus-one. Canapés and prosecco and a goody bag. I'm going for the bag, obviously. You should come. Free night out. With free stuff.'

'Thanks,' Carla said, 'but fuck no. Kim K wannabes chewing one too many teeth-whitening strips? I'd rather be at work.'

Natalie felt her cheeks colour.

'It's not *that* bad,' she said. 'Most of the girls are lovely. And smart, hard-working businesswomen.'

Carla rolled her eyes.

'Yeah, I'm sure it's *incredibly* taxing to be at home on your phone all day in your pyjamas without anyone bossing you around. God. Won't someone start a charity for them or something?' She saw Natalie's face. 'I don't mean *you*. Obviously.'

'No, I know.'

The pause that followed was more than long enough to qualify as an awkward silence.

'I really like her glasses,' Carla said then, jerking her head towards the front of the café.

Natalie got the distinct impression Carla was just saying something to fill the dead air, but she played along. When she turned to look, she saw a woman a few years older than them seated on the other side of the café, blonde and slim, wearing a sharp black blazer over black jeans. Her hair was in one of those perfectly neat, sleek ponytails that Natalie, no matter what length her hair was, had never been able to master. The women's glasses were black too – thick, trendy frames with some designer insignia on the side. She looked to be engrossed in her phone.

'Yeah,' Natalie said. 'They're nice.'

Carla asked how Mike was.

'Oh, he's fine. Obsessed with the house. And we don't even have the keys yet – we're supposed to be getting them this weekend.'

'That's exciting,' Carla said in a tone that didn't match the words.

'Yeah …'

Natalie didn't want to go on too much about the house. Not when Carla was still stuck in her childhood bedroom and years away from being able to afford to buy. And *she* had just bought a place with four bedrooms in the most expensive postcode in the country and was paying her half with the money she made off playing with her phone.

She was trying to think of a topic of conversation that wouldn't immediately run aground when Carla's phone started to blare, interrupting the pleasant, clinking hum of café background noise.

When Carla said, 'I have to go,' Natalie felt sorry for her friend.

But also, a little relieved.

———

The house was finally theirs, but also a jungle. Cardboard boxes of all shapes and sizes were stacked in every room, kept company by the odd suitcase, overstuffed refuse bag, plastic carton and hanging rail. Each morning for the last five, Natalie had got up, shared a coffee with Mike before he ran to the DART and then started thwacking away at it, box by bag by case.

This morning, she was going to make a start on her office.

She'd been neglecting And Breathe ever since they'd got the keys a week ago; by now there were probably hundreds of direct messages and comments clamouring for her attention, as well as a stack of emails from PR contacts awaiting her response. She also needed to get back to Ellie, who'd sent on an official contract.

Natalie was hoping that if she got things in the office sorted, she'd be motivated to spend some solid time at her desk.

She'd commandeered the smallest of the three bedrooms to be the new And Breathe HQ. Mike had kindly spent yesterday evening piecing together IKEA bookshelves and securing them along one wall in there. The room was filled with more boxes than any other, but here the boxes were small and had their old address on them: deliveries. Stuff Natalie had been buying online for the office, or stuff she'd been sent for it. It was going to be like Christmas morning opening them all up and she was childishly excited about it.

Before she did anything else, Natalie picked up her phone and took a 360-degree video of the room. 'Good morning, everyone!' she narrated. 'I know, I know – I've been a bit quiet on here the last few days but as you know, we moved into our new house and it's just been crazy. We're drowning in boxes but progress is being made. And guess what I'm doing today? My office! I'm trying to act cool but I'm actually really excited about this. Stay tuned!' She posted the video to Instagram and set the phone aside on a shelf.

Natalie was slicing through the tape on the first box when she heard the doorbell go.

She thought, *Postman.*

She *assumed* postman.

But a short, broad woman was who she found outside. She was dressed in an unflatteringly long and shapeless raincoat that reached her ankles, and sporting a head of frizzy, too-bleached shoulder-length hair. It was impossible to tell what age the woman was. She could've been anywhere from twenty-five to forty-five.

'Hi,' she said cheerfully.

'Ah, hi ...?' Natalie had no idea who the woman was.

The stranger's eyes raked her up and down. Natalie crossed her arms, feeling exposed. She was dressed for unpacking dusty boxes: a pair of grey, baggy sweatpants and a wrinkled, misshapen T-shirt in mourning for its bright white past. She hadn't brushed her hair or teeth yet and her feet were in mismatched socks.

'I hope I haven't disturbed you,' the woman said, frowning.

'No, no. I was just – we just—' Natalie took a breath, smiled, restarted. 'Unpacking. I'm unpacking. We've just moved in.'

'Oh, I know. That's why I'm here. I wanted to give you this.' The woman raised a small pink flowerpot with two hands, like it was a religious offering. It was filled with pink and white carnations and sprays of wilting baby's breath. A mini 'New Home' card was resting among the blooms and the handle had been wrapped in ringlets of Barbie-pink ribbon. It looked like something you'd give your grandmother that you'd picked up last minute in a petrol station forecourt on the way to her house, but Natalie appreciated the gesture.

She thought, *Neighbour*.

She *assumed* neighbour.

Neighbours were a new thing. Mike and Natalie had spent the last five years in the effortless anonymity of city centre apartment blocks, where they might nod and smile and murmur, 'Hi, how are you?' to the other residents they passed in the hall or the car park or met at the letterboxes, but that was it. If even that. Natalie had once had a conversation with the woman who'd lived directly opposite and this had made her feel justified in saying, *Well, I do know* one *of my neighbours* … until the day she saw a completely different person emerge from the same door and realised that the woman had packed up, moved out and moved on without her even knowing. Now they were homeowners, on a residential street, in a *mature area,* as the estate agent had said a hundred times. There was a duty to be neighbourly.

'Thank you so much,' she said, taking the pot. 'That's very kind of you. I'm Natalie, by the way.'

The woman beamed. 'Alice.'

When they shook hands, Natalie felt rough skin. When she looked down, she glimpsed cracked, flaky knuckles and flesh swelling horribly around a too-tight gold ring.

'Have you lived here long?' Natalie asked.

'Gosh, I must be in Dublin ten years now. Eleven? To tell you the truth, I've lost track.'

'It seems like a lovely street.'

Alice looked behind her. 'It's a *fantastic* street. Really. I love this area. And this *house*. You're so lucky. I'm in an apartment, myself.'

There was a complex of 1970s red-brick apartment blocks down at the end of the road, facing the beach.

'Is it one of the ones with a sea view?' Natalie asked. 'I always think that must be lovely to wake up to.'

'God, no,' Alice said. 'I *wish*!'

'Still. It's nice to be so close to the water.' She paused. 'Well ...' Natalie glanced back over her shoulder, thinking of the unpacked boxes upstairs. 'Thanks so much for this. It's lovely. And I really appreciate it.'

A shadow crossed Alice's face.

'You're very busy,' she said flatly. 'I get it.'

Natalie realised she'd said the wrong thing. She was failing miserably at being neighbourly and she'd only been at it a couple of minutes.

'Actually, I was just about to make some coffee. Would you like a cup?'

Alice visibly brightened. 'Oh, I'd *love* some. You have one of those fancy machines, don't you?'

Natalie laughed. *Are we that obvious?* 'We do, but I'm afraid it's lost in a box somewhere. We're surviving with paper filters until we find it.' She stepped aside, beckoning Alice in. 'It's Boxes 'R' Us in here at the moment. Please excuse the mess. The living room isn't too bad; there's space to sit down in there, at least.' She motioned for Alice to go and do that. 'How do you take your coffee?'

'With a little milk, please.'

'I'll be right back.'

Natalie went into the kitchen. One of Mike's moving responsibilities had been to prepare a box of kitchen stuff just to get them through the move and, clearly not anticipating company, he'd only put two mugs in there, both of them novelties. His was the present she'd got him from Hairy Baby: the *Jaws 2* poster with the, 'It's a different shark' *Father Ted* quote. Hers was one of the many caffeine-themed gifts she'd got over the years: a black mug that said, in white lettering, 'What do we want? Coffee!

When do we want it? I'LL FUCKING CUT YOU.' She blushed now at the Solomon's Choice of which one to serve Alice. She figured *Jaws* was the lesser of two evils. She was about to rinse them in the sink when she heard the unmistakable sound of a photo being taken with a smartphone, that sharp, faux-mechanical *click*.

She stopped, one hand holding both mugs by their handles, the other on the tap over the sink.

Click. Click. Click.

Alice was taking photos. But of what?

Natalie tiptoed across the kitchen to peek into the living room and saw the woman standing in front of the fireplace, holding her phone out in front of her, smiling manically, snapping away.

Click-click-click.

Alice was taking selfies in front of Natalie's fireplace.

That was strange, but not—

Alice pointed behind her, at the framed wedding photo sitting on the mantelpiece, and smiled even wider.

Click.

Natalie stepped into the room. 'What are you doing?'

'Oh—' Alice was so startled, she dropped the phone. It clattered on to the floor. She bent down to pick it up and then dropped it again. Her cheeks had flushed. 'I was – I was just ...'

Natalie was expecting embarrassment, shame, apology. Or maybe some kind of reasonable, logical explanation. But when Alice straightened up, the look on her face was one of annoyance, and her words, when they came, were dripping with indignation.

'If it wasn't for people like me, you wouldn't even *have* this fucking house.'

The air temperature in the room seemed to drop a few degrees. This wasn't an inappropriately nosy neighbour. This was an internet crazy, one of Natalie's followers, who'd come crashing out of the screen and into real life via her own front door.

And Natalie had invited her in.

She didn't know what to do. Her phone was upstairs, in the office. She could run. As quickly as she could, up the stairs and into that room. The door had a key in it. She'd lock it behind her and ring Mike. No, the guards. They were closer. *Then* Mike. Alice could take as many pictures as she wanted in the meantime because when the Gardaí got here, they'd bloody arrest her.

But before Natalie could move, Alice muttered something under her breath and stalked out of the room, into the hall.

Natalie followed, but kept her distance.

She'd set the pink flower pot on the little console table out there, next to the tray where she and Mike had already established a habit of depositing keys, change, Leap cards and the like. As she passed, Alice knocked the pot on to the floor with a single decisive swoop of her hand, smashing it into smithereens, sending shards of pink pot and crumbs of dark soil flying across the floor.

Then she turned to roar a 'Fuck you' at Natalie. 'You stuck-up, ugly *bitch.*'

She went out, slamming the door so hard behind her that the letterbox rattled on its hinges, leaving Natalie standing dumbfounded in the hall, blood thumping in her ears, shaking.

———

'Crazy bitch,' Madeline muttered. 'How the hell did she find your house?'

Natalie and Madeline were sitting beside each other at a long trestle table covered in starched white cloth and festooned with sweet-smelling floral arrangements, flickering beeswax candles and exquisitely wrapped gift boxes whose calligraphy tags doubled as place-cards.

A cosmetics brand was having a brunch at the Dylan Hotel to celebrate the launch of a new lipstick line. Every seat was taken and the room thrummed with the sound of two dozen women talking. Natalie was relieved to find she'd been seated next to Madeline Creen, a make-up artist who'd amassed a huge following with YouTube tutorials that featured only value brands you could buy in chemists and supermarkets. The two of them were decidedly the elder statesmen at the table. Looking around, all the other women seemed to be under twenty-five.

They were also the only two who didn't currently have their phones in their hands. Madeline had already done her duty, adding a video of the room to her Instagram story and pulling Natalie in for a selfie that she'd post later, when she got home, and Natalie just wasn't in the mood for it.

Not after yesterday.

'I've no idea,' Natalie said. 'But I did post a picture of Sandymount Strand right after our offer was accepted and said something like, "It's going to be great living so close to the beach." Mike thinks this woman may have gone online, on to Daft or something, and looked up recent house sales in the area. There'd have been pictures there she could've matched with pictures I posted later, from the house. Matched up the backgrounds, I mean. Then she buys her potted plant and comes knocking on my door.' She sighed. 'But Mike thinks I'm overreacting. He maintains that she's just a neighbour who's a tad unhinged.'

'Nah.' Madeline shook her head. 'She's definitely a crazy. And look, they come with the territory. We want people to feel like they know us. Otherwise all this, it doesn't work. But if they're a bit, you know' – she made a face – '*unhinged*, they don't understand that they *don't* know us, actually. This Alice may be your first one but, honey, she won't be your last.'

'What a comforting thought, Maddy. Thanks for that.'

She laughed. 'Sorry.'

'Have *you* had any visitors?'

'My crazy's confined to email, so far. There's one woman who's been messaging me every day for weeks now because she ran out and bought all the products I used in a video but she' – Madeline made air quotes with her fingers – '"couldn't achieve the same result". And that's my fault, apparently.'

'What does she want?'

'Me to refund the money she spent on the products.'

'You're kidding.'

'She says I have a responsibility. When I didn't agree – and stopped responding – she started on the insults. I'm a liar. I'm a fraud. I've got three chins. My teeth aren't straight. My skin is disgusting. Oh, and of course the classic *who do you think you are*?'

'Lovely.'

'Isn't it? Gotta love fan mail.' Madeline took a swig of her drink; they'd been handed mimosas as they entered the room. 'So what are you going to do?'

'I don't know …' Natalie shrugged. 'Mike thinks we should get electronic gates. He says they'd deter people from coming up the path and knocking on the door. But to be honest, I'm more worried about walking around the neighbourhood. Walking down to the beach. What if I was on my own and someone approached me? Is it weird to be worried about that kind of thing? Or am I *catching* the crazy?'

'No make-up,' Madeline said. 'Hair in a ponytail. Glasses instead of my contacts. That's what I do when I go out running and no one has ever said *anything* to me. No one even looks at me. I'd bet money my most loyal followers wouldn't be able to pick me out of a line-up when I look like that. And I'm *in* all my shots. You're only in some of yours. So I wouldn't worry about it. Really. Yesterday was just bad luck.'

They heard the clinking of cutlery against glass. A representative from their corporate hosts was standing at the head of the table, waiting patiently for everyone's attention. The chatter tapered off quickly and a handful of women who'd been standing at various points around the table, leaning down to chat – other representatives of the company, Natalie presumed, based on the conversations she'd overheard – straightened up now and started to drift towards the top of the table too, throwing smiles and excited little waves at individual guests as they passed.

Except for one.

One of these women didn't look at anybody. She kept her head turned slightly away, as if studying the opposite wall. And she didn't drift towards the top of the table as much as hurried towards it – and then kept going, past the speaker, through the double doors and out

181

of the room, at a speed that suggested she was trying to get out before anyone saw her leave.

A little voice in Natalie's head said, *She's not supposed to be here.*

Was she a gatecrasher? There was always at least one at these things. It was the goody bags that drew them.

But just as the woman crossed the threshold, she glanced back and Natalie saw that she was older, *too* old, surely, to be bothered gatecrashing a Millennial-filled event like this, and that she was wearing black glasses with thick, trendy frames.

They made eye contact.

And then Natalie clocked the impeccable ponytail, the perfectly neat gathering of sleek, bleached-blonde hair, and she realised who it was, where she'd seen her before.

It was with Carla, in Bestseller, a couple of weeks ago.

It was the woman from the café.

FASTFORWARD

0:01:00

By sticking her head outside the front door, Audrey could see what she hadn't been able to from the bedroom window: that while she was sleeping, a convoy of Garda vehicles had arrived and parked in a neat row at the entrance to the complex. The only actual Gardaí Audrey could see, though, were huddled in a little group of five or six by the side of the van marked TECHNICAL BUREAU. Each of them had adopted an identical stance: legs straight and slightly apart, both hands hooked into the sides of their neon yellow vests.

Well, them and the suited one standing in front of her.

When he flashed his ID, Audrey reached out and snatched it from him.

'You lads always do that so fast,' she said, 'you can never read the names. It's almost like that's what you *want* to happen.'

He raised an eyebrow. 'Meet a lot of us, do you?'

'Detective Sergeant Steven O'Reilly.' Audrey handed the ID back to him. 'To what do I owe the pleasure? Again.'

'I need you to pack up your stuff and leave.'

'You're not seriously kicking me out of a house for the second time in two days? Neither of which were actually yours, I might add.'

'The cottages are closed,' he said. 'You can't stay here.'

'Is that because of Natalie O'Connor? Is this a crime scene?'

'This is official Garda business. Not yours.' The detective held up a splayed hand. 'Five minutes. That's how long you've got to pack up and go.' He turned to leave.

'You can't just kick me out,' Audrey called after him.

Over his shoulder: 'And yet I just have.'

'Wait!'

When he'd reluctantly turned back around to face her, his expression was somewhere between bemused and annoyed.

'What if I've nowhere else to go?'

'Then I'd suggest you go *home*,' he said. 'Or back to work, maybe? I'm sure there's some Pulitzer Prize-worthy arse-related news about Kim Kevorkian that needs writing up.'

'Oh, that's good,' Audrey said. 'The deliberately getting the name wrong. I mean, *I'm* not falling for it, but I can see how it'd work on other people.'

The detective sighed deeply. 'Why are you like this?'

'What?'

'So ... *combative.*'

'I don't like not knowing what's going on.'

'A woman is missing, as well you know, and you are impeding the effort to locate her by delaying me. There. Now you're all caught up.'

'Were your phones ringing a lot in the past twenty-four hours, Detective? I wonder why that could be ...'

'Yeah, they were,' he said. 'Off the hook, actually. Unfortunately it was all crazies and fantasists on the end of the line, so many thanks for wasting our limited resources.'

'Didn't they get you here?'

'No, they did not.'

Either he was lying or it wasn't Orla's tip-off that had brought them to Shanamore.

Thinking about it, though, an email from a waitress would hardly warrant the arrival of a small army without so much as a follow-up first, would it? They had to have something else.

Maybe Mike had called them and told them about Natalie asking him about Shanamore. But wouldn't he have done that already, yesterday? Why would they have waited twenty-four hours to show up here? No, there had to be a new lead. A development.

And Audrey absolutely *had* to find out what it was.

'Aren't you wondering why I'm here?' she asked.

'The husband told you she'd asked him about this place. Mystery solved.'

'But I knew before that. I asked *him* if he'd ever heard of Shanamore. And I was already here when I did.'

The detective said nothing, but his mouth twitched.

Audrey smiled sweetly. 'I'll show you mine if you show me yours.'

'Don't say things like that. Don't you read the news?'

'Don't worry, Detective. You're a little flat-chested for me.' Audrey winked at him. 'Geddit?'

'Please God,' he said, groaning. 'Make it stop.'

'Ask me the question then.'

'*Fine.* Why did you come here?'

'I got a message from a woman named Orla Sheridan. She'd read my article, saw my email on there. She works in the café in The Kiln, next to the church back in the village. She spoke to Natalie last Tuesday and Natalie asked her not to tell anyone she was here. And Natalie told her that *Mike* had been here, but Mike told me he's never been here in his life. And when I rang reception' – she nodded towards Cottage No. 1 – '*he* told me there was no guest here by that name.'

O'Reilly was looking at her now like he was afraid to make any sudden moves.

'So you get this email,' he said, 'and then you get in your car and drive down here in the middle of the night?'

'I drove down this morning,' Audrey said. 'And technically the car is my sister's.'

'Seems like a bit of an overreaction to me.'

She pointed at the Garda vehicles. 'Oh, does it?'

'I think those five minutes are up.'

'You're not going to tell me *anything*?'

'That's the way this works,' O'Reilly said. 'We don't keep the press abreast of every move we make. We're trying *not* to shit all over our own investigation. Or let you do it. And let's be honest here, this is all a bit of a moot point, isn't it, because do you even really qualify as *press*?' He turned to leave for the second time. 'Get your stuff and get out and stop wasting my bloody time.'

'She bought a phone,' Audrey blurted out.

O'Reilly aborted his departure, turned back to her.

'She what?'

'Orla's family own the shop up at the petrol station. Her father sold a phone to Natalie when she was here. Not a smartphone. A dumb one. Cheap. Pay-as-you-go. And, well ...'

Audrey hesitated. This was her last card to play. It was her *only* card. It was also the right thing to do, but she needed something to give to Joel so he wouldn't fire her ...

The detective took a step back, closer. 'Go on.'

'I found a phone. Here. Just now.' Audrey slid the package out of her back pocket. She pulled back the plastic bin liner until O'Reilly could see the phone inside. 'It was in the bin in the bathroom upstairs. It's dead. I did touch it when I took it out, but I put it in this as soon as I ... Well. Here.' She held it out to him.

He looked at it, then back up at her.

Then he reached inside his pocket, pulled out a blue latex glove and used it to take the phone from her without actually touching it.

'We'll have to get your prints,' he said. 'And a DNA sample. For elimination.' He re-wrapped the phone in the bin liner and slipped it into a trouser pocket. 'And I'm going to need your details.' He produced a small leather notebook and wrote Audrey's full name, address and telephone number into it.

'I hear there's a room over the pub in the village for you,' he said then, 'if you want it. On your way out – which better be in the next sixty seconds – stop at the van and one of the lads will take your samples.' He hesitated, as if trying to decide something. 'Her mobile phone activity. That's why we're here. The last time it pinged off a mast was in Shanamore a week ago yesterday. If *this* phone is hers, it places her here. Not just at the cottages, but in this cottage.' He raised an eyebrow. 'Are we even now?'

Audrey grinned. 'Suppose.'

'Don't name me.'

'But I can quote you?'

'You can use that information. No names.'

'What do I call you then?'

'What do you ...?' O'Reilly smirked. 'I believe the term is "senior Garda sources", my dear.'

'"My dear"?' Don't say things like that to me, Detective. Don't you read the news?'

'I'm going to have to take an extra Captopril because of you today, you know.'

'What's that?'

'Get yourself a highly stressful job and you'll find out when you're older. Now please, for the love of God, *get out*.'

'Okay, okay,' Audrey said, holding up her hands. 'I'm going.'

She closed the front door and went back inside. Through the front window, she watched the detective walk back across the complex, towards the cluster of Garda vehicles.

Then she ran around the cottage, taking as many pictures as she could as quickly as she could with her phone.

A headline popped unbidden into her head. Exclusive: Inside the Isolated Country Cottage Where Tragic Natalie Spent Her Last Days.

She should *really* ring Joel.

She would just as soon as she got back to the village.

Audrey pushed open the door of Murphy's pub and walked straight into the past.

This wasn't the actual pub where she'd spent long-ago Sundays playing Barbies with Dee under the tables, but it was like one of them and they were all the same. An Old Man Pub, as she called them now. Dusty bare floorboards. Brown and orange swirls in the seventies upholstery in the snug. The crackle of the open fire and the earthy smell of burning turf. Even the smattering of patrons, all men and all local and all old enough to remember when JFK came to Ireland, seemed to have been transported here from a different time, complete with their half-drained pints of stout and copies of the *Evening Echo*. All Audrey needed was a glass bottle of room-temperature off-brand Coke, a packet of Bacon Fries and Dee annoying the absolute shite out of her, and the time-travelling would be complete.

What she needed now, though, was a place to stay.

The woman behind the bar had a plump, shiny face that had evidently never been troubled by moisturiser or make-up. Her elbows were up on the counter, her head was down and she was forensically examining the newspaper that was spread out in front of her, an index finger tracing her progress on the page. She was reading the death notices, Audrey saw when she got close.

'What can I do for you, love?' The woman hadn't taken her eyes off the paper.

'I was, ah, I was told there might be a room here?'

Only now did she look up, then look Audrey up and down. 'You the one who was up at the cottages? Down from Dublin?'

'Yep.' Audrey smiled. 'That's me.'

'I'm Peggy.' She bent down to get something and then dropped it on to the counter with a clatter. 'That's the key.' She pointed to her right where there was a narrow door marked PRIVATE. 'That's the way. The room's up the stairs, door number one. The key to the bathroom is on there too. The only way in is through here so you'll have to be back by last orders. I'll do a bit of breakfast for you tomorrow if you like. It's twenty-five a night. We can settle up in the morning.'

Audrey was still stuck on the phrase *the key to the bathroom*.

'Thanks,' she said, taking the keys. They were both long and old-looking and attached to a ring with no tag. 'If I needed to stay tomorrow night too, would you have availability?'

Someone to Audrey's right snorted. The only possible source was the elderly man sitting on the last stool, the one nearest the fire. He had the dregs of a pint in front of him and his arms crossed, staring into space.

'*Availability*?' Peggy repeated, sounding out each syllable. 'God, now I don't know about that. I'd have to check the computer.' She pronounced it *com-pute-err*, which Audrey couldn't help but feel was an act. 'We're packed to the bloody rafters here every night of the week, but you might be lucky. Isn't that right, Paddy? Aren't we chock-a-block here every night of the week?'

'Not a room to be had,' Paddy – the man on the stool – said wryly.

They were making fun of her, Audrey realised.

'Well,' she said. 'Thanks. I'll let you know in the morning.'

'You do that, love.' Peggy's eyes were already back on the death notices, her finger searching for the name of the poor unfortunate where she'd left off.

The door marked PRIVATE led into a narrow, windowless passageway that offered three more doors and a set of bare, uneven stairs. Each step was a different height and, halfway up, they turned sharply before spitting Audrey out on to a narrow landing. Here, the light was dim and the air smelled of stale beer.

The door marked WC had a huge pane of frosted glass in it and even now, with only what she assumed was daylight on the other side, Audrey could make out the blurry shapes of a sink and a toilet through it. Turn on a light in there at night and you'd have yourself a right little peep show.

She stuck the marginally shinier key in the bedroom lock, turned it and pushed the door open.

The bed inside was a small double, visibly sagging in the middle. The headboard was upholstered in dark brown velour, and sheets and the pillowcases were from the When Paisley Attacks range, circa 1970. There was no duvet, just a hairy, orange blanket that Audrey instantly decided was going absolutely *nowhere* near her, no matter how cold it got. Laced-edged net curtains under heavy brown curtains. A brown, knobbly carpet, threadbare in places and even ripped in one by the door. And hanging above the bed, the *pièce de résistance*: a foot-tall crucifix from which a particularly lifelike and bloodied Jesus hung.

Audrey dumped her bag on the bed, double-checked her laptop cable was in the other bag hanging over her shoulder and walked straight back out again.

She'd save the horror of the bathroom for later.

'Everything all right?' Peggy asked when Audrey re-entered the pub.

'Yep,' she said breezily. 'Is there wifi here, by any chance?'

'Only our own, in the house. I can get the password off my young fella for you, if you need it. It's about as long as the alphabet, so …'

Peggy gave a little wave of her hand as if to say, *I can't be arsed with all that.*

Audrey couldn't be arsed with it either. She told Peggy it was fine, not to worry, and that she'd be back later. Then she hurried across the road to the car park, got into her car and moved it a few spaces until it was as close as it could be to The Kiln's door. She got out her phone and checked for available wireless networks.

Bingo. The Kiln's network was there, it was strong and it didn't need a password.

She *really* needed to call Joel. She couldn't put it off any longer.

There was only one bar of reception showing on the screen of her phone and, based on her limited time in Shanamore, it might disappear at any second. She sent Joel a text message saying as much and asking him to call her via WhatsApp. Ten seconds later, her phone screen lit up with his name.

'Joel,' she said when she answered.

'Audrey.'

'How much trouble am I in?'

'Were you really at the doctor this morning?'

'Well ...' She decided she'd go with the truth from here on in. 'To be honest, Joel, I wasn't really sick.'

A long, deep sigh drifted down the line.

'Where are you?'

'Shanamore,' she said. 'It's in East—'

'I know where it is. It's all over the news.'

'Online or TV?'

'Online so far. TV tonight, I'd expect.'

'Because of Natalie O'Connor?'

'Because of her husband,' Joel said. 'Didn't you see it?'

'I haven't been online. The reception down here is awful.'

'He did an appeal on social media. A terrible one. Someone needs to get that man a media trainer. Or a *solicitor*, the way things are going.'

'And what way is that?' Audrey switched to speakerphone, set the device on the dash and started tugging her laptop out of her bag. 'What's happening?'

'All we know,' Joel said, 'is she went to Shanamore and they don't think she left. We don't know *why* they think that, that's the problem. And may I say how reassuring it is to know that you've gone all the way there but I know more than you about what's going on.'

'I know *something*,' Audrey said. 'I've talked to the lead detective.' She had no idea if O'Reilly was actually that, or if there was such a thing on a Garda investigation, but it *sounded* good.

'What did they say?'

'That they've traced her to Shanamore.'

'But *how*?'

Audrey had the laptop open now. She pressed its power button, sending its hard drive whirring to life.

'You didn't answer my question, Joel. How much trouble am I in? Do I still have a job?'

'Of course you still have a job,' he said. 'But it's on the Ents desk.'

'But I'm here, on this.'

'It's *Sandra* who's on this.'

'Who's S—'

'The Paper's actual crime reporter.'

'But she's not *here*, is she?'

'She will be soon. She's on her way.'

Audrey cursed silently. That wasn't good news.

'But the story yesterday,' she said. 'The reaction. Don't you want more of that? Don't the spreadsheet guys want another hit? Because that's what I'm trying to deliver here, Joel.'

'Audrey.' He sighed again and she could see him in her mind's eye, rubbing at his temples, his elbows on his desk. 'You have a job. It has parameters. If you don't like them, go freelance.'

Freelance.

The word alone made her stomach swim. ThePaper.ie paid a pittance, but at least it paid the same pittance at the same time every two weeks. She could count on it. And she was going to have to pay rent soon.

And yet …

'She definitely came here, Joel. Natalie did. I was just in the house where she stayed, and I have pictures, so... But you know what? I think you're right. Maybe I *should* go freelance. Starting now, with this.'

'Wait, what—'

Audrey tapped the phone's screen, ending the call.

Then she said every swear word she could think of because she was ninety, ninety-five per cent sure she had just made a massive mistake. She didn't want to go freelance. She couldn't afford to. But she couldn't just drive home and go back to writing stories about cellulite and nip-slips again.

She'd write *this* story and send it to Joel, along with her pictures from inside the cottage. There's no way he could turn that down. He wouldn't. She'd be able to name her price.

And her price was a desk one floor up and maybe a slightly larger pittance than they were paying her now. Plus expenses. A refund on the money she'd spent getting here and staying here. What was that saying? Better to ask for forgiveness than permission? Dee would know.

But for now, Audrey needed to get that story done before Sandra Somebody arrived in Shanamore. She needed to get organised. Make a list of what she had. Make a list of who she needed to talk to. Andrew was number one. Where was he right now? Probably talking to the Gardaí. What had he told them about Natalie? She needed to know that. Would her new friend O'Reilly tell her? She had Orla already. Maybe she should talk to her father too, about the phone. Who was the local Garda again? Sergeant Seanie? Maybe he'd be a bit more chatty than the detective down from Dublin had been. She *had* planned on contacting Natalie's friends – what was the BFF called again? Carla? – but now the story felt like it was *here*, in Shanamore. And she needed to watch Mike's appeal. She'd never even looked at the photos she'd surreptitiously snapped in his house yesterday, Audrey realised. She should start with them.

The camera on her phone wasn't half-bad, it turned out. She could read the text on the larger pieces of crap stuck to the noticeboard. *AIB Bank* on the letterhead of what looked like a VISA bill with something on it circled in red. *Let the notions be-gin* on a greeting card. *Free garlic bread when you spend €25!* on a glossy takeaway menu.

Thrilling stuff altogether.

She swiped on to the next shot. It showed the poetry book lying splayed, facedown, on the seat of one of the dining chairs. The next one was of the sticker and inscription just inside its front cover.

The one after that was of their fridge magnets.

Not exactly the Nixon Tapes, this lot.

She switched to her laptop and opened her email.

Downloading 1 of 378 messages.

She'd have a quick check through those, save the good ones to the hard drive, go back to Murphy's, find a flat surface, some caffeine and hot food, and put in an hour tying together what she had. Then she'd knuckle down and write it up, and get it to Joel by the end of the day.

Audrey saw now that he had sent her several emails. Because he favoured one-word communications, she could read them in their entirety just from the headers.

8:50am: Sick??

11:05am: ???

12:04pm: Call

12:30pm: ASAP

12:43pm: NOW!!!

Audrey selected all five and clicked DELETE. Then she started wading through the rest.

The first message wasn't about Natalie at all, but a pervert's appreciation of Audrey's professional headshot. Ugh. Delete. The second was from a secondary school student asking Audrey if she'd answer some questions about working as a journalist for a project she was doing at school. She moved that one into a folder she'd labelled LATER. The third was from a woman who was convinced she'd sat next to Natalie on a flight to Amsterdam that had left Dublin Airport last Monday, but that Natalie had had an Australian accent now. Nope.

The fourth message was from someone called John Anonymous – subtle – and it said absolutely nothing at all.

But it *did* have a file attached. A massive one. Too big a file to send via email, in fact. What he'd actually sent was a Google Drive link. As Audrey moved the cursor over the attachment's icon, it changed to a PLAY button.

It was a video, then.

But of what?

———

Audrey drove to the Far Strand because she didn't know where else to go. Daylight was fading fast, making the screen of her laptop a bright glow in the front seat. Anyone passing by would be able to see what was on screen. After just a glimpse of it, she knew she couldn't let that happen.

The car park at the Far Strand was deserted. There was only one car parked there, in the space closest to the path that led down to the sand, and no sign of its occupant or anyone else. Audrey parked at the opposite end facing the entrance, giving her a view of the whole place. She'd know if anyone else arrived. She backed the car right up against the perimeter fence to ensure that no one could sneak up on her from behind either. She locked the doors.

She slid back her seat and put her laptop on her knees, waiting impatiently as its inners whirred to life. The video was still on screen, paused where she'd stopped watching it, ten seconds into its eighty-eight of them.

Audrey steeled herself, then pressed PLAY.

The video looked like it was in black and white but the quality was very high. The image was very clear. The scene looked oddly lit, sort of bleached, almost greyscale. It took Audrey a moment to work out that that was because this was night-vision of some sort, that the room which she could see on screen was, in reality, very dim or dark, more so to the right of the screen, as if there might be a window off-screen to the left.

It was a bedroom. Or maybe a hotel room. A room with a bed in it, anyway. The view was from the foot of the bed looking up towards

195

the headboard, from a point a foot, maybe a foot and a half, higher than the bed itself and a couple of feet away.

Someone was asleep in the bed.

Long, dark hair splayed across the pillow. One bare arm outside the blankets, a wedding ring on the hand. The hand looked slim and delicate.

A woman.

Why would anyone record this?

Something moved on the left-hand side of the screen then and Audrey realised that the shadows in the corner weren't shadows at all.

They were a *person*. A shadow-man.

He was standing next to the bed, looking down at the sleeping woman, and every single thing about him screamed that he wasn't supposed to be there, that he didn't belong in this scene, that something terrible and frightening and horrific was about to happen. He was dressed all in black, including the mask or balaclava covering his face and head, and the gloves on his hands. He was holding something down by his side, pressed against his thigh. It was reflective, glinting in what must be street- or moonlight.

A blade. A knife.

Slowly, the figure advanced towards the bed and then reached down to stroke the sleeping woman's cheek tenderly.

She didn't move.

He did something to the woman's face – a short gesture, quick, over in the blink of an eye, like a tap or a flick.

She woke up.

Her eyes flew open and her body started to twist violently and jerk and kick.

The intruder pushed her back down into the bed with a gloved hand, covering her mouth with it, pressing on it.

Audrey could imagine the weight of that hand, considering the differential, position-wise, between the two: one lying on a soft bed, one standing on solid ground. It terrified her.

And that's when the attack really began.

Audrey could only watch, unblinking. It didn't look real. The intruder barely raised their hand before they plunged the knife into the woman's midsection; the stabbing was done in small, quick jabs that reminded Audrey, of all things, of piercing the plastic film over a ready meal before it goes into the microwave. But of course, she'd never seen anything like this before that wasn't actors, special effects and a film or TV set. Her reference points were sequences filmed in studios with syrup and stunt doubles and creative camera angles.

It didn't look real because it *was* real.

Audrey was watching the end of someone's life. In a video clip that someone had taken the time to send to her.

The violence went on for what felt like an hour but was, according to the information on screen, much less than a minute in reality.

The worse part was what came next.

The woman in the bed was all but destroyed, her flesh dotted with wounds and her clothes stained with blood. More stains were soaking into the bed, staining the sheets. There was a spray of droplets on the wall above the headboard. And yet she was still moving, turning slowly on to her right side, extending an arm as if to reach for something, or to appeal to her attacker for help or mercy – or maybe to try to get off the bed – but there wasn't enough life left in her to do that and she stopped and fell back.

And that was it. The end of her.

The figure stood above her, stock-still, watching.

Seconds passed. So many that Audrey looked to the progress bar to check that the video was still playing, that it hadn't paused or stopped.

Then the figure bent at the waist to lay the knife down carefully on the bedside table, straightened up again—

The image froze.

The video had ended.

Audrey's chest burned and she felt mildly nauseous, as if she was suddenly car-sick. She rolled down the driver's side window and gulped a few lungfuls of cold, salty sea air.

What the hell had she just seen? Why had someone wanted her to see it? *Who* wanted her to?

How had *they* got it?

Was it Natalie O'Connor in that bed?

Now she thought she might actually *be* sick. She reached across to open Dee's glovebox and rooted around in there until her fingers found a plastic bottle with some weight in it. A near-empty bottle of water. She swallowed what was left; all she could taste was plastic.

Audrey closed her eyes and slumped back against the seat. She remembered the phone she'd found, the one in the bin. She sat up and replayed the video from the start.

This time, she focused on everything other than the main event. She imagined she was standing in a courtroom, tasked with proving that the woman in the bed was Natalie O'Connor and that the bed was the one upstairs in Cottage No. 6.

Exhibit A: the furniture. Audrey had a photograph on her phone, snapped during her mad dash around the cottage just before she vacated it, which she knew would match up exactly. The same headboard, same bedside table, same bare wall. Same ratios of space between them. But it was entirely possible, even likely, that every cottage was decorated the same way, so that narrowed it down but didn't alone prove that it was Cottage No. 6.

Exhibit B: the light. The room was dark but there was a light to the left. It was too weak to be anything other than the light from outside, the glow of a streetlight, perhaps, coming through the thin curtains. There had been one directly outside Cottage No. 6; Audrey remembered seeing it. But she hadn't really taken notice of where the other streetlights were situated, so she couldn't say for sure that that wasn't the case for all the other cottages too.

Exhibit C: the bedside table. By the end, the bloodied knife was sitting on it – but something else was too. Something that had been there from the start. Audrey didn't think she'd have recognised it if she hadn't already seen it, or one like it, somewhere else, up close.

It was the chunky, plastic phone that Natalie had bought at the petrol station.

If the Gardaí determined that the phone Audrey had found in the bin in the bathroom of Cottage No. 6 had been Natalie's, then it'd be safe to say that this video had been filmed just across the landing, in the bedroom of Cottage No. 6.

In the same room where Audrey had been not two hours ago.

Natalie wasn't in a spa somewhere, hiding out. There was no innocent explanation behind her disappearance. She had come to Shanamore, she had stayed in the cottages, and in the middle of the night someone had come into her room and stabbed her to death.

And Audrey had just watched it happen in real time.

In the very same bed where she'd slept.

What was under the sheets she had laid down on? Was there still blood on the mattress? Had the camera still been there? Had someone watched *Audrey* sleep in that bed too?

If she had stayed there tonight, would the same thing have happened to her?

Something in her chest clenched and Audrey suddenly felt that, despite the open window, there wasn't enough air inside the car to fill her lungs. She couldn't breathe.

She kicked open the door, pushed the computer off her lap and climbed outside, the icy wind whipping furiously at her face as she took a deep breath, then tried to take a deeper one, slowly this time, one hand on the roof of the car to steady herself—

Something moved in the dark.

Someone was coming towards her.

When Audrey's eyes adjusted, she saw it was Richard Flynn.

PAUSE

0:01:05

Jennifer is struggling to concentrate on a spreadsheet that details this month's room revenue when she hears a voice declare, 'We're leaving.'

It's a male voice. Gruff. American accent.

She's in the back office and this voice is coming from the reception desk.

'I'm sorry,' he's saying now, 'but we just *cannot* stay.'

She gets up and moves stealthily to the swinging door that, if she were to push through it right now, would deposit her behind the reception desk, right alongside Benek, one of her most experienced receptionists, who's already out there and tasked with dealing with this disgruntled guest.

'Is there a problem, sir?' Benek asks.

'We're just leaving,' the guest says. 'And that's that. Car keys, please.'

'I'm so sorry to hear that,' Benek says – or rather, *purrs*. His voice is so wonderfully smooth, each sentence comes out sounding like a little lullaby. Soothing. Reassuring. But not at all patronising. And all the better with his Polish accent. 'Has there been a change in your plans or …?'

'Look, it's just not what we were expecting, okay?' The man's voice is rising. 'That's it. That's all. Now, give me my keys. I can see them there. The Hertz tag.'

'It was number twenty-one, wasn't it, sir? The room?'

There's a loud, angry exhale of breath, followed by a muttered expletive.

Then a new, female voice, polite and gentle:

'That's the one, dear. *So* sorry about this.'

The wife, presumably. She sounds embarrassed.

202

'Perhaps we can move you to another room,' Benek says.

'No.' The man again. 'We're not staying here, under any circumstances.'

'I'm so very sorry, sir, but perhaps if I knew what exactly was the source of your displeasure—'

'My *keys*.'

That had practically been bellowed, and Benek knew when to quit.

'Certainly, sir.'

The wife, again: 'I just don't understand you, Tom.' The volume of her voice suggested she was speaking to her husband. 'Why don't you let this nice boy help us? He could find us another room. A better one. For God's sake, we've barely even been here five minutes.'

'Jude, I told you. We're *leaving*.'

'It's not a problem,' Benek says smoothly. 'But you should be aware that Sycamore House operates a twenty-four-hour cancellation policy. I'm afraid that means you'll be charged for tonight's stay.'

'That's fine,' the guest says.

That's when Jennifer pushes through the door.

All three of them turn towards her. Benek's face has his front-of-house smile affixed to it but his eyes say, *Can you even believe this prick?* The wife is in her sixties, with shoulder-length grey hair and a hefty piece of ugly turquoise jewellery hanging from her neck. She's about two foot shorter than her husband, and about that width narrower as well. He's a bear of a man, the smooth, rounded bulb of his stomach straining against his shirt as if he's got an inflated balloon under there. His face has the red sting of a lifelong drinker and his teeth the unnatural white gleam of a Hollywood star.

Jennifer glances at the computer screen.

'Mr and Mrs Feldman,' she says then. 'How are you this evening?'

'Unfortunately—' Benek starts.

'We're leaving,' Mr Feldman grunts.

The wife looks stricken. 'I'm so sorry, dear.' Her tone is conspiratorial, as if the root of the problem isn't standing right beside her. 'But I think we're going to have to leave.'

Jennifer looks Mr Feldman right in the eye and asks bluntly, 'Why?'

'We just are.' He looks away. 'That's all there is.'

A red flush is creeping up his neck.

He puts a hand on his wife's back and turns her around, away from the desk. She turns to mouth a *sorry* over her shoulder as they hurry out the door.

Mr Feldman slams it closed behind them.

Then Benek says, in his actual, everyday voice, 'What the *fuck* was all that about?' He shakes his head. 'People. Are. *Mental.* Is it a full moon tonight? Tell me it's a full moon.'

'It's not,' Jennifer says.

'He didn't even mind that we were going to charge him for the night. Even though they were in that room for, like, what? Ten seconds? It couldn't have been much more. I just checked them in.'

That's what had struck her, too. Anytime one of their arrivals had themselves an immediate shit-fit – there was some third-party website, they'd never got to the bottom of which one, which was taking bookings for Sycamore House, Dublin 4, but showing a photo of the interior of Sycamore *Manor*, a five-star resort overlooking the sea somewhere in Co. Mayo; nine times out of ten, that was the cause – they could be counted on to throw a second one when they were told they'd have to pay a night's rate for their trip up and down the stairs. It was an industry standard that made up for any loss incurred by refusing a booking to someone else, but for a disgruntled guest it was a live grenade. They rarely, if ever, enforced it. It wasn't worth the hassle.

If Mr Feldman had as much as twitched when Benek mentioned the charge, Benek would have immediately said they'd make an exception and waive it.

But he didn't. He'd said it was fine. He was willing to pay it.

'I'll go check the room,' Benek says.

It didn't make any sense to get your knickers in a twist about a perfectly fine room, refuse to say what exactly was the problem but also be willing to pay for it when you were going to have to pay to stay somewhere else.

Jennifer knows she shouldn't do this …

She comes out from behind the reception desk, goes to the door.

… but that guy was a *dick*.

Outside, the Feldmans are at their car. She's already in the passenger seat, head down, face lit by the blue glow of a mobile phone. Probably tasked with looking for alternative accommodation after her husband's little hissy fit.

He's at the boot, just about to shut it closed.

'Here,' Jennifer says, hurrying towards him. 'Let me help you.'

He blinks at her, confused. His mouth opens as if to say something, to protest. But she reaches him before he can, slaps a hand on the boot and yanks it down, slamming it shut just a fraction of a second after Mr Feldman pulls his hand out of its way. She catches his sleeve, grabbing it, squeezing his arm as hard as she can, digging the tips of her nails into the soft flesh underneath.

'What the—'

'You recognised it,' she says, cutting him off. 'Didn't you?' Her mouth is so close to his ear, she can see that he badly needs to clean it. 'That's why you're leaving, isn't it, Mr *Feldman*? Because you *recognised the room*.'

He jerks away, pulling free of her grip, eyes wide.

Confused. Nervous. Frightened.

His eyes move to the passenger side of the car, where his wife is sitting.

'Oh, don't worry,' Jennifer says. She lowers her voice to a whisper. 'Your secret's safe with me so long as *my* secret's safe with you.'

When she goes back inside, she collects €1,000 from Mr Feldman's credit card. She know he won't dare contest the charge.

REWIND

0:00:13

Natalie left the Dylan in the middle of lunch-hour. Upper Baggot Street was bustling with foraging office workers, uniformed secondary school kids and yummy mummies pushing toddlers around in various wheeled contraptions. It was a bright, clear day – cold, but clear – and as part of her plan to get to know the area, Natalie decided to walk home. Reasonably confident in her sense of direction in this postcode, she set off without checking the actual route and found herself meandering through leafy residential streets and, at one point, past the space-age silver curve of the Aviva Stadium. After half an hour or so of pleasant strolling, Natalie emerged into a little triangle of a village green, surrounded by upmarket restaurants and shops.

The trendy deli there gave her an idea for dinner: let someone else make it. It had been a fun morning, for the most part, but being 'on' for hours at a time could be exhausting. She'd be half-asleep on the couch by the time Mike got home. She wouldn't feel like cooking and his repertoire was limited to things so spicy you needed to clear half the next day for side-effects, so picking up something ready-made was a much safer bet.

Natalie was trying to choose between a lasagne and butter chicken when she looked up and saw the woman in black glasses for the second time that day.

She was standing side-on, just a couple of feet away. Studying the label on a bottle of red wine. Replacing it. Frowning at the next bottle along.

And now, turning slowly towards Natalie.

Staring at her.

'I'm sorry,' Natalie said, taking a step closer. 'Do I— Do we know each other? Did I see you at the Dylan just now?'

Natalie didn't know what she expected would happen next, but it was somewhere on a spectrum between '*No ...*' (weird look, quick exit; the mystery deepens) and 'You were there too? How funny!' (warm handshake, excitable introductions; mystery solved). It certainly wasn't that the woman's face would harden into what looked like barely contained rage before she suddenly turned and stormed out of the shop.

It was so alien an event, the aftershock felt physical. The woman may as well have slapped Natalie across the face.

'Miss?' a voice said from somewhere behind her. 'Miss, you haven't paid—'

By the time Natalie got outside, Black Glasses was gone.

———

Right on cue at a quarter past six, Mike's keys rattled in the front door.

His routine since they'd moved in here was to call out, 'Honey, I'm home,' in a terrible American accent, empty the contents of his pockets into the bowl in the hall, flop down on the couch, put his feet up on the coffee table, put them down again after Natalie said, '*Shoes!*' and then ask what was for dinner, to which Natalie would respond that it wasn't the fifties.

But today his footsteps came to a halt just inside the front door and he said, a little uncertainly, 'Natalie?' and then, 'Why is it so dark?'

'In here,' she called from the living room.

She was curled up in one of the armchairs, staring into the fire – fire*place*, really, because no fire was lit.

'What's going on?' Mike stood on the threshold; he made no move to sit down. 'What are you doing sitting in the dark?'

'Is it dark?' Natalie reached out to flick the switch on a table lamp. The room was transformed by its golden glow; she hadn't realised how late it had got. 'Will you light a fire? You've been saying you will since the night we got the keys and I really—' Her voice cracked on the *really* so she swallowed the rest of the sentence, then chased it down with a gulp from her glass of white wine.

Mike came and sat on the coffee table, facing her.

He touched her knee. 'Nat, what's going on?'

'Oh, nothing much.' She waved a hand. 'I'm just going crazy. Or being pursued by crazy. I don't know which.'

'What happened?'

She told him about Black Glasses Lady. Three sightings now altogether. The one in the café just under two weeks ago, and the event and the deli today. And about the woman's reaction when Natalie had approached her.

When she was done, she took another swig of wine.

When she lowered the glass, she saw that Mike was smiling.

And then, trying not to laugh.

'What's so funny?'

'Sorry,' he said. 'But what exactly are we talking about here? You were at an event. So was this woman. Then afterwards you went to another place. So did this woman. And she didn't like it when a complete stranger approached her while she was going about her business. What am I missing?'

'She was also in that café,' Natalie said. 'The day I met Carla.'

'But so were *you*.'

'That's my point.'

'*My* point is that if you were in both those places, what are the odds that someone else was in both those places too? They're pretty good, Nat. This is Dublin, not Manhattan. And for all we know, she could think *you're* following *her*.' He shook his head. 'Natalie, have you been eating the dishwasher tabs again?'

'*Michael*, this is serious.'

'I agree. You're seriously losing it.'

'No, really.' Natalie looked into her wine, swirled what was left around the bottom of the glass. 'After that woman was here ...'

A beat passed.

'Okay, okay,' he said then. 'Let me in.' He squeezed himself on to the armchair next to her. He took the wine, transferred it safely to the side table and then wrapped his arms around her.

She let her head fall against his chest.

'So what's really going on?' he said into her hair.

'I don't know.'

'Maybe things are changing.'

She looked up at him. 'What?'

'Look, you always said you loved this. That you can't believe this is your job, you're so lucky, etc., etc. But if that's changing, then …' Mike shrugged. 'Maybe this has gone as far as it can. Maybe it's reached the end.'

'What are you saying?'

'You always knew that that's what was going to happen eventually, Nat. This gravy train can't last for ever. A new social network will come along and everything will change. You think all those girls with their pouting and their Pumpkin Spice are going to be around in twenty years showing us school lunchboxes and grey hairs and the recycling bin?'

'What the hell are you saying?' Natalie stood up, turned to face him. 'I'm confused, Mike. Because I'm here trying to tell you that I think someone is following me and you're telling me I should *quit my job*? This is all just a joke to you, isn't it?'

'No.' Mike stood up too. 'No, it's not. I just think you're overreacting.' His tone was gentle. 'It's not improbable that someone would be in a café in Dawson Street, and then at your event this morning, and then at that deli – because *you* were, too.' He reached for her. Reluctantly, she let him. 'This is because of our visitor, I know. She has you paranoid. But everything's fine. And we'll get that gate. And maybe a guard dog. Something scary that barks and bares his teeth a lot. Or how about a burly bodyguard? One of those ones with mirrored aviators and an earpiece.'

'You weren't there,' Natalie said. 'You didn't see her face.'

'Whose?'

'The woman today. She looked at me like …' She took a breath. 'She looked like she *hated* me.'

'I'm sure that's not true.'

'But she—'

'I'm going to order some dinner. And get another bottle of wine. And light the fire. Okay? And we'll just sit down here and have a nice, relaxing night for ourselves. Watch a movie. Something funny.'

'I thought you were meeting Shane tonight.'

'I was. But I'll cancel.'

'Don't cancel on my account.'

'I can't be arsed going,' Mike said. He winked. 'I'll use you as an excuse.'

'Oh, gee *thanks*.'

But she was glad.

They drifted into the kitchen, Natalie to the fridge and Mike to the pile of junk mail they'd been steadily building on top of the microwave.

'That menu for the Italian place,' he said. 'Is that in here some-where?' He started to sift through it. Then, a moment later, 'What does she look like, this woman? The one with the glasses.'

Natalie described her in as much detail as she could recall. Blonde hair, very straight and sleek, in a long ponytail. Slim but not thin, perhaps a bit stocky. Wearing a suit. Older by a few years, maybe late thirties, early forties. Black glasses in very thick frames. The expensive, trendy kind.

'Thick black glasses,' Mike repeated softly.

He'd stopped going through the menus and now seemed lost in thought.

'Yeah,' Natalie said. 'Why? Does she sound familiar?'

'Ah …' He hesitated. 'A little bit.'

'What? You've seen her too?'

'I don't know,' Mike said. 'Maybe.'

'Where?'

'I don't know.'

'Well, try to remember.'

He frowned, thinking. 'I can't, sorry. Maybe I'm just imagining things. Or picturing someone else. It's just when you said about the glasses, and the ponytail …' He went back to the menus. 'That's probably all it is. I'm thinking of someone else who matches the description. Someone I know. I just can't think of who— Ah!'

He held up the menu, triumphant.

'Yeah,' Natalie said. 'Maybe.'

But she wasn't convinced.

Was there a chance this woman was following *both* of them? Or had Mike just happened to see her on another occasion when she was following Natalie, but Natalie didn't know she was being followed? The latter made more sense.

If any of this did.

Mike disappeared into the living room to get his phone so he could order their dinner online.

Natalie stayed in the kitchen, thinking about what he'd said. The word *paranoid* had stuck in her gut. *Was* she being paranoid?

The visit from Alice *had* unnerved her. She kept thinking of the look on the woman's face as she swept that flower pot off the table, the force of it sending shards as far as under the sofa in the living room. It was like a mania or something. The kind that could power violence. And what Mike didn't seem to understand was that it wasn't even that woman – or what had she done – that had pushed Natalie off-axis, but the fact that that woman had somehow figured out their address. That was what had really scared her. Because if that woman had, who else could? What if that someone else was actually, properly crazy and wanted to hurt them?

But Mike couldn't understand that, because he didn't believe that that's what had happened. He thought Alice was probably just a neighbour, nothing more, nothing less.

'Half an hour,' he called from the living room.

'Plenty of time to light the fire,' she called back.

She heard him sigh, followed by the scrape of the grate against the tile of the fireplace.

She pulled the half-full bag out of the rubbish bin and swept the rest of the junk mail pile into it, then tied a neat knot in the top of the bag. Their wheelie bin was parked around the back, by the garden gate. She went to unlock the back door, but the bolt wouldn't turn.

Natalie frowned at it, tried again.

The bolt wouldn't budge.

But then she tried turning it in the opposite direction and found that it moved easily.

Click.

The pins of the mechanism had slid into place.

She'd just locked the door.

Which meant that the door had been open.

The problem was that Natalie had definitely, absolutely, positively locked the door before leaving the house that morning. She could clearly remember doing it: before she'd left for the Dylan, she'd let herself out to put a couple of beer bottles into the recycling bin, then gone back inside and locked the door.

'Mike?' she called out.

From the living room: 'Yeah?'

'Did you come home today?'

'Huh?'

'Did you come home during the day?'

'No, why?'

The word *paranoid* materialised before her eyes. Could she *really* remember locking the door? Actually doing it, the action itself? Would she swear on her life that it had been *this* morning she'd put those bottles out? Could it have been yesterday? Was it possible?

'No reason,' she called out. 'Never mind.'

———

Natalie walked into the room that was supposed to be her office and realised that she hadn't crossed its threshold in almost a week.

The bookshelves were still empty. Taped-up boxes littered the floor. Mike had assembled her desk one Saturday morning but it was unceremoniously pushed up against the radiator under the window and drowning in packages, torn-open bills and loose, curling receipts.

Once upon a time, Natalie had imagined that her spirit would lift every time she'd walk into this room. In her mind's eye, she'd be sitting behind that desk bathed in early-morning light, drinking coffee from a delicate teacup and powering through her to-do list with joy in her heart. Or, at the very least, reading the showbiz section of ThePaper.ie while guzzling coffee straight from whatever receptacle had been nearest to hand while still in her pyjamas; hair greasy; yesterday's mascara smeared beneath her bloodshot eyes; not pretty, but happy.

But weeks after their move, the room was more dumping ground than creative haven. Every time she as much as glanced through its open door, she felt an invisible weight pulling on her, slowing her down. Standing in there, in the midst of the mess, the weight grew heavier and heavier, until it began to feel like a ship's anchor tied to her ankles in water far beyond her depth.

Everything had just felt so *heavy* lately.

Intellectually, she knew she was lucky. She had her health, and Mike, and this house. She made a sizeable income from something that took relatively little effort and which afforded her complete freedom and the privilege of being her own boss. And it was something that, until recently, she'd absolutely adored. It had never felt like a job until the day that stupid woman had come knocking on her front door.

At night now, she regularly dreamed of flickering screens with claw-like hands coming through them, like in that horror movie Mike had forced her to watch one Halloween. She didn't need a psychologist to figure out what they meant. Each morning she'd open her eyes with the intention of having a good day, of being her old self, of feeling good and positive and happy. But by the time her feet were on the floor of their bedroom, the invisible weights would fall back into place and she'd become inexplicably exhausted.

But who could she talk to about it? It was the very definition of #firstworldproblems. Who would understand? Carla? As if. She'd think Natalie was inventing problems just to have some, because on paper her life was perfect. How would she even begin to explain to that girl – stuck in an awful job, poorly paid, and going slowly insane living with her parents – that despite the house and the money and Mike, and having a job Natalie was embarrassed to even *call* a job, life had started to feel like one long hangover? Meanwhile, Mike thought she 'had' anxiety and suggested she go to her GP to get something to make it go away.

He'd meant pills, which frightened Natalie. She wasn't there yet. (Was she?) He'd also quoted some motivational poster he'd seen at work. *Worry doesn't take away tomorrow's problems, it only steals today's peace.* She would've slapped him in the face if she could've mustered up the energy.

She had managed to unpack most of the rest of the house, albeit half-heartedly, filing things away rather than finding a home for them. There were a couple of cupboards upstairs where boxes and bags and loose items had just been shoved inside, every which way. Natalie found she only had a few hours in her each morning to Do Life before she was suddenly down to the dregs of her energy levels and only capable of lying on the couch and watching mindless TV.

That's where Mike found her most evenings. He hadn't said anything about it directly and had never mentioned Alice or Black Glasses again. But he had his own problems. *Actual* problems, he'd say. There was something at work, some scandal brewing. She could feel him tossing and turning in the bed beside her at night, sense his distraction when he came home each evening.

It wasn't all in her head.

Two more times since the day of the incident at the deli, Natalie had found the back door unlocked inexplicably. Most recently she'd checked it, gone upstairs to deposit something, then come back down to find it unlocked again. Not even five minutes had passed in between. She hadn't told Mike, but she'd called a locksmith to come out and check the door. The guy had said everything was fine and offered to change the locks, but she'd declined, purely because she didn't want to have to explain why she'd done that to Mike.

And things were missing. The biggest was a box of books, treasured ones: a few signed editions and special gifts, including the book of poetry she'd given Mike on the night he'd proposed. Moments before he did. They were in Rome and, on the morning of their last full day, they'd visited the Keats–Shelley House at the bottom of the Spanish Steps. She'd bought the book because it seemed so impossibly romantic and the perfect souvenir of what had been a blissful weekend, conveniently forgetting that Mike didn't like to read, let alone read *poetry*, and that it was destined to sit untouched on a shelf for ever more. Now she couldn't find it, sitting on a shelf or anywhere else, and the more she looked, the more items she noticed were missing. Some clothing, including one of her favourite dresses. A bottle of perfume she'd received as a gift that she'd never even got around to opening. One of her handbags. Mike's explanation was that moving house always resulted in things going astray. He told her they'd turn up eventually. And no, he didn't think it was weird that the only thing of his missing was the poetry book.

The days bled into one another. Each one managed to feel interminable but also ephemeral and inconsequential. Natalie felt, for the first time in a long time, that she was *wasting* time, wasting her life. Some days, she literally was. After Mike left for work, she'd crawl back into bed and wouldn't get out again until the sky began to darken.

She was still posting to Instagram once a day, but she was phoney in it. Sometimes she even reposted old photos with new captions. If anyone had noticed, they hadn't said anything. Thankfully, on social media, it was easy to make it seem like everything was okay. The contracts Ellie Fox had sent on were still sitting on a shelf somewhere, still sheathed in the envelope they'd come in, still unblemished above the dotted line.

And then the bill arrived, changing everything.

Again.

———

She found it sitting face up on the mat in the hall not long after Mike had left for work one Friday morning: a plain white envelope. It had a stamp, but no postmark. Their address was on a sticky label that had been run through a printer but there was no addressee, no name. There wasn't even a *To The Residents*. The first line of print on the envelope was the first line of their address.

Natalie took it to the couch, sitting down to open it up.

Inside was a single sheet of A4 paper, still crisp and smooth except for the two sharp creases that had made the page small enough to fit inside the long, narrow envelope. It was immediately obvious it was a bill or a receipt of some kind, from a place called Shanamore Cottages. There was only one item listed: ACCOMMODATION COTTAGE #6. This had cost €632.41 on October 24 and had been paid with a Visa card that ended in 3711. A slip of a receipt, printed from a credit card terminal, was stapled to the upper right-hand corner of the page, further evidence of the transaction.

Mike's Visa card ended in 3711.

Natalie stared at the page, trying to force the ink on it to rearrange itself into something that made even a little bit of sense, because this made none at all.

The obvious, easy explanation was that this was just a mistake. A mixed-up name or a stolen credit card. Identity theft. Natalie should call Mike and tell him about it, tell him to call his bank right now and report the fraud.

But she didn't.

Instead, she picked up her phone and checked the calendar. Every couple of months Mike would go to Cork for a night or two; his company had a branch down there. Since it was cheaper to bring the Dublin staff down south than vice versa, if there was a training day or an all-in meeting, they held it at the Cork offices. Natalie always made a note of these trips because she didn't have her own car – she'd never got her full licence, so there was little point in her having one – and she would have to plan accordingly. But as far as she knew Mike always had his accommodation arranged for him by his employer, and she didn't think he'd even been down to Cork that recently.

And where the hell was Shanamore?

According to her calendar app, Natalie was right: on October 24, Mike had been at home. She opened her phone's internet browser and typed 'Shanamore Cottages' into Google. Shanamore was a village in East Cork, near the sea. A tiny one, by the looks of things. Natalie had never heard of it and she was pretty sure Mike had never mentioned it.

The cottages were a complex of holiday homes a kilometre outside the village and three more from the beach. One of the search results was tonight's rate for staying there as per Booking.com; it seemed like you'd have to stay there for a long time, maybe more than a week, to rack up a bill that high.

Or maybe this was a bill for several shorter stays, Natalie thought. After all, this was a receipt, not a reservation. Maybe Mike had stayed at the cottages for a night here and there, paying as he went, and then requested a receipt for the total amount. Natalie had been back and forth to London a lot over the summer and often times she was away at a hotel or a resort for a PR event or a junket. Could he have gone to this place then? Why wouldn't he have told her about it, though? It just didn't make any sense.

It made even less sense when she heard the swing of the letterbox and the gentle *thud* of post landing on the mat. When Natalie went into the hall, she found a collection of bills, a small packet from Amazon and the latest issue of her *Stellar* magazine subscription fanned out on the floor. Whoever had put the receipt from Shanamore Cottages through their letterbox, it wasn't their postman.

She would just ask Mike tonight, when he came home. No doubt there was some simple explanation, something obvious she'd failed to think of.

Natalie brought the newly arrived mail back to the couch. She refolded the page from Shanamore Cottages, slipped it back into its envelope and tucked it under the couch cushion she was sitting on for safekeeping. Not to hide it, but because it was the closest spot to hand.

But that night, Mike walked in the door looking particularly tired and annoyed and stressed, and when Natalie asked him about his day he began to unload, telling her about how someone who worked under him had paid a large sum of money into the wrong account and although they'd got it back, he was getting the blame for the mistake, for what could have happened. Natalie imagined she could feel the receipt beneath her like the princess had felt the pea. It may as well have been whispering: *Ask him. Ask him now.* But the timing wasn't right, so she decided to leave it until the following day. Come Saturday morning, Mike's mood had improved but it seemed delicate, precarious. So Natalie waited. Saturday slipped into Sunday and, before she knew it, she was waking up on Monday morning without having said a thing about it.

She came downstairs while Mike was in the shower, flicked on the coffee machine and then went to retrieve the bill from the underneath the couch cushion.

But it wasn't there.

Natalie lifted all the couch cushions and stared, disbelieving.

She got down on her hands and knees and looked under the couch.

She checked under the seats of both the armchairs, even though she knew she hadn't put it under there.

Had Mike found it and moved it? Why would he have done that? *When* would he have?

Natalie didn't know what to think.

When Mike appeared, hair still wet from the shower, moving in a cloud of that cologne he put on too much of in the mornings, she asked him about it.

'Did you see a white envelope? It just had our address on it, typed. I left it under one of the couch cushions ...'

He shook his head, *no*. 'Why would you put something under the couch?'

'Under the couch *cushions*. You didn't see it, at all, anywhere?'

'There's post in the kitchen, isn't there?'

Natalie knew the little pile of mail on the kitchen counter did not include the Shanamore Cottages receipt.

Mike started opening and closing cupboards, looking for his travel mug.

'Did you get up last night?' she asked.

'No, why?' He had poured his coffee and was now screwing on the mug's lid. His back was to her. 'Did you?'

'No.'

He turned around, raised his eyebrows. 'Then why do you ask?'

'I was just wondering.'

'Did you sleep okay?'

'Yeah.'

'You didn't wake up?'

'No. Don't think so. Why do you ask?'

He smiled. 'I was just wondering.'

'Shanamore,' Natalie said then. 'Have you heard of it?'

'What's with all the questions this morning?'

'*Have* you?'

'What?'

'Heard of Shanamore.'

Mike shook his head. 'No.'

'Never?'

'No.'

'So you've never been there?'

Something crossed Mike's face then. Confusion? Or annoyance?

'Why are you asking me about – what's it called?'

'*Shanamore*.' Natalie pronounced each syllable distinctly. 'It's in East Cork. By the sea.'

'And you want to go there?'

'What? No.'

'Then why ...?' Mike rolled his eyes, exasperated. 'Look, Nat, I've got to go. We can continue this – whatever this is – later. Okay?'

She didn't answer.

He came to her, bent to kiss her lightly on the mouth. 'Are you okay, Nat?'

She nodded. 'Fine.'

He studied her face. He clearly didn't believe her.

'I'm fine,' she said, forcing a smile. 'You better go. You'll be late.'

He kissed her again. 'See you later.'

'Bye.'

She waited until she heard the noise of his car's engine fade, then she sprang into action with an energy she hadn't felt in weeks.

She moved room by room, floor by floor, checking every nook, cupboard and drawer.

It took her less than ten minutes to find it stashed in a drawer in the spare bedroom.

At first, Natalie stepped back in shock, slamming the drawer shut again in the process, as if there was some lively, deadly, terrifying creepy-crawly creature in there that she just couldn't let out.

That she didn't want to let out.

But she had to.

How was this possible? Mike hadn't even been home when the envelope arrived. She hadn't told him about it. He couldn't have seen it, wouldn't have known where she'd hidden it. Unless … Had he been expecting it? Had he known it had arrived and it was just a case of finding where she'd put it? Had he gone looking for it during the night, moved it?

Natalie felt sick.

He'd hidden it from her and then denied its existence. He was *gaslighting* her. Isn't that what they called it?

She thought back to that moment in the kitchen, Mike searching for the menu, asking her to describe the blonde woman with the ponytail … He'd said the woman sounded familiar but that he didn't know where from. What if he *did* know? What if all this crap about work lately wasn't actually about work at all? What if there was something else going on?

He'd called her paranoid. More than once.

But it wasn't paranoia if something really *was* going on.

Natalie had thought the woman with the black glasses was following her because she was Natalie O'Connor. It was that Alice, coming to the house – that's what had made her think that. But what if the woman with the black glasses was following her because of *Mike*?

The stranger wasn't behind her on the street, or sitting across from her in a café.

The stranger was in her house, in her bed.

And in the midst of all the pain, there was a strange kind of …

Was that *relief*?

This was something she could prove. This was something real, something tangible, something no one would dismiss as #firstworldproblems. She could pin her unease, her unhappiness, her anxiety to this and people would *get it*.

They'd believe it.

But first, she'd have to prove it.

She'd have to *get* proof.

Natalie threw some things in a bag. Clothes, her make-up bag, the T-shirt she'd slept in last night. She sent an email to the organisers of the event she was due to attend later in the week to cancel; she couldn't even contemplate putting on a face for such a thing right now. Immediately after she pressed SEND, she felt bad and called them to do the same thing in person, feigning flu.

The last thing she did before she left the house was scribble a note for Mike on the notepad in the kitchen. She didn't want to give anything away, didn't want to give him another opportunity to mess with her head, so she wrote:

Someone dropped out of a spa night at a place in Killarney. [It had to be far away enough that he couldn't come check up on her.] *They've asked me to fill in and, to be honest, I could really do with it.* [Only half a lie.] *It's a digital detox thing so my phone might be off, but don't worry.* [This way, she wouldn't have to talk to him and fake that everything was fine.] *I'll be back late tomorrow, I think. I'll call if that changes. Nx*

He might think it was weird that she'd left him a note instead of calling or texting him to tell him – and it was, but she didn't want to give him the opportunity to talk her out of it.

Moreover, he might figure out where she was going and if he did, she'd need this head start.

Natalie checked the timetables on her phone. Trains to Cork left on the hour, every hour, and then a bus would take her from the city centre to Shanamore. If she got to Heuston in the next forty-five minutes, she'd be at the cottages before dark. She briefly considered booking a hotel in Midleton, the biggest, nearest town, and paying for a taxi to bring her to Shanamore and back, but she didn't know exactly what she was looking for and until she did, she didn't know how long it might take to find it. She'd have to stay in Shanamore for a night, at least.

She went to the cottages' website for a second time, to get the phone number.

A male voice answered after only one ring.

'Shanamore Cottages.'

'Hi,' Natalie said. 'I'm just wondering – would you by any chance have a vacancy tonight?'

FASTFORWARD

0:01:08

'I didn't meant to startle you.' He flashed an apologetic smile stocked with crooked, yellowed teeth. 'My name is Richard. Richard Flynn. Local *artiste* and blow-in. No doubt you've already heard of me. By another name, though, I'm sure. This little backwater *delights* in its gossip. You were in The Kiln earlier? Sincere apologies for not introducing myself then but that girl in there, she's the worst of them.' He mimed a mouth moving with both his hands. 'I often say, we don't need a parish newsletter when we've got her. She's the one who told me who you were, right after you left. Audrey, I believe?'

While he spoke, Audrey was discreetly scanning the car park. Her decision to park right at the end of it, in the spot furthest from the entrance – and so the road, and help – now seemed a foolish thing to have done in the dark. There was still only one other car here and it was as far away as it could be while still being in the car park, next to the path that led down to the beach. There was no sign of its owner and now Audrey wondered if that was Richard's car.

There was no one else around that she could see and the only sounds were the whipping of the wind and, just barely discernible underneath it, the crashing of distant waves. The only saving grace was that they were standing not far from the beam emitted by the only light in the entire car park, the one that had been erected to illuminate the NO DUMPING sign, and that, feet away, the light was still on inside Audrey's car.

She'd been saved from total darkness then, but not yet from *him*.

Richard had come to a stop just a fraction too close, a single step past the boundary line of comfortable and on into her personal space. He was close enough that even in this light she could see the plume of red soreness on either side of his mouth and flakes of dandruff lifting from his scalp at his hairline. When he spoke, he carried a pungent, sour smell on his breath. What was most disturbing, however, was not any particular detail of his appearance or his lack of oral hygiene but the sense that, with this determined proximity, he was forcing her to look. He didn't seem at all self-conscious or uncomfortable with his physical self but yet seemed intent on making *her* feel that way about it.

It felt like a cruel, deliberate game and Audrey was in no mood to play.

She took a step back, putting a hand on the open driver's door. She made like she was leaning against it but her real motivation was to position herself for an emergency ingress, poised to jump back into the car, slam the door, lock the door and speed off, just in case.

'Can I help you with something?' she asked.

'In fact, it is I,' Richard said, twirling his hand theatrically as if he were performing Shakespeare, 'who can help *you*.' He paused. 'I have a story. A big one. An exclusive.'

Audrey raised her eyebrows. 'Really?'

'Really.'

'But you don't like gossip.'

His face hardened. 'This isn't gossip. It's *news*.'

'What is it?'

'You'll want to record this. And' – he smiled – 'I have a few terms.'

'ThePaper.ie doesn't pay for stories.'

'Perhaps *conditions* would've been a better word. I'm not looking for money. What I want is for you to acknowledge where you got this information. You must refer to me by name in the piece. If any other media outlets contact you after you've published your story looking to get in contact with me, you must supply them with my details so that they can. I'm prepared for this to be an exclusive for you in the first instance, but after that I want to be able to tell my story to whoever wants to hear it. I take it that's agreeable?'

If circumstances were different, Audrey would have burst out laughing, but she was standing in the middle of nowhere with a man described by the woman whose disappearance she was investigating as 'creepy' and she was certain she'd just watched a video of that woman's violent and brutal death. So instead she said, 'Sorry, but I'm a journalist, not a publicist.'

Richard took a step even closer and whispered, 'Young lady, I think we both know you're neither.'

Audrey's body tensed involuntarily, an evolutionary alarm warning her that danger was near. Her phone was in the car. The keys were in the ignition. She had nothing in her hands or her pockets, nothing she could use to defend herself. Richard was so close now that she doubted she'd get inside the vehicle in less time that he'd need to stick his body into the apex of the open door, preventing her from closing it.

She had one defence left, a move as old as time. She took a step back on her right leg, keeping the heel off the ground, planting her left foot firmly, ready now to bring a knee right up into his balls with as much force as she could muster – which, considering how annoyed she was that he thought he could behave this way and get away with it, was going to be an absolute *fuckload*.

Her knee would make sure that Richard's only intimate relationship in the foreseeable future would be with a catheter. She almost wanted him to try something, just so she could do it.

Go on, give me an excuse.

Richard said, 'I saw her.'

'Who?'

'Don't insult me with stupid questions.'

'I asked that because I heard you in the café earlier. When you said you hadn't seen her at all.'

'I told *Orla* I hadn't seen her. As previously stated, I don't like gossip. Listening to it or providing it.'

'So you lied.'

'Then, yes. But I won't lie to you now. And you should probably be recording. Do you have one of those little recorder things?'

His tone couldn't have been any more patronising.

'How about,' Audrey said, 'you tell me your story first and then, if I *want* to, I'll record you telling it again?'

'I can assure you of one thing, sweetheart, I won't be repeating myself.'

'It's 2018. I'm not your sweetheart.'

'Of course.' Another cold, reptilian smile. 'Apologies.'

The light in the car went off, abruptly turning him into little more than a silhouette before her. The light above the NO DUMPING sign was behind Richard, which meant its beam was illuminating her for him.

The car must have some kind of automatic cut-off system. Audrey needed that light back on, now.

'Let me get my phone,' she said.

She moved her body inside the driver's door, bent down and reached into the car to flip the light back on.

Every muscle was tensed, braced for a blow to the back of the neck or hands closing around her throat.

But none came. She was able to pick up her phone – no reception, of fucking course – and even pull the keys from the ignition.

The moment she slipped them into her pocket she wondered if she'd made a mistake, whether a weapon in her hand was really better than a getaway car ready to go, but it was too late for second thoughts now.

Deep in the warmth of her pocket, she rubbed the pad of her index finger against the tip of the car key and reassured herself with the thought that it could do some serious skin-scratching if the need arose.

Stealing a car, watching snuff films, arming herself against a potential murderer … It struck Audrey that, in the last twenty-four hours, life had taken quite the turn.

'All right,' she said, straightening up. She set the Voice app recording on her phone and then held it out and at an angle, in a bid to minimise the roar of the wind. She looked at Richard. 'Tell me what you know.'

———

Richard exhaled and looked off into the distance, in the direction of the water. Audrey turned to look too, but there was nothing to see. It was cloudy; there was no real moonlight. And impossible to differentiate sea from sky. The only light other than the one inside

Dee's car and the one they were standing underneath was the lighthouse, miles offshore, a flickering, mid-air orb.

'I met her,' he said. 'Natalie. On two occasions. We spoke. The first time I was up at the cottages—'

'Doing what?'

'This will go better if you *don't interrupt me.*' He glared at her, then cleared his throat. 'As I was saying ... I was up at the cottages. Last Tuesday morning. Early. I'd say around eight. And to answer the question that is undoubtedly forming in your head – what was I doing there? – the truth is I wasn't doing much of anything at all. I just like to walk up there sometimes. The cottages all back on to the same stretch of grass. A *communal garden*, he calls it. Hardly. Anyway, I was walking along there. I thought the cottages were empty. I saw something moving through the window and I went to have a closer look. It was her. She saw me and, well, I suppose I gave her a bit of a fright. Unintentionally, *obviously.* I promptly apologised and then I left immediately.'

He stopped and looked at Audrey, which she took to mean as permission to ask questions now.

'You went up to the glass?'

He nodded. 'Yes.'

'Why?'

'I'm not sure what you mean ...?'

'They're holiday cottages,' Audrey said. 'People stay in them all the time. Surely *movement* equals *guest*, especially that early of a morning. So why go up to the glass?'

'I can assure you people don't stay in them *all the time*, and most certainly not in November.' Richard gave a little shrug. 'I thought it could be Andrew. I was just going to say hi.'

'Are you two friends?'

'No, but ...' He hesitated. 'I went for that job too, you know.'

'Managing the cottages?'

'But they gave it to him. Judged a book by its cover, didn't they? Or two books, I should say. And I was the one found wanting.'

'That doesn't explain why—'

'I like to keep an eye on him, okay?' Richard snapped.

There was clearly more to this story but Audrey didn't want to get him sidetracked.

'When you say you apologised to Natalie,' she said, 'did she come outside?'

'No. I sort of, you know, motioned through the glass.' He held up both hands and lowered his head, as if miming the act of an apology.

'So you two didn't actually speak?'

'Not *then*,' he said, 'no.'

Audrey waited for him to elaborate but he just looked at her, patient and waiting, a smile tugging at the corners of his mouth.

He was going to make her ask the question. Dick indeed.

'When then?' she asked flatly.

'It was at the beach,' he said. 'Later that same day. Not long afterwards, actually. I drove there to go for a walk. I saw her sitting on a bench. I thought, this is an opportunity to apologise – properly – for frightening her, so I went and did that.'

'And?'

'And we had a pleasant conversation.'

'About what?'

'Oh, nothing of import, really. The usual.' He waved a hand. 'The weather. Shanamore.'

'How did she seem?'

'Fine.'

'How long did you talk for?'

'Perhaps five minutes? Maybe less.'

'Can you remember anything specific she said? How about why she'd come to Shanamore?'

He shook his head. 'It was just all, you know, *pleasantries*. Although, she did say something curious, in light of where we find ourselves now. She told me her husband would be joining her later that day. Isn't that strange?'

Audrey made a *hmm* noise.

Richard didn't know it, but he'd just inadvertently revealed something about his interaction with Natalie that he either didn't want to admit to Audrey or wouldn't acknowledge. Natalie's little white lie confirmed what Orla had said: that Natalie found their encounter unpleasant and Richard as creepy as hell.

'Who left first?' she asked. 'You or her?'

'Her.'

'And you, what? You stayed on the bench? Kept walking?'

His eyes narrowed. 'Why is that relevant? I didn't *follow her*, if that's what you're getting at.'

'I'm just wondering if maybe Natalie was on her way somewhere specific. Or to meet someone else.'

'I don't know,' he said. Which, of course, didn't answer the question. 'What do *you* think?'

'Of what?'

'Of my story.'

Audrey thought, interesting choice of word.

'I mean,' Richard continued, 'say you were our friends, the Gardaí.' He lifted his chin. 'What would you think?'

'Well ... I suppose I'd be confused as to why you went for a walk on what must surely be private property and then, almost immediately afterwards, got in your car and drove to the beach to go for another *walk*, and at both locations you happened to cross paths with the same woman who was a visitor here and previously unknown to you, a woman whose *whereabouts* are now unknown.'

'You talk just like them. Did you know that?'

'Like who?'

'The pigs. Although the one we have here is probably best described as a pig*let*, wouldn't you agree?' He looked down at Audrey's phone. 'Now, I'm afraid you'll have to turn that off for this next bit.'

'Why?'

'Because I said so.'

'But what if I need—'

'Turn it *off*.'

The hand that had been holding up the phone was freezing cold and the arm attached had long been burning with lactic acid from the effort, and so Audrey was happy to drop it now. She needed to keep recording, though; she had no idea what Richard might come out with next. She made a show of pressing a button and then slipped the device into her coat pocket, microphone-end out. It was the volume button she'd pressed. She had no clue whether or not she was about to record anything except the sound of voices muffled by the material of her coat, but she figured it was worth a try.

When Richard had her full attention again, he said: 'The truth is, I knew she was there.'

'Where?'

'If I might speak,' he snarled, 'without the constant threat of *interruption*.' He exhaled through his nose before restarting. 'I knew she was here, in Shanamore. Because I had heard she was. I was in Murphy's on Monday evening having a pint at the bar when someone came in – I couldn't tell you who it was – and said a girl had got off the last bus and started off up the lane dragging a suitcase behind her. They were ... Well, they were *amused* is probably the word. Or *be*mused, perhaps. As in, where does she think she's going, up there, in the dark, in silly shoes with a heavy case? But I knew there was only one place she could be going, unless she was horribly lost, and I thought to myself, a young girl—'

Audrey had to bite her lip to keep herself from screaming: *She was thirty-one!*

'—all alone up there, with *him*.' Richard made a tut-tutting noise. 'Well, I thought it was my duty to warn her. About him. Andrew.'

He paused.

Audrey was getting sick of the amateur dramatics and refused to indulge him. After a few seconds, he had no choice but to continue.

'He's a little peeper, you see. That Andrew. He has cameras, hidden in the bedrooms. It all feeds back to his computer so he can watch them. His guests, I mean. While they sleep. And ... and do other things.' He sighed sadly. 'But I didn't get to warn her. I just couldn't find a way to say it. Not without frightening her, and perhaps unnecessarily. I never imagined ... But now ...' He looked away. 'Now I feel like I have her blood on my hands.'

Audrey felt a chill that hadn't come from the cold.

'Blood on your hands,' she repeated. 'Are you saying you think she's dead?'

He turned back to her, met her eyes. 'Oh, I *know* she is.'

Audrey wanted to ask how but she didn't trust herself to speak. And *did* she want to know, really, when she was standing in an empty car park with him, off a desolate beach, in the dark?

Richard took another dramatic pause, his most interminable yet.

Then he lifted a hand and pointed towards the sea.

'I know she's dead,' he said, 'because I just found her body.'

REWIND

0:00:07

The black oil.

That's how Andrew thought of it. Thick and slick and so dark that it sucks up all the light around it. Consumes it, even. A true black.

It was like a sludge living in the deepest chambers of Andrew's heart, filling it just to the point before overflow, always there but, mostly, contained. Its presence, the weight of it, sometimes made it hard to breathe. Sometimes a trickle of it escaped, leaking through a tiny pinprick of a hole made by the recall of a dream or the blur of a fragmented memory.

And then there were the days when he woke up feeling as if, during the night, the black oil had leaked out while he'd slept and now that was all that was pumping through his veins. Flooding his chest cavity. Adhering itself to the crevices in his brain, making his thoughts sluggish and sticky. It descended like a curtain behind his eyes, clouding his vision, a pulsing migraine. Every cell was a little black hole, swallowing up everything else around it. His own body turned predator and its prey was the light.

Bad things happened when the black oil leaked out.

Andrew would lie in bed and wrap the sheets tight around himself, trying to keep it all inside, keep it contained, like the people he'd seen on TV who'd died of some horribly virulent disease in sub-Saharan Africa. Layers upon layers of constriction, a barrier that would hopefully halt the spread. A mummification of sorts, only he wasn't dead yet.

Underneath it all, he felt like he was rotting from the inside out. And underneath that, he felt like he deserved it. Because of the things he'd done.

The things he still wanted to do.

And then, invariably, after a few days of trying to hold himself together, he would go and do those things.

He considered it Caroline's parting gift to him, this black oil. After all, it was because of her that he had this problem. She was the only girl he'd ever loved and he'd loved her when she was a *girl*. He didn't know how to love women and had little interest in trying.

What he really wanted was to go back, to go back to Caroline then, but that was impossible. So other girls of a similar age to the girl in his memories …

Andrew considered it the next best thing.

Afterwards, every time, he dreamed of Caroline. Snatches would come back, suddenly, hours later and, whenever he felt the oil recede long enough to allow a clear thought, he'd try to piece them together.

It was always one of three scenarios:

Caroline when she was right, sitting at the water's edge, skimming stones, rubbing the back of his neck with her free hand because, she said, she just wanted to touch him.

Caroline when she was wrong, cowering in a hotel bed, inexpertly applied make-up smudged beneath her eyes. Shifting and rearranging and morphing into someone, some*thing* else, before him. A reverse changeling.

Caroline, looking like she did the first day he saw her, white socks pulled up to her knees, red hairband holding back straw-coloured hair, pleading with him to stop, to stop hurting her.

There had been three adult women, total, over the first decade of his adult life. He'd meet them online, get chatting. Go through the motions for a while. Suggest meeting up. He always travelled to Dublin to do this so he could practise in private, so that no one he knew would see his pathetic, bumbling attempts to interact with women his own age, so the excruciating shame was his and theirs only, a relatively private show.

The most recent excursion had been in August. Mary. She said she was a student nurse. Flat-chested. Make-up-free skin. A spray of freckles across her forehead. Her profile said she was twenty-five.

Andrew had made a reservation at a cheap hotel in the city centre, a nicer place than he usually stayed, seeing as he wasn't, for a change, worried about cameras in the lobby or credit cards or ID-checks.

It didn't matter if he left a trail because he wasn't doing anything wrong, not this time. He was just a normal guest. A normal man. It took some getting used to.

They'd arranged to go see a film in the cinema on O'Connell Street, a plan which quickly revealed itself to be the most terrible of ideas. She was a little late, hampered by a car stuck on the Luas tracks, so after identifying each other they rushed to buy their tickets and snacks and go on inside. The trailers started almost immediately, outlawing conversation and giving Andrew nearly two full hours to incubate his anxiety undisturbed.

By the time the credits rolled, he was sweating profusely and could barely speak. She took one look at his wet, flushed face and said she was tired and had an early start.

Back at the hotel, alone, Andrew had undressed, brushed his teeth, turned off the lights, set an alarm for the morning and got into bed. He would do what he was supposed to do on this trip, no more, no less. He lay awake in the dark dissecting his evening and feeling, in a strange way, a little proud of himself. But the black oil liked the dark. He could sense its approach, its advance, a slick and glistening tide, rushing up the sheets, getting ready to slither inside him, flooding his veins.

Andrew reached for his phone.

———

The video arrived exactly one week after he returned to Shanamore.

It came attached to an email sent to his personal address that included his full name, telephone number and the URL of the Shanamore Cottages website.

Even at that, Andrew would've dismissed it as spam if it wasn't for the subject line. *A souvenir for you from your night in Dublin!* He clicked on the message and scanned the rest of the text, at first confused, then disbelieving, then struggling to breathe as wave after thunderous wave of abject terror crashed over him, shaking him to his core.

Guess what, Mr Paedo? I made you a little souvenir from
your night in Dublin. This copy is just for you. But I have one
for the Gardaí, and one for everyone you know, and one for
everyone you don't know too. I will send it the moment you
refuse to do as I say. Instructions to follow. I look forward to
working with you, you sick fuck!

With a shaking hand, Andrew traced a finger across his laptop's
trackpad and clicked PLAY.

It took him four attempts to watch the whole thing through.

He was clearly identifiable. The girl didn't move around as much as
he did so her face wasn't as readily seen, but there was no mistaking
the fact that her body was years too young to be subjected to what
he was doing.

By the time he finally reached the end of the recording, he'd
vomited into his own lap. He felt like he was spinning and couldn't
stop it. The world had tilted crazily and now everything had lost its
purchase and was sliding off, and he was going with it, and he didn't
know where he was going to end up.

His phone began emitting its angry buzz.

To his surprise, the voice on the end of the line was female.

In the next moment, he understood why: it wasn't the sender of
the email he was talking to. It was the receiver of another, similar
email. She didn't go into details. She just cried and sobbed and said
they were forcing her to do this, and she was sorry, and she had no
choice because she had a video too.

She said they said to say he must listen carefully.

Then she gave Andrew his instructions.

FASTFORWARD

0:01:11

The television in the station was busted, so Seanie went home to watch the *Six-One* news bulletin and to make himself something to eat.

It was the second story in the headlines preview at the top of the programme. An older male reporter was standing at the entrance to the cottages, broadcasting live, unflatteringly lit by an intense white light. He told the anchorwoman in the studio that Gardaí now had reason to believe that Natalie O'Connor had come to Shanamore and, following an initial forensic examination of one of the 'holiday homes' behind him (the screen changed to footage, captured much earlier in the evening going by the light, of figures in white overalls carrying equipment into Cottage No. 6), her case had been upgraded from missing person to murder investigation, although Gardaí were denying that a body had been found. A local man, who local sources said was the live-in manager of the complex, had been detained for questioning and a wide-scale search of the area was due to commence at dawn.

A knock at the door.

Seanie was, at first, surprised and then embarrassed to find DS O'Reilly standing outside.

'Sorry,' O'Reilly said, pointing to his right. 'I could see you weren't in the station, so ...'

'Is there news?'

O'Reilly shook his head, *no*.

The detective's eyes fell to the remaining half of a sloppy chicken sandwich Seanie had in his hand.

'I was, ah, just grabbing something to eat while I could.'

'Good idea,' O'Reilly said. 'You wouldn't by any chance have another one of those, would you?'

The two men ate with plates balanced on their knees, sitting side by side on the couch in front of the fire. Seanie kept his eyes fixed firmly on the news – he'd rewound the bulletin to the start so they could both watch it in full – and tried not to react to the absurdity of the situation: the big detective down from Dublin sitting in *his* little living room, the unexpected spotlight on his sandwich-making skills, a murder in Shanamore. They didn't really speak at all until they'd both finished their makeshift dinners and Seanie had brought out dessert: a pot of strong tea and a packet of digestive biscuits.

'Thank God,' O'Reilly said. 'I couldn't drink another coffee today.'

'There's something you should know about me,' Seanie started. He hadn't yet sat down; he was *looking* down on O'Reilly. 'I know I should've said something before ...'

O'Reilly froze mid-pour to look at him questioningly.

'I used to come here. *Stay* here, I mean. In Shanamore.'

Now the detective put down the pot and raised an eyebrow.

Gardaí couldn't be stationed any closer than 50 kilometres from anywhere they'd ever lived; before they joined the force, they had to disclose an exhaustive list of home addresses. This wasn't technically a violation, but Seanie was the only member here. He should've said something.

'We never lived here,' he clarified. 'We stayed a week at a time, a few times every summer. And not every summer, just for a few years until I was, like, sixteen or so. I didn't know him. Andrew Gallagher. But I did ... I saw him around.'

'Okay ...'

'There weren't too many living in the village back then,' Seanie said, 'and hardly any lads my age. You'd notice the ones that were. Sure you'd meet half of them around the pool table in Murphy's. Well, it was sort of in Murphy's – Peggy's sons had one in the house, and she'd let the summer kids in to play on it if she was in the mood. But Andrew was always off to the side, on the edges. And there were ...' He stopped to take a breath. Why did it suddenly feel hard to breathe and talk at the same time? 'I don't want to use the words *rumours* because I'm not sure anyone ever said anything to me. I just picked it up somewhere, somehow, that, um, that he liked young girls. He was young too then, of course. I mean girls younger *than* him. *Much* younger.'

Seanie sat down on one of the armchairs, opposite the detective now.

'I was, ah, I was sixteen,' he said, 'when it happened, so Andrew would've been … probably eighteen? Could've been nineteen by then, I suppose.' Seanie knew he was just imagining it, but his throat felt like it was threatening to close. He took a swig of his tea so he could trace the momentary burn of the hot liquid as it travelled down his oesophagus, proving to him that the airways were still open and clear. 'My sister, Aoife, she'd just turned thirteen. I was thinking about this today and there's something about that "-teen" that makes this … I don't know, *less*? But the truth is her birthday had just been three days before. I still hadn't even got used to the idea of her being a *teenager*. In my head, she was still a child. She was *twelve*, you know? But not in her head. In her head, of course, she was already feckin' sixteen.'

O'Reilly nodded.

Then he asked, 'What happened?'

And finally, Seanie told him. Someone.

That night was a Saturday night and every Saturday night in Shanamore followed the same routine. Around eight o'clock, the rumbling of empty stomachs would force the Flynn siblings up from the beach and the smell of fish and chips would lure them directly to the kitchen table. Seanie's mother and grandmother would've already eaten something better, something more sensible, like a salad ('It's too hot for warm food,' was one of his mother's favourite summer refrains when what she meant was she didn't want to get hot cooking it), and while the younger generation tucked into their trans fats, mother and daughter would say their goodbyes, get in the car and head to Murphy's for a few glasses of wine and a natter.

At the height of the summer it could remain bright for another two, two and a half hours, so contrary to what their mother might have believed, Seanie and his younger brother, Cathal, and sister,

Aoife, would run back down to the beach once the food was polished off. Seanie was in charge but he was an easy-going guardian. The rule was there were no rules other than, one, stay within sight of the swing-set outside the hotel and, two, be in that spot at half past ten or before dark.

That evening Seanie and Cathal waited by the swings as ten thirty came and went without any sign of Aoife.

Ten forty.

Still no sign, no familiar figure running towards them at high speed, flailing her arms and apologising for being late.

Ten forty-five.

Perhaps the bright lights of the hotel were responsible but it suddenly seemed as if darkness was here, not threatening or descending, and within minutes the sea was no longer blue but a pitch-black horizon on which shards of broken moonlight were floating lazily.

Ten fifty.

Ten fifty-five.

Eleven.

Seanie began to panic.

Truth be told, it wasn't concern for his sister that was the driving force of this anxiety but the threat that, in less than half an hour, his mother and grandmother might return to an empty house. A couple of lads he knew were lingering over long-gone cans of cider smuggled out of their respective houses by the picnic tables around the side of the hotel. Seanie enlisted their help, left Cathal on a chair in the hotel's lobby and took off towards the beach with a torch.

'We found her pretty quickly. In the dunes on the east end of the strand, all tangled up with him. He was drunk. She said she hadn't been drinking but her eyes ... Her pupils were like saucers, so. And I, uh, I remember seeing her—' Seanie had to stop here to take a deep breath. He hated even knowing this detail, let alone saying it out loud (he had never) but O'Reilly needed to know the truth about Andrew Gallagher. He looked down at his hands. 'I remember seeing her underwear crumpled up on the sand.'

'What did you do?' O'Reilly asked.

'I grabbed him. Started just, like, pummelling him. And roaring at him, "She's thirteen, you sick fuck. Thirteen!"' Seanie rubbed the knuckles on his right hand, remembering the way the skin had torn, broke open over them, and left him with scabs that his mother had never believed had come from a fall off his bike. 'I thought I could kill him with my bare hands, I was that angry. I might've done if the other lads hadn't pulled me off him.'

O'Reilly sighed, long and loud. 'Did you report it?'

'Report it?' Seanie snorted. 'I never even *said* it. To anyone. Until tonight. Aoife begged me not to tell, and I didn't that night, and then I didn't say anything the next day and then … Then it felt like it was too late. And everything seemed fine. *She* seemed fine. She always said she was, but—' There was a lump in his throat now and it felt so big, it was painful. 'A couple of years later, around Transition Year, things started to go south for her. She got in with the wrong crowd, my mam says. And she did. I mean, that's true. But we never talk about *why* she did. Or why she kept getting in with them, one crowd after another, until it was too late for her to get out.' Seanie paused. 'I worry it was *him*.'

'What happened to her?' O'Reilly asked quietly.

'She jumped off a bridge in London. Well, she was pulled from the water. Whether she meant to go in there or she had an accident, we don't know. We'll never know.'

Both men were silent for a moment.

'Sergeant,' O'Reilly said, 'tell me one thing and tell me the truth. Did you put in for this because of what you've just told me?'

'No.' That *was* the truth. 'Really, no. I was sick of Dublin, and the rent on this house … But look, I can't pretend I wasn't keeping an ear out. I knew he was still here, I saw him around. I thought—'

A doorbell sounded.

'That's the station,' Seanie said.

No sooner had they both stood up than a pounding started. Fists thumping hard against wood. It sounded like someone was trying to break down Seanie's front door.

They looked at each other, then hurried into the hall.

The pounding ceased.

Seanie threw open the front door and stepped outside.

A woman was at the station's only window, hands cupped to the glass, peering inside. The first detail he noticed about her was how her jeans were soaking wet, dark with water and clinging in patches to her skin, all the way up to her knees. The second was that she'd left her car parked haphazardly in front of the station entrance, the engine still running, the driver's door still open, headlights still on.

'Hey,' he called out.

The woman turned towards them.

'It's that bloody reporter,' O'Reilly muttered from behind him. 'What *now*?'

REWIND

0:00:27

'Where is it?' Natalie demanded.

Andrew frowned at her, confused. 'Where's what?'

He was standing just inside his own front door, one hand on the frame, the other holding the door tightly against him, allowing only a narrow view of the dim space beyond.

She had dispensed with pleasantries and greeted him with her question. It looked to her like he was still catching up.

'I had a book,' she said. 'A book of poetry. I put it in a drawer in the kitchen last night and it was still there this morning before I left but now it's gone.' The words were tumbling out in a rush of breath and anger. 'Where is it? Did you take it? Or was it Richard just now when he was *breaking in*?' She was clutching the slightly crumpled *LEAVE* note in her hand; she thrust it at him and he took it from her. Smoothed it out. Lifted it to his face to study it intently. 'And who wrote *that*? Was it you? Look, my husband stayed here. I *know* he did. He got a bill from this place. You charged his credit card. It was only a couple of weeks ago and yet you deny ever seeing him—' She felt tears threatening and her voice cracked as if to let Andrew know too. 'Tell me what the hell is going on here and tell me *now*. Did Mike ask you to lie to me? Did he …?' Suddenly a thought occurred to her that was so awful, the weight of it crushed something deep in her chest. 'Did he *ask* you to go and get that book? Is that…?' Her eyes were heavy with tears and when she blinked, they began escaping. She was so angry, she didn't even care. Let him see her cry. What difference did it make now? 'Is that why you took it?'

Andrew hadn't looked up since Natalie had given him the note.

Now, finally, he did.

And said, 'Come in.'

He pushed the door open all the way and retreated into the dim. After a beat, Natalie followed him.

Inside, this cottage was the mirror image of hers, down to the furniture. But despite the time of day, Andrew had his curtains closed and only a couple of lamps on. The TV was tuned to a news channel and on mute. The air was musty with distinctly unpleasant base notes of smelly socks and sweaty armpit. Natalie tried to breathe through her mouth.

And there was so much more *stuff* in this cottage. No chair, table or remotely flat surface had escaped it. Each step of the staircase had a little stack of something gathered on one end of it: magazines, towels, loose papers. The coffee table was piled with soiled plates, empty Coke bottles and opened cereal boxes. Andrew was hurriedly removing layers of clothing from the nearest armchair, collecting them in his arms before transferring them to the couch where they were added to an existing collection. He motioned for her to take a seat in the space he'd just cleared.

'I'm sorry about the mess,' he said. 'I haven't been well.'

Natalie sat down. He remained standing.

'So,' she said. 'Is she here?'

'Who?'

'The woman I saw last night.'

Andrew looked at her blankly.

'The woman,' he repeated slowly, as if sounding out a foreign word.

'Yes, the *woman*. The woman I saw from my window about an hour after I checked in last night.'

Now: confusion. 'You mean, like, another guest?'

'I mean like the woman I saw standing *in your bedroom*. Upstairs. Looking out. At *me*. Who is she? Does she work here? Is she the woman my husband came here to see?'

Andrew swallowed. 'Natalie—'

'I just want the *truth*, okay, Andrew? Enough with the act, with all the bullshit. Let's just draw a line under it right now. I'm going to find out anyway so we can stop with the farce, with all this' – she threw up her hands – '*pretending*. You can stop lying for him, okay? There's no point. Not any more. I know what's going on, I just need you to confirm it for me because—' She had to stop to take a breath. If she didn't, more tears would come and she might not be able to stop them this time. 'Because I feel like I'm going mad, okay? Like I'm losing my mind. Can't you understand that? I just … I just need you to tell me the truth. That's all. Please. *Please*.' She paused. 'Don't make me beg.'

For a moment Andrew didn't say or do anything.

Then he moved to the couch and perched himself on the arm of it, facing her.

'Okay,' he said, rubbing at his temples. 'Okay … The book. You said it was a … a poetry book?'

Natalie nodded.

'Was it blue?'

'Yes! Yes, it was. Blue. Did you see it? Do you know—'

'I saw it,' he said, cutting her off. 'I saw it when I was cleaning your cottage. Yesterday morning. Before you arrived.'

This statement drenched Natalie in cold relief. The book *had* been there. It existed. It was real. She wasn't just imagining it.

But then she saw that Andrew was biting his lip, that he seemed mildly embarrassed about something—

'Oh no, I know,' she said quickly. 'It was there before I arrived, yeah. I didn't bring it with me. But you see, it was his. *Is* his. Well, ours. It was in our house. And I couldn't find it because he'd brought it here. My husband, I mean. I—' Natalie knew she sounded confused, unhinged, upset. She stopped, restarted. 'I bought that book for my husband.' She was speaking slower now, more deliberately, working to keep her voice even. 'I noticed it was missing from our home a couple of weeks ago and last night, when I checked in, I found it here, in the same cottage where he stayed. Where I know he stayed because he got that bill from you.'

'I don't send out bills,' Andrew said.

'Well, we got one. I have it with me. It's in my cottage. I can go get it.' She moved to go. 'I *will* get it.'

'It's okay,' he said, holding up his hands. 'Just … just describe it to me.'

Natalie did.

'And did you check your credit card?' he asked when she was done. 'Was there really that charge on it?'

'No. I couldn't, I don't have access to that. It's my husband's card. But there was a receipt stapled to the page. From a credit card machine. And it said "Shanamore Cottages" at the top. Actually, you know what? It didn't. It said "Shanamore Cottage." Singular.' She looked around and after a second spotted that, amid the mess, there was a handheld credit card terminal sitting on a small table just inside the door. 'Print me a receipt. I bet that's what it says.'

'That *is* what it says,' Andrew said. 'I entered it wrong when I first got the machine and I never changed it. But I didn't send you – or your husband – anything. I swear I didn't.'

'Then who did?'

He fell silent, looking lost in thought. Then: 'That's why you came here. The bill?'

'Yes.'

'Did you ask your husband about it?'

'I don't think that's any of your business.'

'No,' Andrew said. 'No, it's not. Sorry.' He exhaled slowly. 'I believe you about the bill, but it didn't come from me. Maybe it's identity theft or something. Like those emails you get pretending to be from your bank? I'll call *my* bank and try to find out more, see if they have an explanation for how someone could've made a receipt that looks like it came from my machine. But look …' He paused. 'If your husband is the man in the photo you showed me, he didn't stay here. We only have five cottages to rent out, we're never that busy and I have a good memory. I would recognise him. Remember him.'

'But maybe you didn't see him. Maybe *she* checked them in. The woman.'

'He came here with a woman?'

'I don't know!' Natalie threw up her hands, frustrated. 'That's what I'm trying to find out.'

'There were no guests here recently that would fit that scenario,' Andrew said. 'And before, all I saw was that your front door was open. I didn't see Richard, or anyone else. And ... Look, Richard doesn't work here. I'm sorry if I gave you the impression that he did, I just didn't want you to think that I let every Tom, Dick and Harry wander around the place. He just likes to have his nose in everyone else's business and he can get a bit aggressive when he's had a few drinks, so I'm probably not as firm with him as I should be. So I'm sorry about that. I'll have a word with him.' He paused. 'What else was there?'

'The note,' Natalie said tersely.

Andrew was still holding it and he looked down at it now.

'I don't know,' he said. 'Maybe a previous guest left it there and I missed it when I was doing my clean? That happens. One time—'

'What about the book? The poetry book that was there but now isn't.'

'It was there before you arrived.'

'But it's *mine*. I know it is because it has a special bookplate stuck inside and I signed it. And that doesn't change the fact that it's gone now.'

'But because it's gone, we can't check, can we?' Natalie opened her mouth to protest vehemently but was silenced by what Andrew said next, very quietly, with his gaze fixed firmly on the floor: 'And there was no woman here last night.'

This was so absurd that Natalie laughed out loud.

'That's impossible. I *saw* her. Here. Upstairs.'

Andrew's face was steadily turning a shade of beetroot.

'No,' he said. 'You didn't. I was home alone.'

He bowed his head so low that the only part of his face Natalie could see was his forehead, which had suddenly sprouted a sheen of sweat.

'But I saw—'

'*I* was home,' Andrew said into his chest. '*Alone.*'

'Oh,' she said, realising. '*Oh.*'

And now *she* was embarrassed, a hot flush creeping up her neck

254

and moistening her armpits and lighting the burners under the skin on her face.

Followed at high speed by a rushing panic.

Because now there was nothing left. There was no woman. A previous guest had probably left the note and she just hadn't seen it until today. The poetry book didn't belong to her, it was just someone else's copy of it that they'd left behind. Had she ... Oh my God. Had she *hidden* the book from herself so she could keep pretending that it was her one, the one she'd given Mike? Had she opened her *own front door* earlier too? And what about the bill that had sent her here in the first place? She couldn't figure out how Mike would've known that it had arrived and where she'd hidden it. Did it even *exist*? Was it really folded deep in her handbag beside the bed back in Cottage No. 6 or had it only ever been in her head?

Mike was right. She *was* imagining things.

No, it was more than that. She was losing it. Losing her mind.

Reality had become a moving object that was darting around just beyond her grasp and it was absolutely terrifying.

Natalie's legs began to shake uncontrollably, her boots mapping a rapid, dull tapping noise on the hardwood floor.

What was wrong with her?

How could something that felt so real not be?

What were you supposed to do when you couldn't *tell*?

'I have to go,' she said.

She stood up, half expecting her legs to go from beneath her, feeling relieved when they didn't.

The move made Andrew *look* relieved. And of course he was. She thought *he* was the crazy one but he'd been the one dealing with the crazy.

'I'm sorry,' she said. 'I don't know what's ...'

But then she stopped, feeling something tugging at her, pulling on her train of thought.

'Natalie,' she whispered.

'What?'

'Natalie,' she said, loud and firm. 'You called me Natalie.'

Andrew blanched. 'Did I?'

'I told you my name was Marie.'

'Well, I ...' He ran a hand through his hair, held out the other hand, shifted his weight. 'I saw it on, um ...' A quick breath. 'I knew it from the, ah ...'

If Andrew had denied it, if he'd protested, and if he was even a tiny bit convincing or managed to do it with even a *smidgen* of righteous indignation, Natalie would've believed him because she couldn't believe herself.

But he didn't.

Evidently, he *couldn't*.

Instead, he said, almost in a whisper, 'I'm not supposed to talk to you about her.'

Blood rushed in Natalie's ears, a thunderous roar of a wave. For a moment she thought it might annihilate her altogether. But then it retreated, and she found herself standing strong on solid ground for the first time in a long time.

Feeling utterly calm.

And with a clear head.

'Who is she?'

Andrew sighed, defeated. 'She's ... She's in charge.'

'I thought you were.'

'Not of everything.'

'And she knows me?'

He nodded miserably. 'She knew your name was Natalie.'

'She was here with my husband. She brought him here.'

'No, that's the thing. She's never stayed here. Not once. I swear. And I've never seen your husband. Really.'

He looked desperate for her to believe him.

'Does she wear glasses?' she asked. 'Black ones, with thick frames.'

'Why?'

'Just answer the question, Andrew.'

'Yes,' he admitted. 'Sometimes.'

'What do they look like?'

'I don't know ... They're black. And, like, big?'

'Big like thick?'

'Yeah.'

'Was she here today?'

'No, she left last night. I told you: she never stays here.' He looked at her pleadingly. 'I swear, that's the truth.'

She believed him, for whatever that was worth.

'I don't suppose you'll give me her name and her phone number?'

Andrew turned as pale as she'd ever seen him, practically translucent.

'Please,' he said. 'Don't make me.'

He sounded like a small boy being scolded by his mother.

'Okay,' Natalie said. 'But only if you tell me when she'll be here again – and you tell me the *truth*.'

Now Andrew looked like he might be sick.

'You can't tell her,' he said quickly. 'You can't tell her I told you. You'll have to leave me out of it.'

'She can't fire you because you told me she was coming.'

'She can do whatever she wants.'

'No she can't. There're laws.'

But Andrew didn't look convinced about that. Whoever this woman was that Mike was apparently attracted to and willing to risk everything to be with, she evidently had Andrew under her spell as well.

'*When* will she be here?' Natalie demanded.

'Tomorrow morning.'

'At what time?'

'She always arrives around half nine. But you won't … The thing is, you won't see her. She doesn't drive in here, she always parks in the site next door. The building site. She doesn't want to run into any guests, so … If you come here and demand to see her, she'll know that I—'

'She comes in the back door here, then?'

He nodded. 'Yes.'

'Knocks or comes in?'

'She has keys.'

'But you'll be here?'

'Yes, I have to be.'

'I'll make sure I'm at around the side here at half nine. I can pretend I've just come from the front door because I got no answer. I can make it seem like I've casually run into her. I'll act all surprised.'

She held her hand out for the LEAVE note and Andrew handed it over.

'And you'll leave me out of it?' he asked.

'You know you could just get another job, right? Why stay working for her when she's such a bitch?'

Andrew suddenly reached for her, touching his hand to her upper left arm, and when he spoke he was looking her right in the eye, his voice urgent.

'You have to leave me out of it. If she finds out that I—'

'Fine,' Natalie said.

She turned away from him, yanked open the front door and strode outside.

Her mind was racing but for the first time in a long time, she felt like she had more answers than questions. Black Glasses Lady hadn't been following her, at least not in the way she'd feared. She was The Other Woman just trying to get a look at The Wife.

But Andrew maintained the woman had never stayed here. And he seemed to be telling the truth about not sending the bill.

Had *Black Glasses* sent it, then?

Why would she do that?

Natalie paused outside the door to Cottage No. 6, the key in the lock and her hand on the key.

If Mike hadn't stayed here, what reason would there be for that charge, for the bill?

Was Black Glasses trying to let her know what was going on?

She thought back to their encounter in the deli in Sandymount. The way the woman's face had flashed with what Natalie had identified as contempt, maybe even rage. But what if she was wrong about that? She didn't know this woman well. She didn't know her *at all*. What if the woman had just been caught off guard? What if the expression Natalie had seen was shock?

She unlocked the door and went inside, collapsing into the nearest armchair. The first stirrings of a tension headache were gathering at her temples. Her heart was heavy with the knowledge of what Mike had done.

But things felt clearer now. They were clearer and they'd be clearer still tomorrow, when Natalie would engineer a casual meeting with this woman and they'd have a chance to talk. She'd ask everything she needed to, then she'd get herself on the noon bus out of Shanamore and head back to Dublin to confront Mike.

It would be easier to do it when she had all the information.

More information than even he had himself.

Coming to Shanamore like this was probably the craziest, most ridiculous thing Natalie had ever done. She'd barely stopped to think before she'd walked out of the house yesterday and started the journey here. And until a few minutes ago, all this trip had done was prove Mike right. She *was* crazy. She *was* paranoid.

But now she knew that he'd just wanted her to think those things.

Now, she knew the truth.

Now, Natalie knew that she'd done the right thing.

It had been a good idea to come to Shanamore.

FASTFORWARD

0:00:33

Andrew liked to watch documentaries. He especially liked ones about terrible things that had happened to people – terrorist attacks, natural disasters, plane crashes and train derailments – because there were always people for the documentary-makers to talk to, to interview. People who had had these terrible things happen to them but who had, somehow, survived. The people in these documentaries always said things like, *My instincts just took over* or, *I thought to myself this can't be how it ends* or, *I guess it was just flight or fight.* In the terrible moment when they were put to the test, they all did things they'd never thought themselves capable of. Fear fell away and they took action. Andrew had always imagined that he'd be the same. He'd be on a bus that swerved and overturned, or on a train that jumped the tracks, or in a supermarket when the *pop-pop-pop* of rapid gunfire cracked the air, and he'd – in an instant – become a stranger to himself. No fear. All action. Selflessly save other people but, in doing so, also save himself. 'I don't know what it was,' he'd tell the documentary-makers afterwards. 'I can't explain it. My instincts just kicked in. It was like someone else just took over. I wasn't even thinking. I was just doing what needed to be done.'

He'd be a good person, he thought, for a change. Or at least able to act like one.

But when the time came, he didn't do any of those things. He did absolutely nothing.

He just sat there and watched.

A knife plunging into flesh, again and again. Dark blooms spreading on pale clothes. An intruder in one of *his* cottages, murdering one of his guests.

The fear didn't fall away at all.

It rose up all around him, stronger than ever.

It rose up all around him and it locked him in. A cage made of fear, pumped full of panic. Impenetrable.

The time-stamp on the video told him this had happened less than fifteen minutes ago. He should call the Gardaí. Or an ambulance. No, the Gardaí. He could say he'd heard a strange noise, a shout or a scream. Any noise at all was easily heard out here. He wouldn't have to go over there, wouldn't have to … to see her. That new sergeant would drive out here, look around and discover the woman.

But it was the middle of the night. How long would it take for someone to get here? And that's if they took Andrew seriously – about a scream in the night? – and came out straight away. It could take half an hour, maybe more. It could take another hour before whoever came discovered that room. There'd be no point in calling an ambulance then.

And once the sergeant walked into it, it'd be an official crime scene. Crime scenes got meticulously searched; Andrew watched cop shows too.

They'd find the camera.

He couldn't let them find the camera.

If they found that, they'd find out what he was doing, and then surely they'd find out *why* he was doing it, and what he was.

No.

No.

No.

He couldn't let that happen.

He replayed the video while he wondered what he should do. The moment at the end, the very last one, is what made the decision easy: the destruction of the camera. That changed everything because that's how Andrew knew that all this wasn't some inexplicable, random event.

This had happened for a reason and that reason was *him*.

His body jerked forward and he threw up all over the floor.

———

He didn't know how long he sat there for but by the time he finally moved, the vomit had started to dry and harden on his jeans and a frame of grey light had appeared around every set of drawn curtains in his living room. There was a sour taste in his mouth and his throat felt raw and sore. A red-hot poker of pain had been slipped inside his spine and his muscles ached.

The digital clock on the TV screen said it was gone seven o'clock in the morning. Daylight was coming. The *day* was coming. People would be waking up, leaving their houses, moving around ...

Someone might see something.

The monitor that had shown him the murder was switched off now, a lifeless black rectangle in which he could make out a poor reflection of himself and the room around him. Had he turned it off? He couldn't remember.

If there was something to see.

Had all that happened? Andrew wondered now if anything actually had.

When he recalled what he'd seen on the screen hours before it felt distant and weightless, like a news report from the other side of the world.

It could've just been a nightmare, he told himself, and hope rose eagerly in his heart. He'd been under a lot of pressure lately. Not sleeping right. Having nightmares. This could just be the latest. He'd go check.

He swapped his jeans for a pair of sweatpants from the laundry basket and picked up his keys and his phone.

Then, on second thoughts, he decided to leave the phone. They could track those now, couldn't they? He didn't know on what sort of scale and it was better to be safe than sorry. Fingerprints and all that he could account for – he was the person who cleaned the cottages. But going over there at this hour of the morning would be harder to explain away.

He left the phone and took a torch instead.

Outside, the sluggish breaking dawn cast everything in the same shade of dark blue. The streetlights were still on. It was silent save for the odd car in the distance, the quiet chirping of hidden birds and the clip of Andrew's own footsteps as he crossed the road from Cottage No. 1 to Cottage No. 6.

There was nothing unusual about its outside. All the lights were off, the curtains were drawn and the front door was closed and – he tried to push it inwards – locked. There were no signs of forced entry, no broken glass or damaged locks.

A nightmare, he told himself. Just a nightmare. It must have been.

He started to put his key in the door but then thought better of it and knocked instead. Two firm, loud raps.

Waited. Listened.

Nothing.

He knocked again. He took a step closer to the door and pressed his right ear against it. Waited. Listened.

Still nothing.

He slid his master key into the lock and slowly pushed the door open as quietly as he could.

Everything inside Cottage No. 6 was silent, still and in shadow. Andrew switched on the torch and swung the beam of it about in a large arc, but everything looked as it should. The wall of glass to the rear seemed intact and the backdoor appeared to be shut properly. There were no bloody footprints on the floor, no knife missing from the block on the kitchen counter.

A nightmare. Just a nightmare.

Andrew started up the stairs, careful to keep the torch focused on its steps.

When he reached the landing, he paused again to listen. His heart was beating fast and loud, a primal *thump-thump-thump* in his ears. It was the only sound he could hear.

On his left, the bedroom door was closed.

On his right, the door to the bathroom was as open as it could be.

He scanned the small, tiled space with the beam of the torch. There were some toiletries around the sink and a towel had been thrown over the side of the bath, but otherwise it looked as he expected it would, as it should. Andrew stepped inside to study the sink for traces of ... Well of *anything*, but it looked perfectly clean to him.

265

He turned back towards the bedroom door.
Reached for the handle.
Pushed.

———

Much later, Andrew would marvel at his complete lack of a plan. What would he have done if he'd opened the bedroom door only to discover that she was fine, that it had just been an unforgettably vivid nightmare, and that he was an intruder with a torch in the bedroom of a woman to whom he was a stranger, that *he* was now the bogeyman? What if she'd woken up? What would he have said? The fact that he hadn't given this any thought at all was proof positive that, deep down, he knew what he was going to find in the gloom beyond.

The smell of wet pennies.

A shock of brown-red spray on the wall above the bed.

A pale limb pockmarked with wounds and smeared with drying blood.

The morning light was filtering through the thin curtains; Andrew couldn't see everything clearly, but he could see enough.

His knees buckled and he slumped against the doorframe for support. His mouth was filling with the taste of acrid bile, the signal that whatever was left in his stomach was trying to force its way up.

He wanted to run. Get in his car and drive away. But he couldn't leave. Where was there to go? They'd just think he'd done this then. And what about—

The camera.

It was hidden in the clock atop the chest of drawers that stood against the wall opposite the bed.

Exceedingly careful about keeping his gaze away from the mess on his right, Andrew took one, two, three steps into the room and pointed the beam of the torch behind the door.

The clock was gone.

He checked on the floor. He shone the torch in the narrow space between the drawers and the wall. He went to the window and lifted the ends of the curtains to check it wasn't hiding there.

Then, swallowing hard, he pointed the torch back at the bed.

A sob escaped his throat, startling him. The clock was nestled in the crook of the dead woman's left elbow. Its power cable was wrapped neatly around it and tied, like a ribbon on a gift.

Unthinkingly, he picked it up.

It was slick with drying, sticky blood; he had to hold it in both hands. He felt his skin accidentally touch her skin, which wasn't cold but had a strange quality to it, an empty lifelessness, like a waxwork.

When he stepped back from the bed he heard a squelching sound and looked down to see that he'd left two perfect shoeprints in blood on the bedroom floor.

His vision blurring with tears and his knees weak and shaking, Andrew hurried back to his cottage, walking quickly with his head down, trying – but failing miserably – to swallow the panic that was rising up, coming up, threatening to overtake him completely.

He locked the front door behind him, leaving the curtains closed and lights off, touching as little as possible.

He looked at the bloody clock in his arms. He didn't know what to do now or next.

A full ten seconds passed before he realised he wasn't alone.

'What …' He blinked in the gloom. 'What are you doing up?'

She was standing by the window, looking out into the road. She must have watched him cross it just now. She must know where he'd just been.

She turned to face him, looking him up and down, taking everything in. When she reached the clock, she raised a single eyebrow.

'Oh, Andrew,' she said disdainfully, 'what did you *do*?'

FASTFORWARD

0:01:21

Tentative steps, first on the rough, broken gravel of the path and then on the sand that gave a little beneath their feet. The eerie white glow from her phone's torch function illuminating the hem of Richard's dirty coat, the back of his jeans, his sand-encrusted boots as they hurried a few steps ahead, leading her in a diagonal line towards the shoreline. The inky blackness of actual dark encroaching on all sides just beyond the glow's reach, yawning open like the mouth of a great abyss. Threatening to consume her. Dwarfing the threat of him, the threat of what he had said he was bringing her to see. The small, flashing orb of the distant lighthouse revealing the location of the water every other beat. The biting wind. The undulating topography of the rock pools, covered in mounds of slick and slimy seaweed and the pale, naked limb that shouldn't have been in the middle of them, that looked like it had been Photoshopped in from an image of a woman with one leg casually hooked over the side of her bath.

The scene wouldn't stop replaying in Audrey's brain.

She'd followed Richard down the beach with three nines already tapped into her phone, half thinking he was luring her to her death, half believing that she was about to see a body. He claimed he hadn't called the Gardaí yet because he didn't have a phone, that he'd approached her initially in the car park to ask *her* to make the call, but that he knew once they did he'd have to talk to the detectives and, when he saw that the person in the car park was Audrey, he realised this might be his only chance to tell his 'story' so he decided to do that first. She'd taken one look at the leg and started backing away, then turned and started running up the beach, screaming over her shoulder for him to stay there, to not touch anything, to not let anyone else touch anything either, the shifting sand beneath her feet impeding her progress. Back up at the car park, the call wouldn't connect. So she'd jumped in her car and roared her way back to the village, where she pulled into the Garda station – she could see from the road that the lights were on in both the station and the house adjacent – and started banging down the door.

'We're *here*.'

The tone implied that this wasn't the first time the female Garda in the passenger seat had said this.

'Oh,' Audrey said, coming to. When she looked, she saw they'd pulled up outside a hotel. The something PARK, the lettering on the glass doors said. 'Yeah. Thanks.'

She'd driven back to the beach, tailed by a Garda car. The two Gardaí – Seanie Flynn, she assumed, and her old friend from earlier, Steven O'Reilly – made her stay in the car park while they went down the path. By the time they'd come back up, the place was swarming with flashing lights, white vans and reflective vests with GARDA printed on the back and chest, with more arriving every minute. They'd been waiting to start a search in a few hours' time. Now they'd been deployed earlier than expected, and to a crime scene. It was only when O'Reilly reappeared, pulling off a pair of those same blue gloves he'd used to take the phone from her earlier, that Audrey thought to tell him about the video.

The car door opened and the female Garda – she might have said her name was O'Halloran? – was indicating with a tip of her head that Audrey should get out.

She waited in a corner of the lobby while the guard spoke to the man behind the front desk, and then they both took a silent elevator ride to the second floor. Her room was at the far end of the corridor. The Garda slid the plastic keycard into the lock and pushed open the door for her.

'Someone will be by in the morning,' she said, handing Audrey the key. 'I'd lock this door behind me. The station is less than five minutes' drive away from here. Ring us if there're any problems, okay?'

Audrey nodded.

Once inside, she immediately did what she'd been told. She turned the deadbolt until she heard the reassuring *click* and then flipped the safety latch into place too, just for good measure.

If the room had any features above and beyond the standard chain hotel, Audrey didn't notice and she didn't care. Unless there was already another guest in there, it would do. Sleep was tugging on her limbs, weighing down her eyelids, clouding her thoughts. All Audrey could see were the white, smooth sheets of the double bed and the pillows piled high on it. All she wanted was to not be awake.

She flipped various combinations of light switches until the room fell completely dark, then kicked off her shoes and shimmied out of her sand-encrusted, still-wet jeans, which had probably deposited half a beach in the backseat of the Garda car now that she thought about it. She left them where they fell. She went directly to the bed, yanked back the duvet – why were they always tucked so bloody tight? – and crawled underneath it, stretching out her arms and legs. Sighing contentedly in anticipation of the hours of deep, warm and, most importantly, *ignorant* bliss she was about to sink into.

But as soon as she closed her eyes, she saw the leg.

Sticking out of the rock pool.

And exposed and bloody on a computer screen, captured by a camera that had been concealed in a room in which Natalie O'Connor was a guest.

Audrey opened her eyes.

Then sat up and reached out to turn on the lamp by the bedside.

Then she got out of bed and pushed at light switches again until every square inch of the room was blindingly illuminated.

She started her sweep in the bathroom, working methodically and systematically, examining the ceiling first, then the shower cubicle, then all around the mirror above the sink. There was a smoke detector or something mounted on the ceiling just inside the door; she pulled over the chair from the desk and stood on it so she could examine it closely for marble eyes. (Is that what it would look like? She was only guessing.) No part of the device looked like it shouldn't be there, but then she hadn't noticed anything back in the bedroom of Cottage No. 6 either and, for all she knew, the camera that had captured Natalie's final moments had also recorded *her* afternoon nap. Audrey checked inside the wardrobe, then realised that didn't make any sense. (Or *less* sense, because had this made any sense to start with?) She opened the curtains, revealing a view of what looked like a staff car park and a loading bay. She closed them again, checking to make sure that they had completely covered every inch of the glass. She unplugged all the electronic devices in the room: the television, the alarm clock beside the bed, the phone on the desk. Finally, she fished her own phone out of her bag and climbed back into bed with it, burrowing down until the duvet was almost completely over her head.

When she tapped the phone to life, she saw she had numerous WhatsApp and text messages, five missed calls and a migraine's worth of new social media notifications. She ignored them all and started typing a text to Dee that promised everything was fine and that she'd call her in the morning. She was halfway through when she noticed the minuscule lens eyeballing her from just above the screen, and she stopped and stared at it staring back at her.

She stuck her thumb over it before continuing.

A phone was ringing.

The sound reached through the realms of sleep, piercing it, before rudely shaking Audrey awake. She opened her eyes to a pitch-black room and an expanse of unfamiliar bed that offered no clues as to where or even *when* she was.

Then it started to come back to her, in pieces:

Shanamore.

A ride in a Garda car.

A bluish white leg sticking out of a rock pool.

She could feel the hard shell of her phone stuck uncomfortably beneath her left shoulder blade but when she pulled it out from there, the source of the ringing didn't move with the motion.

Confused, Audrey hoisted herself up on her elbows and looked around, her eyes struggling to discern shapes out of shadows.

There was a blinking red light on the other side of the bed.

It was the *hotel* phone that was ringing. She'd missed it during The Great Unplugging the night before.

273

She picked it up.

'Hello?'

'This is Ava at reception,' said a female voice. 'I'm very sorry to bother you at this hour, but you have a visitor. A Miss Sandra Cotter?' Someone away from the phone said something inaudible and then Ava added, '*Ms* Cotter.'

The name rang a distant bell.

'What time is it?' Audrey asked, rubbing sleep out of her eyes.

'Almost half five. Five thirty a.m.' The person in the background – *Ms* Sandra Cotter, Audrey assumed – spoke again. 'She, ah, she says she's from the paper. Sorry, *the* paper. She says to tell you that Joel sent her. And that she has coffee.'

The crime reporter, then. The proper one.

What was *she* doing here?

'*Does* she have coffee?'

'Yes,' Ava said. 'She does.'

'Tell her to come on up then.'

Audrey dumped the phone back in its cradle and patted the wall until her fingers felt a switch. The lamp there, the lamp on the desk and the ceiling light all came on; there seemed to be no rhyme or reason to the wiring in this place. She got out of bed and touched an exploratory toe to her crumpled jeans, but her skin met rock-hard, gritty denim. She dug around in her bag until she found the only other pair of pants she'd brought with her: black leggings that had been rendered loose and misshaped by their double-duty as pyjamas. She went into the bathroom to pat down her hair and swill some mouthwash.

She was brought back out by two sharp knocks on the hotel-room door.

Sandra Cotter was fortyish, Audrey guesstimated, and sporting the kind of short, razor-cut, white-blonde hairstyle that should really only work on edgy Swedish popstars and models for conceptual clothing stores whose name no one quite knew how to pronounce. Sandra was pulling it off effortlessly but Audrey wondered if it was more to do with time-saving than style. The

T-shirt under her leather jacket looked like it had last been in a ball under her bed and there were smudges of mascara at the corners of her eyes. She had probably left Dublin in a hurry, like Audrey, and not stopped moving since.

There was a cardboard tray in her hands with two enormous takeaway cups wedged in it, which she held out now like an offering.

'Audrey?'

'Sandra.'

'We meet at last.'

Audrey motioned for her to come inside.

Sandra set the cups down on the desk and pulled the chair out from under it.

'Latte or Americano?' she asked.

'What has more caffeine in it?'

Sandra gave her the Americano. Audrey took it back to her still-warm spot in the bed and took up a position with her back against the headboard.

The coffee tasted like it had come from a petrol station kiosk and had been brewed the night before – which it probably had, and it probably was – but she sipped it gratefully, thankful for the caffeine buzz she hoped would kick in soon.

'Are you up early,' Audrey asked, 'or late?'

'I don't know ... What day is it?' Sandra lifted the lid off her cup and sighed into it. 'I think I've been up for almost twenty-four hours now.'

'You're the proper crime reporter.'

Sandra laughed. 'That I am.'

'Did you just come from Shanamore?'

'Yep. I think they gave me your old room at Murphy's.' She nodded towards Audrey's bag, its contents pulled out and dropped as if in some kind of explosion. 'I think the imprint of that is still on the bed.'

'They thought it'd be a good idea to get me out of the village,' Audrey said. 'The Gardaí, I mean. I have to go in and give a statement first thing in the morning about what happened down by the beach and they didn't want the locals trying to get it out of me first. Oh, and I have to get my bloody laptop back too. Hopefully.'

Sandra raised an eyebrow. 'The guards have your laptop?'

'The video is on it.'

'In an email, though. Did they really need to take the machine?'

'I don't know, I was too tired to argue.' Audrey took another slug of coffee. 'So. Sandra. The suspense is killing me.'

'You want to know why I'm here.'

'Joel sent you to stop me.'

'*The Paper* sent me and Joel asked me to *help* you, actually.'

'Help me do what?'

'Write a story. Three thousand words. It'll go online as The Paper's first ever long-form piece on Saturday morning and they're going to promote it full blast all weekend. You'll get paid for it, a premium. It's almost a certainty you'll be moved upstairs. We can all get the facts, but only you can tell your story. You met the killer. *Alleged* killer, but come on. You slept in the room where it happened. In the very *bed*. They know how valuable that is and, in turn, how valuable you are. They'll look after you. And it's a mutually beneficial arrangement, because you'll have a job to pay the bills for the next few months or year, while you work on your book.'

Audrey raised her eyebrows. 'My what now?'

'True crime is' – Sandra put on an OTT American accent – '*so hot right now*. Anything could happen for you. I'm willing to bet a book deal will. In the meantime, I'm supposed to fill you with caffeine, set you in front of a computer and help you write your piece.' She paused. 'This is going to be national news, Audrey. And not just for the weekend. In the last hour, Gardaí found a cache of over two hundred hours of hidden camera footage on a hard drive belonging to Andrew Gallagher. He tried to throw it off the cliffs in Ballycotton but it didn't make it into the sea. A local hill-walker had found it a few days ago and brought it home, but he didn't know what he had until he saw the news last night. And that might not be the only illicit thing on there, if you know what I mean. Seems our Andrew likes girls and I'm not using that word like thriller writers do. I mean, like, *actual* girls. Very young ones. I'm also hearing that Richard Flynn is a made-up name and that the guy calling himself that was involved in some major bank robbery in London years back.'

'Shit,' Audrey said.

'My point is that this is only going to get bigger and bigger. What we know is only the tip of the iceberg. The real story is what we've yet to find out. Like, why did Natalie O'Connor come to Shanamore in the first place?'

'Why are you doing this?'

'What, waking you up at five o'clock?'

'Helping me.'

Sandra shrugged. 'I'm just sending the elevator back down, aren't I? Mind you, there's a charge for the ride. I want to see the video.'

Audrey sighed. 'No, you don't.'

'How bad is it?'

'Worse than you can imagine.'

'I still need to see it.'

'Need or want?'

'I'm a crime reporter.' Sandra gave a half-smile. 'So, both.'

'You'll have to watch it on my phone,' Audrey said. 'They took my laptop.'

'It was sent to your email, right?' Sandra hopped up and went for her bag. 'Here, we can watch it on mine ...'

———

Sandra lifted the computer's lid and moved her finger across the trackpad, then sat back down in the chair to watch as the video played. With her eyes on the screen, she said, 'Does this make sense to you?'

Audrey frowned. 'What, the video?'

'Andrew Gallagher as the murderer. You met him. What did you think?'

'Well ...' Audrey considered the question. 'I didn't think, Oh, this guy is definitely a serial killer, if that's what you mean. And I don't know why he'd admit to finding the body, dumping it and cleaning up the scene if he hadn't killed her. And if it's not him, who could it be?'

'But why didn't he just go the whole hog and admit that too?' Sandra said. 'Or not admit anything at all and try to get away with it?'

'Maybe because he doesn't like jail?'

'I detect sarcasm.' Sandra sighed. 'I'm just not buying him as the killer. Sorry.' She pointed at the screen. 'I mean, do you even think that's him?'

Audrey really didn't want to watch that video again, but she didn't have to. She could recall it perfectly, replay it in her mind.

And now that she thought about it, actually, she wasn't sure.

There was nothing that ruled Andrew *out* as the figure in black, but then there was nothing that proved it was him either.

They watched it through in silence, and then again at half-speed.

'It's not Richard Flynn,' Audrey said. 'I'm sure about that. He's bigger, taller. Wider.'

'But is it Andrew Gallagher?'

'You know ...' Audrey squinted at the screen, then got up so she could look at it more closely. 'There's something weird about the clothes. The shape of them ...' She clicked until the video had gone back to about a third in, when the figure began to advance towards the bed, pausing it in mid-stride. 'Look.' She pointed. 'Something's off, isn't it?'

Sandra squinted at the screen now too. 'Yeah. But what?'

'Could it be ...?' Audrey paused. 'Could that be a *woman*?'

They turned and looked at each other, then back at the screen.

'*What* woman, though?' Sandra asked.

'This was an opportunist thing, right?' Audrey said. 'Andrew is Norman Bates the Second, just without the mother stuff, and he killed one of his guests, randomly. Who was there, randomly.'

'*Was* she there randomly? She was chasing down suspicions about her husband, wasn't she?'

'All I know is she asked him if he'd heard of Shanamore the morning she left.'

'So where did *she* hear about Shanamore?'

'I don't know.'

'Does Mike?'

'I don't think he did when I spoke to him,' Audrey said. 'Or maybe he did but he just didn't want to tell me.' She paused, thinking. 'There are other women in this story, though. When I spoke to Mike, he said that Natalie had a few crazy followers. One of them apparently called to the house … He didn't get to finish telling me about it, some Gardaí arrived. Well, some *more* Gardaí because there were two already there. Because … because that morning, the morning the appeal went out, some woman tried to break into their house.'

Sandra's eyes grew wide. '*What*? Who was she?'

'Don't know. Mike wasn't there when the first one came to the house. And actually, he wasn't there when the other one tried to break in. Unless… Could they be the *same* woman?'

They were both quiet for a moment, considering this.

'She was in the back garden,' Audrey said then. 'A neighbour spotted her. So presumably she was trying to get to the back door. It has glass in it, it wouldn't have been that hard to smash a pane and reach in to unlock it. Hang on …' She moved to get her phone. 'I have a picture of it.'

Sandra raised her eyebrows. 'You took pictures inside the house? Mike gave you permission for that?'

'Those,' Audrey said, 'are two different things. Here.' She sat next to Sandra and held the phone so they both could see it. Then she started swiping through the photos she'd taken inside the house on Sydney Parade Avenue, looking for one that included the back door.

But she stopped before she got there.

The photo of the noticeboard.

The Visa bill with something circled in red.

'What?' Sandra said, looking from the phone to Audrey's face. 'What is it?'

'What does that say?' Audrey stretched two fingers across her phone's screen to zoom in, then handed it to Sandra so she could take a look. 'Doesn't that look like "Shanamore Cottages"?'

'Maybe ...'

'And it's circled in red. So, what? Natalie found a charge on the credit card and went to investigate?' Audrey paused before answering her own question. 'No, that doesn't make sense — because according to Mike, she asked him about Shanamore. If she knew there was a charge from there — if she'd found this bill — why didn't she just ask him about that?'

'Maybe she did,' Sandra said. 'Maybe Mike wasn't completely truthful with you.' She paused. 'Or his wife.'

Audrey turned to her. 'You have your car here, right?'

'Yeah. Why?'

'Feel like driving to Dublin?'

'*Now*?' Sandra looked horrified. 'Not even a little bit.'

Audrey grinned. 'But you'll do it anyway?'

'You have to give your statement, don't you?'

'That can wait. I need to talk to Mike.' Audrey pointed to the photo of the Visa bill. 'About *that*.'

FASTFORWARD

0:01:25

The door to the interview room opened and two Gardaí walked in, one Richard didn't recognise and one he did: Sergeant Seanie. He wouldn't trust either of them with a rental car. Where were all the senior Gardaí? Why had they sent teenagers to tackle a case of this magnitude and complexity? This outfit was as good as the Keystone Cops.

'Richard,' Seanie said, taking one of the two seats opposite. 'Thanks for coming in to talk to us this morning. We really appreciate it.' He had a thick file in his hands and he lay it down now on the table.

Richard pressed his lips together to hide a smile. As if he didn't already know that trick – and every other trick in the book.

'Sergeant Seanie,' he said. 'Good morning.'

'I think his name is Flynn,' the other officer said.

'Sergeant *Flynn*,' Richard said. 'My sincere apologies.'

'There're just a few things we need to go over,' Seanie said.

'Am I under arrest?'

The other officer raised an eyebrow. 'Why, should you be?'

Richard fixed him with a stare. 'And you are ...?'

'Detective Sergeant O'Reilly.'

'Pleasure.'

O'Reilly grunted. 'I fucking hope not.'

'We have a few questions,' Seanie said.

Richard sat back, folded his arms, smiled. 'Fire away.'

'You told the reporter – Audrey Coughlan – that Andrew Gallagher was, quote, a *peeper*, and that he recorded his guests with cameras hidden in their rooms.' Seanie paused. 'Can you tell us how you knew that?'

'So he was? He did? I was right?'

No one answered him but the implication was in the question: they had found cameras up at the cottages, *making* Richard right.

The little pervert.

'Thought so,' Richard said. He touched his tongue to his front teeth.

'Did you ever see any evidence of these cameras?' Seanie asked. 'Or was this just a suspicion?'

'I saw him once, looking at footage on his laptop.' Both Gardaí shifted in their seats. Their eagerness to hear the rest was coming off them in waves. Richard hoped neither of them played poker. 'He was in his living room, at the table. I could see the whole thing. At first I thought he was watching, you know, porn or whatever, but then I realised what it was.'

'How familiar were you with the interior of the cottages?'

'I did a bit of work on them,' Richard said, 'when they were being built.'

'What work, specifically?'

'Oh just, you know' – Richard waved a hand – 'whatever was going. Day labourer, you could say. But I was inside for the second fix. I know what they look like. I could identify the bedroom from the video, if that's what you're getting at.'

'Where were you when you saw Andrew watching the video?'

'At the window. Outside.'

'Front or back?'

'Back.'

Seanie raised an eyebrow.

'I just like to walk around up there, okay?' Richard said. 'Is that a crime?'

'Yes,' O'Reilly said flatly. 'Trespassing.'

'Charge me with it then.'

'I just might.'

Richard threw the detective a filthy look. Big man on campus, was he, yeah? Swinging your dick around, *Dick*? He might want to try being polite or Richard might let a few pertinent details fall right out of his head.

'You like to walk around down by the beach, too?' Seanie asked.

'Doesn't everyone?'

O'Reilly snorted. 'At this time of year?'

'We must be made of hardier stuff down here, Detective.'

'Tell us how you found the body.'

Richard shrugged. 'I was just walking along, and I saw something up ahead. I went to look. It was her. I don't have a mobile phone so I went to get help. I saw a person in the car park, standing by their car. It was the reporter. I told her and she raised the alarm.'

'You were walking along,' O'Reilly said. 'In the beach, in the dark, in the freezing cold, across *rock pools*—'

'I never walked on the rock pools. I saw the body from a distance.'

'Then how did you know it was her? Audrey Coughlan said you identified her. You said, "I know she's dead because I just found her body."'

'Who *else* would it have been?' Richard scoffed. 'Did we have *two* murders this week?'

'How did you know she was dead?'

This, Richard didn't answer immediately – because he had known as early as the morning after that Andrew had killed that woman. It was *obvious*. She had disappeared, Richard hadn't seen her leave – and, when he asked around in the village, no one else had either, even though she was known to have not brought a car – and Andrew had spent nearly the whole day inside Cottage No. 6, cleaning furiously. Richard had thought it might be wise to keep an eye on the boy. Which is what he was doing when, in the middle of the next night, he saw Andrew hoisting something large and heavy out of his cottage into the boot of his car.

Richard said, 'She just looked it. The colour of the skin, perhaps.'

'Right, right,' O'Reilly said. 'The colour of her skin, even though it was dark and you were nowhere near the body because you didn't walk on to the rock pools. Got it. And then you decided that the best course of action was to go up to the car park, find a woman half your age, frighten the life out of her by approaching her in the dark, chat for a bit and then entice her down to a *crime scene* so she could be traumatised by that, too?'

Richard shrugged. 'She's a reporter, isn't she? I was doing her a favour. Handing her a scoop.'

'How much time passed between you finding the body and you approaching Audrey Coughlan in the car park?'

'Minutes. I left the beach as soon as I saw the body.'

'That's quite the coincidence, isn't it? That she was there?'

'Is it?'

'*Yes*,' O'Reilly said, nodding, as if talking to a child. 'Yes, it is.' He paused. 'You like having your name in the paper, don't you, Richard?'

'Is my name in the paper, Detective?'

O'Reilly smiled coldly. 'It might be, yet.'

Richard returned the smile. 'You know, for Good Cop, Bad Cop to work, I think perhaps you're supposed to be a bit more subtle than this.'

'Orla Sheridan,' Seanie said. 'You told her that you'd never met Natalie.'

'I would never tell *her* anything. That café may as well be on Fleet Street.'

'What I don't understand is why you didn't come and tell me about the camera and your suspicions long before now. And I *really* don't understand why you didn't do that as soon as you heard that a previous guest of the cottages was missing.' Seanie paused. 'Can you explain that, Richard?'

Richard shifted in his seat.

'Could it be,' O'Reilly continued, 'because you don't like talking to the police? Could it be because you've been in trouble with the law? That you *are* in trouble, for something else, somewhere else?'

———

Good Cop, Bad Cop were right – in *some* ways. Richard hadn't gone to them because he distrusted the police and he was loathe to do their job for them. Come and ask him questions, okay. He'll answer them. But expect him to go to them to report something they'd no idea had even happened? Now that was just laziness.

Furthermore, he knew that Natalie hadn't liked him. That little stuck-up bitch thought she was too good to even *talk* to him. And with the world the way it was, she could've recounted the story of their meeting to anyone, with God knows how many embellishments, maybe even put it online – and you know what that place was like now, the lit torches of the Outrage Brigade just lying in wait for fresh flesh – and done God knows what to a man's reputation. He'd only been trying to have a polite conversation with her, for God's sake. And the thing at the window – well, that was just a misunderstanding. But if she'd said that, if she'd complained about him, wrote about him online, no doubt the keyboard warriors would get to work, investigating and searching and uncovering, running checks. Joining dots that hadn't been joined in a decade, following a trail that led to a different name and a long-ago crime. Not one of this nature, but still. Richard, as he called himself these days, was happy where he was. Being *who* he was.

So he had held back. Waited. Watched. Then the girl was dead; she couldn't say anything about him. And he *had* just happened upon the body – that was true. But he didn't call the Gardaí. He'd waited, thinking. There were reporters swarming around the cottages. What if he alerted one of them, instead? Then he'd gone up to the car park and found that Audrey girl, just standing there, practically wrapped up in a bow.

But now Richard was wondering if he'd made a mistake. Perhaps he should've just ignored it. Walked on. Let someone else find the girl and call it in.

He was realising that he needed to extricate himself from this whole situation before anyone took the time to look too closely at Richard Flynn.

He especially needed to get out of this room, to end this interview. It wasn't quite the casual chat he'd been led to expect.

So when Sergeant Seanie fixed him with a dead-on look in the eyes and said, 'Is there anything else you can tell us that could help our investigation?' Richard opened his mouth and lied for the first time:

'No.'

'Are you sure?'

The second:

'Yes.'

'No one saw Natalie alive after Tuesday afternoon,' Seanie said. 'And from his initial assessment, the pathologist thinks she died not long after that. So tell us, Richard: where were you Tuesday evening?'

Richard wanted to scoff and say how preposterous the implication was, but he said, 'In Murphy's.'

'Until when?'

'Closing.'

'And then?'

'Then I walked home and went to bed.'

'What time was that?'

'I couldn't say. But I had my phone with me. You can track those things now, can't you? I was nowhere near the cottages that night.' He folded his arms to display his confidence. 'You can check.'

'You think Andrew did this,' O'Reilly said.

'Yes,' Richard said. 'I don't see how any thinking person could come to a different conclusion.'

O'Reilly snorted, presumably at the phrase *thinking person*.

'Do you recall,' Seanie asked, 'ever seeing anyone else up at the cottages? Shortly before Natalie arrived or at any point after she did?'

Richard let a beat pass.

Because here it was, now. The big one.

The third lie:

'No.'

But he *had*.

He hadn't gone to the cottages the night Natalie died, but he had the night before. Her first night there. And he had seen the figure in the window. The bedroom window. Not Natalie's, but Andrew's. She was standing in a darkened room, looking across the complex into the bedroom where Natalie had just flicked on the lights.

The woman.

From where Richard had been standing – or hiding – around the side of Cottage No. 5, he could see Andrew too: standing in the living room, looking up towards the ceiling, and then calling out something, calling out to her.

Natalie had drawn her curtains. He'd watched as this woman had joined Andrew downstairs. They'd talked for several minutes. It was hard to tell from that distance, but Richard got the impression that Andrew was upset, and that the woman was reassuring him.

But he wasn't going to say that now.

Not to Laurel and Hardy here. They liked Andrew for this anyway, he could see it. And *he* liked Andrew for it too.

That boy was a pervert and he needed to go away. Let them take him. Let this all be over. Let Richard – *Richard* – go back to being that without the threat of being exposed as someone else.

He might even get the job that little shit had stolen out from under him, if there even was a job after all this, because who was going to want to stay in those godforsaken cottages now?

'Okay, then,' Seanie said, sliding back his chair. 'In that case, I think that's it.'

REWIND

0:01:16

Andrew had no idea how much time had passed since they'd put him in the cell. It didn't look like it did on TV; there were no sliding bars. The door was solid steel. Inside there was a little seat made out of concrete and a thin mattress covered in a kind of plastic that clearly could be wiped clean, like everything in those soft-play areas for children. There was a hole in the ground which he thought might be the toilet. There were no windows and the fluorescent light made his eyes sting. The only other thing in the room besides him was all that was left of his dinner: a crumpled McDonald's bag and an empty cup of Coke. He thought it might be very late now, maybe eleven or even later.

They'd brought him to Midleton Garda Station, he remembered that much. He'd assumed he was here because Shanamore Garda Station was too small, or maybe it was just easier to get him out of the village, out of the scrum of reporters and onlookers and nosy neighbours, and bring him to a proper station in an actual town instead.

The bolt in the door slid open and a Garda in a uniform beckoned him out. Directed him down the hall. Into yet another windowless room.

This one was different, but desolate in a similar way. There was a glossy-topped table, fake wood effect, the kind they had in school. A black leather chair fixed to the floor; he was sitting in it. Two more chairs on the opposite side, awaiting, he assumed, his interrogators. An old, stained brown carpet and crumbs stuck on it. Pockmarked ceiling tiles, square. Plain walls with nothing on them except for chipped magnolia paint. A little black machine with buttons. A black fish-eye mounted in the furthest corner of the room which Andrew thought must be a camera.

The camera.

He wondered if they'd found that yet.

He'd driven to Ballycotton, walked a little along the cliffs there and flung it into the sea. The following evening he'd done the same thing with the little hard drive he'd been supplied with.

He wondered if anyone had spoken to his mother. The silver lining, if there was one, was that the woman was well past understanding any such thing now.

Footsteps outside the door, the low murmur of voices.

Sergeant Seanie entered, followed by another, bigger, taller Garda he didn't know but who he'd seen earlier, back at the cottages, when he was getting arrested. The two men nodded to the uniformed Garda who'd brought him from the cells; he nodded back then left.

They sat down opposite him. Andrew remained slumped in his seat, eyes fixed on the floor.

Seanie had carried in a small laptop which he put on the table in front of him.

'I'm Detective Sergeant Steven O'Reilly,' the bigger man said, 'and, as you know, this is Sergeant Sean Flynn. We'd like to ask you a few questions ...'

Andrew tuned out whatever O'Reilly said after that because he was watching Seanie load CDs into the little black machine. They were going to record what he said. Audio and – he looked up at the camera – maybe video too.

'I need you to actually say yes,' O'Reilly said.

'Yes.'

'It's been explained to you that you have a right for a solicitor to be in here, but you have waived that right at this time?'

'Yes.'

The two Gardaí exchanged a glance, which made Andrew wonder if that was really the right thing to say.

Maybe he should ask for a solicitor. They'd told him he was entitled to one but that, it being the middle of the night, it would delay things. He just wanted to get this over with. And what was a solicitor going to do for him anyway? It wasn't like he was going to be walking out of here a free man. He'd been caught.

The question was, what for?

O'Reilly had brought a pad of paper and a pen in with him and he poised over it now, ready to write something down.

'You are the manager of Shanamore Cottages, Andrew,' he said. 'Am I correct?'

'Yes.'

'And last week you had a guest named Natalie O'Connor.'

'Yes.'

'Did she make a booking in advance?'

'That morning, she made it.'

'How?'

'On the phone.'

'Is that the normal method?'

Andrew shrugged. 'Sometimes people do that, yeah. Usually, it's the last-minute people.'

'What exactly did she say?'

'That she needed a room for the night. She told me her name was Marie. Marie Kerr.'

The two Gardaí exchanged another glance.

'When did you learn her real name?' O'Reilly asked.

Andrew didn't answer right away. What was the right thing to say? He didn't have time to speed back through his memories of Natalie's stay to figure out if he could get away with this lie and he was so tired …

The two men across the table were staring at him intently. He had to say something. He went with, 'From the news. I don't remember exactly when.' A pause. 'Sorry.'

'Did she provide you with credit card information on that call?'

'No.'

'Did she ever?'

'No. I usually do that on check-out. And I had no other guests. If she didn't arrive, it wasn't like I was going to lose business.'

'But you didn't take it from her when she arrived either?' O'Reilly raised an eyebrow. 'Wouldn't that be standard practice, in case they drive off during the night?'

'I didn't think that was going to happen. I just ... This time of the year ... It's quiet, you know.' Andrew shrugged. 'It was fine.'

'Were you aware that Natalie's husband had a charge from Shanamore Cottages on his credit card from a fortnight or so before?'

'Yes. No. I mean, not then. But I am now.' He pointed at Seanie. 'He told me about it.'

'And your explanation for that is ...?'

Andrew hesitated. 'I don't have one.'

'You'd agree it's an astronomical coincidence, though, right? If it's just an error. His card gets charged, she arrives ...'

Andrew said nothing.

'What time did she arrive, that day?' O'Reilly asked.

'Late that afternoon. It was just dark.'

'So, what? Five, six p.m.?'

'Around that, yeah.'

'And you put her in Cottage Number Six.'

'Yes.'

'Why?'

'What do you mean?'

'Why that one in particular?'

'It's just easier to use the same one in the off-season when you only have one guest at a time. And more economical. I can close down the other ones until spring. Not worry about cleaning them, or whatever.'

Technically, that wasn't a lie.

'Is there a difference,' Seanie said, 'between that one and the others?'

'No,' Andrew said after a beat. 'All the cottages are identical.'

O'Reilly's mouth twisted with satisfaction. That must have been the wrong answer.

'Now,' he said, 'my colleague is going to play you a video. Please watch it carefully.'

A video.

Andrew's stomach dropped like a stone.

'Are you all right, Andrew?' O'Reilly's eyes had strayed to Andrew's hairline, where he could feel beads of sweat forming. His chest felt like it was growing smaller and smaller, trapped in a vice.

Andrew nodded. He didn't dare speak.

Seanie lifted the lid on the laptop and turned it around so Andrew could see it. A video was queued up already to play.

A still of the bedroom in Cottage No. 6.

Relief flooded Andrew's body. He let his shoulders sag.

Not *that* video, then. Maybe they didn't have that. Maybe *she* hadn't sent it to them at all.

Maybe he could get out of here yet.

'This was recorded in the bedroom of Cottage Number Six,' O'Reilly said, pointing at the screen where, now, a figure clad all in black was violently murdering Natalie O'Connor. 'Right? That's Natalie O'Connor there, in the bed.'

But now that the wave of relief had receded, Andrew was confused. Where had they got this video? He'd never sent it anywhere. It had been saved to his laptop, which was in the sea somewhere off Ballycotton Bay.

Had *she* sent it to them?

If she had, then where did she get it? He'd never sent her this one. He hadn't had time to.

'Where did you get this?' he blurted out.

O'Reilly said, '*We* ask the questions, Andrew. So here's one for you: why were you recording your guests?'

If she *had* sent the video, he thought, that changed things.

Andrew felt the buzz of gathering panic.

'Security,' he said tonelessly. 'The camera is for security.'

'Security?' O'Reilly scoffed. 'Yeah. And I'm fucking Santa Claus.'

She was setting him up for this. He saw that now. The other stuff, the other video, she didn't care about that. That was nothing compared to this.

If you murdered someone, you went away for life.

For *all* of your life.

Andrew felt a rising nausea reaching up into his throat.

'We know that's not why you have it,' Seanie said. 'Don't try to spoof us, Andrew. We have our tech guys round there now examining every square inch of that place.' He pointed at the figure in black. 'Who is that?'

'I don't know,' Andrew mumbled.

'Who is that?'

'I don't know!'

'Have you seen this video before?'

Andrew shook his head, no. His eyes were fixed firmly in his own lap now. He couldn't face the relentless glares of the two Gardaí any more.

Then O'Reilly placed a large colour photograph in front of him.

Natalie O'Connor's body, pierced and bruised and bloated. Some skin pale with a bluish tinge, other skin crimson with blotches. Limbs exposed. Seaweed tangled in her hair. Eyes, mercifully, closed. Lips thin and receding, stretched back in a ghastly, clownish smile.

Andrew tasted bile.

O'Reilly tapped the photograph.

'You moved the body,' he said.

Andrew took a deep breath.

'I did,' he said. 'I did move the body.' He could sense the air in the room change, charge. 'But I didn't kill her, I swear.'

The two Gardaí looked utterly unconvinced.

'Well,' O'Reilly said, 'let's take this one step at a time. Tell us about moving the body.'

Andrew described discovering what had happened. He'd been panicking, terrified that the police would think the murder was his doing. He recounted rolling Natalie up in the sheets from the bed, and then putting more clean sheets around that bundle, and then putting the body into two large refuse bags, one on each end, taping them together at the joint in the middle. The effort of sliding the body down the stairs, the surprising weight of it, struggling to get it into a wheelbarrow that he kept around for doing the gardens. Going back into his own cottage to change. Going back to Cottage No. 6 to clean up. Spending hours and hours scrubbing every floor and surface, washing the things that could be saved, burning the things that had to be disposed of. Then, when it was finally night again, wheeling the body across the road and lining it up with the boot of his car. Transferring it from one to the other.

All he left out was his first visit to the crime scene. And the fact that the reason he'd returned was because *she* told him to.

She had made him do all that.

'Tell us about the beach,' Seanie said.

Andrew had driven to the cliffs above the Far Strand, until the tide was in as far as he knew it would come. He'd checked and checked again that there was no one around. Then he'd dragged the body out of the car and pushed it over the cliff edge.

'All by yourself?' O'Reilly asked.

Andrew nodded.

'Must have been a lot of work, that.'

Andrew didn't respond.

'And after all that effort, she didn't go very far.' O'Reilly slid another picture across the table. This one showed a white, waxy body, driven through with stab wounds and mauled by the sea, lying half-in, half-out of a shallow rock pool. You couldn't see Natalie's face in this one, thank God. 'Didn't take her long to come back to us, now did it? Lucky for us. And for her family. Her husband. Her friends.'

'I'm sorry,' Andrew said.

He meant it.

'So,' Seanie said, 'you admit to moving the body, cleaning the scene and disposing of the body at the beach – or attempting to?'

Andrew nodded, then said, 'Yes,' quickly and firmly, before O'Reilly could warn him again.

'And that's you in the video?'

'What? No.'

'That's *not* you in the video?'

'No. No, no. That's not me.'

'The man in black,' Seanie said, pointing at the laptop with his pen. 'That's not you?'

'No.' How could they even think that? *'No.'*

'You're saying you didn't kill her,' O'Reilly said.

'I didn't.'

'Then help us understand, Andrew,' Seanie said, leaning in closer. 'Why did you do it then? Clean the scene, dispose of the body. Get rid of the camera. Why not just ring us? Why not ring an ambulance? Why, if you weren't the killer, would you do all that? It just doesn't make any sense.'

'I know,' Andrew said miserably.

How could it when he'd left out the worst bit?

It was because of her, he said silently. *Because she told me I had to. Because she said if I didn't clean up the mess, they'd find out and they'd release the video.* The other one, his one. This was their mess and they wanted him to get rid of it.

At some point since, of course, Andrew had realised that there was no *they*.

There was only *her*.

But how could he explain that to the Gardaí? How could he prove it? He didn't even know her name. No one had ever seen her at the cottages. Everything exchanged between them was encrypted.

'I didn't kill her,' Andrew said again. 'I would never do such a thing.'

'What kind of things *would* you do?' O'Reilly asked.

Andrew saw Seanie shift in his seat and look away, and he recognised why. Unease. Disgust. Hatred.

And he realised that they already knew.

They knew about *him*.

The girls.

What surprised him, though, was how he felt about that: relieved. He hadn't been able to contain the black oil by himself but, if he was locked away, there'd be nowhere for it to go. It would have to stay in his head.

This was probably for the best.

Is that why she'd done this? Did *she* want him behind bars? Was this some kind of vigilante justice? How did a murder fit into that?

Andrew's head swam with confused thoughts. He was just so, so tired. He wanted this to be over. He wanted to sleep.

He slumped in his chair.

Across from him, the two men exchanged one final glance.

Then O'Reilly put down his pen, checked his watch.

'Interview concluded,' he said. 'For now.'

FASTFORWARD

0:01:31

It had been a relatively quiet night at Sycamore House.

Room Two, a solo man, had had a visitor just after ten, but they'd both managed to get under the covers fully dressed and then they'd managed to stay under there throughout. Aside from a bit of humping action and the odd bare leg, there was nothing to see.

DELETE.

Room Twelve, a solo woman, had watched porn, presumably, on her phone before bed and acted accordingly, rather enthusiastically, but she'd turned the lights out first and sunk low beneath the covers and the angle didn't offer very much for the spectator.

DELETE.

But she was staying again tonight. There might be something there yet.

Room Sixteen, a couple, had gone at it for over an hour, on top of the covers, various positions, both completely naked. She even faced the lens full on for at least ten minutes and both of them were young, slim and strong. If it wasn't for them, there'd have been nothing at all. Everyone else had just climbed into bed and gone to sleep.

SAVE TO FILE.

But that was slim pickings, truth be told. One short clip on a night when Sycamore House didn't have one vacant room. It had been like this a lot lately. It had been fine when Shanamore Cottages – or Shanamore Cottage No. 6, specifically – was supplementing her stock, but now that that was gone, she'd need to take action.

Another seller on the forum swore by backpackers. There was a third-party booking site aimed just at them. If you listed there, you wouldn't get as much money for the rooms but you'd get a much younger, much more adventurous, much more energetic clientele.

The kind who liked to book in and then go out to find a stranger to bring back.

Jennifer made a note in her diary. She'd look into that.

Yes, there was a lot going on, but she couldn't afford to neglect her business. Her *real* business.

She watched the footage from Sixteen for a second time, at high speed. She extracted a twenty-second segment that would best serve as a teaser, trimmed it, scrubbed it and then uploaded it through the secure server. It went live on the forum with a reserve of a thousand dollars. They were young and attractive, it was a clear shot, yes, but straight and boring. Vanilla. She'd be lucky to get that amount for it.

Jennifer shut everything down, locked the laptop away in the safe and left the room, double-checking the door was locked behind her.

Then she went downstairs, let herself out of the back door of Sycamore House, her private residence, and crossed the courtyard to the backdoor of Sycamore House, bed and breakfast. A commute of less than twenty seconds.

Breakfast hadn't hit its full stride yet so the place was relatively quiet.

Jennifer relieved the night manager and half-listened as he passed on his report from the night before, gibbering on about a dripping tap and some guest whose luggage was still in Amsterdam. In summary: nothing interesting. Then she sat down at the reception desk and started on her morning tasks: reading emails, checking arrivals, closing out departure bills.

That's where she was when she heard it, drifting across the hall from the TV lounge.

'Gardaí in East Cork have arrested a man in connection with the murder of Natalie O'Connor, the Dublin woman and popular blogger who went missing from her home in Sandymount on the fifth of November last. Although the man's name has not yet been released, sources say he works at the holiday village near Shanamore Strand, where a woman's body was found late yesterday evening. Locals say Ms O'Connor had been staying there. For more on this, we can go now to—'

'Can I trouble you for a washcloth?'

Jennifer looked up at the voice.

The guest standing on the other side of the reception desk was American. Somewhere southern, going by her drawl. Seventy if she was a day. Silver hair carefully coiffed into a low bun. Wearing a shiny tracksuit top over a T-shirt with the Guinness toucan on it and – Jennifer could only assume, as the desk was in the way, but she'd have bet money on it – pastel-coloured cropped pants with an elasticated waist and slip-on runners with socks. A pair of gold-rimmed reading glasses hung from her neck on ruby-coloured beads and a wide, kind, earnest smile stretched across her face. She was part of a coach group overflow from the chain hotel across the street that had taken three rooms the night before.

Room Eighteen, as far as Jennifer remembered.

'A washcloth,' the woman said. 'Would you have one?'

A *facecloth*, Jennifer corrected silently. For some reason, American guests always asked for them. Sycamore House kept a small stack in the laundry room expressly to satisfy these requests, but Jennifer usually lied and said they didn't have any because, well, what the fuck? It's a smaller version of a towel, people. There're four of them in your room. Just use one of them instead, for God's sake. Who had the time for this kind of crap?

But this time, Jennifer stood and said, 'Of course. Let me grab one for you. I'll be right back, okay?' because she needed some time to think about what she'd just heard: they'd arrested Andrew.

The woman beamed. 'Thanks *so* much.'

Jennifer pushed against the door and entered the back office. She reached out and grabbed the first warm body she encountered which happened to be Louise, one of the waitresses. She told her to get a facecloth for the woman waiting at reception and then to stay there until she got back.

Louise's eyes widened to the size of saucers. 'Stand out *there*?'

'Just for a few minutes, Louise.'

'But what do I *do*? I don't know how to use the system, I—'

'Just *stand there*,' Jennifer said, 'and write down anything I need to do when I get back because you can't. I won't be long.'

'But what about check-outs and things?' Louise was getting panicked. 'Money and credit cards—'

'*Louise*!' Jennifer shouted. The girl stepped back, stunned. 'Go to the desk and just figure it out, okay? I'll be back in half an hour. At least *pretend* you're not completely helpless, for fuck's sake.'

Jennifer turned and followed the corridor to her right until another door deposited her back into the yard between the two buildings. She used her key to open her back door and then walked through her kitchen and into the hall, where she grabbed her coat off the banister and kept going, out the front door, down the drive and out on to the footpath, into her car and away.

Andrew has been arrested and charged.

It was all over now, surely. The body had been found. The culprit was in custody.

Her and Mike were free now, free to be together.

The plan had worked perfectly.

But she needed to see him. She couldn't wait any longer. She gunned the engine and headed for Sandymount.

———

She'd started out as a mere viewer, back when she used to frequent The Club.

Members met once a month. Usually in a large house out in the countryside somewhere. Never the same venue twice. Background checks required. Regular testing expected. You could do what you wanted, with whoever you wanted, and then go back to your normal, mundane, everyday existence with no one around you knowing a thing.

It was Peter – or the man who gave his name as Peter – who'd first told her about the forum. Hidden sex-cams, he explained. In all sorts of places. Some vanilla, some taboo. Some downright disgusting. Hotel rooms. Private homes that were rented out to holidaymakers. Student dorms, the kind at college and the kind in boarding schools. Peter claimed to have once seen footage from a camera in a cell in a women's prison. Truth be told, Jennifer liked a lot of things, but this didn't appeal to her at all. Mainly because she didn't believe for a second that any of it was real.

Peter told her how to access the forum and two nights later, that's what she did. And she saw that she was right. Most of the footage, the vast majority of it, featured people who were clearly just pretending to be unaware of the lens. It was all in the details. The room that was supposed to be in a hotel, but that also appeared in a video that was supposedly a dorm. The schoolgirls who seemed inexplicably concerned with keeping their long hair from obscuring the shot and who looked old enough to be *teaching* teenagers. The prison cell with a fire evacuation plan on the back of an interior door – and, heck, an interior door.

There were only a handful of videos that seemed like they could be the real deal, like they could actually be from cameras hidden in the most private of places, their subjects unaware.

Jennifer noted with interest that these had the highest view counts; the audience for these things could clearly sniff out authenticity.

Then she discovered the most interesting thing of all: that these weren't the actual videos, but teasers for them. Trailers, like in the movies. If you wanted to watch the whole thing, you had to pay up. Sizeable sums. And that would only give you access for a limited time. You couldn't, apparently, download the footage. This thing was a money machine.

Jennifer couldn't even say she *came up* with the idea. It was there, on a platter, presented to her for the taking.

All she'd had to do was turn her head and look at it.

———

It had just hit the hour and all that was on the radio news was Natalie this, Natalie that. People were horrified. Jennifer was already over it. She switched it off and thought about mistakes instead.

Everyone makes mistakes. That's what people believed. But Jennifer didn't. She didn't believe it because she didn't make them. She was too careful.

Instead, she made sure to take advantage when others did.

Mike's mistake, she was willing to forgive. He shouldn't have let things get this far. He should've just left that silly bitch before she ran off out of the house and he had to tell a nation that he loved her and missed her and wanted her home.

That had really hurt. It hurt Jennifer now, just thinking about it. As had the radio silence. As it continued to do.

That, though, she understood. Too risky. It wouldn't look good. And it wouldn't *be* good either, would it? Mike was concerned with such things.

She knew he was hurting too, though. She could understand that much, even though she didn't like it. Okay, so, his marriage had effectively ended, but he'd been with Natalie for a decade before that. It was natural that Mike would be grieving her death, that it would be intensely painful for him and confusing, what with his feelings for Jennifer mixed up in everything as well.

Whether it was right or wrong, appropriate or not, she wanted to be there for him now. To comfort him. To be able to hold him and tell him that everything was going to be all right. Because everything *was* going to be all right now that they could be together.

Jennifer had seen to that.

———

Andrew's mistake, meanwhile … Christ, take your pick! That idiot was *made* of them. Mistakes were in his DNA. Checking into a hotel with a thirteen-year-old girl was probably the best place to start. That sick fuck. And Andrew had unwittingly doubled down on that whopper, because the hotel he'd checked into was *hers*.

Jennifer had never actually blackmailed anyone before. To be honest, it hadn't even occurred to her to do it. Selling the footage was cleaner, quicker and much less work – but Andrew had been asking for it.

He was astonishingly stupid and had taken no steps to conceal his identity. He'd paid in cash but, when she'd asked for an email address to put on file, he'd not only readily provided one, but *handed her a business card* to read the address off.

Shanamore Cottages, Shanamore, Co. Cork. He was in hospitality too, it turned out. And he'd done something truly terrible, despicable and ferociously illegal that she'd captured on camera.

This idea, she came up with all by herself.

Jennifer had visited the website. It was a bare, ugly, rudimentary thing. But there were six cottages. That meant six master bedrooms, and six more cameras meant a lot more footage to trade.

That's how it had started: extra stock. In the beginning, that's all she'd been after.

She'd sent him the video, then posed as a fellow victim forced to deliver Andrew his instructions – that was still a performance she was proud of – and explained the actions he needed to take to keep the video of him committing a heinous, shameful crime off the internet and away from the Gardaí. She had a video like that too, she'd told him, that *they* were going to release unless she got him to do what she'd been told to tell him to do. She was nervous, teary-eyed, forever frantic.

And he'd fallen for it hook, line and hidden camera.

That was her genius move, really: to keep her real identity from him. They'd started with just the one camera, to see how he handled that. She'd cried and apologised throughout the installation process. She'd thought that was a nice touch.

The answer, though, it soon became clear, was that Andrew couldn't handle it *at all*. Within days, he was a nervous wreck. And he did stupid things, careless things, like using the same computer for this as he did for everything else. She was tempted to just cut him loose and leave it be. More trouble than he was worth, that idiot.

But then she'd met Mike. And Mike had a wife. And Mike was too good a man to leave the woman who'd made their lie of a perfect life her business plan. And Jennifer had begun to think that maybe Andrew could prove useful after all.

Natalie's mistake had been the same one she always made, in everything, as far as Jennifer could figure out: she'd thought this was all about *her*. That everything always was. That the weird things that were happening were happening because of her online 'fame'.

Come *on*.

After Mike had walked into Sycamore House – and into her life, changing it for ever – Jennifer had Googled his name. She was desperate to know more about the man she knew now was her future.

She'd known right from the get-go that he was married, but unhappily so. He and Natalie had been together for years and for the last few they'd been focusing on their wedding, her increasing fame. There'd been distractions. They hadn't smelled the rot, had been oblivious to it. You could see it in the pictures she posted online. The more perfect they got, the more fake the smiles seemed.

But Mike had seen the truth, although he feared taking action. She knew that was the problem before he did.

So Jennifer decided to take it for him.

There was a Garda car parked outside Mike's house and a uniformed officer standing by the garden gate. She hadn't been anticipating that and, for a moment, Jennifer considered driving past and going home. But then she thought of Mike and her heart tore a little in her chest and she knew that, for both their sakes, she had to take this chance.

She checked herself in the rear-view mirror. Fixing her hair, swiping away a stray eyelash. She rubbed balm on her lips and sprayed a light dusting of the perfume she knew he liked on her neck and wrists. She didn't like how tired she looked. All the back and forth, the driving up and down from Shanamore ... The lack of sleep had caught up with her, had crawled deep into her bones and settled there.

Play it cool, she told her reflection. Now would be a terrible time for her to lose it. They'd got this far. She couldn't run dramatically into his arms, she knew that, but she could at least *see* him. Talk to him. Let him know that she was there for him, that she was ready when he was.

She got out of the car and crossed the road, immediately attracting the attention of the Garda.

'Can I help you?' he said when she was near.

He couldn't have been more than twenty, twenty-five. He didn't even look like he was shaving yet, for fuck's sake. What age did you have to be to become a guard? He looked more like a Confirmation boy playing dress-up. When did the guards all get so bloody *young*?

'Is Mike in?' Jennifer asked. 'I'm a friend of his. I just wanted to see how he was doing.'

The guard lifted his chin. 'Name?'

Her first instinct was to lie, but there was no need to now, was there? There was nothing to connect her to what had happened in Shanamore. And Mike needed to know it was her, here.

'Jennifer,' she said. 'I'm an old friend. I know – knew – Natalie too. I just wanted to pop in for a few minutes, to check on him ...'

The guard walked her up the path to the front door where, after he'd knocked lightly, it was opened by a second officer. A female one. She was young too and really pretty, with more make-up on than Jennifer would've thought Gardaí were supposed to wear.

She felt a pang of jealousy that this bitch was locked up in this house with Mike, but she pushed it down.

'A friend of Mike's,' the male guard said. 'Jennifer.'

The female guard looked her up and down while Jennifer's hands slowly clenched into fists.

'This way,' she said then.

———

The problem was Natalie just didn't seem to be taking the bait. Not at first. She'd apparently ignored unlocked doors, things disappearing, coming back. There'd been a lot of interest in the house and it had been on the market long enough for a bidding war to play out; it had been easy to get into the house numerous times and, on one occasion, palm the key for the back door, get it copied and return it on her next 'viewing'. This time of the year, it was easier to come and go, slinking down the side of the house and around the back under the cover of early-afternoon or early-morning darkness, letting herself in, doing what she needed to do, sneaking back out. It was helpful that Natalie kept a schedule of all her movements online for the world to see, so Jennifer could pop in when she was out.

Jennifer, of course, hadn't told Mike what she was up to. She knew he wouldn't go for it; his and Natalie's lives were so entwined, business threaded through the personal, that it seemed like too big a devastation to cause. So she'd just had to wait, wait Natalie out, waiting impatiently for her to get a fucking *clue*.

But she couldn't do it for long. Enter Shanamore Cottages.

She already had Mike's credit card number from his stay at Sycamore House. She charged it again using Shanamore's credit card terminal; Andrew, who she no longer trusted with anything, didn't even know about that. She thought maybe Natalie would see the charge on the bill and freak out.

Nothing.

Jennifer printed out a mocked-up bill on Shanamore Cottage letterhead and posted it through the letterbox herself.

Still nothing.

Early the next morning she'd chanced going inside – a big chance, she knew that, probably her riskiest one – just to see what had happened to the bill. She saw a slip of white sticking out from beneath a sofa cushion. What the hell was it doing there? Either Mike had met the post and hidden it, knowing what she was up to, or Natalie had hidden it from him. She'd moved it, just because she didn't know what else to do but she needed to do *something*. She needed to move this along.

Hours later, she'd been parked across the street outside the house when she saw Natalie rushing out, looking frazzled, towing a small suitcase behind her. Just outside the gate she stopped, and for a moment Jennifer thought she might be waiting for a taxi. But she'd taken off down the road.

Jennifer followed her. Saw her getting on to the 145 bus, which would take her all the way to Heuston Station.

Trains to Cork left from there.

Where was she going? Could it be …?

The voice in her head told her it was. She called Andrew and got confirmation: Natalie had just made a booking at Shanamore Cottages, arriving today, staying for two nights. Under the name of Marie Kerr, which was amusing, but actually helped Jennifer with her cover story.

She told Andrew that *they* had arranged this, that for some reason this woman had angered them, and tonight they wanted Andrew to capture a video of her, for leverage. Insurance. Just in case.

She said she was on her way to Shanamore now to help him with it.

And she told him to ready Cottage No. 6.

Jennifer hadn't actually expected Natalie to *go* to Shanamore. That was pure luck. She thought maybe Natalie would confront Mike, who would of course deny ever being there – and he'd be telling the truth about *that* – but it would be the tug on the thread that would unravel everything.

The truth would out. They'd admit to each other that their marriage was over. Mike would leave. He'd come to *her*.

But Natalie actually went to Shanamore, the lunatic. Jennifer had the poetry book she'd taken from the house, the one that she knew Natalie could never mistake for anyone else's. She would put it in No. 6 and wait for Natalie to find it. The camera would just keep an eye on things, maybe even pick up an upset phone call to Mike. Help her stay on top of it all.

But on the way to Shanamore, a new plan began to form.

After all, Jennifer considered, no one knew where Natalie was going, especially since Jennifer had taken the time to double back to the house and dump the note she'd found left on the kitchen table. And Andrew could be forced into doing almost anything. Neither Andrew nor Natalie had any idea who Jennifer was. Andrew didn't even know her real name.

Now Natalie was gone, Andrew had got the blame, Mike hadn't had to even get involved and Jennifer's hands were clean. Bleached clean. She was a goddamn *genius*.

Everything had worked out perfectly. There'd been a couple of speed bumps, okay – like Andrew growing a conscience and writing that stupid note to Natalie, trying to get her to leave, but she forgave him for the good job he'd done in persuading her to stay another day when she actually went to do it.

And that reporter not checking her email all damn night and day, so it was much later than Jennifer would've liked when someone finally watched her little feature film.

Aside from that, it had all gone to plan.

But it was always going to, wasn't it? Because Jennifer wasn't like everyone else. She didn't make mistakes.

She found Mike in the kitchen, sitting at the table, an array of paper things spread out in front of him. Official-looking documents slipping out of a file folder. A couple of newspapers with Natalie's face on the front. He was sitting very still, holding his head in his hands. He looked up at the sound of footsteps and Jennifer's heart clenched when she saw that his eyes were rimmed red and swollen. He'd been crying, the poor thing. Her arms ached to reach for him.

'Hi, Mike,' Jennifer said, just the shape of his name on her tongue bringing her some relief, deflating the tension of separation, of anticipation.

She'd waited so long for this.

He looked at her, then at the female guard who was still standing by the door.

'Could you give us some privacy?' Jennifer said to her. 'Thank you.'

After a moment's hesitation, the guard nodded and turned to leave. When Jennifer heard the door close behind her, she advanced into the room, pulled out the chair closest to Mike and sat in it.

He seemed to pull back from her, a little uncertain.

'It's okay,' she soothed. She dropped her handbag on to the table and turned to face him, to meet his eyes, to let herself fall into them. 'It's okay. Really.'

He blinked at her. 'I'm not sure I—'

'Mike, don't.' She put a hand on his arm. She couldn't help it, couldn't wait a moment longer. Half on, half off the cuff of his long-sleeved shirt. Slowly she pushed it up until all five of her fingers were touching his bare skin. Jennifer stroked it lightly, feeling the heat transferring from his body to hers. The rest of her body ached for all of his. 'It's fine, really.'

For a moment he let her do it, looking down at her fingers, watching them.

Then, abruptly, he jerked his hand away.

'I'm sorry,' she said, 'I just needed to—'

'*I'm* sorry,' he said, 'but who the hell are you?'

———

Mike was such a good man. Here was yet more evidence of it, as if she didn't have enough already. She knew what this was, what he was doing. He was suggesting they start from scratch. Go forward from this point. Erase all the messiness that had gone before.

It was so thoughtful of him. He didn't want to contaminate their new love with all the darkness that had ended his old one.

Jennifer smiled to let him know that she understood.

Mike blinked back at her.

And then, from behind, footsteps in the hall. Coming into the kitchen. It was the female Garda, rinsing a cup out in the sink. From the speed at which she was doing it and the odd cock of her head, it was stupidly obvious that she was eavesdropping.

Fucking prissy bitch.

Mike was staring at Jennifer.

'So,' she said to him, nice and loud and clear. 'What's all this then? Anything I can help you with? Maybe I could help sort through these cards ... Gosh, there's so many of them, aren't there? Are these from strangers or people you know? Aren't people lovely? So considerate ...' As she talked, she drew her bag to her and started feeling inside for her glasses case. Her fingers found the smooth, curved plastic. 'Natalie was so popular. I bet this is only the start of it.' She snapped the case open, took out her black glasses, unfolded their arms. She'd used them recently as a sort of disguise, but she did actually need them to read. 'You'll have to come up with some kind of plan. Are you going to respond to them? No, never mind. We can think about that another time. Let's just have a read of them for now.' She lifted the glasses and slipped them on, pushing her hair back off her face.

She glanced at the guard, who was still in the same spot, still listening.

But Mike had moved. *Was* moving.

Up off his chair. Back from the table.

While staring at her, open-mouthed.

'Mike,' she said. 'What's wrong?'

The guard turned around.

From somewhere behind her, a doorbell went.

'You,' he spat, pointing a finger at her. 'It was *you*.'

PLAY

0:01:35

From the other side of the door, Audrey could hear voices and then the clack of footsteps, hurrying her way. They sounded like high heels. But when the front door opened it did so suddenly and the woman who came out ignored Audrey completely, pushed past her and hurried off down the garden path. She looked upset. A long, sleek blonde ponytail whipped back and forth behind her; it was the same woman that Audrey had seen leaving the house the one other time she was here, two days before. Two for two now. The woman must be one of Natalie's friends. Perhaps one of her relatives.

Audrey turned back just in time to see a young female Garda in uniform approaching her, her face full of concern. She opened her mouth to introduce herself but before she got a chance to, the Garda said, 'Which way did she go?' and then pushed past without waiting for an answer. She shouted something at her colleague, the male guard who'd been standing like a bouncer at the garden gate, and then the two of them hurried after the woman, him lifting his radio to his mouth as he went.

Audrey blinked.

What was *that* all about?

Now she was standing outside the open front door, alone. She knocked on it and called out, 'Hello?'

No answer. No movement.

She took a step, two, into the hall. 'Hello?'

Still no answer. No movement.

No anything.

'Hello?' Audrey called again. 'Is anyone home?'

Finally, then, a shuffle of footsteps.

A moment later, the door at the other end of the hall, the one that led into the kitchen, opened. Mike was standing there, white as a sheet, staring at her uncomprehendingly.

'Mike,' she said, giving a little wave. 'Hi. How are you? I'm … I'm so sorry about Natalie, I …' She wondered if he knew that she'd seen the body and – oh, God – been sent the video. What if he asked her about them? What would she say? Surely it was better for him to never know any specific details about either of those horrors? But how could she refuse to give him information?

'The reporter,' he said flatly.

'Yes.' Audrey took another step in. 'I'm sorry to bother you, especially at a time like this, but I think that, um … Well, I've come from Shanamore and I was just wondering—'

'Did you see her?' Audrey thought Mike meant Natalie but then he said, 'Where did she go?'

'Sorry, I …' She looked behind her, then back to him. Did he mean the guard? Or the woman, the friend? 'I don't know. Do you – should I go look for her? I can go get her if you—'

'It was her,' Mike said. 'That was her. That just left.'

Audrey wasn't following. But she could see that something wasn't right here, beyond the obvious. Mike looked like he'd seen a ghost. He looked like he could *be* a ghost: he was so pale, and he was swaying slightly.

Slowly, Audrey advanced into the hall until she was standing just a couple of steps from him.

'Come on,' she said, taking him gently by the arm. 'Let's sit down.'

'It was her,' he said again.

'Let's go and sit down and then we can talk about it, okay?'

She led him to one of the kitchen chairs and then gently pushed him down on to it. He didn't protest or say any more. She poured him some water, hoping he wouldn't notice that she went to the right cupboard for the drinking glasses on her first try, remembering its location from her illicit search of the kitchen two days before.

After he drank the water down, Mike seemed to come back to life.

'That woman,' he said. 'With the black glasses. Did you see her leave just now?'

'Yes. Is she a friend of Natalie's or ...?'

Mike shook his head, *no.*

Then he said, 'She was following her.'

Again, Audrey thought he meant the guard. That the guard had left because she was following that woman, but that didn't make any—

'She was following *Natalie.* Before she ... Until she—' His voice broke. 'And I didn't believe her.' Tears now, glistening in his eyes. 'I didn't believe her.'

He dropped his head.

Audrey felt a tingle drop down her spine.

'Mike,' she said gently, 'can you tell me why you think that? Why you think that woman was following Natalie?'

He sniffed, wiped at his face. 'Natalie told me a woman with blonde hair and black glasses – thick frames – was following her. She'd seen her in ... I think three places, over a couple of weeks.' He shook his head. 'I didn't believe her.'

'Is that what Natalie was upset about? Before she left?'

Mike nodded miserably.

'Shanamore,' Audrey said. 'Did Natalie tell you why she was asking about that?'

'No,' Mike said. 'Not at the time. But when I came home that night, the Visa bill was in the post, and I just had a quick look at it, like I normally do, and I saw "Shanamore Cottage" ... There was this big charge, six hundred euro and something. I didn't understand but I presumed that must have had something to do with why Natalie asked me about it, so I left it' – he pointed at the noticeboard, although there was no sign of the bill there now – 'up there. I was going to ask her when she came back. But she' – his voice cracked – 'didn't.'

'So who was the woman? Why was she following Natalie?'

'I don't know,' Mike said. 'I don't know her. But she ... she acted like I did, even though I don't think I've ever met her before in my life. There's something wrong with her—' He stopped, seeing Audrey's expression. 'What? What is it?'

'I saw her too. The first time I came here. Two days ago. She was leaving just as I was arriving, just like this time.'

Mike's eyes widened. 'What? That was—'

'The morning of the break-in, yeah.' Audrey's blood was fizzing with adrenalin. She took a breath. 'Mike, there's something else. I don't know if I should tell you this, but … I've seen the video. Have they told you about the video?'

He swallowed hard, nodded.

'Well,' Audrey continued, 'I don't think the person who … I don't think the person who attacked Natalie was a man.'

He stood up abruptly and pushed back his chair, stepped back from the table, from Audrey, moving away as if she'd just revealed she was contagious.

'Are you saying—'

'Yes,' she said. 'Were there only two guards here? I think we should ring them.'

He nodded again. It seemed like he couldn't speak.

Audrey got out her phone and dialled the number O'Reilly had given her. She'd put it in as a contact on the way up from Shanamore so she'd know when she was getting an angry 'Why the hell did you delay your statement appointment?' call without having to actually answer it. It was a mobile. She assumed his own.

Mike leaned against the wall. He looked like he was being held together only by his clothes.

The call rang once, twice.

Then, suddenly, Mike's face changed.

'Jesus Christ,' he breathed. 'I *have* met her. She was standing behind a desk…' He put his hands to his mouth, then covered his eyes with them. 'Oh, my God. Oh, my God.'

In Audrey's ear, a click signalled the call had been picked up.

'Yes?' O'Reilly's voice said.

'It's me,' she said. 'Audrey. I'm with Mike in Sandymount. You need to get your people here. *Now.*'

STOP

0:01:38

REWIND TO BEGIN

By Audrey Coughlan

Last November, the body of Irish Instagram star Natalie O'Connor washed up on a Cork beach the same day a graphic video of her murder was sent anonymously to media outlets. The investigation into her death would uncover not only the culprit, but the twisted crimes of a man Natalie barely knew and a woman she had never formally met. Yet many mysteries still remain. As murderer Jennifer Blake marks the first weekend of her life sentence and her accomplice, Andrew Gallagher, waits to hear the details of his, we share an extract from reporter Audrey Coughlan's upcoming book, *The Follower*, which promises to be the definitive account of the strange and tragic case that has captivated this nation – and shaken our Instagram generation to their core …

The nameplate of Belleview House, built in pitted red brick in Donnybrook in 1981, tells two lies. It is not a house and, if it offers any attractive views, I spied none of them from its top floor. It is, in reality, a block of flats and not a particularly attractive one. The units inside are studios if we're being generous, bedsits if we're not.

The letting agent who shows me around one of them – available to rent for 'just' €1,350 per month – doesn't use those terms, however. He says things like *light-filled* and *intelligently proportioned* and, for reasons I don't quite understand, *Scandinavian living*. His megawatt smile only dims when I enquire after the water tank on the roof. A former tenant, I explain, has filled me in: back when he lived here, not that long ago, the water supply would cease without notice at least once a month, leaving him and his fellow tenants with no working taps, no heating and no showers.

That former tenant is Michael Kerr and, as unlikely as it may seem, Belleview House's water tank is the reason his wife, Irish Instagram star Natalie O'Connor, is dead.

I first set foot in Shanamore in November 2018, one day before Natalie's body washed up on the stretch of beach the locals call the Far Strand, and about one week after she herself had arrived there for the first time. We both stayed in the same place: Shanamore Cottages, a small U-shaped arrangement of six holiday homes, built originally to sell as private homes. We both stayed in Cottage No. 6, the house directly opposite Cottage No. 1, where Andrew Gallagher, the manager, lived and greeted his newly arrived guests. We both slept in the king-sized bed in No. 6's only bedroom but only Natalie died in it. I saw this happen, after the fact, via a computer screen. Unbeknownst to both of us there was a camera hidden in that room, concealed in an alarm clock sat atop a chest of drawers at the foot of the bed. It was gone before I arrived, dumped along with Natalie's lifeless body. I suspect the same person who killed her sent me the video it captured.

I had written about Natalie's disappearance for ThePaper.ie and then followed a report from one of her many thousands of Instagram followers that claimed Natalie had been in Shanamore since. I had two questions: had Natalie really been there and why had she gone there at all? It was easy to answer the first one. She had indeed gone there; spoken to various people; had a coffee in The Kiln, the local design store; and walked on the beach. The second was harder to answer and that answer, when I eventually pieced it together, was confusing and complex.

But the short version is this: she was lured there.

———

Andrew Gallagher does not look thirty-something. The first time I met him – shortly after Natalie did for the first time – he was pale and lanky, wearing oversized clothes and sporting longish, floppy hair. He seemed innocent, perhaps even naïve. He didn't seem at all suited to a job in hospitality. What I didn't know at the time – what, it seemed, almost no one knew – was that Andrew had a sexual preference for very young girls and, on regular trips to cities like Cork and Dublin, he would satisfy it. His victims, the youngest of which was three days past her twelfth birthday, nearly all first encountered him online, via a video game or social media app. He was careful to conceal his identity and left these girls with very little in the way of concrete detail to report to authorities. When one of them found the courage to tell her mother, almost as soon as she had returned home, she could only give a physical description. The accounts on which he'd contacted her had already been deleted and the 'hotel' where they'd stayed never checked IDs and had no cameras inside or out.

But someone was watching him. In the summer of 2018, Andrew Gallagher travelled to Sycamore House in Donnybrook, Dublin 4, a somewhat grubby bed and breakfast based in a converted Georgian townhouse (now closed) that had enticed guests with its postcode but made no effort to impress them with the reality. The young girl he took there has never been identified but what he did to her was captured in horrifically high definition by a camera concealed in the room. A week after he'd returned home to Shanamore, Andrew received a copy of the footage via email along with instructions that, in order to avoid the video's public dissemination, he should begin capturing similar footage of *his* guests. He was to send 'fresh' footage at least once a week to his anonymous blackmailers, the crying woman on the other end of the telephone explained. She didn't give her name but she claimed that she, too, had been videoed doing something similarly shameful and this was how *she* was supposed to avoid *its* release. Andrew did as he was told.

This was why, when a faceless killer entered Cottage No. 6 on the night of 6 November, 2018, and murdered Natalie O'Connor in her bed, someone was watching – or, at least, some*thing*. A lifeless black marble in the dark. A lens.

———

Richard Flynn said he did various things – he was a painter, a handyman, a labourer – but what he did the most was lie. His name wasn't Richard at all, but Martin, and although Flynn was his last name, officially it came with an 'O'. He'd fled London in 2001 after a series of ATM robberies left a red-hot trail leading police to his door. He changed his name midway across the Irish Sea and settled in the sleepy seaside village of Shanamore, where locals were unimpressed by his unkempt appearance, lack of personal hygiene and – if you were a local female – failure to observe the concept of personal space.

In the autumn of 2008, Flynn was on the verge of leaving Shanamore. He was sick of the cold, hard winters and the lack of paying work. Then, over a pint in one of the local pubs, Murphy's, he heard of an opportunity: the new housing estate 'up the lane' had failed to sell a single home and was being rebranded as a holiday village. The developer was looking for someone to manage the place, and although the pay was minimal the role would be live-in and come with one of the cottages, rent-free. Richard thought it was the answer to all his problems and set out to secure the job, going so far as to invest in a suit (from a charity shop) and cut his hair. But someone else wanted it too: the son of the family who had owned the land. He was younger ('and *cleaner*' one of the locals would later say) and much more suited, it was thought, to the role. Andrew Gallagher became the manager of Shanamore Cottages, leaving Richard out in the cold, still.

Richard took this as a personal slight and began to nurture a grudge which, a decade later, would inadvertently help solve a murder. He was obsessed with assessing Andrew's effectiveness in the job he felt he could've done better and, as a result, spent an inordinate amount of time hanging around Shanamore Cottages. Andrew, while wary of him, was thought to be too intimidated by the older man to risk a confrontation and so never asked him to leave, even when some of the guests complained that they'd found him loitering outside their windows or relaxing on their patios.

Richard was there the night Natalie O'Connor arrived at the cottages and he, by chance, witnessed a strange thing. Andrew had a visitor, an older woman, who had parked her car, not in the complex, but in the abandoned building site next door.

He wondered what she was doing there.

He wondered why she didn't want to be seen.

Andrew Gallagher and Richard Flynn were, understandably, prime suspects in the murder of Natalie O'Connor. Andrew quickly admitted to having removed the body and cleaned the scene, and Richard was the first to happen upon the body when it washed ashore.

I was the second. Richard had had no phone with which to raise the alarm, had gone to get help and found me. I had parked nearby to watch a video I had just been sent, anonymously, via email: the video of Natalie's murder. When I watched it again hours later with another journalist, we both agreed: the figure on screen was not Andrew or Richard. We weren't even sure it was a man.

Natalie had been lured to Shanamore, but how, and by whom? Was it the same woman who had murdered her? What was the motive? Was it someone she knew? Those first twenty-four hours I spent in Shanamore I spent following, sometimes unknowingly, in Natalie O'Connor's footsteps. I stayed in the same cottage. I went to the same café. I walked along the same stretch of beach.

I was going forwards, I thought, into this investigation. But what I've come to realise in the months since – the months I've spent immersed in this case – is that the truth is behind me. To get it, you must go back. You must rewind all the way to a warm night in April 2018 when Mike Kerr returned to the apartment he was sharing with his then-fiancée, Natalie, flushed and sweaty from a day at work followed by an hour at the gym, and discovered that, yet again, Belleview House's water was out.

Natalie was away in London for the night on a work-related trip. Mike had an important meeting in the morning and, if past incidents were anything to go by, the water might not even be running again by then. He later described to me how he stood in the kitchen, considering his options: take a chance and stay there, go back to the gym and shower, stay with a friend. He eventually decided all three options had annoying downsides and elected instead to check into a chain hotel on Burlington Road, less than a five-minute drive away.

But they were fully booked for the night. The staff on reception suggested he try Sycamore House, a nearby bed and breakfast. Mike remembers it as being slightly rundown, but he got what he needed: a bed for the night and running water. The following morning, his meeting went well. He was on his way to the airport to collect Natalie when he realised he'd left his phone charger behind him at Sycamore House.

When Mike called the number on the website, he connected with someone who spoke English with a Polish accent and said he was at the reception desk. The proprietor herself, he explained, dealt with Lost & Found, for security reasons. Would he like her mobile number? He could call her on that. Mike said yes and called the number as soon as he'd hung up, before he could forget it. When he heard the woman's voice, he realised it was the same woman who'd checked him into his room the night before. Jennifer, her name-tag had read.

Mike returned to Sycamore House later that evening to collect his charger. He was in and out within the space of a minute, he thinks, and cannot remember any specific detail of this second visit. It's likely, however, that Jennifer Blake remembers it well. She had been, according to court-ordered psychological reports submitted during her trial, attracted to Mike instantly and had, that day, stored his number in her phone alongside his professional headshot, which she'd taken from his employer's website.

What started in Sycamore House was an obsession, a fantasy in which, her therapist says, Jennifer came to fully believe. In her mind, she and Mike had embarked on an illicit affair. They were in love, he with her as much as she with him.

The only problem was that they couldn't be together openly until his wife, Natalie, was out of the way.

————

The Follower will be published by Henry Books early next year

Irish Times Weekend Review, 31 August, 2019

ACKNOWLEDGEMENTS

This book would not be in your hands were it not for three wonder women: Jane Gregory, Sara O'Keeffe and Susannah Hamilton. I might never have made it to Book 3 without the friendship/support/gin-infused therapy of Hazel Gaynor and Carmel Harrington; getting to know you two has been one of the highlights of my writing life. Special thanks to everyone at David Higham & Associates, Corvus/Atlantic Books and Blackstone Publishing, and to all the wonderful booksellers, bloggers, readers, reviewers and authors who have so generously supported me and my work. Thanks to Casey King – Garda procedure consultant extraordinaire – Erin Mitchell for sending me the BEST text messages and Andrea Summers for pointing out the PostSecret that gave me the initial idea for this book. Sheena Lambert: that *cacophony* was just for you – enjoy! Barry O'Connell: I *told* you I'd get your name in here. Sheelagh and Iain: you're BY FAR my favourite disembodied voices from far away.

Thanks also to Mum, Dad, John and Claire. They really didn't have anything to do with me writing this book specifically but I get the feeling they wouldn't be too impressed if they got to the end of this page and didn't see their names here, so ...

And thank *you*, for reading!

Praise for Catherine Ryan Howard's *The Liar's Girl*

'Gripping' Elizabeth Haynes

'A clever and intriguing tale.' Liz Nugent

'A killer premise that 100% delivers.' Caz Frear

'Dark, yes, but tender too. *The Liar's Girl* is tightly plotted and crackles with suspense.' Ali Land

'An absolute belter of a book!' Gillian McAllister

'Expertly plotted, with a series of stunning twists.' *Daily Mail*

'Slick, smart and stylish suspense.' Holly Seddon

'Absolutely fantastic.' Jenny Blackhurst

'The Liar's Girl is a tightly structured, highly suspenseful follow-up to Howard's excellent CWA Dagger-nominated debut, Distress Signals.' *Irish Times*

'Heartstoppingly brilliant ... An extraordinary talent.' Jane Casey

'Incredibly pacey.' Sinéad Crowley

'Astonishingly good.' Jo Spain

'[A] sharp and modern thriller, cleverly plotted and completely immersive ... Magnificently murky.' *Sunday Independent*

'*The Liar's Girl* is brilliant. It's even better than the Dagger-nominated *Distress Signals* and that's saying something!' Michelle Davies

'Absolutely terrific.' Pat Kenny